Search for the Shadow Key

OTHER BOOKS BY WAYNE THOMAS BATSON

THE DREAMTREADERS SERIES
Dreamtreaders

THE DOOR WITHIN TRILOGY
The Door Within
The Rise of the Wyrm Lord
The Final Storm

PIRATE ADVENTURES
Isle of Swords
Isle of Fire

THE BERINFELL PROPHECIES
Curse of the Spider King (with Christopher Hopper)
Venom and Song (with Christopher Hopper)
The Tide of Unmaking (with Christopher Hopper)

THE DARK SEA ANNALS
Sword in the Stars
The Errant King
Mirror of Souls

IMAGINATION STATION
#8: *Battle for Cannibal Island*
#11: *Hunt for the Devil's Dragon*

OTHER ENDEAVORS
Ghost

SEARCH FOR THE SHADOW KEY

THE DREAMTREADERS SERIES
BOOK#2

WAYNE THOMAS BATSON

THOMAS NELSON
Since 1798

NASHVILLE   MEXICO CITY   RIO DE JANEIRO

Search for the Shadow Key

Published in Nashville, Tennessee, by Thomas Nelson. Thomas Nelson is a registered trademark of HarperCollins Christian Publishing, Inc.

Excerpts are featured from *The Prince and the Pauper* by Mark Twain.

Thomas Nelson titles may be purchased in bulk for educational, business, fund-raising, or sales promotional use. For information, please e-mail SpecialMarkets@ThomasNelson.com.

Library of Congress Cataloging-in-Publication Data

Batson, Wayne Thomas, 1968-
Search for the Shadow Key / Wayne Thomas Batson.
pages cm. -- (Dreamtreaders ; #2)
Summary: As the only living Dreamtreader, fourteen-year-old Archer must protect the waking world from the evil lurking in the Dream, but when his family and friends begin to disappear, unexpected help comes from the Wind Maiden, a mysterious angelic being who seems to know how Archer can rescue his loved ones and defeat the new Nightmare King.
ISBN 978-1-4003-2367-8 (pbk.)
[1. Dreams--Fiction. 2. Fantasy.] I. Title.
PZ7.B3238Se 2014
[Fic]--dc23
2014031874

Printed in the United States of America

14 15 16 17 18 19 RRD 6 5 4 3 2 1

Ex Misericordia Dei

CONTENTS

The Laws Nine   ix

Chapter 1 · Seeing Things   1

Chapter 2 · Whac-A-Mole   11

Chapter 3 · The Inner Sanctum   18

Chapter 4 · Snow Falls Gently   31

Chapter 5 · No More Nightmares   47

Chapter 6 · Visis Nocturne   61

Chapter 7 · Old Wounds   73

Chapter 8 · Broken   85

Chapter 9 · Ice-Fire   91

Chapter 10 · The Silentwood   99

Chapter 11 · The Paravore   113

Chapter 12 · A Wake-Up Call   121

Chapter 13 · The Darkening   133

Chapter 14 · The Shadow Key   143

CONTENTS

Chapter 15 · The Third   151

Chapter 16 · Taken   164

Chapter 17 · First Priority   177

Chapter 18 · Search and Rescue   186

Chapter 19 · Hourglass Sands   204

Chapter 20 · Demands   219

Chapter 21 · Powers   225

Chapter 22 · Master and Student   231

Chapter 23 · The Price   242

Chapter 24 · The Deepest Wells   257

Chapter 25 · Enslaved   268

Chapter 26 · Dinner Is Served   277

Chapter 27 · Just Desserts   285

Chapter 28 · A Dark Impasse   293

Chapter 29 · Stone Cold   301

Acknowledgments   309

THE LAWS NINE

Law One: Anchor first; Anchor deep. Construct an anchor image that is rooted in a deeply powerful emotion. It must be dear to you.

Law Two: Anchor where you may find it with ease, but no one else can. If your anchor is destroyed or otherwise kept from you, your time may run out.

Law Three: Never remain in the Dream for more than your Eleven Hours. Your Personal Midnight is the end. Depart for the Temporal . . . or perish.

Law Four: Depart for the Temporal at Sixtolls or find some bastion to defend against the storm. The Nightmare Lord will open wide his kennels, chaos will rule, and the Dreamtreader shall be lost.

Law Five: While in the Dream, consume nothing made with gort, the soul harvest berry. It is black as pitch and enslaves your body to those of dark powers.

Law Six: Defend against sudden and final death within the Dream. Prepare your mind for calamities that may come or else be shut out from the Dream forever.

Law Seven: Never accept an invitation from the Nightmare Lord.

Not even to parley. He is a living snare to the Dreamtreader. There is no good-faith bargain. With him, the only profit will be death.

Law Eight: By the light of a Violet Torch, search yourself for tendrils, the Nightmare Lord's silent assassins.

Law Nine: Dreamtread with all the strength you can muster, but never more than two days in a row. To linger in the Dream too often will invite madness. Temporal and Dream will be fused within you and shatter your mind.

ONE

SEEING THINGS

THE TERRAIN IN THE DREAM ON THIS NIGHT WAS LIKE
the ocean's surf during a riptide, only twice as violent.

"This is crazy!" Archer shouted. He kicked out his surfboard,
carved a hard left on the Intrusion wave, and nearly wiped out.
Relentless Dream winds whipping his dark red hair into his eyes, he
circled back to see what had caused such a jolt in the Dream surf.

There it was: a breach the size of a manhole cover had burst
right off the tip of his board. This rip in the Dream fabric, the layer
of matter between the sleeping and waking worlds, spewed glowing
blue, purple, and crimson particles. The thing was huge, like a giant
wound gushing . . . or a mini-volcano erupting. Only this volcano was
spewing right in the middle of a dense Dream forest, strobe-lighting
all the sloped trunks and gnarled limbs with a flickering sheen of
creepy. As a Dreamtreader, one of three human beings selected each
generation to patrol this realm, Archer was duty-bound to sew up this
breach—and fast.

The shockwave from the breach surged beneath him, tossing his board sideways. Archer stumbled to one knee and almost fell off. Somehow, his grip on the board held.

"Enough of this!" Archer growled. He leaped off the board, used his sheer will to batten down the waves, and landed next to the gushing breach. "Razz, I need you again!" Archer cried out into the air.

"Coming, boss!" a shrill feminine voice answered from the air. There was a double puff of smoke, a scattering of swerving sparks, and Razzlestia Celeste Moonsonnet appeared. A twin-tailed flying squirrel with an acorn hat and a fashionable gray pinstripe ensemble, Razz flew to Archer's shoulder.

"Like my new outfit? It's perfect for the season—" Then she spotted the raging breach and squeaked. "Ewww, ugly one!"

Archer thrust a fist into the satchel he always wore, pulling out his favorite barb needle and a spool of ether silk. He went to work, binding up one lip of the breach. "Razz," he said, "thickest gauge thread, spiral technique!"

Razz might be mercurial, but when she showed up, Archer knew he could count on his little Dream assistant. And now that he was the only active Dreamtreader—and just fifteen years old—Archer needed Razz more than ever.

"Got it!" she squeaked. With a flap and snap of her tails, Razz leaped from Archer's shoulder and shot high into the air above the breach. Then, the barb needle already threaded, she plummeted around and around and around, jamming the needle into the loosely flapping fabric and creating a kind of loose seam.

"Great, Razz! That's perfect!" Archer yelled, feeling like the roar of the surging Dream matter would steal his voice. He pulled his first thread tight, strained to get as tight a seal as possible, and knotted it.

It wasn't over, though. This breach was powerful. Beastly, even. The knot held, but served only to make the Dream matter's only escape point that much narrower. Now, it shot into the sky like a mighty torrent.

"Cross breach!" Archer cried out. "Gotta be now, Razz!"

Razz zigzagged like a shooting star, driving the needle within loops of thread and then pulling taut across the opening. She flew in and out of the violent blast without seeming to care for herself. By the time she handed off the thread to Archer, she glistened and pulsed as if dipped into stardust.

"I think I'm going to be sick," Razz muttered, gliding in a slow circle through tree branches and coming to rest on a hillock nest of tangled roots and waving purple grass.

Archer had no time to check on her or he'd completely render her efforts worthless. He held Razz's thread, what he called *the boss thread*, and took a deep breath. He had a job to do. This task would cost a glob of Archer's mental will—the creative energy of the mind that enabled a Dreamtreader to do just about anything in the Dream—but it had to be done. Fortunately for Archer, he had plenty of will left in the tank. He hoped.

Archer secured the boss thread with a two-fisted grip and called up his will. In response, the flesh of his hands and wrists turned gray and knobby. He felt the hardening as his lower arms became stone. The thread anchored, Archer turned his will to generated pure aggressive power.

For a moment, the Dreamtreader drew a mental blank. *What will give me the thrust I need to seal this off?* He thought about wings. But no. That wouldn't do it. He thought about dropping himself into a Lamborghini. But on the Dream terrain, traction would be iffy. Besides, he couldn't afford a spinout with a huge breach at stake. That's when the perfect concept came to mind.

Archer concentrated. He'd never created this exact combination before, so it would cost him something extra. With a groan, Archer let his will loose. His surfboard melted and morphed into the caterpillar treads of a bulldozer. Archer fell backward into the machine's cockpit, the thick glass canopy immediately closing over top of him. With a rush, the rocket engines he'd imagined appeared on either side of the vehicle and burped white-blue flames.

The machine lurched forward, pulling the boss thread taut. The breach spouted and spewed like a fire hose, but Archer hit the thrusters. They responded with a slow but relentless creep forward. Slowly, the stitches grew tight, cutting off the flow of Dream matter to a trickle . . . and, finally, to nothing. Archer ejected from the cockpit, and the machine vanished. He dove for the now-sealed breach and tied it off like a rodeo jock hog-tying a steer.

Archer took a peek over his shoulders as he worked. Fortunately, he saw none of the breach-eating, beetle gub-esque scurions in the area. They'd apparently eaten their fill of matter in the process of chomping open that massive breach. Given the size of it, Archer figured the scurions would be in a food coma for at least a week's worth of Dream time.

"Good riddance," he muttered. Packing up his ether thread and needle, he raced to Razz's side. "Hey, you okay?"

She lifted her squirrelly head and blinked her big dark eyes. When she spoke, the words came out a little slow and slurred. "Aye, aye, chief," she said, saluting weakly. "Sergeant Razz, zzhu-reporting for duty-shhhh."

"Look at you," Archer teased gently. "You get splashed with Dream matter and you go all loopy."

"Sszh . . . sorry, Archer," she squeaked. She sat up and adjusted her acorn beret. Ever so slowly, she got back on her feet. "I'm beat, tuckered, whooped! Other than the quick snooze break you gave me, we've been at it nonstop. Covering two Dream districts, alone? This is nutball Looney Tunes! How many more breaches tonight?"

"No clue," Archer said with a deep sigh.

Little paw-hands on her little hips, Razz frowned and asked, "Well, when is Master Gabriel waking up two new Dreamtreaders?"

Archer's answer was the same: "No clue."

"What?" Razz blurted. "How can he just—I mean, that is, what's he doing? Leaving the whole Dream to one Dreamtreader? That's . . . unprezzy . . . uh, unpresidential . . . er—"

"Unprecedented," Archer said, smiling in spite of the stinging reality. "You're right: this hasn't happened before. We're spread too thin, and we're going to miss breaches. The breaches will multiply, and every breach not sewn up will push the Dream closer and closer to a rift."

"Don't say that," Razz said, shuddering. "Please don't say that."

Her reaction gave Archer a gut check. He knew what a rift would do to his world. The fabric of the Dream would be torn. The Temporal and the Dream would begin to mix. People would begin to confuse dreams and reality. They'd gain abilities they wouldn't know how to use and wouldn't have the safety net of simply waking up. It would be chaos.

Ten thousand heart-stopping rift scenarios played out in Archer's imagination. Little kids thinking they could fly and diving from rooftops; an angry employee suddenly causing his boss to burst into very real flames; wars being waged over illusions—it would be absolute chaos.

But Archer had never given any thought to what would happen in a rift to the beings who inhabited the Dream. Beings like Razz. They were made of the same stuff as the Dream fabric. If the Dream were completely torn by a rift? Archer looked down at his little companion and couldn't let his thoughts go there. "Don't worry, Razz," he found himself saying. "Even if we have to do it alone, we'll handle it. We've got each other, right?"

Razz nodded. "I know," she said quietly. Then she took off her acorn beret and held it over her heart. "But I miss Duncan and Mesmeera."

He felt it too: an ache, the creeping sadness of fraying emotions. Duncan and Mesmeera were his previous Dreamtreading partners. They were efficient, hardworking Dreamtreaders, to be sure. But more than that, they were friends. They'd stayed far too long past their Personal Midnights in the Dream—trapping themselves, seasoned Dreamtreaders who should have known better.

But, mistakes aside, Duncan and Mesmeera didn't deserve their ultimate fate. The familiar leaden cold pooled in Archer's stomach. He'd never forget his friends . . . or his own role in their ultimate loss.

He shook those guilt-laden thoughts away and said, "We've covered Verse District and Forms now . . . in record time too. But we've still got Pattern left, and that could be the worst. You never know with the Lurker roaming free."

Razz bounced twice and looked warily over her shoulder. "But the Lurker's no threat now . . . right, chief?"

Archer didn't answer.

Razz frowned. "Right, chief?"

"I don't know, Razz," Archer grumbled, a little more bite to his words than he'd meant. "I'm sorry. Just frustrated. All I know about the Lurker is what Rigby tells me . . . and honestly, I know I can't really trust him anymore. With the Nightmare Lord gone, the Lurker is no longer under his control. He's acting on his own will . . . but that might not be a good thing. Master Gabriel is still very concerned about the Lurker. Therefore, so am I."

Razz crossed her arms. "And now we have to go patch up the breaches in the Lurker's backyard? You sure we have time?"

Archer looked up, scanned the darkening crimson sky, and found the ancient tower clock, its pale face looming in the haze to the northeast. "Old Jack says we have three hours left," he said. "Might be enough. It'll have to be. We can't let breaches go unchecked. If a rift forms, then it's game over. We won't . . . we, uh . . . won't . . ."

Archer's words trailed off. He'd spotted something odd through the trees.

"Boss?"

"Just a sec, Razz." He raced forward, ducking low boughs and leaping roots, but always keeping his eyes riveted ahead. Eighty yards later, he broke the tree line and found an unobstructed view of the horizon.

Razz leaped into the air and came buzzing after him, dropping awkwardly onto Archer's shoulder. "What's the deal, boss?"

"The horizon," he muttered. "It look strange to you?"

"Most days," she said. "The Dream is kind of big on *strange*."

Archer nodded absently, staring. Old Jack loomed on high, as usual, and there were many crimson vortices, the tornadolike entry paths used by Dreamtreaders as portals. But there was something else, a kind of silvery shimmer following the line of the horizon. It was faint and spidery, and Archer wasn't altogether certain he was seeing it.

"What . . . what is that?" he asked. "You see it, right?"

"*That? It?*" Razz grumbled. "You use too many pronouns."

"The silver shimmer!" Archer growled, pointing emphatically. "Right at the horizon. I've never seen that before."

Razz twirled in the air once and then hovered, stretching her tiny neck out. "I think I see it, boss," she said. "Kind of sparkly like." She crossed her arms and rubbed her shoulders. "Makes me feel chilly."

SEARCH FOR THE SHADOW KEY

"Yeah," Archer said. "I felt it too. Have you ever seen it before today?"

"I don't think so," Razz replied. "But I find something new in this place every day."

"True," Archer said, turning reluctantly away. "Anyway, we have bigger problems to deal with. Let's get back to work."

Razz leaped into the air, and her twin fuzzy tails twirled. "Well, all right then. Off we go."

Archer summoned his Dream matter surfboard, flexed his will, and found an Intrusion wave to ride west.

Like a sea of mist with islands of craggy rock, the moors of Archaia stretched out before Archer's board. He and Razz had been searching the villages and territories of the Pattern District for just over two hours, but they'd found no breaches. Not a single one.

"I don't like this," Archer said. "This happened before, when the Nightmare Lord was still on his throne."

Razz bounced impatiently on Archer's shoulder. "Why are you complaining? No breaches to fix! This is a good thing, Archer. Now, we can go home!"

"Still have Archaia to check."

Razz brushed some dust off her pinstripe blazer. "None of the other twenty territories had any breaches. Why would Archaia? Let's leave it."

"We can't take the chance," Archer replied. "There are no Intrusion waves here, but still . . ."

"No buts, Archer. You've got, like, forty minutes."

Archer glanced up at Old Jack, the always-visible tower clock that showed Dreamtreaders how much time they had before their Personal Midnight, their deadline. Archer frowned. "A little less, actually. We need to motor."

The Dreamtreader dismissed his board and started running: running like Olympic gold medalist sprinters *wished* they could run. In the Dream, Archer could harness his will and move with the speed of a cheetah and the coordination of a mountain lion. With Razz tucked into his trench coat pocket, Archer stormed the moors, bounding from crag to crag, leaping the low, rooty trees, and flashing across any flat land. He ran a tight spiral, stopping now and again to make sure he wouldn't miss a breach.

At last, he came to a steep incline, leading up to a wide overhanging ridge of black stone. "That," Archer whispered, "is the Lurker's home."

Razz let out a surprised squeak. "L-looks like an old, old tomb dug into the rock."

"Might as well be," Archer muttered. "Last time I was here, the Lurker had a pack of ghostly wraith things as a welcoming party for me."

"G-ghostly . . . wraith . . . things?" Razz let out another squeak. "But we've seen enough, right? No breaches. We're good to go, right?"

"I'm not sure," Archer said. "I've got a bad feeling here."

"You know why you have a bad feeling, Archer?" Razz shivered. "Because it *feels* bad here. We gotta leave. You can't have much time. How are you going to get back to your anchor?"

That, Archer thought, *is a very reasonable question.* His anchor, an image of the old well his mother had loved, was all the way back in the Forms District. Archer glanced again at Old Jack . . . and growled. Even if he sprinted back across the border and surfed the rest of the way to the anchor, it could get dicey. Minutes had a way of flying by in the Dream, but Archer had his circuit to complete. He'd risk it but needed to be smart.

The mist had been creeping over the lower half of the incline. Now its shrouded fingers were reaching down even to Archer's feet. He lifted his foot and prepared to take a step.

"No, Archer!" Razz squealed.

His foot suspended in the air above the writhing mist, Archer frowned. "Don't be silly, Razz." He lowered his foot.

"Don't!"

Archer deepened his frown to a scowl and decisively thumped his foot down into the mist.

TWO

WHAC-A-MOLE

"OH, NO!" RAZZ SQUEAKED.

The landscape was silent. "There. You see?" Archer said. "It's no . . . big . . . uh . . . deal—"

Archer's words were cut short by a whisper. It was not wind or an Intrusion wave. It was a shivering, whirling breath that seemed to flow through the rippling mist.

Archer didn't need to look behind himself to know that something was there. He didn't need Razz to tell him that something enormous was rising up out of the mist.

Without a thought, Archer summoned his sword. Its blue flame kindled to life and flared up the blade. Archer almost laughed at how reflexively he called up his sword. A hint of danger and— *WHOOSH*—the sword.

"Y'know, Razz," he said, "this is my favorite Dream weapon."

"Archer . . ." Razz said, her voice a strangled whisper.

"I mean, I use it all the time," Archer went on. "Seems like I should have a name for it, y'know?"

"Archer?"

"I always call it 'The Sword,' but that's just cheesy. I mean Arthur had Excalibur, Aragorn had Andúril, and Aidan had Fury. My sword should have a name. Funny how so many heroes have names that begin with *A*. Hey, my name begins with—"

"ARCHER!" Three unnerving sounds shattered the quiet and rendered Archer and Razz mute: a dire howl, a shrill screech, and a thunderous roar.

Razz disappeared in twin puffs of purple smoke, and Archer spun on his heels to face the threat. His skin went cold, and his mouth dropped open. Archer had seen many strange and horrifying things in the Dream, but this was something new. Something wholly unexpected.

A wide span of the mist rose up like a massive bubble. Something was underneath, and the mist clung to it as it rose. Soon, it began to bulge in several places, and the mist fell away like overstretched gum. As the haze vanished, a living shape emerged. There were spiderlike legs as long and as thick as tree trunks. A serpent torso appeared, ending in a knobby appendage tail, like that of a scorpion. Enormous bat wings extended from the creature's back, and its long reptilian neck ended in a snarling, spitting wolf's head the size of a truck.

Archer tried to spring into the air to engage the creature but never left the ground. Instead, he stumbled and took a nosedive. In that crashing moment, he understood why he'd heard those three distinct sounds. Another long neck uncurled from behind the creature. Upon it hung a fierce hawk's head. Its glittering eyes fixed on Archer. It gave a shrill cry that sounded to Archer like it was hungry.

Archer readied his sword and revised his attack strategy to deal with the two-headed creature. It occurred to him, a bit too late, that he'd heard not two strange noises . . . but three. Archer jumped up and flew toward the hawk's head. He cranked the sword around in a lethal right-to-left, two-handed slash that never connected. A massive red shape crashed into Archer's side, knocking him end over end until he disappeared into the mist and slammed into the mossy turf.

Archer gasped in pain, slowly becoming aware of his injuries: dislocated shoulder, broken upper arm, and three cracked ribs. In the Waking World, Archer might not have had the will to continue the fight. But this wasn't the Waking World. This was the Dream, and Archer had plenty of will.

He rose up, waist deep in the mist, and flexed the mental energy surging within. With each heartbeat, his wounds healed. In the span of moments, they just weren't there anymore. But the creature was.

Archer blinked. It was a three-headed beast now; the third—more terrifying than the others—was that of a dragon. Two long, slightly curved horns thrust back above its ears, while a shorter, sharper one protruded from its snout. Much like a unicorn, only ugly.

"You're going down first," Archer growled. In a blur, he sprinted a wide arc around the dragon-head side of the monster. It rained fire down upon the spot Archer had just vacated, missing by a gasped breath. The Dreamtreader took to the air, surging behind the creature. The dragon head turned, but not before the blade flashed white hot and sliced through its lethal path. The dragon's roar fell silent, and as Archer made a quick turn, he heard the heavy thud of the creature's head on the moors below.

The creature reeled, the two remaining heads respectively snarling and screeching. Archer did not idle. He somersaulted over the beast, tapping it on the back of its hawk's head. When it turned, Archer was ready. He silenced the screeching with a wicked lunging chop.

A vise grip of canine teeth snapped closed on Archer's leg. The wolf creature flung the Dreamtreader back and forth, shook him vigorously, and threw him to the ground. Dazed and bleeding, Archer stumbled to his feet. His flaming sword was gone, hidden somewhere under the rolling mist.

One of the beast's spider limbs jutted out, plowing into Archer's chest and pinning him to the ground. Archer felt the creature's weight bearing down and couldn't breathe, but he knew better than to panic. Instead, he used his mind. Seeing the legs, Archer thought he knew just the thing. He mind-crafted a can of Spider Slayer spray and sent a jet of the bug killer right into the wolf head's face.

It yelped and growled but did not let up the pressure on Archer's chest. *Strike one*, Archer thought urgently. Still he didn't panic. With a little more thinking, the idea came. Archer imagined a lit torch and suspended it in the air in front of the creature's face.

The monster's tail swung around and cocked backward. It was like an arrow set to the bowstring, and Archer felt certain that those nasty scorpionlike barbs were targeting his face. The tail twitched once and whipped forward.

Not wasting another split second, Archer willed the giant bug spray can to spew its contents once more. This time, the insecticide went straight through the flame of the floating torch, flaring into a gusting storm of fire.

Everything around Archer burst into flame. With frantic steps, the creature staggered backward. It loosed a gurgling, strangled yelp, collapsed into a heap, and went still.

Archer exhaled, feeling quite a bit better without the beast's foot on his chest. "You can come out now, Razz," he said. "The creature is toast."

A deep, sonorous bell rang out—Archer knew that was Old Jack, and he knew that it was his Personal Midnight. He was late for getting back to his anchor. Not good. Missing that deadline—even by a little—was something a Dreamtreader could not do. He had to get back to his anchor. Every second mattered.

Then, with a double *poof* and a rush of air, Razz materialized. "Archer, what's going on?" Razz yelped. "That's Old Jack. You can't be here! Oh, no. Oh, no. Oh, no!"

From behind, there came three more sounds: a guttural feline growl; a high, thin hiss; and something that sounded like a freight train's horn. The scorched creature had risen upon its spider legs once more. Its vast bat wings flapped and kicked up gusts of debris. Its scorpion tail whipped menacingly. More troubling still were the creature's new heads: a lion, a wide-hooded cobra, and some kind of freakish dinosaur with a crown of luminous white crystal.

"I don't have time for this," Archer muttered. "I don't have time at all." He called up his will and felt a weak surge. Of all his Dream abilities, flying took the most will. It forced the mind to cover so many details: height, weight, wind resistance, drag, propulsion, Intrusion blocking . . . Archer knew what will he had left wouldn't be enough to fly all the way back to the anchor, but it would hopefully get him over the beast.

"Disappear, Razz!" Archer yelled. "The monster is back!" He leaped skyward and soared well above the creature. He didn't dare get within range of a lightning-fast cobra strike. No, he gave himself plenty of altitude.

"Archer!" Razz shrilled.

Wicked sharp agony lit up his legs. Incredulous, Archer shouted and wrenched around to see as the cobra head's fangs sank in. He understood. *Wings*, he thought. His mind began to cloud with a sleepy haze. The creature has wings. Duh.

Archer called on his will to cleanse his bloodstream of the venom, but that wasn't good enough. He had no focus left for flying or fighting off the three-headed monster.

The cobra jaws tightened, and Archer felt himself wrenched violently through the air. Then, suddenly, he was loose . . . and falling.

He turned end over end and plummeted. On one revolution, he caught a glimpse of the cobra head snapping back and forth, unable to dislodge the branch stuck in its eye.

Good old Razz, Archer thought. The misty ground below raced up to greet him. He had enough will to slow his fall, but the whipping motion made his left arm go numb for a moment.

He scrambled to his feet and sprinted away, but the lion head craned down, cutting off his escape. Archer turned back just in time to see the third head light up.

The white crystals flared bright, as did the creature's eyes. It reared back and opened its jaws. A solid stream of bluish-white flame gushed outward. Whatever the breath touched exploded. The stream didn't stop, carving a fiery furrow and marching right toward Archer.

"What are you, some kind of Godzilla clone?" Archer yelled. "Who dreams of this stuff?"

The turf exploded in front of the Dreamtreader. Archer cartwheeled backward, smacking into the snarling face of the lion.

"Razz!" Archer cried out.

I am here, Archer! a voice answered, but it wasn't Razz.

Suddenly, a blade of lightning flashed, and the head of the Godzilla thing careened into the mist. The cobra head bounced away next. The beast and its one remaining head tried to dodge the final cut but was too slow. It roared and shrieked but fell silent.

Go now, Archer! the voice commanded, and he recognized it: the

Windmaiden, a mysterious ally who had rescued Archer before. *I will help.*

Archer scanned for Razz, but she was nowhere to be seen. He sprinted away, giving the fallen creature a wide berth. As he ran, he saw the headless necks writhing and flailing. But in a moment, a knobby clump formed at the end of each neck. Flesh peeled back, and new heads appeared: a bear, a hornet, and some kind of jelly thing with three yellow eyes.

"This is like Whac-A-Mole!" Archer growled, trying to sprint past.

I've got this! the Windmaiden called. *Go, Archer. Go, now, with my aid!*

Archer took all his remaining will and used it for a monumental leap. But as he rose into the sky, he felt a sudden pressure behind him as if an invisible hand was behind him, pushing and pushing, faster and faster. Archer felt he'd passed through a kind of elastic membrane.

Then he fell face-first in the grass next to the old wishing well.

His anchor.

Knowing he was past his Personal Midnight, Archer lunged for the well, caught its cool stone wall, and vanished from the Dream.

THREE

THE INNER SANCTUM

"WE MUST MAKE AN ODD COUPLE, EVEN FOR THE DREAM,"
Rigby said, smirking at Bezeal as they trod down the slope of hill lit
by the Dream's two moons.

The top of the resourceful merchant's hood barely reached
Rigby's elbow. His eyes, just pinpricks of yellow light in the blackness that hid all other facial features, glimmered and then dimmed
slightly. When Bezeal spoke, his voice was rich and smoky, and, as
always, he spoke only in rhyming triplets. "I care not for what these
others think. Ignorance is the poison they choose to drink. For us,
greatness awaits; we are on the brink."

"I still don't understand," Rigby said, scratching the thick side-
burn that knifed down past his ear to his square jaw. "Why shouldn't
Kara be with us for this?"

Bezeal's eyes flared slightly, a glimmer of white teeth appeared,
and he said, "As we have already thoroughly discussed, no one can
make this choice, but you . . . you must. And who can be certain who
else you can trust?"

"I trust Kara," Rigby said. "More than I trust you."

Bezeal's white grin appeared, broader and whiter than the Cheshire Cat's smile. "Wise you are to be cautious with Bezeal. And while I do not doubt the things that you feel, be wary for not all promises are real."

Rigby made a dismissive snort. Kara had been his closest friend since he'd arrived at Dresden High School. Since then, he'd shared his Lucid Dreaming secrets with her, and she'd become his trusted business partner. "I may be only sixteen, but I'm not stupid," he said.

"When many more seasons you have seen, we'll know just how wise you have been, for Bezeal knows much, much more than the average teen."

Rigby ignored the slight as they trod under shadow. He looked up. "This the place, then?"

Bezeal nodded, but Rigby didn't really need the confirmation. He'd traveled to the Central Library of Garnet Province once before, just never to the Inner Sanctum deep within. His Uncle Scoville was well known in the Dream—feared even—and given a sinister nickname: the Lurker. But even the Lurker couldn't get Rigby into the Inner Sanctum.

Rigby had spent his share of time in libraries, mostly in England before the move. Garnet's Central Library reminded Rigby of Haddon Library at the University of Cambridge. It was all serpentine arches made of faded red and gray brick, tall banks of windows that looked like half-lidded eyes out upon the world, and a stately mansion sort of roof topped off with a wrought-iron weather vane in the shape of a rooster.

Similar in so many features, Rigby thought. *Well, except for one detail. Central Library is up in a tree.*

As if in the palm of some godlike hand, the entire building was nested within the massive curling limbs of the sprawling sequoia tree. The gnarled green-brown trunk of the tree was fifteen feet thick but didn't look remotely large enough to support the huge library. Somehow, it did. The library rested up there as if it had grown right out of the tree.

Weird, Rigby reflected. *But that's the way things are in the Dream.*

Bats fluttered out of the treetops, as if to make the picture whole. Or rather, they looked like bats. "I really don't care much for these things," Rigby muttered. "Why can't we just fly up ourselves?"

"Sages' rule," Bezeal replied. "Not so cruel, to hitch a ride upon a grool."

Rigby watched the creatures spiral down to the ground. They were black, leathery, and broad, but had no visible torso, head, mouth, or eyes. How they saw, Rigby had no idea. They seemed like a pair of thick wings joined in the center by a marbled stone tile.

Rigby stepped up onto the nearest grool and tried to ignore the queasy wobbly feeling. He heard the grool's gurgling growl and wondered where the sound came from exactly.

When Bezeal boarded his own mount, the two creatures rippled. Their wings began to flap, stirring hundreds of dead leaves. Slowly, Rigby and Bezeal rose into the air.

Rigby could barely restrain the joy bubbling up inside. The Inner Sanctum. The throbbing heart of the Dream. If any place in the Dream held the answers he'd been searching for, it was here. Ever since his first Lucid Walk, Rigby had longed to search its deep lore. *It's in there*, he thought. *I'll find it, Uncle Scovy. I will.*

Beneath his confident thoughts, however, Rigby wondered if there really was a way to free his uncle. "Mad Doc Scoville," as he was known to the Waking World: Rigby's uncle had been the first to discover the secrets of Lucid Dreaming. He'd mapped out the Dream realms and even drawn conclusions about the physical laws that governed the Dream.

Unfortunately, he'd learned too late about the dangers. Scoville had gone Lucid Dreaming far too often, fraying his mind. And then, he'd stayed well beyond his session limit of eleven hours. His consciousness, his thinking mind, had been imprisoned within the Dream . . . forever. If not for the machines keeping his body alive in the Waking World, Rigby's Uncle Scoville would die. And unless Rigby could find a way to release his uncle's consciousness, his body would remain enslaved to the machines, just an empty shell of the brilliant, vigorous man he had once been.

The grools rose gently through the lower boughs of the tree and floated toward a deck platform at the library's main door. Rigby and Bezeal stepped off onto a large branch dotted by cobbled stone.

Rigby blinked as they entered the library, trying to ward off the disorientation of the sight. From the outside, Central Library seemed a large structure but nowhere near large enough to house what was inside. The vaulted ceiling was more than a hundred feet high, and the cavernous interior sprawled on left and right to distant horizons obscured by towering bookshelves. It was a labyrinth of shelving, some twenty to thirty feet tall, some reaching near to the ceiling. Others were less regular, more like great spirals of shelves, winding in and out of view and sweeping away to points unseen. The sheer number of books seemed beyond count. Hundreds of thousands . . . millions, maybe. Maybe more. It was, in all, a massive panoramic view.

"Manchester United could play in here," Rigby muttered, "and still 'ave room for practice fields."

"It is the collected wisdom of all the ages, scribed and stored within these pages. Guarded fiercely by the Sages."

"Where are they?" Rigby asked Bezeal. "The Sages, I mean."

"The Inner Sanctum is where they dwell. Among the deepest secrets they keep so well. Who else might they admit . . . only time will tell."

Bezeal led on through the maze of bookshelves. Here a left, there a right. A U-turn, followed by a long diagonal path through piles of scrolls that climbed into the air. The merchant never wavered or hesitated. It seemed to be a complex route he had handled many times before.

As they walked, Rigby watched with wonder as the many citizens of the Dream busily searched the shelves throughout the library. Some clambered like spiders up an array of eighty-foot ladders. Others who possessed limbs like insects didn't need the ladders. Still others used the grools to fly to the higher shelves. It was almost as much a sight to behold as the library itself.

At last, Bezeal's complicated path led to a strange corner. Every interior line of the library's floor and ceiling turned and angled down to this one simple arched doorway. And beyond it, was a dizzying, vast spiral stair. Carved with splendid detail and engraved with the runes of some ancient language that Rigby didn't know, each step had been made of some gray stone, though each in a different shade: charcoal, slate, storm, smoke, silver, wolf, gunmetal, and ash.

Rigby stood on the verge of the first wide step and gaped down . . . and down . . . and down. Between the endless round-and-round of the stairs, there were slivers of open air, revealing a plummeting drop.

Rigby swallowed deeply. "I know . . . I know I'm in the Dream," he said, "but something looks different down there. I 'aven't a clue why it would be different, but it is. Fear seeps up from it like a deadly vapor. I could die down there, couldn't I?"

Bezeal's white toothy grin appeared. "Many have died upon the

Gray Stair," he said. "Take not a single step without urgent care. And meddle not with the Sages' work; don't you dare."

As if on cue, two spectral gray figures drifted down and lighted softly upon the first step. They wore hooded cloaks. No, Rigby reflected, they didn't so much "wear" the cloaks. They were enshrouded by them. Tatters of gray material shifted constantly around the Sages, giving them a ghostly wavering outline. The hem of their cloaks hid their feet, and their hands were drawn up into voluminous hanging sleeves, as if in wait.

They hung in the air in front of Bezeal and Rigby, but did not look up. In fact, their hoods completely hid their faces. Synchronized perfectly in movement and timing, the two Sages crossed their arms. It seemed clear that they meant to bar the way.

Bezeal stepped forward and pulled something from one of the many deep pockets of his own cloak. It was a silver metallic cube with some kind of engraved markings.

Rigby squinted at it. He asked, "Is that the Karakurian Cham—"

"SHHHHHH!" The Sages looked up abruptly. Each one sliced a hasty finger to its lips like a blade. Except they had no visible lips.

To Rigby's dismay, there were no faces at all beneath the Sages' hoods. It was a pale blank mask filling each hood but bearing no features. Rigby stared, and it seemed to him that their faces might not be solid. It was like staring into some liquid, cloudy with milk or some other pale mix. That and their fierce shushing combined to raise every hair on Rigby's neck.

Bezeal cleared his throat. The Sages turned to stare at him and what he held in his palm. The merchant calmly moved three greenish fingers along the metal. There came a tinkling of bells like a music box, light and pretty, and the cube began to unfold into platforms. Tiny silver skeletons appeared and began to dance.

"Ahhhh," the Sages said at once. "Descend."

The Sages whispered, but Rigby felt each vowel, consonant, and syllable as if being pelted with hailstones. He couldn't wait to get away from the creepy library keepers.

Bezeal felt around beneath the box's skeleton platform. There was a metallic click, and one by one, the skeletons leaped and then fell down through a hole in the platform. The puzzle box reformed into a simple cube.

"Come," Bezeal whispered. "And be very, very quiet."

Given the Sages' frightful reaction to his voice and Bezeal's uncharacteristic lack of rhyme, Rigby decided to honor the old saying, "Silence is golden."

From the moment his booted foot hit the first step, Rigby felt a fierce gravity working. Any fall would be deadly, he knew, even if he had the will to fly at the moment. Small gaps in the steps revealed as much. Rigby held on to the smooth granite rail and cautiously placed each and every step. In a few moments of descent, the close wall surrounding the spiral stair came to an end, and the Inner Sanctum was at last revealed.

Impossible, Rigby thought, gasping. The stairs were in the exact center of a colossal round chamber, hundreds of feet in diameter and a thousand feet deep. And it was all bookshelves, wall to wall and floor to ceiling. Here and there, an arched stained-glass window cast colorful light beams across the chamber, revealing the Sages at work. They floated or flew, carrying armfuls of books for re-shelving. Back and forth, up and down, the Sages hovered, moving with incredible precision. It seemed to Rigby like watching an ant farm or maybe a beehive: constant motion, but everything purposeful.

"Whoa," Rigby whispered. He had watched a Sage place a book on the shelf, and the moment the volume left the Sage's hand, it sent a wavelike ripple surging through all the shelves. Each time a book was delivered to its proper place, a new ripple traveled round and round the chamber.

Rigby was so intently watching the Sages at work that he stumbled. His foot hit nothing but air as he went down. He didn't even have time to yell. Bezeal was there at his side, grabbing Rigby before he could fall. Rigby fought back to his feet, stood, and found himself surrounded by a dozen Sages.

"SHHHHH!" they hissed in unison. Their faces—their blank, pale faces—changed. The roiling cloudy mask morphed into a black-eyed skullish shape.

"I . . . I apologize," Rigby muttered.

"SHHHH!"

"Come quietly, I told you so," Bezeal whispered. He ushered Rigby away. "No time for gaping at this show. Our destination waits below."

Rigby kept his head on a swivel for the rest of the long journey down the Gray Stair, watching the Sages and staring back at the steps so as not to stumble again or make any noise whatsoever.

At the bottom of the Gray Stair, a broad floor stretched fifty yards in every direction, its white stone glistening. Rigby noted imperfections in it; spidering cracks lay scattered here and there. They looked like the marks of impact. Rigby glanced up at the height of the curling stair and shuddered.

"This way," Bezeal whispered. "No delay. Heed . . . what I say."

"You know," Rigby whispered back, "that whole rhyming triplet thing? It gets kind of old."

Bezeal turned, and a frosty white grin appeared in the blackness beneath his hood. He led Rigby to the outskirts of the marble floor and stopped at the sheer blank wall. Bezeal inhaled deeply, leaned forward, and released the breath.

The wall moved.

It was as if it weren't a wall at all but some kind of powder that could be disturbed by a breath. Bezeal stepped forward and, in a whirling cloud of white, disappeared into the wall. Rigby shrugged and followed.

On the other side, darkness waited. Darkness broken only by a torch at the distant end of a narrow corridor. Rigby followed Bezeal until they stopped just a few yards away from the flickering, spitting torch.

Rigby wasn't sure what happened then. Emotions—prickles of nerves and something else—flooded his body. Something drew his gaze down. There, in the floor, sat a door. Not a trapdoor but an honest-to-goodness, full-sized door. It was framed in a kind of faded gray-blue stone, carved with ornate renderings of symbols, markings, and designs, none of which Rigby recognized in the least.

The door, an extremely dark wood with hints of red, was divided into eight equal panels. These, too, were carved with marvelous detail. So intricate was their design that Rigby felt like he couldn't look at them for long without his eyes playing tricks. Faces appeared in the wood. Moaning, anguished faces. When Rigby blinked, they were gone.

Where the door's knob might have been, there was instead a rack of deer antlers. These were gnarled and twisted and wickedly sharp. "At last," Rigby said. He took hold of the antlers and pulled. The door didn't move.

"Pull and pull with all your might," Bezeal said, "the door won't open; it's locked tight. The Karakurian Chamber requires a key . . . and a price that's right."

"Karakurian Chamber?" Rigby echoed, ignoring the not-so-

WAYNE THOMAS BATSON

rhyming end of Bezeal's speech. "I thought that was the little puzzle box you carry around."

"I told the Dreamtreaders that was its name. It was the only way they would play my game. But the real chamber is here . . . all the same."

Bezeal held out the silver puzzle box. His green fingers roamed its surface, and again, the silvery skeletons began to dance. Soon, a tall ship with many sails popped up and seemed to move on undulating waves. Bezeal's fingers worked once more. The metal of the skeletons and the ship began to twist and move as if of its own accord. The familiar images unraveled but began to wind anew into another form. The color changed from pure silver to a weathered bronze. In a flurry of clinking and clicking, the threads of metal wound tighter and tighter until, at last, a solid eight-inch key remained.

"Perfect," Rigby whispered. He held his hand out.

Bezeal's pinprick eyes glinted back, but he did not hand over the key.

"What are you waiting for?" Rigby asked. "I need to get inside the Karakurian Chamber. I need to research."

Bezeal held on to the key and did not reply.

Rigby moved a few steps toward Bezeal and towered over him. "You told me of this place, Bezeal. You brought me here. You said this was for me, and I want it. I want it now."

"Good, good, your ire climbs, as it should at certain times. But to give the key for free would be a crime."

"I'm warning you, Bezeal," Rigby growled, stepping closer. "Cut the games. Give me the key."

"You may use the key for now," Bezeal said, his voice warbling more than usual and dropping an octave. "I'll even show you how. But each time requires of you . . . a vow."

27

"Whatever, Bezeal," Rigby grumbled. "You want a deal? Fine. If it's within my powers to grant, I'll do whatever you want."

The Cheshire Cat smile returned, and the merchant beckoned for Rigby to kneel. When Rigby did (with a sigh), Bezeal whispered into his ear.

Rigby's eyes bulged. "What? Kara?" he blurted. "But . . . I can't."

Bezeal whispered again.

Rigby shook his head, but he said, "All right. I'll do it, but I'm certain you're wrong. About her, that is. If she proves me out, the deal's off."

Bezeal drew back from Rigby and held out his palm. "Take now the Shadow Key. For one hour, delve the chamber, for you are free. So many secrets wait for thee."

"One hour?" Rigby scoffed. "But I've got six hours left in the Dream."

"The vow you've made is . . . ah! So small. Next time, the Shadow Key will cost a greater haul . . . and I'll come to collect, collect it all."

Rigby rolled his eyes and took the key from Bezeal's hand. He stopped smiling a moment. The key was heavier than he'd expected, and the metal was icy cold. But there was more. Taking the key felt somehow like a transaction. In accepting the key, Rigby felt as if he'd just given away a part of himself. He had a fleeting thought of his Uncle Scovy wasting away on that sterile bed and tethered to all those cursed machines.

Rigby dropped to a knee and jammed the key into the matching keyhole just beneath the antler rack. Nothing happened.

"Push the key in; force it deep. Twist it left in a long, fluid sweep. Unlock the secrets for you to reap."

Rigby did as instructed. The Shadow Key sank deep, all the way to its bow, the intricate handle pinched between Rigby's fingers. It would go no deeper, so Rigby began the turn to the left. The movement felt strangely exhilarating, like making a perfect kick in soccer or finally solving a difficult math problem. There came a chimelike click, and Rigby heard a ghostly chorus of moans.

"There something alive in there?" Rigby demanded. "Something behind the door?"

Bezeal laughed. "Several somethings there might be. Wondrous sights are what you'll see. Open up, and set them free!"

"Wait, wait," Rigby said. "I don't want to open this door."

All eight wooden panels of the door began to tremble. One by one, they popped open on hinges of their own. Rigby jumped back, but not fast enough or far enough to avoid the onslaught.

Shrieking and seething, the creatures spewed up and out. They were almost transparent, vaguely shaped like men but seemingly boneless in the way that their features and limbs stretched and surged. Several of them found Rigby at once, clinging to him, embracing him. Their long, sinuous limbs each ended in a kind of black patch of barbs, like fingers and toes made of pitch-colored sea urchins.

Rigby groaned, fell backward, and writhed, crying out for help.

"That is enough, pesky Scath," Bezeal commanded. "Off you go now on a different path. Depart now, or face my wrath."

The shadowy man figures immediately unraveled from Rigby. With a flurry of angry, red-eyed glints, the creatures fled. They disappeared into thin air, each with a thin popping sound.

Rigby rose to his hands and knees. Coughing and grimacing at first, he soon began to laugh. "It's . . . it's in there," he gasped. "The book I need. It's in the Karakurian Chamber! Ha-ha, I knew I'd find it, Uncle. I knew it!"

"Yes, yes, yes," Bezeal whispered.

"Those . . . those things," Rigby said, clambering to his feet.

"The pain was nearly unbearable, but they made me see things . . . see inside the Sanctum. I know just where to look now."

There came a great creaking, and the dark wooden door wrenched open, revealing a thin stairwell lit in red light.

"Go now and get the knowledge you seek," Bezeal said. "The Scath are away, dream havoc to wreak. And there is but one hour for you, so do not be meek."

Rigby stood at the top of the stairs, took a deep breath, and began his descent. When he was gone from view, Bezeal turned the Shadow Key back to the right and removed it. The heavy door to the Inner Sanctum swung slowly back and shut tight within the floor.

FOUR

SNOW FALLS GENTLY

"DUDE, LOOK OUT!" BUSTER YELLED. HE CARVED A tight, snow-spraying curl right between the old well and two goggle-eyed teenagers dragging sleds: Archer and his good friend Amy Pitsitakas. Buster's move covered them both in fresh powder.

"Thanks a lot, Buster," Archer grumbled at his eleven-year-old little brother. "You know, we were *trying* to stay out of your way by walking back up behind the well."

"But you got us good anyway," Amy said, shaking piles from her knit cap. "Real good, yep."

Just then, Kaylie's plastic sled arrived with a crusty stop. Putting a mittened hand on the well for balance, Archer's eight-year-old sister clambered to her feet. She held up her iPod and grinned. "I got the whole thing!" she shouted triumphantly, bouncing so that her strawberry blond hair swung around to cover half her face and then back behind her ruddy cheeks. "That was perfect, Buster."

"You post it yet?" Buster said, holding up his thumb and pinkie, giving her the *hang loose* sign.

Kaylie had taken off her mittens and was tip-tapping on the touch screen. "Done," she said.

"Great," Archer said. "Another embarrassing video of me for the whole world to see."

"Rock on!" Buster exulted. That was Buster. Born to surf and snowboard. Little Mr. Extreme Games, Buster was the only one of the kids to avoid the red hair, pale-skin-with-freckles Keaton gene. His hair was blond, and he had naturally dark olive skin—an all-the-time perfect tan—something most people did not have in Maryland in December.

"You two look like Mr. and Mrs. Jack Frost," Kaylie said, giggling. "Though, technically, you're covered in snow . . . not frozen water vapor."

"Like I would ever marry Jack Frost," Amy said, giving Archer a playful shove.

Archer's cheeks, already ruddy from the cold, turned beet red. "Enough marriage talk!" he said, shaking his snowy glove above Amy's head.

"Hey! Like I need more snow in my hair? Really?"

"Race to the bottom?" Buster challenged.

"I'm in!" Amy said. She dropped her sled and lay on top of it. "But I get the left side. It's more packed down . . . faster."

"Sure!" Buster said. "Still have no chance."

"Neither one of you has any chance," Kaylie said as she plopped into her sled and shoved off. She was ten yards away when she called back, "I'll beat you both!"

"Kaylie!" Buster growled. "That's just so wrong." He gave a twist of his torso and took off after her. Amy did too.

But not Archer.

The surprise snow day off from school had been a great blessing.

Chocolate chip cookie dough waited in the fridge for baking. Hot cocoa too, but Archer just wasn't feeling it. He stood alone by the well, watched the snow falling, and was enveloped by the forlorn silence.

I am alone.

The thought came unbidden, but Archer couldn't shake it. Kara Windchil, his old best friend, avoided him now. His father was still detached and distant. And, of course, Archer was the only Dreamtreader left. Duncan and Mesmeera were gone, and Master Gabriel had yet to select two more to fill their roles. The events of the previous summer came rushing back in a fiery vision.

The Trees of Life and Death. Archer had been deceived into thinking that destroying those trees was the key to taking down the Nightmare Lord. The inferno Archer created had reduced the trees to smoking cinders, but among the ashes were the remains of Duncan and Mesmeera.

My pride, Archer thought, *my impulsive . . . desperate need to win, and it all turned to death . . . and ash.* Archer laughed humorlessly at the irony. *And now, I almost took myself out.*

He shook his head and exhaled, muttering, "The Windmaiden got me to my anchor ten times faster than I ever could have, but I heard Old Jack's toll. I missed my Personal Midnight. So why didn't I get trapped in the Dream?"

It was one of a dozen questions that would have to wait for his next meeting with Master Gabriel.

Archer leaned over the cobbled stone edge of the well and gazed absently into the darkness below. This old well had been on Keaton property for more than a hundred years, long before the Keatons owned the land. It was nothing fancy, just an artesian well built of cobbled stone with a wooden frame where the rope and bucket hung beneath a little shingled roof. But it was Archer's mom's favorite. She said it made their house a home and their property something to be proud of. The water from it, she claimed, was the purest and coldest freshwater to be found anywhere. She'd always believed it was special.

"It is special, Mom," Archer whispered. He picked at a little fleck of mortar from the seams between stones and then dropped it into the well. It made a dull plunk in the yet unfrozen water. "It was special because you loved it."

He listened to the snowy silence. Snow falling always muffled the noise: traffic, neighbors, wildlife. It was peaceful, but not pleasant for Archer. The cancer had taken his mom away eight years earlier . . . on a snowy morning.

But Archer had kept the well close to his heart, making it his Dreamtreading anchor and, through all the crazy stuff of life, always bringing Archer back to the important things.

Like family and friends, maybe? The thought broadsided Archer. *What am I doing being so mopey on a snow day?*

As Archer walked away, the roof of the well caught his hat. He spun to grab it but accidentally knocked it over the edge. It disappeared into the well.

"Snot rockets!" he exclaimed. "That was graceful." He laughed and winced. "Ribs are still sore." Archer shrugged it off as best he could, plopped down on his sled, and shoved off. "Oh, Buster, I hope you're walking back up the hill. I have a little something for ya!"

☥

"That was crazy!" Amy said, raising her fist in the air. "But I won, yep."

"I thought we had, like, a no-contact rule," Buster replied. He huffed to catch up to Amy on the hill, by the well.

"You had it coming," Archer said, right behind them. "Trying to cut in front of us like that."

"She knocked me clear off my snowboard!" Buster complained. Then he grinned and winked. "Gnarly bump though. Kinda fun."

Kaylie giggled and bounced at Archer's elbow. "Hot cocoa time!" she said, her breath in little puffs of white. "Can we, Archer? Can we now?"

Archer shook his head to get the snow out of his hair. "Yeah, I could use a break," he said. "Getting cold out here."

"Where's your hat?" Amy asked.

Archer laugh-snorted.

"Awww," Amy said. "Your laugh is so cute."

"Ewww," Kaylie said. "Sounds like a cat when it has a hair ball."

"Does not," Archer said, but his snorting laughter continued. "Okay, maybe it does a little."

"What's so funny?" Amy asked.

"My hat," he said. "I accidentally dropped it in the well."

"Nice one, chief," Buster said.

Amy tromped to the side of the well and looked down. "It went all the way down?"

"Afraid so."

"It's dark down there," she said. "Can't see anything. We could get some fishing line and a hook . . . maybe fish it up out of there?"

"It can wait," Archer said, chuckling.

They continued walking up the hill, far past the well, when Kaylie stopped dead in her tracks. "Hold on."

Archer didn't like the tone of her voice: high, thin, and brittle. She was afraid. "What's wrong?"

Kaylie pointed down into the snow near the base of the well. "Weird footprints," she said.

Archer shook away the chill and went to Kaylie's side. He put his arm around her and asked, "Where?"

"There," she huffed impatiently. "By the well . . . it kinda goes off into the pine trees."

Archer stepped around to Kaylie's right and gazed down. The chill came right back, sliding down his neck and spine like icy drizzle. There could be no doubt. There were footprints. The way they were spaced, like a right foot then a left and so on, showed something had walked in the snow there.

"I didn't see those before," Buster said. "Creepy."

Creepy *doesn't begin to cover it*, Archer thought.

"There are more." Amy pointed to several other tracks. Some of them overlapped or crisscrossed the others. But they all led into the pines.

"Kaylie," he said quietly, "what could make prints like these?"

"I'm not sure," she said. "They're bipedal."

"What?" Buster blurted. "Speak English."

"Bipedal," she repeated and rolled her eyes. "It means they walk on two feet. You can tell from the spacing."

"But they're smaller," Archer said.

"I don't think these are human," Kaylie said, bending over and pointing. "Look. These aren't toes. These are claws or maybe talons. Look closer."

Kaylie was right; Archer had never seen footprints like these. They'd had deer on the property, rabbits, squirrels, raccoons, and even a stray black bear cub once. But those critters left prints any western Marylander could recognize. Each of these was long, like the mark left by a person's bare foot, only smaller, like a child's size. But where the toes would have been on a human footprint, there were six blade-thin gouges. Two similar cuts dug into the snow at the heel.

On top of that, the snow was discolored to an ashen gray tint. It reminded Archer of the nasty chemical-infused slush left on the roads by snowplows and salt trucks after they passed.

"In fact," Kaylie went on, her eight-year-old fears giving way to her off-the-charts-advanced intellect, "with the ones near the heel, I'm thinking these might be from some birds."

"Birds?" Amy echoed.

"Had to be," Kaylie said as if the conclusion were obvious.

"Strange birds . . ." Archer didn't get it. "Why?"

Kaylie blinked up at him, squinted, and said, "The prints are all one direction."

"So?"

"So, whatever they were, they didn't walk out of the trees up to the well and then back. The footprints all lead from the well to the trees. They had to fly in."

"Why would birds fly to the well?" Amy asked.

"Maybe to get water," Kaylie said. "Maybe there are bugs down there."

"Whatever," Buster muttered. "Let's get some cocoa." The most energetic Keaton sibling charged up the hill.

Amy and Kaylie followed, with Archer just behind. He walked slowly, the gears in his mind still spinning. Kaylie had said the footprints leading away from the well meant that birds had flown to the well and then walked back to the woods. For all her brilliance, Kaylie had seen only one possibility. But there was another possible conclusion.

Something might have come up out of the well.

Six cups of hot cocoa and fourteen cookies later, Archer felt much less worried about creepy things crawling out of the well. At least he hadn't lost his legendary appetite. Besides, he had other, much more important concerns.

He passed through the den and looked to make sure his father wasn't around. Archer hadn't seen him all morning, but he could never be too sure. With the coast clear, Archer shrugged and marched up the stairs and stepped into his room. He shut and locked the door. He closed his blinds and curtains and then went to his closet. With one more look over his shoulder, Archer reached up to the highest shelf and felt around until his fingers touched a metallic edge. It was the new silver case he'd gotten for his birthday. His father had told him the case was military grade: tamper-proof, fireproof, even bulletproof—perfect for an extremely valuable comic book collection. Only Archer had chosen to use the case for something a little more important than his comics.

Of course, Archer knew, no matter how strong and tamper-proof the case was, it wouldn't be Kaylie-proof. More than a prodigy, Kaylie was smarter than anyone Archer knew. She was particularly brilliant with electronics and puzzles. The simple combination lock on his old case was no problem for her. More than once, she'd cracked it open to read his *Dreamtreader's Creed*, the textbook of lore studied by all Dreamtreaders. Hence all the secrecy with his new case and its contents.

Archer opened the silver lid, releasing a hiss of breathy air, a glimmer of blue light, and a hefty leather-bound book.

At least she doesn't know about the Summoning Feather, Archer thought, turning all the pages of text to get to the back of the book. There, a long pocket held a single white feather. Archer tossed the feather toward his ceiling. It spiraled down for a moment but then sparkled and transformed to a pair of radiant golden wings. These fluttered upward until disappearing through the ceiling.

"What do you want now?" Master Gabriel asked from behind.

"Why . . . do you always show up behind me?" Archer grumbled as he turned. "You could give a guy a heart attack—uhm . . . okay . . ." Archer was speechless for a moment. He'd been expecting the master Dreamtreader, commander, and teacher to appear in his Incandescent Armor, the glowing, medieval-cool battle gear he usually wore. But not today. "That's different."

Master Gabriel straightened his bow tie and said, "What on earth is the matter this time?"

"A tuxedo?" Archer asked. "Really? You going to an awards show tonight?"

"I fail to see the humor. You know I am permitted but two garbs: the armor and the style of the day."

Archer looked his guardian over. It was a nicely tailored black-tie tux. Gabriel wore his wavy white hair back in a tail, and it seemed even his mustache and beard were neatly groomed. The dark shades were a nice touch too. *Gabriel and his sunglasses,* Archer thought before saying, "Look, that's still not the style of the day. I mean, for a big dinner or some kind of event, maybe. Honestly, if you want the style of the day, just go casual. You know, jeans and a T-shirt or a hoodie."

Master Gabriel arched one eyebrow above the rim of his shades. "A . . . hoodie?"

"Never mind," Archer said, shaking his head. "We need to talk."

"The breaches. I know," Gabriel said. "They continue to worsen."

"Hundreds of them . . . every night now," Archer explained. He placed his Creed back in the protective case and then stretched to put it back on the closet's top shelf. He groaned slightly and rubbed his side. "It's insane. Even with Bezeal's paste, I'm falling behind. And that paste doesn't hold for long. Honestly, it's like Whac-A-Mole up there. No sooner do I sew a breach up than another one rips open. We can't go on like this. I need help."

"And help you shall have."

"No, you don't understand," Archer continued. "I need more than Razz. I need partners. I need—"

"You need two more Dreamtreaders," Gabriel said, finishing Archer's sentence. "Of course you do, and it's long overdue that you muster the courage to ask. You cannot do it all because you were never intended to do it all. But this is a lesson hard learned for you, is it not?"

Archer laughed sadly and winced again. "So . . . all this time . . . all I had to do was ask?"

"Don't be absurd," Master Gabriel replied. "Do you think I would risk letting breaches go unpatched just to teach you a lesson?"

"Uhm, the thought had crossed my mind."

Master Gabriel glowered. "As you should know, Dreamtreaders are rare. It takes time to identify them, time to awaken them, and much more time to properly train them. But, as it happens, I have found a new Dreamtreader for Pattern. And you will train him."

"Me?" Archer plopped down onto his bed.

"I will be quite busy with other things," he said. "I think I have identified the third Dreamtreader, but there are concerns. You will begin with Duncan's replacement for the Pattern District. His name is Nick Bushman. You'll have to find him in the Dream and awaken him."

"I've never done that before," Archer said. "How will I find him?"

"You have enough skills and knowledge to get started, but . . ." Master Gabriel reached inside his tux coat pocket and took out a short roll of parchment. He seemed to weigh it in his hands for a moment before holding it out for Archer. "This will explain where to find Nick and how to awaken him safely."

Archer reached out for the parchment and felt a twinge of pain again in his ribs. "Safely?"

Gabriel stared thoughtfully. "There's a small chance that you could . . . drive him mad. But really, it's an insignificant and unlikely chance. Just follow the instructions."

"Great," Archer muttered. He coughed and held his ribs. "That sounds . . . fun."

"Fun is beside the point. Dreamtreading is a high calling, Archer. And we both have our jobs to do."

Archer fiddled with the seal on the scroll, tugging at the parchment on either side. "Hey, it won't open."

Master Gabriel took off his sunglasses and gave Archer a flat stare. "It will open when the time comes. Keep it with you at all times and read it when it opens. And, Archer? Read it carefully. It will disintegrate in a matter of minutes."

"What is this, *Mission: Impossible*?" Archer laughed and winced.

"Certainly this mission will be difficult but not impossible."

"It was a joke," Archer explained, laughing harder and holding his ribs.

"I fail to see the point of this humor. It's in poor taste to laugh at my—" Master Gabriel cut his words short to glare at Archer. "What are you doing? Stop all that wincing. What's the matter with you?"

"Sorry," Archer said. "It just hurts to laugh. My ribs are sore from Dreamtreading last night. That's all."

The master of Dreamtreading lost his scowl and any hint of color in his face. There was a long, cold moment before he said, "You are not supposed to be sore from Dreamtreading."

"Well, anyone would," Archer replied, squinting. "I mean, it was this nasty three-headed—well, it was multiheaded, actually—but anyway, I took a few hard shots to the ribs and—"

"Archer Percival Keaton, listen to me. You are a Dreamtreader. You were in the Dream. You are not supposed to be sore."

Archer's mouth snapped shut. He ran his fingers lightly over the sore spot on his ribs. Then, slowly, he lifted the corner of his T-shirt. The hem passed the pale pink of his abdominal muscles, rose a few inches more where his skin became a smoky bluish, and then rode over his ribs, which were an ugly dark purple.

When Archer gasped, pain rippled across his ribs. He dropped the edge of his shirt. *Duh*, Archer thought, rolling his eyes. *I should have thought of this earlier.* He knew that wounds in the Dream should never have produced wounds in the real world. *What's going on?*

"Think, Archer," Gabriel commanded. "Could that injury have occurred in some other way? I mean, some other way in the Temporal?"

Archer felt as if Buster had shoved a handful of snow down the back of his shirt. "No," he said finally. "I can't think of anything I've done that could've cracked a rib. The bruises are right where the creature struck me. I healed them in the Dream, like always. But . . . wait."

"What is it?"

Archer expelled a deep breath. "No . . . no, no, no. It wasn't in the Dream. Sheesh, I'm an idiot."

"That is beside the point. Would you please get to it?"

"I was sledding all morning," Archer said. "The sled is an older one, all made of wood and metal. I let Kaylie ride on my back a few times. Must have put too much pressure on my ribs."

Master Gabriel sighed. "That is a relief. A huge relief. But you be mindful, Archer. There's no telling what could happen if the Dream fabric is allowed to weaken."

Archer pondered that a moment.

"When will you go Dreamtreading again?" Master Gabriel asked.

"I can't go tonight," Archer said. "Law Nine. Tomorrow night for sure."

"Very well. Keep me posted. I will return soon with news of your new Dreamtreading partners."

"What about number three? Who's going to take the Verse District? I was hoping you'd reconsider—"

"I said I will return with news, Archer. Not wait around to deliver the news . . . now."

Gabriel vanished in a scattering of tiny shooting stars. Archer watched them streak, brighten, and go out. Somehow the stars seemed angry. Master Gabriel certainly had been.

Archer unlocked his bedroom door. When he opened it, he found Kaylie on the other side. She immediately began to whistle. She grinned innocently. For a moment, Archer thought a little halo might appear over her head. He wasn't buying it for a second.

"Kaylie, were you eavesdropping?"

"Who . . . me?" Kaylie giggled nervously. "I was actually looking for Dad. Oh, but I guess he's in the basement. Nope, not eavesdropping on you and Mr. Gabriel at all."

Archer crossed his arms. "Kaaay-lieee, if you weren't eavesdropping, how did you know who I was talking to?"

Kaylie just smiled. "Well, duh, silly. It was the weird blue glow around the door. Hello?" She pranced away without another word.

Bluish glow, he thought. *She's not supposed to see that. Or . . . maybe she was.* Archer thought back to the fateful battle against the Nightmare Lord. It seemed so long ago, but it wasn't. Not at all. Things would have turned out very differently if Kaylie hadn't helped out. She was a natural. If only Master Gabriel would see . . .

Archer went back to his room to check his text messages. Nothing new appeared on his phone. All in all, the visit with the Master Dreamtreader had gone pretty well. The prospect of finally getting some help was encouraging. But still . . .

Archer couldn't banish the unsettled feelings that were crawling around in the pit of his stomach. Gabriel had said things could go very wrong "if the Dream fabric is allowed to weaken." Archer knew if he didn't get help sealing up the breaches soon, it wouldn't be a question of "if," but "when."

DREAMTREADER'S CREED, CONCEPTUS 6

Temporal, Ethereal, and Dream.

Three worlds, separated by the unseen fabric from which all things are knit together. Your domain, Dreamtreader—your charge—is, of course, the Dream. But in patrolling and safeguarding the Dream, you shepherd also the Temporal . . . your waking world. Have a care, for this is no small thing. Either by purposeful attack or by sheer decay over time, breaches will appear in the fabric. Dream matter will intermingle with what you would call reality, creating peculiarities that neither world will be able to explain. As a Dreamtreader, your chief concern is to find and seal each and every breach.

Leave the breaches to rot and fester, and they will expand. Like the tide eating away at a castle in the sand, the fabric will weaken. It will grow unstable. Breach will tear into breach, form—ing larger and larger ruptures in the Dream fabric until, at last, a rift will form. Dream and Temporal will merge, and no citizen of one will know for certain which realm he is in, whether he is asleep or is awake.

All will be chaos as the people of the Temporal realize their new abilities make them feel invincible when they are far from it. People will die by the thousands. And in the Dream, whether a Nightmare Lord sits on the throne or not, there will be terrifying storms. Intrusion waves churned up by the sudden and simultaneous nightmares of millions will boil up and rage across the Dreamscape.

If a rift be allowed to form, all will pay a dear price.

FIVE

NO MORE NIGHTMARES

"WHAT'S WRONG?"

Archer glanced up from the lunch table and found Amy's owlish gaze surveying him. "Nothing," he mumbled, again letting the buzz of the cafeteria—teachers droning on the PA, staccato bursts of laughter, the clatter of trays, the slurp of milk, and a hundred conversations—wash over him like a tide.

"Nothing?" Amy echoed. She put her lunch tray down on the table. "I'm not buying it, Archer. You look like you just swallowed a sea urchin, yep. So what's the deal?"

He exhaled deeply and said nothing. He didn't mean to be rude to Amy, didn't mean to stare, but he couldn't help it. Kara and Rigby sat at the corner table where they always sat at lunch. Today, like always, they were deep in conversation. And, like always, there were grins, laughs, and knowing glances. It made Archer sick. It was—

"Excuse me?" Amy's voice pierced the cloud. "Earth to Archer. I'm right here, y'know." She followed his gaze. Behind her round wire-rim glasses, her eyes narrowed. "Oh, oh, I see it now. You're still nursing an old crush, aren't you?"

"What?" Archer snapped suddenly from his thoughts. "Wha-a-t crush? Me? No. Of course not."

Amy put a hand on her hip and tilted her head to the side. "As if I weren't here all last year? C'mon, Archer, you were totally crushing on Kara Windchil. I mean, who could blame you, really? Long, perfectly straight, silken black hair . . . dark eyebrows and lashes . . . those weird but alluring blue eyes?"

"Stop it, Amy," Archer said. "You make her sound like a goddess."

"She is," Amy replied. She smirked. "Or at least she thinks she is."

"Cut it out, would ya, Amy? You're just as pretty. And I am not still crushing on her. I'm—"

Amy picked up her lunch tray and walked away. It was a strange walk, slow and measured. And then, the look. Amy turned her head just enough for Archer to see a glimmer from her left eye. There was profound happiness in that eye: a kind of joyful lightness and a kindling fire of hope.

What did I say? he wondered frantically. *She was the one describing Kara like some kind of gorgeous movie star. I didn't . . .* That's when Archer got it. *I told Amy she was just as pretty.*

Archer gave himself a wicked facepalm. "I can't believe it," he muttered crossly. He had to admit it was true. Sure, Amy was pretty in a mousy kind of way, but still . . . And her personality, her heart was so much kinder—

Stop. Archer dropped a nuke on those thoughts.

When he looked back at Kara and Rigby, he had a completely different mind-set. Archer shook his head and wondered how he ever could have trusted either one of them. He glanced up at the clock. Five minutes left of lunch. He hadn't even touched his food. That was something of a tragedy for Archer because food . . . well, food was glorious. But the churning in his stomach warned him that eating something now . . . would not end well.

But, Archer reflected, he had trusted them. His decision. Thanks to his Uncle Scoville's groundbreaking research, Rigby had learned to Lucid Dream. He could enter the Dream consciously, just like a Dreamtreader. And he'd taught others: Kara . . . and a whole team of kids from his old school. Archer had called them allies, and together they'd routed the Nightmare Lord from his fortress at Number 6 Rue de la Mort.

Routed, he thought. *Not quite.* The Nightmare Lord had tricked them all. He'd tricked Archer most of all, tricking him into a foolish, tragic move that cost the lives of his Dreamtreader allies, Duncan and Mesmeera. Still, in the end, the Nightmare Lord lost. Archer took some solace in that.

But even that victory felt hollow because Rigby and Kara had claimed the rulership of the Dream. And worse still, they'd begun to market Lucid Dreaming . . . as a business venture. They'd begun taking some of the world's richest and most privileged on Dream safaris and making buckets of money from it.

Safaris. Archer rolled his eyes. How could Rigby and Kara be so shortsighted? Taking more and more private citizens into Lucid Dreams as if it were no more dangerous than watching lions and gazelles from a touring bus?

They pretended to be just advisors to the company, Dream Inc., but Archer knew better. Rigby Thames was too ambitious, too controlling to let others manage what really amounted to his family's secret heritage. Rigby's Uncle Scoville had begun the research and had discovered the methods and most of the rules to Lucid Dreaming, but he'd paid a hefty price for it. His consciousness remained trapped in the Dream, while his body stayed hooked to life-support machines in a wing of Rigby's basement. No, Rigby was the brains and the will of Dream Inc., and Kara had become Rigby's right hand.

It's their fault, Archer thought. *Their fault the breaches are multiplying like they are. And if someone doesn't stop them, they're going to tear up the Dream so badly that a rift forms.*

"No," Archer muttered. "I'm not going to let that happen." He stood up, left his tray where it was, and headed for the corner of the cafeteria. On the way, he reached into his jacket pocket and tested Master Gabriel's scroll. It was still sealed tight. *Figures*, Archer thought. *Well, while I'm waiting for Master Gabriel to get things ready for the new Dreamtreaders, I'm going to take care of things here.*

Just then, the bell rang. Rigby and Kara were already moving, taking their trays to the lunch line window. Archer cut them off.

"Hey!" Rigby jerked his tray to the side. "What're you doing, Keaton? You almost got painted with barbecue sauce."

"We need to talk," Archer said. He glanced at Kara. She looked away.

"The bell's rung," Rigby said, his voice still spiced with England, where he spent most of his life. "You 'ad to wait until the end of lunch, did you?"

Archer stood his ground, glanced over his shoulder, and lowered his voice. "Look, Rigby, this Dream Inc. stuff has to stop. You're ripping too many breaches in the Dream fabric."

Kara gasped. "Archer!"

Rigby was suddenly there in Archer's face. "Shut up, Keaton!" he hissed. "Or I'll—"

"Or you'll what?" Archer challenged. And that was a risk. Rigby was dangerous. He'd once taken down David "Guzzy" Gorvalec, the school's worst bully, with one punch. But Archer knew how to defend himself. He figured he could pretty much hold his own with anyone.

"The teachers are watching," Kara warned.

Rigby's brown eyes smoldered. Archer did his best to match, fiercifying his own glare. Their faces were just inches apart. Finally, Rigby looked away.

"Fine," he said. "We'll talk. But not here."

"Where and when?" Archer demanded.

"My house. After school today. Be there at four. Don't be late."

Scoville Manor perched like a gargantuan gargoyle on a hill a few blocks away from Archer's street. It was a towering Victorian mansion: three stories, two protruding gabled roofs, two tall brick chimneys, some kind of attic sub-roof with a widow's walk, and the whole thing was topped by a dark wrought-iron weather vane in the shape of a galloping horse.

Archer trod up the slushy uneven walk, with Kaylie rushing up onto the porch to push the glowing doorbell button. They waited, puffs of breath appearing and vanishing like ghosts in the unseasonably frigid air. The bell triggered the usual ruckus of barks, squawks, chirps, and growls—the welcome from Rigby's basement full of exotic animals—until the door eased open.

"You're early," Rigby said through the crack in the door. "Kara's not even here yet. And . . . what's she doing here?"

Archer put his hand on Kaylie's shoulder. "She wanted to see the pets," he said. "Kaylie loves your little zoo so much. She even considers several of the meerkats to be family. And Doctor Who, of course. You don't mind, do you? She volunteered to feed and clean all the animals."

"Please," Kaylie mewed.

"You'll feed and clean, hmm?" Rigby asked.

Kaylie nodded vigorously, and Archer saw her blue eyes widen and her tiny button lips go to level five pouty. He knew Rigby had no chance.

"I guess it would be all right," he said. "C'mon, then."

He led the way down the hall to the kitchen and turned to the basement door. He turned the knob but paused, a wily look in his eyes. "Wait a moment. You aren't playin' at something now, are ya?"

"What are you talking about, Rigby?" Archer asked.

Rigby remained undaunted. "Listen both of you," he growled. "You best not be thinkin' of trying to visit Uncle Scoville. I've rigged a new system on his door. If you so much as touch it, I'll know about it."

Kaylie blinked, little beaded tears forming. She shook her head. "I wouldn't go near him. Never. He scares me."

"She's going to see the animals," Archer said, lowering his voice an octave. "That's all."

"Right then," he said. "Down you go."

When Kaylie was safely in the basement, Archer turned on Rigby. "If you ever threaten Kaylie, I'll—"

"You'll what?" Rigby asked, a cruel smile forming. "You Dream-treaders have some sort of code, don't you? An oath to do no harm or some such?"

"That's for doctors," Archer said. He waited a few heartbeats for Rigby to get the point. "Dreamtreaders *may* have something similar, but my family comes first."

Rigby turned and went to his fridge. He pulled out a can of soda, sat at the kitchen table, and popped it open. He didn't offer a drink to Archer, and they waited in silence for several awkward minutes.

At last Kara arrived. She joined Rigby on his side of the table, crossed her arms, and avoided Archer's eyes.

"So what's all this about, Keaton?" Rigby asked.

"I told you," Archer said. "Your company, Dream Inc. You've got to shut it down."

"Shut it down?" Rigby echoed. "Are you mad? It's the entertainment sensation of the century. Besides, we're making a killing."

"Why do you want it shut down, Archer?" Kara asked.

It was the first time she had spoken directly to Archer in months, and to his surprise, there seemed to be a touch of kindness in her voice. That threw him off stride for a moment. "The Dream," he said, "it's not for sightseeing."

"Why not?" Rigby asked. "We're doing good there, Archer. We've set all of the Nightmare Lord's other captives free. They've gone back to their dreamy little lives."

"While you took the Nightmare Lord's throne," Archer growled. "You used me to get rid of him, and then you took over. How can I trust you? You might just turn into the new Nightmare Lord and his queen."

"Archer, that's not fair," Kara said. "We weren't using you. We stormed his castle together."

"And left the Nightmare Lord for me to finish off."

"Is that all you see, Keaton?" Rigby asked. "You think the Nightmare Lord was the only remaining threat? What about the rest of his hounds and henchmen, eh? Who do you think took them out?"

Archer's words stuck in his throat.

"Yeah, that's right," Rigby said. "And it was no easy task, let me tell you."

"In your wildest dreams, how could you imagine us becoming a Nightmare King and Queen?" Kara asked, an odd tremble in her voice. "Nightmares are the last thing either of us would ever want. Ever."

Rigby glanced thoughtfully at Kara, but she said nothing else. Archer stared too. He hadn't heard that vulnerability from Kara for a long time. He studied her. Her expression seemed honest and sincere, but something about her words felt wooden . . . kind of hollow.

Undeterred, Archer pressed on. "We had a plan: finish the Nightmare Lord. That was it. That was the whole thing from the beginning. There wasn't a step two: take his throne for ourselves. At least there wasn't one that I knew anything about."

"The plan changed, Archer," Kara said. "If there's anything we know about the Dream, it's that things can change in an instant. When the Nightmare Lord took us captive, I saw his other prisoners. They were desperate for help . . . we couldn't just leave them."

"Your compassion is touching," Archer quipped.

"See here, Keaton, there's no call for that. We made a choice in the heat of the moment. So did you."

"In the heat of the moment?" Archer replied. "Right."

"That's exactly right, Archer," Kara added. "We wanted you to stay with us, remember? You might have chosen that path with us. Then, when the Nightmare Lord returned for his castle—and you know he would have—we could have defeated him together."

"I needed your help against him," Archer said, his words simmering. "And you left him to me alone. I could have been killed. My family could have been killed."

"We couldn't predict that," Kara said. "We didn't even know that physical things could already pass through the Dream fabric, much less that the Nightmare Lord himself could come through."

"But no one died," Rigby said. "Your family ended up fine,

right? The Nightmare Lord is gone, his captives are free, his hounds are run off, and best yet, there are no more nightmares."

"What?" Archer blurted. "Of course there are still nightmares. I had one . . ."

Rigby snickered at that. "When?" Rigby leaned back in his chair, crossing his arms. "When was your last nightmare?"

"It was . . . I . . . I can't remember," Archer said.

"When you took out the Nightmare Lord and we took over Number 6 Rue de la Mort, we stopped nightmares from forming. Forever. Do you know what incalculable good we've done?"

Archer was truly speechless. *No more nightmares? Ever?* He thought back. No one in his family had reported a nightmare. And, now that he'd thought it over, Archer was reasonably certain he hadn't had a nightmare.

"Are you sure about this?" Archer asked.

Rigby glanced sideways at Kara and grinned. "Not a single one. Ask anyone you know. Anyone. Dreams are free from fear now. Thanks to us."

An eerie muffled howl halted the conversation. Archer tensed, remembering the three-headed monstrosity in the Dream.

Rigby laughed. "That's just Licorice," he said.

Archer lowered his eyebrows evenly. "Licorice is a candy. It doesn't howl."

"It does when it's a rare black coyote," Rigby said. "Mum and Dad got a call from a collector and had her sent over."

"Your mother and father are home?" Archer asked.

Rigby glanced sideways. "No," he said, "they're still in England, doing what they always do."

"Their loss," Kara said. "They'd be proud of you, you know."

Rigby sat up stiffly. "To use an American idiom: as if."

"Well," Kara said, "they ought to be. You've done great—no, amazing—things with Dream Inc." Kara put a hand lightly on Rigby's forearm and made eye contact with Archer.

That's it, Archer thought. *She's totally gone now.* "You know," he said, anger simmering in every syllable, "it would be nice to think that all's well that ends well. It'd be nice to think that we all did something heroic and deserve a little payback. But I can't join you in this delusion."

"Delusion," Rigby spat. "Is that what you think about—"

"I *know*. Not think. Know. Dreamtreaders have been around since the dawn of time, and our job is to protect the Dream and the Waking World. My Dreamtreading commander tells me that now—right now, as we're talking—the breaches are spreading, threatening to decompose into a full-on rift. Do you even know what that is?"

Rigby sighed, and Kara shifted uncomfortably in her chair.

"You really don't get it, do you?" Archer asked. "The Dream fabric is in the worst condition it's ever been in. Do you hear me? It's damaged more than anytime in history. Damage the Nightmare Lord began and damage continued by Walkers."

"Walkers?" Kara blurted.

"Lucid Dreamers," Archer explained. "Dreamtreaders call you Lucid Walkers. And each and every time you go skipping through the Dream on your 'safaris,' you tear new breaches into the Dream fabric. I know. I've seen them. I've had to patch up most of them myself. But breaches are appearing and growing at a rate that even the Dreamtreaders can't keep up with forever. If you don't shut down Dream Inc., you're going to destroy the world."

"Don't be so blasted dramatic, Keaton," Rigby chided. "You think you're the only one who knows about the breach problem?"

Kara turned and gaped at Rigby. "You knew?" she asked.

"Of course I knew," he said. "Uncle Scoville knew, and he passed it on to me. It's not a big deal."

"Not a big deal?" Kara practically spat. "Archer says it might cause the end of the world."

"Look, love, Keaton here is right that there's a danger," he said. "But I've got it under control. It's all about equilibrium."

Archer had just about had enough of Rigby's nonsense. "Explain."

"It's like this," Rigby said. "The Dream fabric is real and all, but it's much stronger than you let on. Sure, Lucid Walking causes a bit of damage, but so what? The fabric handles it, heals, and moves on. If it survived for centuries with a Nightmare Lord actively punching holes in it, surely it can survive a little Lucid Walking."

"It's not that simple," Archer countered. "With multiple Lucid Walkers going in and out, the number of breaches increases exponentially."

"Again with the drama, Keaton. The Dream fabric can sustain damage and still hold strong. We just have to maintain the equilibrium, the balance. Not too much Lucid Walking so that we avoid a rift and not so little that we have to shut down Dream Inc. Look, every time I go, I take readings and collect data. When I get back I feed the information into an application I created on my computer. It tells me where the balance is, and I make sure I schedule the Dream Inc. safaris when it's safe to do so."

"Wait," Archer said, "you have an app for that?"

"Sure," Rigby replied. "I'll e-mail it to you, if you like."

Archer crossed his arms. "Yeah, please do," he said quietly. "But does it show readings in real time? I mean, suppose the readings show that the Dream fabric is not in any danger. How do I know what I'm looking at isn't old data?"

"Would it work if I said you just 'ave to trust me?" Rigby asked.

Archer glared at him and muttered, "No."

"Ha! I didn't think so. Look, the data I enter makes it as real time as each and every visit I take into the Dream. It'll be listed by date."

Archer chewed over this revelation. Was it really possible to monitor the condition of the Dream . . . by computer? Even with dozens of new Lucid Walkers doing the tourist thing in the Dream each week? Archer frowned. "Wait," he said, "how do you keep track of all the Lucid Walking?"

Rigby frowned back. "I don't follow you."

"I mean, how do you know how many Lucid Walkers are in and out over time?"

"Carefully controlled, Keaton," Rigby replied with a dismissive wave of his hand. "At Dream Inc. we have a meticulous schedule. We know just how many Walkers the Dream can tolerate at any given moment. We never let in any more than acceptable."

Archer blew out an exasperated breath. "That's not what I mean. What if your clients go to the Dream on their own time?"

"Archer," Kara said, squinting, "you're not making sense."

"Your clients," Archer repeated. "Once they learn how to Lucid Dream, what's to keep them from going in any old time they want to? What's to keep them from teaching their friends how to Lucid Walk? They could overwhelm the equilibrium before your data readings can catch up. They could trigger a rift without any warning."

Rigby opened his mouth and shut it with a snap. When he spoke, his words had a thick, wet quality to them. "As I said, Keaton: carefully controlled. Successful corporations do not give away their secrets."

"I'm going to talk to my Dreamtreading Master about this," Archer said, getting up to leave.

"You can do what you want, Keaton," Rigby said. "I'm not shutting down Dream Inc."

"You should have come down to see Licorice, Archer," Kaylie said, stomping slush with each step she and Archer took as they walked home from Rigby's. "She's such a sweetie-fluffer-muffin!"

"She's a coyote," Archer muttered. "She could eat you."

"Licorice would do no such thing!" Kaylie said indignantly. "She's just a pup."

"Uh-huh," Archer replied distantly. He was unhappy about the icy water seeping into his shoes. He was unhappy about a lot of things.

"Archer, are you listening to me?" Kaylie asked.

"Yeah," he replied. "I've heard everything you said."

"Hearing and listening are two distinct entities," Kaylie said, switching on genius mode.

Archer said nothing.

"Boy, Rigby must have really made you mad," Kaylie said.

Archer walked the rest of the way home with his mind churning. Yes, Rigby had made Archer angry. So had Kara. Part of him had secretly hoped he could salvage their friendship, but that seemed out of the question now. He felt like he didn't know Kara anymore. She was too hard to read, too hard to understand.

And there was something she'd said, something that Archer found intensely curious. Kara had said, "We didn't even know that physical things could already pass through the Dream fabric, much less that the Nightmare Lord himself could come through."

Archer had confronted Rigby and Kara about the Nightmare Lord's intrusion into the Waking World, but he'd never said anything about physical objects coming through. And what had Kara meant when she used the word *already*, as if she'd been expecting things to come out of the Dream for a long time?

Everyone has secrets, Archer reminded himself. Rigby had his Uncle Scoville, among others. But Archer knew almost nothing about Kara's secrets. Archer wondered if that would come back to haunt him.

"Take her?" one of the raspy voices asked.

Rigby stood in front of his basement door and stared down into the darkness. "I hadn't wanted to begin with something so extreme."

"You said to distract," whispered another voice.

"Taking her would distract," came still another.

Rigby was silent for several moments. Archer was getting way too curious, and he wasn't stupid . . . not in the classical sense. He needed other things to keep him busy.

"Go ahead," Rigby said, shutting his basement door. "Take her but don't hurt her."

"We hears!"

"And we obeys!"

SIX

VISIS NOCTURNE

"THIS CAN'T BE RIGHT," ARCHER MUTTERED, STARING AT the computer screen in his room. "Maybe I'm looking at the wrong graphic."

Rigby's Dream Fabric Monitoring App—Equilibris, he called it—was very professional. It opened in a typical metallic gray browser window and showed a graphic representation of the Dream territory. The three districts glowed in different colors from cool blue to violet to red.

The closer an area was to the color red, the more numerous the breaches. Archer tinkered with the app's preferences and its settings, but the results still showed the same. There were a few hotspots, flares of violet or red, but overall, the Dream seemed to be in good shape.

If Rigby's app were to be believed, that is.

Maybe this is just a snapshot, he thought. *Not real time. For all I know, Rigby gathered his data right after I'd finished a dreamweaving tour. Maybe it would appear more stable then.*

Archer left the app running and the window open and went for his *Dreamtreader's Creed* and the summoning feather within. He tossed the feather up into the air and waited.

A border of sparkling blue sealed Archer's bedroom door signaling Master Gabriel's arrival. Archer wondered what outfit he would dream up this time. He didn't have long to wonder.

The master Dreamtreader appeared in a storm of bluish white fireflies. He wore a smooth black fedora, the brim pulled low, his trademark sunglasses, and a long, black trench coat.

Gabriel crossed his arms and scowled. "What?" he demanded. "What's wrong with this one?"

"Uh . . . actually, nothing's wrong with it," Archer said. "I'm surprised."

"Surprised?"

"Yeah, I mean, that's pretty cool. You look like Morpheus from *The Matrix*."

"Never heard of him," Gabriel said, shoving his hands deep into his coat pockets. "Now then, why have you summoned me?"

"Trouble," Archer said. He explained Rigby and Kara's refusal to close down Dream Inc. He even showed Master Gabriel the app on the computer.

"That isn't even close to accurate," Master Gabriel said. "Not at that time and certainly not now. The Forms and Verse Districts are teeming with new breaches."

"But not Pattern?"

"No, nothing in Pattern," Gabriel replied. "You may recall that both Pattern and Verse went dormant before the fall of the Nightmare Lord. For a time, Forms, your district, was the only place in the Dream with a continuous need for Dreamweaving. But now, Verse has flared up violently, even more than Forms. Yet Patterns remains undisturbed. I find this fact both curious and troubling."

"Could the Lurker have something to do with it?" Archer asked. "That's his territory."

"I cannot imagine how," Master Gabriel replied. "Whatever the Lurker has been doing since last year, it has been for his own interests, not the benefit of the Dream and certainly not for our benefit."

"Maybe he scared all the scurions away," Archer said with a throaty laugh. "He's ugly enough."

Master Gabriel didn't return the laugh. He lowered his shades and fixed Archer with a smoldering glare. "There is no humor here, Archer. In spite of what your friend Rigby tells you, the Dream is sliding slowly toward a rift. It is as unstable now as I have ever seen it. You've got to get back to work tonight."

"What about the new Dreamtreaders?" Archer asked, staring at the floor. "I'm trying. Razz and I are pushing ourselves, but it's too much. We can't do this alone."

Gabriel turned, took a few steps, and placed his palm flat on Archer's bedroom door. Threads of sparkling blue trailed out of the door's border to his fingertips. "Nick is almost ready to awaken," he said quietly. "You still have the scroll?"

"Of course," Archer said. "And it still won't open."

"Soon, Archer, soon. For now, you will have to make do with Razz. As I said, there has been a wild flare-up of breaches in Verse. The most volatile area is Garnet Province. Make that your first priority."

"The Libraries?" Archer asked.

"It is likely," Master Gabriel replied. "There is great power there. The Inner Sanctum holds many secrets. And, Archer, there is some talk that Bezeal has recently made visits to Garnet Province. You must be careful."

"Careful?" Archer echoed. "It's just Bezeal we're talking about here. I'll be sure to keep chocolate handy." He laughed. "He's a fool for chocolate."

"Bezeal is what he chooses to reveal to you for his purposes. You must not underestimate him, Archer."

"Seriously?" Archer swallowed back a laugh. "I mean, I know I've screwed up in the past, but I'm sure I can take on Bezeal."

"It is precisely that attitude that has hurt you in the past," Master Gabriel replied. "Or have you forgotten the blood pact?"

"I haven't forgotten." Archer stared down at his right palm. There was no scar, of course, because the wound happened in the Dream. But he remembered how it felt. Bezeal had offered a deal and held out his hand. When Archer shook, a small hidden blade pricked and stung his palm. His blood had flowed, had mingled with Bezeal's blood. "No, I'll never forget," he said. "But I satisfied my end of the deal. I got him that stupid, useless puzzle box."

"Are you so certain it was useless?"

Archer's open, ready-to-argue mouth shut with a snap. He knew many things about Bezeal, but did he really know him? And if there was anything true of the shifty, little merchant, he never—ever—got the worse end of the deal. Why had he wanted that puzzle box, the Karakurian Chamber, so desperately? And why was there a sudden burst of breaches in the Verse District's Garnet Province . . . at just the same time as Bezeal's recent visits?

"You are thinking before you speak," Master Gabriel said. "That is very reassuring."

Archer gave a thin smile and sighed. "Okay, I think I've got the mission: hit Verse hard, especially Garnet Province. Keep an eye out for Bezeal and investigate the Libraries. Got it. But what about Rigby and Kara? His company is sending more and more people Lucid Walking. The breaches will keep forming more and more. What do I do about it?"

"I am not certain," Master Gabriel replied. "But you are right:

you need help. It will come soon. But, in the meantime, forget Rigby's computer program. You will need a more accurate vision for the conditions in the Dream."

"What do you mean?"

"Tell me, Archer," he said, "how much of your time in the Dream do you spend searching for breaches versus weaving them up?"

Archer thought a moment. "Well, I get around pretty fast on my surfboard, but yeah, I waste a ton of time hunting the breaches."

"This will no longer do," Master Gabriel said. "I think it is time."

"Time?" Archer echoed. "Time for what?"

"You must have Visis Nocturne."

"Never heard of it."

"No," Master Gabriel replied, pacing the room, "you wouldn't have. Remember, you are still very young for a Dreamtreader. Visis Nocturne gives you the vision to track breaches more precisely. Duncan and Mesmeera called it 'Seeing Sideways,' and that is not altogether inaccurate. You must be able to see the Dream as I see it. And for that, you need Visis Nocturne."

"Seeing sideways, for real?" Archer asked. "Snot rockets, I can do that?"

"Not before," Master Gabriel said. "It would have been too draining on your mental energies. But now, you've matured. You've come to a new level of strength. You will be able to handle it. Yes, I'm sure you will."

"You don't sound sure."

"Yes, yes, you will. You must. I will teach you, but I warn you with all caution, Archer: use this power sparingly. It takes ten times the energy as flight. More than a few seconds of Visis Nocturne will make you very weak. Using it too often could knock you right out of the Dream . . . or worse."

"Okay, Master Gabriel," Archer said, mentally stuffing the indignation and impatience that threatened. He took a breath and tried to act with a little more dignity. "I will be careful."

"Come."

Archer complied. Master Gabriel reached out his hands and placed them on the sides of Archer's head.

"Close your eyes."

Archer blinked a moment but did as he was asked. He felt Gabriel's thumbs resting lightly on his closed eyes. He felt his fingers near his ears. Then there was light, bluish-white sparks and flashes, swirling and racing. Like a series of dot-to-dot pictures, the sparks came together in strange, recognizable shapes: mountains, trees, cliffs, forests, and lakes. Only for moments, and then they dissolved into random whirling sparks once more.

Master Gabriel removed his hands and said, "Now, slowly, open your eyes."

"Whoa," Archer gasped. His entire room coursed with the racing sparkles, but more than that, he became aware of tunnels that had appeared in the corners of his eyes. He was looking straight forward—at his bed, the window just above—but those peripheral tunnels added a new dimension. He suddenly had startling clarity, and he saw . . . more.

His pillow became a hillside of braided cords, winding and looping and intertwining. And among the corded strands, squat, baked potato–sized, eight-legged lumps marched. They had no visible eyes, but gaping beaklike jaws that continuously opened and closed.

"Yikes! What are those things?"

"Probably dust mites," Master Gabriel replied drolly. "Nothing to be concerned about. They've been there all along."

"Eww," Archer said. "I'm sleeping on those things? Every night?"

"If it makes you feel any better, an army of them are probably roaming around on your head right now."

"Thanks," Archer muttered. "I feel loads better."

He blinked, and the strange, ethereal glow faded. He blinked again, and his vision returned to normal. His room was just as it always had been, and only the door retained its glowing border. It was as if his peripheral vision had magnified and streamlined what he could normally see. "Huh," Archer said. "Seeing sideways."

"Now, you know," Master Gabriel said. "Use it sparingly, Archer. Quick glimpses, that's all. Remember what I've told you."

Archer felt suddenly exhausted. He glanced at his bed and thought it looked like the most inviting place on earth. He could feel the blankets and pillows, and they seemed to call to him. "So tired," Archer said. "I'll remember."

"Sleep then, Archer," Master Gabriel said. "Renew your strength in the Dream, and test your new abilities. I am counting on you."

Archer's eyes were closing before the last of Master Gabriel's form vanished from his room. He was nearly asleep in moments, drenched in that gray twilight where he could still hear things in his room but the sounds weren't distracting or even distinct. Like having a fan on in the room; after a while, it became white noise. But now, in this hazy, pre-sleep state, everything was like that.

He was still thinking a little bit, but his thoughts were running, bouncing, and ricocheting off each other. He saw Rigby and Kara walking arm in arm in some kind of tropical garden. Then Kaylie and Buster were sitting on a pier with fishing rods and their legs dangling over the side. And then he saw his bedroom closet. The door was open, and shadow people stood there. No eyes. No features. Just slightly lighter shadows in the darkness of the closet. And they were moving, getting closer to the foot of Archer's bed.

There came a shriek. Archer's eyes snapped open, and he gasped for air. The bifold doors of the closet were shut tight. But the shriek still echoed in his mind. It slowly resolved into a more familiar sound.

"My cell," he whispered, seeing the glow on his desk. The ringtone sounded shrilly once more. Archer grabbed it, saw that Amy Pitsitakas was calling, and thumbed the green *talk* button.

"Amy?" Archer mumbled. He was still breathing heavy. "It's almost midnight."

"I'm sorry, Archer," she said. "But something terrible's happening at the house behind ours, the Gambers' place."

"Gamber?" Archer echoed. Images from elementary school came flooding into his mind. Mr. Gamber had been his favorite teacher. He'd been everyone's favorite teacher because he did experiments that set off the fire alarm. "What's going on?"

"I don't know yet," she said. "But my mom's checking on them. Archer, there are police cars everywhere. I can see their flashlights in the backyard. I'm really scared."

"Is there an ambulance there?"

"I can't see. Window's fogged." A few squeaky moments later she said, "No, no flashing lights, no ambulance."

"That's a good sign."

"You think?"

"I do," Archer said. "Besides, if I remember Mr. Gamber well enough, he'll be taking good care of his family."

"I don't know, Archer. This feels . . . wrong."

Archer frowned. He wanted to do something to help. "Should I get my dad?"

"Hold on," she said, her voice suddenly whispery and harsh. "I hear something. Archer, there's someone in my house!"

"Amy?" Archer said. There was no answer. "Amy, what's going on? Amy?"

"Sorry," she said, returning suddenly. "It was just my mom. I gotta go, Archer."

"Wait, just—"

But she had already ended the call.

Archer immediately switched on every light in his bedroom. Chills spiking gooseflesh on his arms, he went to the closet and slid open the doors. Clothes, shelves, shoe boxes, etc. Nothing unusual. The shadow figures had seemed utterly real. The shriek too.

"What *was* that?" he whispered.

Archer looked down at his phone, thought about calling Amy back, but eased back into bed instead. He had to get to sleep, had to get Dreamtreading, but how? He was still too wired from the strange experience and Amy's phone call. That's when he heard talking coming from the hallway.

It sounded like Buster, but Archer couldn't tell what his little brother was saying. He heard a lot of half-mumbled words but could only discern a few: *wave*, *maverick*, *channel*, and *rip* . . . something.

"Sleep talking," Archer whispered. He turned on his side and shut his eyes—for about a half second. His phone rang again, still shocking in the midnight quiet. He snatched up the phone and sat up. "Amy?"

"Oh, Archer! Someone . . . someone took him!"

"Wait, wait," Archer said. "Slow down. Someone took who?"

"Mr. Gamber . . . that's why the police were there. Someone took him."

"What? That doesn't make any sense. Why would anyone kidnap an elementary school teacher? He probably just went out for a late-night snack."

"No, Archer," she said. "My mom told me. Mr. Gamber's truck is still in the driveway, and there were signs of a struggle."

Archer's thoughts spun. He thought for a second he heard footsteps in the hall. But Amy spoke again. "My mom said Mr. Gamber's wife and kids heard a lot of yelling, but when they checked his office, it was wrecked. And Mr. Gamber was gone. Strangest thing was they said his house showed no signs of forced entry. All the doors and windows were locked up tight."

"Okay," Archer said, feeling the chills again, "that doesn't make any sense. How'd they get in then?"

"Archer, I'm really scared. I hope he's okay."

"Me too," Archer said. "Is there anything I can do?"

"I don't know," Amy said. "I don't think so. It's just a messed-up night. I was having a horrible dream when the sirens woke me up."

Horrible dream? So much for Rigby ridding the world of nightmares. Almost like a reflex, he asked, "What was your dream about?"

"Ghosts," she said. "At least, I think that's what they were. There were these shadows reaching out for me and—"

"YAAAAAH!"

The yell gave Archer such a jolt that he sent his phone careening across his bedroom floor. But that shock was nothing compared to the horrific crash that came next. Somewhere down the hall, there had been a *smack-thump*, followed by breaking glass. Archer tore out of his bedroom and found himself a step behind his father, racing to the stairwell. Archer flipped the hall light on as he ran and watched his father stop suddenly at the top of the steps.

"Buster!" his father cried out, turning the corner and stumbling frantically down the stairs.

When Archer got to the top, he saw his father cradling Buster's limp form. Several other images blinked into focus: blood, a broken surfboard, and the wrecked remnants of a family picture that had once hung on the wall at the bottom of the stairs.

"Call 911, Archer!" his father yelled. "Now!"

Archer spun on his heels and nearly tripped over Kaylie, who had come up behind him. "Archer, what'samatter? I heard a thump."

"Kaylie, uhm, just go back to your room."

"Why? But I heard Daddy on the stairs."

"Never mind. Come with me to my room," Archer said, taking her hand and pulling her back to his room. He found his cell on the floor, half covered by a blanket.

He grabbed it up and heard, "Archer? Archer? What is it? What's going on?"

"Amy? I'm sorry. I've got to go." He hung up and dialed 911.

The next twenty minutes went by in a fearful blur. Keeping Kaylie occupied was one thing, but Archer could barely calm down himself. He bounced back and forth between her and Buster, his mind spinning and his heart racing.

"He's breathing," his father reported. "But he's shaking. I'm afraid he's having a seizure."

Archer raced back up the stairs. "Is Buster gonna be okay?" Kaylie asked, her big blue eyes wide and teary.

"I . . . I think so," Archer replied.

The ambulance arrived, and the EMTs took over. They had Buster in a neck brace and on a stretcher in no time. As they wheeled him over the threshold out into the night, Archer's father stared up the stairs. "Stay here with Kaylie," he said, his face looking haggard, haunted. "I'll call you when I can."

Archer went to Kaylie's bedroom window and watched helplessly as the paramedics loaded his kid brother into the back of the ambulance. Kaylie tugged on Archer's T-shirt. "Is he gonna be okay? He's not gonna die, is he?"

"Oh, Kaylie," Archer whispered, kneeling to look her in the eye. He pulled her into a hug, squishing her stuffed scarecrow doll, Patches, between them. "I think Buster will be fine. He's got a real hard head."

"That's true," Kaylie mumbled into his shoulder.

Archer held her tight and said a prayer. He hoped he hadn't just lied to Kaylie. He thought about what he'd seen: Buster sprawled at the bottom of the stairs, the shattered family picture, the broken surfboard—broken surfboard? Archer tried to put all the pieces together, but none of it made any sense.

He'd heard Buster talking in his sleep, heard him yell, and then the crash. What did it all mean?

Archer picked up Kaylie and brought her into his room. He let her snuggle into the covers while he sat on the edge of the bed and stared at his cell phone. There was no way he could fall asleep. Dreamtreading would have to wait.

Something very strange was happening. Strange and frightening. Both he and Amy seeing shadow people. Mr. Gamber being violently abducted. Buster falling down the stairs. There was a thread tying it all together, Archer felt sure.

He thought about Buster: how small and vulnerable he looked on that stretcher. Archer prayed again but found himself chased by a creeping thought: that this night might be the last time he'd ever see his brother alive.

SEVEN

OLD WOUNDS

KAYLIE WAS ASLEEP. TURNING OVER AND STIRRING FIT-
fully, but asleep. There was no such refuge for Archer. Waiting for
his father to call with news about Buster was torture. Over the hours,
Archer had whipped off a half dozen texts but gotten no response.
Still, he clutched the phone and waited.

The phone began to feel warm in his hand. At first, he thought
it was his imagination. He'd been nervous, holding the phone too
firmly in his grip. But the heat intensified rapidly. In an instant, it
became a flare of white-hot pain.

"Agh!" Archer yelped. He dropped his phone onto the bed and
shook his throbbing hand.

A raw red welt smoldered in the exact center of his hand. *No way*,
he thought. Tablets and laptops sometimes got hot, Archer knew, but
he'd never heard of a cell phone heating up enough to burn. He glared
suspiciously at the phone, half hidden in blankets at the foot of the
bed, and wondered if it might be a fire hazard.

The burn still stung, so Archer used his left hand and carefully
picked the cell up by its outermost corner edge. Then, trying not to

startle his sleeping sister, he eased off the bed, tiptoed to his desk, and laid the phone on a plate full of potato chip crumbs. He waved his hand back and forth just above the touch screen but felt no radiating heat. He tapped the phone and laid his fingers on the keyboard: nothing. It wasn't hot. It wasn't even warm. Archer shook his head and exhaled. It made no sense. But his hand still stung, and the welt was still red and angry.

Heading for the bathroom, Archer slipped down the hallway and paused at Buster's room. The bed in there was a mess: sheets and covers strewn about, pillows flung all over, and the mattress itself jutted away from the headboard. Luminous blue clock numbers revealed it to be 4:16 a.m.

Dad and Buster had been gone since midnight, and yet no word had come from the hospital. Not good news. Archer stepped into the hall bathroom, refusing to look at the stairwell. The water from the sink felt shockingly cold on the burn, but as it continued to run, it became more soothing.

After a minute, Archer looked at his hand. The welt had shrunk to a reddish-purple pinhole in the very center of his palm, with a corona of little pink tendrils. It felt different too. No longer a continuous, edgy sting, the wound felt more like a spot of sunburn. The surrounding skin had that kind of overstretched discomfort, and it hurt to open his hand wide. Archer snagged a tissue, gently patted his palm dry, and returned to his bedroom.

Archer stood next to the desk and stared down at the phone. *How could a cell phone get hot enough to burn like that?* He reached down and let his hand hover over the cell again. Still no heat at all. Maybe it was something electrical. Maybe the battery had given off a rogue shock. Or maybe . . .

Maybe it wasn't the phone at all.

The thought rang like a bell in the fog. Archer didn't want to think about it, but now that the thought had come, it opened up a cascade of others. *It might not even be a burn,* he thought. *Maybe a spider's bite. Maybe—*

The phone rang. Shrill and sharp as ever, the sound made Archer jump. He yanked his hand away as if the cell had burst into flame. "Snot buckets," he muttered. Then he saw who was calling.

Archer pressed the green button and said, "Dad?"

The only reply was his father's brittle whisper: "Archer . . ." followed by weeping, raw and breathless.

⚷

The limousine navigated the suburban neighborhood like a mechanical shark and left a twisted trail of white exhaust in the lingering December cold. The chauffeur behind the dark windshield wore even darker sunglasses, and his chiseled face bore no expression as he deftly maneuvered the slushy streets. Cold as it was outside, the interior behind the chauffeur, the passenger section of the limo, was toasty warm and richly appointed with a forty-inch Internet/TV monitor; a refreshment bar stocked with water, juices, and soft drinks imported from London; and a long, luxurious bench seat.

On the right side of the seat, Rigby Thames smiled and handed Kara Windchil a business card. "I just 'ad these made up. Tell me what you think."

Kara traced her finger across the raised type of the card. "Rigby Thames," she read. "Dream Inc. President, Chairman of the Board of Directors, Chief Executive Officer, Chief Creative Officer, Chief Technology Officer, and Chief Human Resources Officer." She coughed. "That's a lot of officers. Save any for me?"

Rigby laughed. "Of course, love," he said. "You're the Chief Information Officer and Chief Marketing Officer. Not to mention: Chief Keep Rigby from Screwing Up Officer."

"The CKRFSUO?" Kara smiled. "That's too many letters."

"But a very important role nonetheless," he said.

"The card's nice," she said, handing it back to him. "Very professional looking. But why shout out about all the titles you hold?"

A velvety smooth voice floated back from the front seat of the limo. "Three minutes to arrival, Mr. Thames."

"Thank you, Smithers," Rigby replied, still staring down at his business card. "These titles equal respect, Kara. It's 'ard enough getting respect from normal adults. Really, it's no easy thing to get respect from juniors and seniors at school even. It wasn't until I took care of Guzzy Gorvalec that anyone took me seriously. But in the corporate world, it's ten times harder. I guess the titles are my way of letting the bullies in business know that I am no one to be trifled with."

Kara swept the curtain of dark hair out of her eyes and stared from Rigby to the limo window and back. She said, "Maybe I should get some cards made up, too."

"Done," Rigby said. "You'll 'ave them by Monday afternoon. Oh, and something else I wanted to show you." Rigby clicked out of his seat belt and clambered halfway over the backseat. After some rummaging, he slid back to his seat and held something in his hands.

"A top hat?" she blurted. "Why do you have . . . a top hat?"

"This isn't just any old top hat," Rigby said. With a well-practiced flourish, he twirled the hat from its brim and it came to rest snugly on his head. "This is a vintage, Victorian-era John Bull gentleman's top hat. It belonged . . . *belongs* to my Uncle Scoville, but he's given it to me." He tugged once on the brim.

"But, uhm . . . why?"

Rigby raised an eyebrow and smiled patiently. "Trademark," he said. "It's like Steve Jobs' black turtleneck or wire-rim glasses. Every technology guru has to have a trademark. This will be mine."

Kara wore a vague smile and absently twirled the business card in her fingers as the limousine drove on. Kara and Rigby didn't speak, but the air was thick with deep thought for the rest of the drive.

The building that housed Dream Inc. headquarters had once been Washington County's trendiest restaurant, the home of roasted Rockfish Rockefeller and a spectacular view of Antietam Creek. It still had the view, but now it was a technological fortress surrounded by electrified fences and surveillance towers. Armed guards patrolled the perimeter day and night, and its rear parking area was filled with armor-plated Humvees.

Rigby and Kara stepped out of the limousine and found a large black umbrella over them, denying the constant sleet. The Dream Inc. logo was understated but stood out tastefully among the angular glass and brushed aluminum that covered most of the building. The letters were modern and very modular, made of sleek black metal that looked wet and were divided horizontally by a bolt of silver lightning: a bold look for a bold company.

The guards outside, their arms bulging even in oversized black trench coats, nodded at Rigby and Kara as they approached. Rigby gave them each a tip of his top hat.

Once inside, Rigby and Kara passed by a luxurious waiting room where a few executives sat tip-tapping on their smartphones. Rigby knew a couple of them by sight, billionaires who had already paid a premium fee for Dream Inc.'s unique service and were now anxiously waiting their turns.

"Any chance Frederick won't be there?" Kara asked.

"Frederick doesn't miss these meetings," Rigby said. "There'll be a handful of other shareholders as well." Rigby paused and turned to Kara when he finally noticed the distaste in her voice. "What've you got against Frederick?"

"I don't trust him," Kara said. "It always seems like he's hiding something."

Rigby laughed. "He's no worse than Bezeal."

"I don't know about that. Bezeal is cheap and tricky and annoying, but I feel like I know his ways. Frederick is a mystery. A dangerous one."

"Better the devil you know?" Rigby raised an eyebrow.

"Something like that."

Rigby glanced at his phone. "We're early yet. Follow me. I want to show you something." He led a meandering course through the facility and used his key card to get through several sets of double doors.

"Where are we headed?" Kara asked.

"The Neural Command Center," he said.

"I've seen it."

"From the client side," he said. "Not from this side."

The last set of doors opened with a hiss of pressurized air. Several guards waited on the other side, standing next to a heavily wired gateway.

"Metal detector?" Kara asked. "Looks like what Homeland Security uses at airports these days."

"Similar," Rigby said. "But this detects magnetism. We'll 'ave to leave our phones in the tray."

"Why?"

"The computers on this side are absolutely sensitive to magnetic fields," Rigby explained, handing his phone to one of the guards and walking through the detector gate. "We're monitoring each client, you know. We make sure they don't bring things back from the Dream."

"How?" she asked, handing off her phone and following.

"My uncle was the first to theorize it," Rigby said. "But I confirmed it through trials. Anything created in the Dream that comes back gives off a subtle magnetic field. We don't know why. We only know that it does. And we can track it with our sensors and equipment. That's why we can't bring anything magnetic in here."

"That's bizarre," Kara said.

"Not bizarre," Rigby said. "Simply unexplained. The data we get from each Lucid Walking session is incredible. We can tell exactly how self-aware each client is in the dream. If they get too close, we wake them up."

"Too close?"

"You know," Rigby said. "Dr. Gideon from London is walking in the Dream and he sees one of our other clients, say, oh, Alicia Kerr, the actress. In most cases, Dr. Gideon would simply assume she was part of his dream, maybe something he conjured up himself. But if he began to understand that Alicia was Walking as well, that they are coexisting in the Dream, then we could have trouble."

"I don't see the issue."

"Power, Kara," he said. "If Dr. Gideon and Alicia are both in the Dream and they both recognize that they are Lucid Walking together, they might start to combine their mental energies, and they could change things in the Dream. Worse still, they might realize how to Lucid Walk on their own. They would be out of control—Keaton had that part right, at least. Our clients are not idiots. They'll figure it out . . . if we let them. But we won't."

Rigby led Kara through the rest of the security checkpoints and they arrived at an octagonal split-window recessed into the wall. "Prepare," he said, tapping a sequence of numbers into a colorful keypad beside the door, "to be awed."

There was a hiss of pressurized air and a pulsing mechanized tone, and the door slid open. Chrome gleamed, banks of servers hummed, and holographic images hovered across six identical stations. Rigby watched Kara's eyes widen, saw the hitch in her breathing. She was awed.

"I've never been in here," she mumbled, her head turning slowly.

People in stark white clothing, a style Rigby called "military meets scientist," sat at colossal workstations against the far wall and hovered over tablet computers in the aisles between. The ceiling was hard to see through all the intricate ductwork: huge hanging tubes, ventilation fans the size of merry-go-rounds, and spiderlike hubs. Beneath the ducts was a network of more pipes, but these were thin and dotted with sprinkler heads.

"What are those?" Kara asked, pointing up toward the closest corner of the room. "Those angled panels?"

"Sound dampening," Rigby said. He held his arms up in a Y shape and turned slowly, gesturing to the slabs that hung in every corner of the chamber. "Wouldn't want to disturb our clients sleeping on the other side of the wall."

Kara nodded, her mouth still slightly open. Awe and more awe—Rigby loved it. He wanted to savor more of the moment, but he had a bit of business to attend to and led her to one of the holographic stations. "Anything come through?" Rigby asked one of the technicians.

"Oh, Mr. Thames," he said. "I didn't know you were inspecting today."

"Not inspecting, Timothy," Rigby said. "Just curious."

The technician reached up into the hologram and, like a pair of luminous anemones waving undersea, his hands manipulated the strands of data until he found what he was searching for. "A few leaves," he said. "Pebbles, twigs—just flora and fauna. Nothing purposeful. Not since Mr. Carnegie brought back the gold coin three weeks ago."

"Good," Rigby said.

"But . . ." the technician hesitated.

"What?"

"There have been more of those anomalies."

"What anomalies?" Kara asked.

The technician said, "Very infrequently we've discovered shadows in the data. Well, not shadows really, but more like digital trails moving from the Dream into real time. We call them shadows because they don't take up space like someone bringing back a coin would. There's no displacement value in the data."

"Wait," Kara said. "You're saying these shadow surges happen at night, after closing?"

"If there's no displacement," Rigby said, "there really isn't a problem."

She nodded, but her expression clouded. "If none of the clients are hooked up to the machines and dreaming, there shouldn't be any way for anything to come out of the Dream."

"That's what I'm saying, love," Rigby explained. "There's nothing tangible coming out of the Dream, so nothing to worry about."

"But," Kara countered, "what if some ambitious billionaire dreamed up some creature, robot, or mutant virus that becomes self-aware and tries to escape?"

"We'd catch it," Rigby said. "We'd know right away. Monitors, sensors, all this shockingly expensive equipment. Isn't that right, Timothy?"

"It is true," the technician confirmed. "We monitor everything."

"But what about the weird shadow anomalies?" Kara asked.

"We won't be afraid of shadows." Rigby laughed. "All under control, love. No fears. And . . . we've got our meeting in five, so we'd better leave Timothy here to his very important work."

In the conference room, a balding man looked up from his tablet computer and said, "You'll be happy to note, Mr. Thames, for the second quarter in a row we have tripled our profitability."

"Very happy to know," Rigby replied, stifling a yawn. "Thank you, Harrison, for your always . . . *detailed* . . . report." He saw Kara smile. They'd joked privately about how long-winded Harrison could be.

"Well," Rigby said, beginning to stand. "That covers security, data, R & D, and the bottom line. Thank you, all for your diligence and loyal—"

"They're asking again," Frederick interrupted. He was a big man, wearing a dark suit that made his shoulders look unnaturally wide. The cut of the suit and his buzz-cut hair gave him the bearing of a military commander. He tented his fingers and leaned forward. "That kind of money leads to a lot of pressure."

Men and women in expensive tailored suits leaned forward as well and nodded.

"Money isn't a concern," Rigby said. "We have a waiting list of investors a mile long."

"Political pressure *is* a concern," Frederick said, washed-out blue eyes blazing. "If certain influential people get involved, permits could disappear, and patents could be delayed or outright denied."

Rigby sneered. "If they want to play politics, fine. There's no reason we need to base Dream Inc. in the United States. We can pull up our tent stakes and go elsewhere. But I will not put any Dream Inc. customer in control of our patented method."

"Why not?" Kara asked. "Some of it's already public record."

Rigby's frowning intensity deepened. "How do you know that?"

"Chief Information Officer, remember?" She smiled sweetly. "I don't have business cards yet, but it's my job to know."

Rigby nodded. *Touché.* "Still, I've read Uncle Scoville's articles. There's not enough of the specifics there for just anyone to start Lucid Dreaming."

"Not just anyone, no," she said. "But, like you told me before, we're dealing with bright people. Why not let them have their fun?"

"Fun?" Rigby blurted. "It's not fun. It's business."

"Mr. Thames is correct," Frederick said, his voice high and thin but not thin in a brittle sense. More like a thin blade or a razor. "This is a business, and, as such, we aim to raise as much money for our shareholders as possible. The more money for our shareholders, the more money becomes available for future research and development."

"We weren't going to discuss this today, Frederick," Rigby said quietly.

"I understand," Frederick said. "But it bears noting to someone as highly placed as Ms. Windchil. Governments around the globe are offering staggering sums for Lucid Walking site licenses."

"What would governments use Lucid Walking for?" Kara asked.

Rigby sneered. "Nothing good—"

"Nonsense," Frederick interrupted. "In the hands of the right agencies, Lucid Dreaming could open up new treatments to fight depression and anxiety, mental illness of all kinds—"

"Yeah," Rigby said, "that's right. But it could also be used to dig deeper into people's privacy like drones in the brain."

"We select who gets the licenses," Frederick said.

Rigby crossed his arms. "If we turn over the secrets of Dream Inc. to anyone outside of our inner circle, we're done. We'll no longer control the market. Dream Inc. clone companies will appear overnight. We'll get priced out of our own industry."

"With all due respect, Mr. Thames," Frederick said, sitting up painfully straight in his seat, "you're jealous for your family's invention. I get that. But there's a bigger picture here that you're not seeing because . . ."

"Because what?" Rigby asked.

"Because you're young," Frederick said. "You're brilliant and ambitious and used to being right, but you're young. If you cling to this thing too tightly, you're going to regret it. Someone else will come along and discover what we're doing. They'll compete without us getting compensation."

"No, they won't," Rigby said. "That's one of the things I pay you for. It's all about control, Frederick."

"Of course it is," Kara muttered.

"What?" Rigby hissed. "What was that?"

"Forget it," she said, turning her back. "It's your company."

"That's right," Rigby said. His voice dropped an octave. "It is."

EIGHT

BROKEN

THE TEARS HAD BEEN TEARS OF JOY AND RELIEF.

In that eventual phone conversation, Archer's father reported that Buster's fall had been serious but far from fatal. If the remaining tests came back clear, he'd be able to bring Buster home in the morning. Exhausted and utterly relieved, Archer had dropped into an easy chair in the living room to wait.

Some time later, during a dreamless gray sleep, Archer heard someone calling his name.

"Archer, Archer!" It was Kaylie. She squealed and bounced at the living room window. "They're here!"

Archer bounded out of the recliner and raced for the door. He was outside in a flash, barefoot in the snow, but he didn't care.

His father was in the driveway, already walking around to the backseat door of their dented-up SUV. He opened the door.

"Buster!" Archer shouted.

"Dude, not so loud, 'kay?" Buster said. He wore dark sunglasses that somehow fit his beachy personality perfectly. "No loud noises or bright lights, Doc said."

Kaylie half ran, half skidded past Archer and hugged Buster.

"Yo, careful, Sis," Buster said, but he returned the embrace with gusto. Archer and his father joined in. They stood in the cold for what seemed like hours, but Archer didn't feel cold at all. A half hour later, Archer and his family sat at the kitchen table and hovered over mugs of hot chocolate and a box of muffins.

"Surfing down the stairs?" Archer said. "Buster, what were you thinking?"

"Easy, bro," Buster replied. "I'm concussed, remember?" He gave a snarky laugh.

"A concussion is no laughing matter," Kaylie said, looking somehow profound and absurd at the same time. "It is a traumatic brain injury that alters the way your mind functions."

"Well, it's not like I think straight anyway," Buster said.

Archer and Kaylie couldn't help but laugh too, but not Archer's father. He managed a weak crooked smile. It was all he could manage, Archer knew, since his mother's death eight years ago.

"The doctors say Buster has to stay out of school for a couple of days," Archer's father said.

Buster held up a peace sign and said, "Rock on!"

"And, once he's back in school," his father explained, "he won't be able to do gym for a while, either."

Archer watched the steam from his mug for a thoughtful moment. "So . . . can you tell me about what happened? Do you remember?"

"It's kind of a blur, but I had this killer dream, y'know?"

Archer sat up straighter. "Like a nightmare?"

"Nah, nah. It was a cool dream. I was in Australia at the Big Wave Championships, you know, at the Tombstones in Gnaraloo?"

Archer shrugged. "Never heard of it."

"Aww, it's such a cool place. I've seen it on the Surfing Channel, but this dream, it was like I was really there. I could feel things, y'know? The sand, my smooth board, the spray—it was so real."

Archer nodded. "I know a thing or two about dreams that feel real."

"So, anyway, I saw this swell rise up, and I was like, 'Dude, I am SO catching you!' I paddled like crazy and got up on the board, but . . . ah . . ."

"But what?" Kaylie asked, her eyes big as saucers.

Buster shook his head. "So the Tombstones are known for epic waves, right? But this thing, it rose up like Godzilla, and I was up there on my board, like way up there."

Archer asked, "Then what happened?"

"The wave curled, and I rode it but . . ." He frowned and rubbed his temples. "All I remember is it was like the wave took me toward shore and was heading for this rocky cliff. I felt like I was falling. I heard a bang, like a gunshot. Then I woke up in the ambulance."

Archer's dad took the family out for a late breakfast to celebrate Buster's return from the hospital, but Buster lacked his usual appetite. What he did eat, he threw up an hour later at home. After his father cleaned up the mess, he disappeared to the basement. Archer helped Buster get into some new clothing and then took him to the living room couch, his new bed. No stairs for Buster for a while.

"No more stair-surfing, okay?" Archer said, easing a chair over next to the couch.

"Nah, broham," Buster said, his words garbled. A second later, he was sound asleep.

Archer watched his little brother rest. He listened to Kaylie in the next room as she narrated an adventure starring Patches the Super Scarecrow Doll. Then Archer's eyes wandered over the long shelf above the sleeper sofa to all the framed family photographs, and his gaze lingered one photo in particular: their last family portrait. There was his mother, just a few months into her treatment, and a little gaunt but still beautiful: a kind and playful glint in her big brown eyes. Her hand rested lightly on her husband's shoulder. He held Kaylie in his arms. *Gosh*, Archer thought, *when was she ever that little?*

Archer thought Buster's lopsided grin in the picture looked kind of cheesy. Then again, so did his own smile. If memory served, he'd shoved an Oreo into his mouth just before the photographer took the shot. Archer thought he could detect a little bulge in his cheek. *Figures,* Archer thought.

But again and again, Archer kept returning to the image of his father. How content he'd been in that photograph. Holding his pride-and-joy daughter and his wife's hand on his shoulder— so happy. But not for long. His mother died just over a year later. They'd never taken another family portrait, and his dad had never really recovered.

It didn't surprise Archer to see his father surface from the basement only to have a cigarette out on the porch. That was all he did lately: hibernate in the basement and take smoke breaks. Archer wasn't sure what his dad did in the basement. There was a computer down there and, sometimes, he'd play online card games, like bridge or hearts. But lately, he'd been spending multiple hours down there. So what *was* he doing?

Archer wasn't about to investigate. He hated the basement for the memories it represented. It was the site of the scariest event of Archer's life.

Archer blinked. *This is not what I need to be thinking about right now.*

But the memory jolted into his consciousness vividly, especially the sounds. The sounds were the worst.

It had been right after the funeral. Archer had gone down to the basement, the side where his father kept a woodshop. Archer wanted to look at the wishing wells. In honor of his wife's love of the family well in the backyard, Archer's father had put his considerable skills to work, crafting all manner of replica display wells. Not working wells, of course, these were ornamental, decorative—the kind people put in their yards to give their property a little character, a little homey charm. All variations on the design of the family well—round, knobby turret, tall hooded canopy with shingles, a spool, a length of rope, a bucket, and a crank handle—they were so lovingly crafted, so intricate and beautiful, that word got out and he ended up making a tidy profit selling half a dozen of them. But not the ones his mother liked best. He never sold those.

Archer had gone down to the basement just to be among those wells that night. He didn't understand death. He didn't understand how a live person could be there one day and gone the next. He didn't understand any of the psychological pain of such a loss. All he knew then was to be near the wells made him feel near to his mom. He'd only been down there for a few minutes when he heard heavy footsteps on the basement stair.

The door to the work side creaked open, and Archer's father stood there. He'd worn a mask, expressions ranging from slack-jawed anguish to eyebrow-bunching fury to unblinking, fixed-eye, faraway numbness. "Archer, go on upstairs," was all he'd said.

Archer backed away from the wells and edged out of his father's way. The man had never been considered a big man, but he seemed somehow swollen. Fists bunched, forearms bulging, he strode toward the wells and, without looking back at Archer, exploded.

CRACK! With both hands joined in a single giant fist, he came down on the roof of a well, and the support beams snapped. The second blow crushed it with a series of sharp snaps and crackles that sent Archer reeling onto his backside.

"No, Dad," he whimpered.

But Archer's father went at the next well with a violent, clumsy backhand, knocking it onto the ground. He lifted a foot and stomped on the well as if it was the most wretched, hated thing he'd ever seen. CRACK!

One by one, he obliterated the loving works of his own hands. And Archer watched it all. His eyes blurred with tears, he'd muttered, "Why, Dad, why?"

His father had said nothing, but left the work in ruins. In the years that had passed since, Archer had looked in on the room a few times. The wreckage of all the wells was still there. His father never even cleaned up.

Archer blinked. No, as curious as he was about his father spending so much time downstairs, Archer wasn't about to go down there now. The sounds of grief and viciously cracking wood haunted the basement. Archer didn't have the heart to face them.

NINE

ICE-FIRE

IT WAS NOON BEFORE ARCHER FINALLY MADE IT BACK TO his room.

When he shut the door and turned, Master Gabriel was there.

"Snot buckets!" Archer exclaimed. "Don't sneak up on a guy like that."

"It's time," he said.

"Time?"

Master Gabriel glared. "Nick Bushman is waiting."

Archer blinked. "Oh," he said. "Oh! The new Dreamtreader? But it's noon. Kind of early for sleep."

"Not in Australia. It's three o'clock in the morning there. Nick is in his deepest sleep. It'll be best for him—and you—to meet him now."

Archer went to his closet, opened his lock box, and retrieved the parchment Master Gabriel had given him. The wax seal was split. "I can read it now," he said.

"Of course you can read it now. I told you it would open when it was time. Remember, read it before you enter the Dream. Study it while it remains. Do exactly as it prescribes."

"What if he doesn't believe me?" Archer asked. "What if he doesn't want to be a Dreamtreader?"

Master Gabriel took a deep breath. His Incandescent Armor flared to life. "Show him, Archer. Open his eyes. Trust me on this: Nick Bushman will want to be a Dreamtreader."

"Okay," Archer replied. "I'll do my best."

"That is all I could ever ask."

"What should I teach him first?" Archer asked. "Anchoring? Dream Lore? Weaving?"

"Anchor first," Gabriel said.

"Anchor deep," Archer replied, finishing the most important Dreamtreaders' law.

"Be swift about it. You will not have the luxury of time. There are breaches that need your attention. Use Bezeal's patch if you must, but get them locked down fast."

Archer unrolled the parchment. "This is it?" he muttered, staring down. "Just a handful of lines?"

He looked over his shoulder, but Master Gabriel had disappeared. That's when the parchment began to tear. No, not tear, but rather disintegrate. Even as Archer watched, bits and pieces of the scroll broke off and fell away. "No, no!" he gasped. He hadn't read it yet. He locked his eyes down on the text and tried to take it all in, but the bottom line disappeared in flurry of dust.

> In the Silentwood just south of Garnet,
>   Seek the Hunter's Stone.
> Beware the law of tooth and claw
>   And the dell where shadows roam.
> When the winding path delivers,
>   You must climb the ever-swaying tree.
> Above the clouds . . .

"No, no, no!" Archer growled. But it was done. What was left of the parchment turned to dust in his hands. He grabbed up his phone and tip-tapped what he had seen—what he could remember anyway—into a notepad app.

He'd done reasonably well, he thought. The first few lines were right, he thought. But the last line was just a few words: Above the clouds . . . what? Archer had no idea.

Why didn't I pay more attention? Then Archer gave himself a facepalm. *Why didn't I take a picture of the scroll with my cell phone camera?*

He shook his head. One facepalm didn't cover it. Not even close. Archer knew he could probably just summon Master Gabriel, and he would finish the text. But, of course, that would mean admitting—yet again—that he'd blown it.

"Maybe I should ask Bezeal," Archer grumbled to himself. "He's good at rhymes." But Archer knew involving Bezeal in the awakening of a new Dreamtreader would be worthy of far worse than a pile of facepalms.

As far as Archer was concerned, there was really only one thing to do: go to sleep.

Turbulent crimson vapors rotated around Archer. He couldn't help but think it funny that L. Frank Baum had been so close to right when he wrote *The Wonderful Wizard of Oz*. After all, a tornado had taken Dorothy to a land of wonder.

Once the Dreamtreader fell into the deepest possible sleep, a vortex erupted, churning the Dream fabric until breaking through and forming a funnel cloud. It was a personal Dreamtreader slide, and Archer always enjoyed the ride. "Booyah!" he cried out, careening recklessly in the swirling wind.

On the ground, Archer stepped out of the vortex and took a deep breath of Dream air. He imagined it smelled like raspberries. So it did. He had hit the ground in a bare stone canyon, but now it had clumps of full raspberry bushes. He thought his companion would appreciate the humor.

He called for his surfboard and his little Dream helper. "Razz!"

"Here I am!" came a squeak from thin air. A double puff of purple smoke later, and Razz was there. She perched on Archer's shoulder and looked around. "Raspberry bushes, Archer, really?"

Archer shrugged.

Razz frowned for a few moments but then started giggling. She descended into full body-shaking belly laughs and held her sides. "Okay, okay," she said. "It was a little funny. Now, let's get this party started!"

Archer found a good Intrusion wave, kicked his board over, and hopped on. Speeding southeast, carving down the steep wave, Archer said, "It's no party tonight, Razz. We've got to quick-patch tonight. We still have enough of Bezeal's paste?" It was a viscous translucent substance with the consistency of toothpaste, but it could temporarily mend small breaches in a hurry.

"Tons," Razz replied. "But why such a rush? Don't tell me . . . you aren't doing something stupid again, are you?"

"Hey!"

"A blood pact with Bezeal, taking on the Lurker by yourself, a duel with the Nightmare Lord . . ." Razz fluffed her tail. "I could go on."

"Don't. Point taken." Archer swerved the board around a craggy peak and picked up speed on the downslope. "No, tonight we are welcoming a new Dreamtreader."

"Really?" Razz leaped in the air and somersaulted so that her twin tails clapped together. "A girl? A girl this time, right?"

"Uhm . . . no."

"Dagnabbit!" Razz grumbled. "We need another girl Dream-treader. Who else can appreciate my tastes in fashion?"

"Sorry, Razz. The new Dreamtreader is a guy named Nick Bushman from Australia. We'll find him in a forest in Verse."

"Okay, well, maybe the third will be a girl," she said. "I suppose we should get to it. Direton first?"

Archer turned west with a grimace. There were always a ton of breaches in Direton. It was where Number 6 Rue de la Morte, the Shadowkeep, still stood . . . the fortress from which the Nightmare Lord himself once ruled . . .

Steadying the board and then crouching, Archer turned on Visis Nocturne, his sideways vision. The landscape darkened, and instantly Archer felt his reservoir of mental energies surging. It felt good. There was great power, exhilarating power, but it was drain-ing away rapidly. He would only be able use the Visis Nocturne for a short time. And what he saw in the Dream fabric was alarming: the web of threads trembled, whole sections swung loose, and others seemed to be fraying . . . or burning. Where the breaches ruptured the Dream fabric, pockets of fire flared. But the west was by far the worst. In the west, the horizon was ablaze.

No, it wasn't quite fire, but more like ice, spreading like flash frost up from the horizon and climbing slowly, flickering and licking upward. Ice-fire, something possible only in the Dream, and it wasn't a good thing.

"So, Archer?" Razz asked. "Direton?"

Archer sighed. "We'll start there," he said. "But we're going to be crazy busy. I can see them . . . hundreds at least. Looks like more than ever."

"Whatcha mean?" Razz asked, raising an eyebrow comically high. "You can see them? From here?"

"I can see them now, Razz," he said. "Master Gabriel gave me Visis Nocturne."

"Oh, that will help a ton!" Razz hovered just above Archer's nose. "C'mon, Archer. We got this!"

"I don't know, Razz," he said. "This is going to test us."

"Snap out of it, Archer," she replied, flicking his nose with a paw. "You used to tell me we don't have time for worrying."

"Sorry, Razz," he said. "I've got a lot on my mind."

"Splattering a few scurions might help," Razz said. "It always makes me feel a little better."

"Come to think of it," Archer said, "I could use a good couple of splatterings."

But after eight solid hours, Archer and Razz both had had more than their fill of breach repairs and scurion splatterings. And the Dreamscape was more turbulent than ever with Intrusion waves.

"Whoa, Archer, look out!" Razz squealed. She struggled to hold on to Archer's sleeve as he maneuvered his board down the slope of a gigantic wave.

"Hold on," he muttered through clenched teeth. He made the turn and slowed the board.

"You watching your time?" Razz asked through huffing breaths.

"Uh . . . yeah, we have like five hours still!" Archer exclaimed.

"You sure?"

Archer glanced over his shoulder at the night sky and Old Jack, the clock tower's image hanging there like a moonlit cloud . . . or a ghost. He swallowed hard. He'd way overestimated his time. "Three hours should be enough. I hope." He shook his head and let out a forceful sigh.

For the first time in his Dreamtreading career, he had lost track of exactly how many breaches they'd repaired. Dreamweaving for the large tears, Bezeal's patching paste for the little ones—Archer and Razz had closed up more than 300 breaches before he'd lost count.

"What do you know about the Silentwood?" Archer asked.

"It's beautiful," Razz said.

Well, that's good, Archer thought. *Makes sense. Verse District was the most scenic—*

"But deadly."

"You wanna explain that?" Archer asked.

"Oh, Archer, it's my favorite place to visit," she said. "But not for long. It's a forest, deep and lush, full of mysterious and stunning things to see. There are dangers at every turn, too. Creatures lurk there . . . and the Tripols."

"Tripols?" Archer echoed, steering south toward Garnet Province. "What are Tripols?"

"Little people," Razz said. "Big ears, big attitudes, and all kinds of trouble."

"I've never seen them," Archer said.

"You wouldn't," Razz said. "You only see them when they let you. And by then it's probably too late. You'll end up a butt of one of their jokes or at the bottom of their cook pot."

"That it?" Archer muttered. "Sounds like a problem for a flying squirrel, not a Dreamtreader . . ."

"Not hardly," Razz squeaked. "You know why it's called the Silentwood?"

"Not really. What? Is it really quiet?"

"Actually, it can be noisy," she replied. "Like I said, lots of wild-life. Then, sometimes, the whole place goes silent. That's when you know you're in deep trouble."

Archer looked at Razz, just to make sure he was hearing right. "Why?"

"Something lives deep in the Silentwood, Archer. Few have ever seen it; I haven't. It's dreadful, whatever it is. Wherever it travels, that part of the woods goes completely silent. Everything hides."

"Sounds like fun," Archer mumbled. He kicked his board off one Intrusion wave and caught a smaller wave headed directly south, where the tall shadows waited.

TEN

THE SILENTWOOD

"YOU'VE GOT TO BE KIDDING ME," ARCHER SAID. HE STOOD at the base of the forest, an uneven border strewn with eight-foot-tall dark feathery ferns, thick tree trunks that forked again and again and again, and a massive tangle of thorns. Archer reached out to one of the glistening five-inch spikes and tested its point. "Ouch!" He shook his hand. "These things are no joke. How are we supposed to get in?"

Archer summoned a bit of will, and a wickedly edged three-foot machete appeared in his hand. He shrugged and lifted the tool, preparing a mighty hack.

"I wouldn't," Razz said.

Archer froze and looked back at the tangled forest. A pair of platter-sized eyes opened in the darkness, and a warm breeze washed over Archer. "Oh," he said. "Oh, there's something alive here. Heh, heh . . ." He stepped backward hastily.

A bubbling growl sounded from the trees.

"What is that?" Archer asked.

"A galoot," Razz said. "What else would live in a thatch of life-threatening thorns?"

"Uhm . . . right." Archer shook his head. "So, hacking into the forest is no good. Can we fly over and drop in? It'll take a bit of my will, but—"

"Not worth it," Razz said. "We'd get caught in the webs."

"What webs?"

"The Silver Orb Weavers," Razz said. "Their webs are everywhere."

Archer shuddered. "Not a big fan of spiders. So, can't walk in or fly in. How do you get in, Razz?"

"I go *POOF!*" Razz vanished in a double puff of purple smoke. Then she reappeared a moment later. "See?"

The galoot in the woods laughed. It was a sound like rustling leaves and distant thunder.

Archer glared at the woods. "Great, so now the forest monsters are laughing at me." He turned back to Razz. "Look, Dreamtreaders can do a lot of crazy stuff, but we can't go *POOF*. Is there any other way into the Silentwood?"

Razz spun in the air once, removed her acorn hat, and scratched thoughtfully at her scalp. "Well, maybe the tunnels."

"Tunnels? There are tunnels into the forest."

"Technically, they are under the forest, but yepperdoodle, you can get in that way."

"Show me."

Razz clapped and sped off to the west. They rounded a particularly nasty snarl of thorny vines and came to a swift stop at a tree stump. "Here's one," Razz said, pointing at the stump.

"Uh, that doesn't look much like a tunnel."

"Silly," Razz muttered. She landed on the stump and her tail twitched. "No, not this. The tunnel is underneath. Just give the stump a smack."

As if that was the most obvious thing. Archer leaned over and slapped the stump. It made a hollow clicking sound, and then flung upward with such velocity that it shot Razz into the forest.

"Razz!" Archer bounded to the woods, skidding to a stop with a thorn just inches from his eyes. "Razz, are you okay?"

Archer heard some rustling around and a strange muffled cry. "Razz, what's wrong? Razz, are you there?"

There came a wet *SPLUT* from the woods, and then Razz said, "Big ugly galoot, trying to eat me, were you? I'll fix you!"

Archer winced at the bluster of noise, smacks, and crashes that splurted out of the woods. They ended with a series of deep whiny squeals, like a dog whimpering after being whacked with a newspaper. Razz reappeared moments later.

Her clothing was stained dark, and her fur was matted. "Don't ask," she grumbled. "Anyway, there's the tunnel."

Beneath the upturned stump, an earthen stair led down beneath the surface. It was as dark as pitch down there, but Archer had no fear of the dark. The Dreamtreader stepped down and held up a hand. A miner's hat appeared on his head and flooded the tunnel with LED light.

The walls of the tunnel were half-packed clay and half-rugged stone. The path beneath Archer's feet was as smooth as sanded wood, with nary a root or splinter. "I've been Dreamtreading here for eight years," he said, "and I had no idea you could actually dig tunnels in the soil. Are there more?"

"Oh, yes," Razz said, buzzing by Archer's ear. "They're all over."

"Who dug the tunnels?"

"Dunno," she replied. "Some say the Nightmare Lord. Some say the Lurker."

"That's not especially encouraging," Archer muttered. "Wouldn't be surprised if the tunnel dropped us into a pit of spears or a vat of boiling lava."

"Nope, this tunnel comes out in a patch of viscer flowers. They aren't as bad."

"Well, that's something, I guess."

Perhaps a hundred paces later, the tunnel sloped upward and became illuminated with a very faint green light. After a slight curve, an arched opening appeared, crisscrossed with vines and broad leafy foliage. A hint of lavender and melon scented the air as Archer pushed through the vines. He found himself in a dark glade overhung with twisted black tree boughs, a thousand loops of vine, and a never-ending canopy of wide leaves. Huge, felty, five-petaled blooms of dark pink or yellow grinned up at Archer from either side of an obvious path.

"Viscer flowers!" Razz warned. "Not too close!"

"Why?" Archer said, reaching slowly for a blossom. "Just a big, pretty—"

A sharp hiss shot from the bloom and, in the same instant, a fleshy tongue snapped toward Archer's hand like a whip. He couldn't move his hand fast enough. But he could think.

The speed of thought was the Dreamtreader's advantage in all situations. If you had the mental energy in the tank, you could create in an instant. Archer's move was a reaction, a reflex that summoned a medieval shield. The flower's attack clanged off the metal once, whipped forward a second time and a third, but couldn't pierce the shield. As the tonguelike appendage retreated back into the bloom, Archer saw the teeth on the end of it, a full set of vampire jaws.

"Snot rockets!" Archer exclaimed. "That would have left a mark."

"Is anything really as it seems here?" Razz chided. "Duh."

Archer exhaled and proceeded a little more carefully through the viscer flower stalks. As they picked their way through the shrubs and trees, Archer recited from the scroll Master Gabriel had given him: "In the Silentwood just south of Garnet, seek the Hunter's Stone."

"I've never heard of the Hunter's Stone," Razz said.

"Anything it could be? Any strange rocks or stony formations?"

Razz circled Archer's head. "Hmmm . . . it might be . . . maybe the pikes."

"Pikes?"

"In the middle of the forest, there are these rocky towers," she said. "They jut up from the pine needles. They look like tall stacks of stone coins. I guess if you could climb one, it would be a good place for a hunter to wait for prey."

"Take me there," Archer said. Razz flittered away, and he followed. As Archer ran, the Silentwood proved itself to be anything but mute. Chirps, buzzes, neek-breeks, gorkles, riddips, snorts, chirps, howls, and growls filled the night. More than once, Archer spotted eyes glistening within the shadows and foliage. The footing was awkward for him, but he still kept up with airborne Razz.

Once, in a particularly tense moment, a shadow passed overhead. Archer skidded to a stop, dropped to a knee, and looked up. He only saw the silhouette of a pair of spindly legs as a gigantic spider disappeared into the trees high above. Archer shuddered and ran on.

The thickening forest overcame the recognizable path, and Archer found himself leaping roots, swinging from low boughs, and bouncing off the large smooth rocks that began to complicate his passage. Soon the single stones became clumps of stone, too tall to leap with ease, and eventually, a few stone towers began to rise up high in the canopy.

Razz landed on Archer's shoulders. "This is the place," she whispered.

"Why are you whispering?" he asked.

"I dunno," she said. "It just feels like I should be quieter here."

Archer said nothing more. He too felt the urge to be silent. *Hunter's Stone*, he thought, moving stealthily through the tall turrets of rock. *Gotta be one of the highest towers.*

Scanning the tower tops, he continued deeper into the shadowy dell. Finally, he came to the tallest stone formations. "Razz," he whispered. "Buzz on up there. Tell me if you see anyone."

"Right, boss." And she was gone.

While she was away, it was so quiet that Archer could hear his heartbeat. It wasn't utterly still, though. Thank goodness. There were still a few chirps, neek-breeks, and riddips, but they were far less enthusiastic than before, and there were no more howls or growls.

Slipping from darkness to moonlit patches to the rippling shadows of the stone towers, Archer mentally recited the parchment. *In the Silentwood just south of Garnet, seek the Hunter's Stone. Beware the law of tooth and claw and the dell where shadows roam.*

Uh-oh.

Archer stopped. He stood now in a dell. There were shadows everywhere. But what was the law of tooth and claw? Try not to get eaten or mauled? By what?

"Pssst!" Razz, suddenly appearing at his side, whispered. "I found him. I think."

"Where?"

"Tallest rock tower," she said. "It's about four back and three over from here. At first I thought it was a big bird nest or a clump of branches. Then it moved, and I saw a really sharp arrowhead sticking out of it."

"That's gotta be him. Let's go." Razz led the way, and they came at last to a stone tower so high that Archer couldn't see the top of it. "Up there?"

Razz nodded. "You'll have to fly. No way you'll climb this."

"I'm already half-spent," Archer muttered. He searched above for Old Jack's clock face. "But we're running out of time."

Archer summoned his will. He'd flown many times before, and that made it easier to get started, but flying always drained the mental batteries. Archer flexed his will, the forest floor fell away, and he soared upward.

He followed the contour of the tower. It really did look like some giant banker had stacked the stones like coins. The ridges between the disks of rock were defined, each stone slightly askew from the one below it. Near the top, the stones increased in diameter, ending with a fairly wide platform at the top. Upon that stone, as Razz had described, was a very irregular clump. Leaves, branches, bracken, vines, and roots were tangled into a lumpy snarl that, as Archer squinted, took on the irregular shape of a person.

"Nick Bushman?" Archer whispered. "Is that you in there?"

A grumbling, gritty growl spilled out of the clump in reply.

"He's in there," Razz said, buzzing around the tower.

"Nick Bushman," Archer repeated. "We need to talk."

"Beat it, ya' ankle biter!" the gritty voice commanded. "I'm fair busy."

"I'm sorry to interrupt your dream here, Mr. Bushman," Archer said, changing his tone. "My name is Archer Keaton and—"

The clump of leaves shifted suddenly. "Look, mate, I don't know how you know me, but what's all this about my dream?"

"You're asleep, Mr. Bushman," Archer said. "You're dreaming right now."

"Right, mate," Nick replied. "I'm dreaming, and you're mad as a cut snake."

"What?"

"Eww!" Razz squeaked.

"Crazy," Nick said, "an absolute nutter. I'm wide awake. Anyone can see that. Now, rack off, I've got work to do."

"This is going to be harder than I thought," Archer mumbled. *How do I convince someone who thinks he's awake that he's really dreaming?* Archer had no idea. He didn't remember how Master Gabriel had done it all those years ago. All Archer knew was that it was absolutely essential for the Dreamtreader-to-be to recognize he was dreaming. It was the first step to controlling elements in the dream. If you don't know you're dreaming, then you aren't conscious within the dream, and then you cannot harness your mental will. Archer decided to try another tactic.

"I'm a Dreamtreader, Mr. Bushman," he said. "I patrol this world. So that makes me kind of an authority on dreams. Believe me when I tell you that you are, in fact, dreaming."

"Dreamtreader, eh? I already told you, I'm not . . . wait . . . are you flying?" A scruffy head poked out of the pile. His skin was painted with crisscrossing stripes of black, gray, and brown, but pale blue eyes shone out from the camouflage. "You *are* flying," he said. "Well, color me gobsmacked. That-that's not possible. For your squirrel thing, maybe, but not for you."

"Squirrel thing?" Razz blurted. "Why, I ought to—"

Archer quickly sidled in front of Razz and came to stand on Nick's platform stone. "Flying's just one of the things you'll be able to do as a Dreamtreader, Nick."

"That's bonzer, mate," he said. "Maybe later I'll give it a burl, but now I've got to stay—"

Bang!

If someone had fired a shotgun just a few feet away, the sound wouldn't have stunned Archer like this. Nick too. His head disappeared back into the pile of bracken. Razz darted into Archer's jacket.

A wave of something had just blasted through the dell. It made no sound of its own but stole sound wherever it struck. Now the forest was dead silent. Nothing moved. Even in the Dream fabric, all became still and silent, the Intrusion waves flattening in an instant.

Archer couldn't understand what was happening. He wanted to call out to Nick but couldn't make himself do it. The physical ability to speak seemed to be there, but to say even a single word seemed too terrifying to contemplate. Instead, Archer dropped down and lay beside the clump that hid Nick Bushman.

Movement. Out in the moonlit forest, something caused the trees to sway. Archer stared, straining to see what had caused the movement. A trail of swaying trees formed. And each time a new patch of trees was thrust aside, there came also a peculiar, unnerving sensation.

Sight, sounds, smell, taste, and touch: Archer felt them all in the Dream just as he did in the waking world. But with the advancing threat in the trees, there came a new sense. It happened again and again, with the frequency of footsteps, a kind of pulse of suction. Each time it hit, it was as if the silence somehow became more silent, and Archer's mental energy grew weaker. It reminded Archer unpleasantly of being caught in a strong undertow at the ocean, except that this was some kind of riptide of the mind.

"C'mon, ya shark biscuit," Nick yelled from his camouflage pile, but his voice just scarcely pierced the silence as a faint whisper. "C'mon."

The nearest trees parted, several snapping at the base and toppling violently into the wood. Archer understood at last: *the law of tooth and claw.*

Like a dark wave of scaly flesh, a mountainous shape lumbered into the dell. Its body was bulky with knotted clumps of muscle and had the rough bulbous shape of a hippopotamus. A hippopotamus the size of a resort hotel. Its four limbs were segmented and thick, each ending with an extraordinarily wide, knobby foot studded with talons. Its fore shoulders were so thick and pronounced that it seemed to have no neck at all. Its head was reptilian, but tapered, more like the head of a horse. It was bigger than a house and had interlocking saberlike tusks on both upper and lower jaws. Tiny beads of fierce red showed its tiny eyes, tucked within folds of more leathery skin.

"You're the one!" Nick gasped. "After all these years."

Hearing Nick speak once more broke the spell of fear over Archer. "Nick, come with me," he begged. "Right now."

"Sorry, mate," Nick replied. "I've waited far too long to sock out of here now. I mean to kill this bitzer."

"You don't have to kill it," Archer said. "I can get us out of here."

The creature reared up on its hind limbs, opened its massive jaws and roared. Freight trains, explosions, windstorms, and car crashes— all put together—that's what the beast sounded like to Archer. He felt the draining on his mental will once more and had a sudden inexplicable desire to close his eyes . . . to sleep.

A rough hand took hold of his shoulder and shook him. "See there," Nick said. "See what it was doing to you, mate? That's what it did to my little Taddy."

"Taddy?"

"You know, mate, a wee friend and compatriot like your squirrel thing."

"I heard that!" came a muffled objection from Archer's coat.

"Taddy was just a cute little fella, never did anyone harm unless they earned it. That thing out there took Taddy right out of the sky and then swallowed him. So don't you tell me I don't have to kill it. Killing it is the only thing I have left to do in this life."

Archer's mind whirled. He had to awaken Nick to Dreamtreading, but Nick wouldn't listen. And Archer had never seen this beast before or felt anything like it. How could a creature of the Dream drain away his will, the very source of his power? Archer didn't know. And didn't care. He needed to get Nick and get as far away from this dell as possible. That's when the idea hit him. He didn't know if his offer was quite true, but it was the only thing he could think of that might sway Nick.

"If you come with me right now," Archer said, "I'll show you power, power that will let you kill this thing any time you want."

"You seem a decent bloke," Nick said. "But I've got to do this, and I can't wait any longer."

Archer was out of ideas. He couldn't take his eyes off the creature to check on Old Jack, but he knew it was getting very late. Nick wasn't coming. The next bell to ring would be Stroke of Reckoning, Archer's Dreamtreading deadline, and he was way too far away from his anchor to get there in time.

"Okay, okay," Archer blurted. "We'll kill it. We'll kill it right now. I'll help you. But once it's done, you need to hear me out about Dreamtreading."

Nick's hand shot out of the pile. "Now, that's an offer I can't refuse. Shake on it."

Archer's heart leaped. "Deal!" He lunged and shook Nick's hand.

"Done and done," Nick said. "But listen, mate, don't take this thing lightly. The paravore don't have a soul. It don't have pity, and it don't have mercy. You get a chance to take it out, you do it right fast."

"Got it," Archer said.

"And one more thing."

"Yeah?"

"You best keep your squirrel thing hidden away," Nick said. "I'd hate for it to end up like my Taddy."

DREAMTREADER'S CREED,
CONCEPTUS 7

A word of caution, Dreamtreader. Beware of Garnet Province in the district of Verse. The Libraries are there, and they are a vast and priceless treasure. Like most treasures, the Libraries of Garnet Province can be dangerous, even for the Dreamtreader. You see, there are many secrets there, especially in the Inner Sanctum. Much of this hidden lore is open to the Dreamtreader, required reading, even. But there are some volumes you must not read. You must not even touch them! These are the *Masters' Bindings*, and these great tomes are as far above the Dreamtreader's wisdom as the stars are above the Waking World.

It is precisely because you must not read the *Masters' Bindings* that you almost assuredly will want to read them. Resist the temptation, dear Dreamtreader. Resist with all your heart, mind, and soul. To give in would be your undoing.

The Sages guard the Inner Sanctum jealously. And well they should, for the temptation to read the *Masters' Bindings* came over them once. It drove them mad. What is left of them became the Scath.

Sometimes called the Soul-stolen or Felshades, the Scath are utterly conscienceless, ruthless, and maniacal. They are bound to evil just as they are bound to the Sanctum. It is their home, their prison, and their tomb.

But becoming a Scath would be a kind penance for the Dreamtreader. You see, a Dreamtreader who delves into the *Masters' Bindings* will become something far worse. But this fate is beyond your reckoning. It is something of which none but the Masters can speak.

Know this, however: the Inner Sanctum has since been sealed behind a door that is impenetrable to the Dreamtreader. It can only be opened or sealed with a particular one of the Masters' keys. And for many Dreamtreader ages, the *Masters' Bindings* have been safely sheltered. But now, the danger is greater. The Shadow Key was stolen . . . and then lost.

Lost, but not destroyed. If you should find this "Shadow Key," use it not. He who unlocks the Inner Sanctum will release the Scath to do mayhem in the Dream and Waking Worlds . . . and will slowly transform into something so wicked that it is beyond imagining.

ELEVEN

THE PARAVORE

RAZZ ZIPPED OUT OF ARCHER'S JACKET. HER EYES WENT huge and focused on the creature, lumbering through the trees.

"We're going to kill it, Razz," Archer said. "You can *POOF* if you need to, but we need to take this thing out." The paravore snapped a copse of trees with a sudden crush of its foreleg. *CRACK!* Archer winced and his confidence drained away. That sound . . . reminded him of his father shattering the wishing wells in the basement.

"Archer, please," she said. "This thing is different. This isn't all Dream."

"What? What do you mean?"

"I can't explain it," Razz said. "But I'm made of Dream fabric, and I can sense other things. Like you, you're not Dream stuff. This creature, there's something weird about it, like it's made of two places at once. It's got Dream fabric all over it, but . . . I just can't tell what the other place is."

"I promised," Archer said. "And I've got to wake Nick up."

"I'm not asleep," Nick said. "Now, cut all this ear-bashing and let's get to slaying."

"I'm sorry, Razz," Archer said. "I have to."

Razz didn't argue. She shook her head sadly and vanished.

The creature roared again, blotting out all sound and making the stone towers tremble. "It's spewing mad now," Nick said. "It scented me out but doesn't like the stone here."

"How do you know?"

"I've been tracking the paravore for years, mate. Either you learn or you die."

"So how do we kill it?"

"Can't pierce the thing's hide," Nick said. "I mean to put this carbon steel arrow in its eye."

"From here?"

"No, not from here, ya goon," Nick said. "It's got to get closer, get caught up in the towers here."

"It doesn't look like it's coming in."

"That's where you come in, Archer," Nick said. "You can fly, right? I need you to fly down there and coax him forward. Duck its roar and, whatever you do, stay out of its eye lance."

"Its what?"

"Eye lance," he said. "That's what I call it anyway. The thing'll sap you, take your strength, sometimes even shut you down, but that's when it looks directly at you."

"Sheesh," Archer said.

"I know!" Nick replied. "It's a nasty beast."

The paravore was nasty—of that, Archer had no doubt—but that wasn't actually what he was thinking about for just that moment. Archer marveled at how self-aware Nick seemed to be. He planned; he reflected; he had emotional reactions—it was like he was in some kind of pre-Dreamtreading state.

"Yo, mate?" Nick said. "You'd better get focused."

"Sorry," Archer replied, blinking rapidly. "Okay, duck the roar, avoid the eye lance—got it. Wait, how do I do that? I can't fly for long."

"Stay in its peripheral vision, and move around a lot," Nick said. "But ya gotta keep it from thinkin' straight. Make it mad, and it'll follow ya."

"I'm good at making things mad at me," Archer said. He stood up and stepped toward the edge of the platform. "Here I go. Don't miss."

"I never miss."

Archer dove from the stone perch, soared out to the creature's right flank, and decided to start with fire.

The paravore emitted a low gurgling growl that Archer felt as much as he heard. But the creature seemed focused on the pillars of stone. It rubbed its lower jaw tusks along the stone as if sharpening them.

It's testing the towers, Archer thought as he banked hard back to his left and made straight for the paravore. But why? It toppled bigger trees without a second thought. Was there something about the stone, something the creature didn't like, didn't trust?

"Here goes nothing," Archer said, flexing his will and calling up a glob of molten rock for each hand. He increased his speed and readied the attack. But as he neared the creature, he found himself overwhelmed by the thing's sheer size. From shoulder to foot, it had to be at least sixty feet. If it turned too swiftly and opened its jaws, it was certain to be able to take Archer in a single mouthful.

Archer drove those thoughts away and steered toward the mid-section. He thought he might come in super low and aim for the paravore's underbelly. Perhaps it was a weak area. At the last second, though, Archer spotted a fan-shaped projection of flesh laying flat against the side of the paravore's head. It was ridged and tapered toward a dark cavity.

An ear! Archer thought. *Gotta be.*

That became the target. Archer swooped up and curled hard, letting loose with the fireballs. The Dreamtreader heaved them both at the creature's ear but couldn't stop and watch the impact. He curled away just as a flare of angry orange exploded. The paravore roared again, but the pitch was higher, more frantic. In pain.

Now for the tough part. Archer had to get the creature to see him without directly fixing him with the eye lance attack.

"C'mon, you stupid, thick beast!" Archer yelled, swerving in and out of the paravore's field of vision. "Yeah, I'm the one who toasted your ear! That's right—whatcha going to do about it?"

Archer risked looking over his shoulder just in time to see the creature snapping its jaws wildly, seemingly in frustration over the burning sensation in its ear. But its massive head whipped back around.

When the paravore turned, its red eyes flared. Archer couldn't see the lance attack, but the evidence of its coming was unmistakable. Wherever the paravore's gaze lined up with a stone tower, flecks of rock blasted outward in little whirling clouds that caught the moonlight.

"Uh-oh," Archer muttered. He tried to rocket upward, but an invisible wave hit him. Hard. All at once, Archer lost the ability to fly and careened out of the air into the foliage.

SNAP! CRACK! Branch and bough shattered on Archer as he tumbled end over end. He slammed into the mossy turf far below and lay still.

The paravore's roar startled Archer back into the moment, but he was dazed. His thoughts bumbled around in his head, and he couldn't focus. *Creature. Big. Move. Run.*

It was enough to get him stumbling to his feet and hands. He rose up on all fours and clambered like a spider over the ferny terrain.

Then he heard it: *KERRACK!* It was the earsplitting shatter of stone. The paravore had overcome its hesitance to cross into the pillars. Archer rose up and turned in time to see a massive stone tower crashing through the treetops right at him.

He dove and fell into a muddy creek bed. The tower came crushing down to the earth, smashing trees and shrubs alike. It slammed to the ground, bridging the creek, and coming to rest just above Archer's shoulders.

"Snot-blasting nose nuggets!" he exclaimed, rolling out from under the fallen tower's shadow, just as a huge section of stone broke loose and fell into the creek bed. It hit the mud and water and sent a gooey spray all over Archer. He blinked and wiped the muck from his face, but he didn't have time to think about the near miss.

The paravore continued its advance. Each footstep brought a minor earthquake; each roar sent ice slivers careening up Archer's spine. The Dreamtreader turned toward the creature. It appeared high above the tree canopy like an unstoppable tidal wave, filling his vision with that gnarled, leathery flesh and those beady red eyes.

Archer leaped for the bank of the creek and slipped. He skidded awkwardly like a puppy on a tile floor, gave up, and sprinted up the creek bed. Another stone tower came crashing down just inches away. Archer winced and jumped at the thunderous impact, but there was no more looking up or back. He had to hope and pray that the falling stone wouldn't just suddenly crush him. He had to keep running.

"Razz, I could really use some help here!" Archer yelled as he ran. "I can't see above this creek bed. I don't know where I'm going!" When she didn't appear, Archer wasn't exactly surprised, but he was disappointed. Razz tended to stick to her convictions. If she thought a certain course of action was stupid or reckless, she stayed away.

Another stone tower crashed through the forest somewhere to

Archer's right. Reflexively, he bounced to the left, slamming into the creek bank again. The paravore's roar sounded closer than ever. Archer kept running but risked a look. The monster's clawed foot slammed into another pillar of stone. The shadow of the great beast loomed above.

Archer stepped on something that wasn't mud or pebbles. That "something" gave a strange crackling beneath his feet, and then Archer tripped. He went face-first into the gravelly mud, flopped over like a fish out of water, and looked back.

Sitting in an uneven circle around what appeared to be the ruins of a picnic lunch of gigantic steamed crayfish were a crowd of little blue people. *Tripols*, he thought. *Just like Razz said.*

With bulbous, angled eyes of blue glass, they glared at Archer and had their floppy, wing-shaped ears pinned back tensely. Archer realized with sudden clarity that he had been the cause of their lunch's ruin. He hadn't been looking and had apparently stepped right in the middle of their food.

"Uhm . . . sorry about that!" Archer said, clambering to his feet. "But, uh, you guys might want to get out of here. There's a really big—"

Archer never finished the sentence. The paravore's foot came down through the forest canopy and bombed into the space between Archer and the Tripols. He heard a chorus of warbling shrieks and hoped the little guys hadn't been flattened. Somehow that thought made Archer mad. Boiling mad.

"Enough of this!" he growled, summoning what was left of his will to create. He reached back over his shoulder. His hand came back with his favorite sword, a broad-bladed long sword modeled after the versatile blades used by the Vikings. But Archer's sword had a little something extra: when he cried out, a blue fire rushed up from the hilt and engulfed the blade.

"I have got to get a name for this sword!" he exclaimed.

He lunged toward the paravore's foot and thrust the blade into the flesh just behind its nearest talon. The beast shrieked in pain, pulling back. The force of the creature yanking its foot out of the creek bed flung Archer upward into the trees, but the sword was still embedded deep in the monster's foot.

Somehow the creature's fury helped crystallize Archer's thought. Finally, he had enough concentration to go airborne once more. He leaped up out of the tree, blasted through the dense canopy, and almost flew directly into the paravore's mouth. Archer careened off an upper jaw tusk and cartwheeled twice in the air before regaining flight control enough to swerve out of mouthful distance.

He felt his will dwindling, but he had to stay ahead of the creature enough to find Nick's tower perch. With the paravore pouncing just behind, Archer moved evasively, darting around and behind the stone towers. He dove skyward to get a look and then plummeted again to avoid the creature's eye lance.

It was on one of the sudden ascents that he spotted the high stone turret where Nick waited with his bow. The paravore screeched and another stone tower fell. Archer turned and hovered, then launched a series of blazing fireballs at the creature's already singed ear. The beast reared on its hind legs and searched for Archer.

"I'm only going to have enough left for one more pass," Archer muttered. "Nick, I hope you're paying attention!"

Archer positioned himself directly between the beast and Nick's stone tower. Finally fixing its stare on Archer, the paravore careened through the forest and other turrets. Archer watched the eye lance striking one tower after another—evidenced by bursts of steam and shattered stone—coming at him swiftly. He dodged to his left and sheltered behind the thickest tower remaining. The paravore did not relent. It roared and charged. The jaws gaped wide. Its eye lance swept just over Archer's head.

The paravore pounced, a red-eyed colossal wrecking ball, coming straight for the stone tower and Archer hiding behind it. Archer had a little will left, but not enough for flying. Not knowing what else to do, he clambered up the stone. With the concussive footfalls and the roars of the beast so near, it felt like climbing a ladder into a thunderstorm. He braced himself for the impact.

There was a sudden, frightening silence. The paravore's gaping maw thrust out from the other side of the tower behind Archer. The Dreamtreader yelped and tried to clamber away but had nowhere to go. Then the creature's face went slack, and its head lurched, banging clumsily into the stone a foot from Archer's clinging hand. The red light in its eyes had gone out and the very last bit of an arrow shaft and its fletching protruded from one dead eye.

The paravore's face slid down the tower. Its body crumpled near the bottom and crashed sideways onto the forest floor. The creature's legs twitched for a moment and then went still. Archer clung to his stone turret and heard two very strange sounds: one was a chorus of warbling cheers from the forest below. These apparently belonged to the Tripols. Archer watched as dozens of the little people clambered up onto the dead paravore.

Razz was right, Archer thought. *Those Tripols really will eat anything.*

The second sound was something that reminded Archer of the old Tarzan jungle scream, an almost operatic yell of triumph and sheer ferocity that ended in "HOOROOO!"

TWELVE

A WAKE-UP CALL

NICK. IT HAD TO BE. ARCHER CHECKED HIS MENTAL reserve. It was very low, but enough to power a few tower-to-tower leaps. He launched into the air and propelled himself toward the highest tower, the Hunter's Stone. Archer at last dropped down next to an exultant Nick Bushman.

"Bonzer, mate!" Nick cried out, clasping Archer's shoulder. "We dropped that bitzer at last! I owe you heaps!"

"Just keep your promise," Archer said. "We need to get you to understand that you're dreaming. You need to become a Dream-treader."

Nick swiped away some of the branches and leaves that still clung to his strange outfit. Archer could see his face much better now. He was older than Archer had thought. Thirty, maybe more. His face was leathery and creased but most likely from care and wear over the years. He had three almost perfect triangles of hair on his face: two slanted eyebrows and one below his bottom lip. And his hair, still mingled with twigs and leaves, was spiked, with a tall mohawk crest leaning in the center.

Nick's eyes darted to the side. His expression changed from

exultant to fretful. "I . . . uh, have to fess up, Archer," Nick said. "I know I'm dreamin'."

"You what?" Archer spluttered.

"Well, I should say I suspected it pretty strongly."

"But . . . you said—"

"Fact is, you kind of confirmed things once and for all, but I needed your help. I'm sorry, mate, but time was short, the paravore was upon us, and I just didn't know what to do."

Archer chomped down on the first comment that leaped into his mind. He remembered all too well the rash decisions he'd made under the pressure of time and danger. Speaking of time, Archer looked over his shoulder. Less than an hour remained.

Archer finally found the right words. "Look, Nick," he said, "when there's time, we'll need to talk about this again. Dreamtreaders have to be able to trust each other. But in the meantime, I need to know just what you know about your abilities and dreaming."

"Right then," Nick said, scratching at the patch of whiskers beneath his lower lip. "So for years, I knew I could dream things when I wanted to. Loads of fun. And I met Taddy; cute little guy knew me. And he kept showing up in my dreams, so I figured something was up." Nick's eyes clouded. "Then that paravore beast showed up, took Taddy away. I grieved for months, mate. Strangest thing, being that I only knew him from my dreams. But I've put that beast in the dunnie at last. And I've got you to thank for it. You've got the truth from me and my friendship from here on. And that's fair dinkum, count on it."

"Fair dinkum?" Archer asked.

"Eh, it's the most honest and genuine kind of a pledge," Nick explained.

"Oh," Archer replied. "Got it. Well, first thing I can tell you is that your ability to dream things at will is a talent very few people have. It's a gift. You were born to be a Dreamtreader, Nick, and this world of dreams is a lot more complex that you've ever . . . uh . . . well, dreamed. But realizing you're dreaming is only part of waking you up as a full-powered Dreamtreader."

"Right. What else do I need to do?"

"It's different for each Dreamtreader," Archer explained slowly. "But I have—had—a scroll that told me how to wake you up. We need to follow the winding path to something called the ever-swaying tree."

"I know it," Nick said. "I know right where it is."

Archer exhaled. "Can we get there in twenty minutes or less?"

"Sure thing," Nick said. "You fly, right?"

"Yeah, but I'm toast. I couldn't fly now more than a few feet."

"No worries," Nick said. "We'll go my way."

"What's your way?" Archer asked.

"Oh, you'll like this," Nick said. He put his fingers to his mouth and let loose a trilling whistle that echoed off the nearby canyon walls.

"What are we . . ." A broad shadow loomed overhead. A fierce wind nearly knocked Archer from the stone platform.

Magnificent pure-white paws clutched Archer's shoulders and lifted him into the air.

"Whoa, hey!" Archer cried out.

"It's all right," Nick said, being lifted similarly from the platform. "They're friends."

Archer looked up and saw the wind-streaked mane of a huge lion, only this lion was the pristine white of arctic snow . . . and it had wings. Massive eagle-type wings. *Griffin?* Archer thought. *Sphinx?* He couldn't remember which one had a bird head or a lion head, if either one. It really didn't matter. These flying white lions were cool. And fast.

The majestic creatures airlifted Archer and Nick over the forest, over the vast silvery webs of the spiders in the treetops. *Glad I didn't try going in that way,* he thought. Soon, their speed and altitude took away fine details like the spiderwebs. The terrain below became a quilt of earthy colors. Far ahead but growing rapidly closer, Archer saw a misty mountain wrapped in a treacherously winding path.

"Snot rockets, these things are fast!" Archer cried out. He dangled beneath the flying lion and blinked at the rush of air.

"The valkaryx are a real ripsnorter, right?!" Nick called back. "Now where do ya want them to drop us?"

"Drop us?"

"No, mate, not like that. Set us down's what I mean. Kinda."

"Kinda?" Archer said, feeling his cheeks reddening. "I can see the winding path, but we don't have time to follow it. Can the valkaryx take us to the ever-swaying tree?"

"Of course they can," Nick replied. He shouted a series of words and sounds that Archer didn't understand. *"Rak-ta, Shak-ta, soonerian, tre aborandum, ne!"*

Immediately, the valkaryx banked right and accelerated toward the mountain. Archer reflexively grabbed ahold of its paws and hung on. As they closed on the mountains, Archer noted a very small tree growing up from its peak. But, closer still, Archer realized he'd misunderstood the scale. The mountain was much bigger than he'd thought. Colossal, really. The "little" tree was actually a towering giant. The trunk was narrow and full of odd bends and curves. There were branches aplenty, each ending with patches of glistening silver leaves. And the tree was indeed swaying.

The valkaryx swooped a swift spiral down to the base of the tree and lightly placed Archer and Nick in a cleft of the peak. The noble white pair landed nearby and folded their wings behind their broad shoulders.

Nick bowed to them and said, "*Gratis, Rak-ta, Shak-ta. Te bonis trel esse.*"

The valkaryx with the longest mane made a rumbly growling sound and stamped its paw once.

"I heard you speak like that when we were flying," Archer said. "You can talk to them, can't you?"

"Yeah, the words just come, but only in the Dream. Doesn't seem to matter the creature. They understand, and I understand them."

"Even the paravore?"

"Yeah, even that brute," Nick explained. "You shoulda heard what he called you when you stuck that sword in its foot. He was spewing, he was. Would ya like to know—"

"No, I'd rather not," Archer replied. "What did you tell the valkaryx just now?"

"I told 'em to wait here till we're done. You're on a time limit, right?"

"Very much so," Archer said, pointing up into the clouds. "See that?"

"What?"

"The old clock tower," Archer said. "You can see it from pretty much anywhere."

"All I see are clouds."

"Oh," Archer replied thoughtfully. He stared across the landscape. Aside from being in an airplane in the Waking World, he'd never been this high up before. The geography below was so distant that it appeared only as vague splotches of color. There were even a few low clouds drifting below. It was an odd sensation, standing above some clouds.

"So what's the deal with the ever-swaying tree?" Nick asked. "Am I a Dreamtreader yet?"

"I don't think so," Archer said. "You don't see the clock yet. Something's not quite right. I think we need to climb the tree."

"'Kay, and then what?"

Archer stared at his boots.

"You don't know, do you?" Nick slapped his knee and let out a deep roaring laugh. "Hoo, hoo! You don't know! There, now, we're even, right?"

"It was in a kind of riddle," Archer said. "But I lost the last line." Archer recited the poem and said, "I don't know the last line."

"Guess it rhymes with tree, right?" Nick concluded.

"Yeah, but there's a lot of things that rhyme with tree."

"Well, here's the ever-swaying tree. Let's give it a burl." Nick showed no fear, diving for the lowest bough and shimmying up.

Archer followed a little less skillfully. Still, his mental will made him stronger than he would have been in the Waking World. He bounded upward, scaling each crook and bough as best he could. Halfway up, it became crystal clear that the tree was indeed swaying. Archer could feel the motion in his body . . . a slow drifting . . . back and forth. It was hypnotic. It made him sleepy.

"No!" Archer told himself. Falling asleep in a skyscraping tree would not be a good thing.

"Hey, you all right, mate?" Nick called down. "You're fallin' behind a bit there."

"I'm okay," Archer said. "Just tired is all."

"'Kay, then. Lemme know if ya need a hand."

Archer focused on the branches and kept his mind off the sway. Soon, he and Nick reached the highest place where they still had both a branch to stand on and a bough to hold on to. The view there was astounding. The Dream Sky was often a violet-tinged crimson, but from where Archer could see, there was a purplish blue that seemed to undulate like a tide. A light breeze even carried a vaguely familiar scent.

Mom's pumpkin pie, Archer thought.

It was that nutmeg spicy-sweet smell he had always loved when he had was little, that he remembered so vividly here in the treetop. He saw his mom in that ratty old red-and-white crisscrossed apron that she refused to throw away. He saw the vapors rising from the hot pies fresh out of the oven. He saw the smile on his father's face as his mother put a big slice of pie in front of him and then proceeded to bury it in whipped cream. He could taste the pie, even. It felt . . .

"Whoa, Archer."

It was Nick, gripping the Dreamtreader's shoulder. "You looked like you were about to doze off there."

"No, I'm okay, I think," Archer said. "I just had the most vivid memories."

"Same here," Nick replied, but he gave no details. "Think I'm a Dreamtreader now?"

"I don't think so," Archer said. "Do you see the clock?"

Nick craned his neck every which way. "Nope. No clock. Just really high up."

But Archer could see the clock. Old Jack hovered out in the distance, a little lower than usual, due to the height of their perch. The time left was not promising. Even with the swift valkaryx, getting back to Archer's anchor before the Stroke of Reckoning would be a difficult feat.

Archer scoured his mind. *When the winding path delivers, you must climb the ever-swaying tree. Above the clouds . . .* and then what? Shout out who you want to be? Stare at the clouds and you will see? No, those don't make any sense.

Something stung his right palm, and he pulled his hand away from the branch. There was no blood, no recent injury, but that reddish blotch on his palm looked redder still. Staring at the ruddy scar sent him back into his thoughts. *When the winding path delivers, you must climb the ever-swaying tree. Above the clouds . . .* there had been a letter *t*. It might be the beginning of any word, but Archer felt an idea forming in his mind. Above the clouds . . .

Wait. It wasn't a letter *t*. It was a letter *f*. It came in a sizzling rush: Above the clouds, face your fears, die to live, and take the faithful leap.

Leap? Leap out of the tree? That seemed crazy. Archer didn't recall much about his own awakening, but it didn't seem possible that he could forget something so dramatic as leaping from a ridiculous height.

But it made sense in an odd sort of way. Archer pondered this while absently itching the mark on his palm. "I think I've got it," Archer said.

"Ace!" Nick exclaimed. "Lay it on me."

"You're not going to like it."

"You never promised me this was going to be a rage. What do I need to do?"

Archer glanced down through the crisscrossing tree branches. "I think you need to leap out of this tree."

Nick's mouth dropped open. In fact, his entire face seemed to grow a foot longer. "You're funning me, aren't ya, mate?"

"No," Archer said. "I think I've remembered the last line of the scroll. 'When the winding path delivers, you must climb the ever-swaying tree. Above the clouds, face your fears; die to live, and take the faithful leap.'"

"Well, I suppose it rhymes," Nick said. "More of a slant rhyme, really. But, ah . . . that's not much to hang a hat on if it means I jump from this tree."

"I'm sorry, Nick," Archer said. "I wish I knew better."

"Well," Nick said, turning round to face the open air, "we are in a Dream, right? What could it hurt? I'll give it a burl. Hoorooo!"

Archer cried out, "Wait!"

But it was too late. Nick leaped from the branch. It wasn't just a raw jump. He actually did a swan dive. The moment the Australian was in the air and out of reach, Archer had second thoughts. The poem's final verse suddenly didn't make any sense at all.

Archer leaped. He used what little will he had left and soared down. He had to catch Nick before he hit bottom. Sudden death in the Dream wouldn't awaken Nick to Dreamtreading. It would probably keep him from ever becoming a Dreamtreader, though. Archer had a chilling fear that it might do even worse.

Archer dodged branches, trying to keep Nick's plummeting form in sight. But it was becoming more and more clear to Archer that he was too late. Nick disappeared from view. Archer poured on the speed and rocketed toward the mountain's peak. Archer heard a sudden cry and gave a choked yell.

When Archer slowed his descent and dropped to the mountain-top at last, there was no sign of Nick. The Dreamtreader gasped. He had just enough will left to gasp for air and fear the worst. Careless mistakes, bull-headed stubbornness, and reckless, spur-of-the-moment ideas—the past came back in a rush. His old Dreamtreading partners, Duncan and Mesmeera . . . and flames.

"Well, that was a closey!"

Archer lifted his eyes, and there, seated on the back of the long-maned valkaryx, was Nick.

"You didn't fall?" Archer yelled.

"Well, yeah, I fell a bit," Nick explained. "But halfway down I got to thinking it was about the dumbest thing I'd ever done, so I called for ol' Rocky here."

"You have no idea how relieved this makes me," Archer said. He turned. "Do you see the clock by any chance?"

Nick shook his head.

"I'll just have to talk to my superior."

"Who's that?"

"He is called Master Gabriel," Archer said. "I'm guessing you'll meet him soon enough. But I need to get back to my anchor. Can the valkaryx get me back to Garnet Province."

"That where the Libraries are?"

Archer nodded.

"Yeah, yeah," Nick said. "We go there all the time." He spoke a few words and sounds to the valkaryx. The short-maned creature nuzzled Archer's shoulder.

"Oh, she wants ya to climb on," Nick explained. "No sense carryin' ya like before."

The journey back to Garnet Province was smooth and swift. The valkaryx were majestic flyers, but there was no questioning their athletic prowess. They flew tirelessly and at a great height, giving Archer and Nick a panoramic view of the Dream landscape.

Feeling more confident about making it back to his anchor before the Stroke of Reckoning, Archer found that he rather enjoyed the ride. It wasn't every day that you were able to ride a flying lion.

But even that brief pleasure took ill when Archer blinked on his Visis Nocturne. The entire stretch of the northern Verse District was dotted with tiny breaches. No single one was problematic: too small to be a threat. But there were so many.

Forms District was just the same. From the splintered landscape of the Cold Plateau all the way to Warhaven and Direton, especially Direton, tiny dot-to-dot diagrams of breaches appeared. And these were areas Archer knew that he and Razz had repaired breaches earlier.

Sure, many of them had been patched up with Bezeal's paste. But . . . and that's when the cold realization hit Archer: Bezeal's paste wasn't holding. Archer had known all along that it was a temporary fix; it leaked Dream matter. But now, it was degrading far faster than ever.

By the time, the valkaryx delivered Archer to his anchor in Garnet, he was consumed with his thoughts and with his anger toward Bezeal . . . and Rigby: Bezeal for making an inferior batch of breach paste, and Rigby for his bold-faced lies about the Dream being in perfect balance.

"You all right?" Nick asked, stepping past Archer's well and around a leaning tree trunk. "You look fit to spit."

"What?"

"Aww, mate, you're spewing mad, aren't you? What's eating you?"

"Nothing," Archer said. "Nothing I can talk about right now. Just someone I need to kill."

Nick barked out a laugh. "That's a ripsnorter, Archer! Ha!" Nick stopped laughing. "Wait . . . you are kidding, aren't you?"

Archer considered the question a little too long. "Mostly," he said. And then, as if a switch had flipped, Archer ran out of anger-induced energy. He slumped forward against the valkaryx's neck. The Visis Nocturne had sapped whatever little bit of mental energy he had accumulated since the battle with the paravore.

"Archer?" Nick said. "Archer, you with us?"

"Huh?" Archer blinked his eyes open. "Awww, man, I am tired."

"This well is your anchor, is it?" Nick asked.

"Yeah," Archer said. "It's the way Dreamtreaders get back to the Waking World."

"You probably oughtta be getting back then, eh?"

"Yeah," Archer said. "Almost out of time, anyway."

"Hey, I don't mean to pry," Nick said. "But why a well?"

"It's not just any well," Archer explained. He explained a little bit about his mother and how important the well had been to her.

Nick nodded along quite a bit. "I understand that completely," he said. "Uh, each Dreamtreader needs an anchor then, right?"

"That's right," Archer said. "Any idea what your anchor would be . . . I mean, for when you're officially a Dreamtreader?"

Nick replied without hesitation. "Yeah, I know just what I'd use. I can see it in my mind just as plainly as I see your well here."

"Good," Archer said, glancing up at Old Jack. "I have to leave now. I'll talk to Master Gabriel and explain what happened. We'll be in touch soon."

Nick nodded.

Archer put his hand to the well, and just as one world melted into another, he thought he heard a voice. It was Nick's voice.

He said, "Hey, I can see the clock now."

THIRTEEN

THE DARKENING

THE NEXT AFTERNOON, ARCHER AND AMY STOOD ON Rigby's front porch. The doorbell's chime faded slowly within the cavernous mansion.

"I still don't think this is a good idea," Amy said.

"Come on," Archer replied. "Since when have my ideas been anything but good?"

Amy adjusted her glasses and gave Archer an owlish glare of disdain. "You don't want me to answer that."

"We're just going to talk," Archer said. "This can't wait."

"Remember, you promised," she said. "Nothing physical. Just words, yep?"

Archer didn't reply. The door opened.

Looking tired and frowning, Rigby appeared in the doorway. "What do you want, Keaton? It's not your day to look after the pets."

"Not here for the pets," Archer said. He kept his voice low, words clipped and tight. "We need to talk."

"Can't it wait?" Rigby asked. "Kara and I are working through some equipment orders for Dream Inc. We're rather busy at the mo—"

Archer stepped toward the door. "Has to be now."

"Well, seeing as how you're halfway in already," Rigby said, stepping aside, "won't you both come in?"

Archer entered, with Amy as his shadow. Rigby went ahead toward the kitchen.

"Remember," Amy whispered, "be diplomatic."

Archer grunted in reply.

At the kitchen table, Kara looked up. Her eyes narrowed, but she said nothing. Rigby gave a flourishing wave of the hand and said, "Keaton here has something to discuss. Oh, and Miss Pitsitakas . . . why are you here?"

"Moral support," she said. "Yep."

Rigby snickered at that. "Well then, please have a seat. I'd offer you something to drink, but I'm rather hoping you won't be staying that long." He sat beside Kara and asked, "So what's this about, then?"

Archer said, "Your computer app reeks."

Rigby's bemused look morphed into confusion and then anger. "Excuse me?"

"It doesn't work," Archer said, leaning forward. "It's bugged or rigged or just plain old broken. But I'm guessing you knew that already."

"What are you talking about?" Rigby asked, the pitch of his voice rising.

"Yes," Kara said, turning to Rigby, "what is he talking about?"

"The app you gave me," Archer said, "the one that's supposed to monitor the so-called balance in the Dream? It's way off."

"It most certainly is not," Rigby replied. "I've verified the data. I've explored the Dream—wait a moment." His gaze shifted to Amy. "Does she . . . does she know?"

"She knows enough," Archer said. "She knows that you're lying."

Rigby stood up abruptly, bumping the table. "Don't you dare enter my home and insult me!"

Archer stood up too. "Would you rather come outside so I can insult you there?"

"Archer!" Amy whispered urgently.

"Calm down, Archer," Kara urged.

"I'm warning you," Rigby said. "I don't know what's flipped your lid so badly, but let's get this sorted out, shall we? What's the problem—as you see it—with the dream app?"

"I told you," Archer said. "It doesn't work. I checked the app the other night before I went in. According to the data you had, the Dream realm was completely stable: lots of blues and dark blues. But when I went in, there were more breaches than two Dreamtreaders together could repair in twelve hours of Dream time."

"That's rubbish," Rigby said. "You just aren't reading the app right."

"Enlighten me."

"Right then," he said, shuffling under some papers and pulling out a tablet computer. He slapped his fingers across the touch screen and held it out for Archer. "See there? The Dream's fine. You probably just didn't adjust for the contrast."

Archer clenched his fists at his side and forced himself not to speak until he had unclenched them. "You aren't listening," he said. "I was there. There were breaches all over the place."

"I was there too, Keaton," Rigby said smugly. "I collected data, just like I always do. The science is on my side."

"This isn't science," Archer said. "What are you hiding?"

Rigby put down the tablet and stepped around the table.

Kara jumped up. "Rigby, no!"

But he was already in Archer's face, inches away. "You get out of my house," he said. He almost sounded calm. "You get out before I throw you out."

Archer didn't back down. He matched Rigby's glare and, in spite of Amy tugging at the back of his shirt, he inched even closer. "I'm a Dreamtreader," Archer said. "I was chosen to protect the Waking World by watching over the Dream. I've learned to see the fabric, to actually see how close to a rift it's getting. It's all unraveling, Rigby. Do you know what that means? Do you know what will happen if a rift forms? Do you?"

Rigby growled something feral and low. "You Dreamtreaders and your bloody creeds . . . you're just so superior, aren't you? As if you're entitled. Hah! Selfish, that's what you are, wanting to keep the Dream for yourself!"

"What's your solution, then? Destroy everything? Because that's what you're doing. Your company is tearing the Dream fabric apart. You've got to shut it down. If you won't, I will."

Rigby shoved Archer. Archer stumbled backward, stepping awkwardly on Amy's foot and colliding with the kitchen wall.

"Rigby, what are you doing?" Kara shrilled. She was up and around the table in an instant.

But Rigby kept his back to her and stayed face-to-face with Archer. "So you're a Dreamtreader," Rigby growled. "So what? Every person should have the right to dream."

"Everyone?" Archer asked with a steaming laugh. "You mean everyone who can pay your price, right? Drop the act, Rigby. You're just in this for the money. Admit it. You're like a strip miner—just tear everything up, take your profits, and let everything burn."

Rigby moved so suddenly and so fast that Amy screamed. His strike, if he'd unleashed it, seemed aimed for Archer's throat. But, like a hammer on a pistol, Rigby's open-handed chop stayed cocked back.

"That how you roll, Rigby?" Archer asked without so much as a flinch. "If you don't like what you hear, you get violent?"

Rigby's striking hand remained in the air and trembled. "You shut your mouth, Keaton. You have no idea. Someone told you that you were special, gave you the title Dreamtreader, and you think you get to run everyone else's lives? You think you know me well enough to know my motives?"

"Am I wrong, then?" Archer growled.

"Yes, you are wrong," Rigby hissed. In his striking hand, a strange, wickedly curved blade melted into existence. He leveled the razor tip toward Archer and scowled.

Archer's eyes widened.

"Rigby, don't!" Kara yelled.

Archer blinked. "How can you do that?"

Rigby raised the blade menacingly. When he winked, the blade melted into thin air. "See, Dreamtreader?" he said. "Don't know everything, do you?"

"C'mon, Archer," Amy urged at his elbow. "Let's go."

"Run along now," Rigby commanded. "Go fix your made-up holes and save the world . . . because Dream Inc. won't stop. See, now, the Dream is my home too."

Archer shook his head slowly. "You are nothing more than a trespasser."

"You're the trespasser," Rigby said. "Now, get out of my home . . . and never come back."

Archer's simmering anger had gone cold. He glanced at Amy and nodded. She followed him down the hall, down Rigby's icy walk, and out into the street. Archer shoved his hands in his pockets and began the trudge home.

"'Your computer app reeks'?" Amy said, hurrying up the street to keep up with Archer. "That was your most diplomatic move?"

Later that night, Rigby Thames entered the Dream alone. He journeyed to the Kurdan Marketplace and found Bezeal in his workshop. The wily merchant looked up and his star-point eyes glittered. "In all the Dream realm so vast, the Walker supreme arrives at last. I wonder if his die is cast."

"I want the key," Rigby said. "And not just for an hour. I want to own it."

"Such a thing could be arranged," Bezeal said. "If you'll risk joining the deranged. But, of course, there must be a particular kind of exchange."

Rigby held up a hand. "No deal . . . yet. I want to know a few things first. If I have the Shadow Key, the Sages will leave me alone, right? I can come and go to the Inner Sanctum as I please?"

"Sages know the key and know it well. Its bearer passes through the Libraries where they dwell. And to the deeps, the Sanctum, that sacred cell."

"What about the Scath?" Rigby asked. "If I own the Shadow Key, will the Scath obey me?"

"Live for mischief, do the Scath, but they will follow your chosen path . . . especially if it leads to wrath."

"Fine by me, Bezeal," Rigby said. "What's your price?"

Bezeal's white teeth appeared. He gestured for Rigby to draw closer. The merchant whispered for several moments, a sound like rats scratching at wood.

Rigby took a step back. "That's a steep price."

"Too rich for your blood, then off you go," Bezeal said. "I have other suitors, some you might know. The Sanctum's mysteries to them I will show."

"I'll do it," Rigby whispered.

"What?"

"I'll do it. I'll meet your price."

Bezeal's smile glistened. From the folds of his cloak, his green three-fingered hand appeared. "You must seal . . . the deal . . . with Bezeal."

Rigby stepped forward, clasped Bezeal's hand in his own, and winced.

Rigby held the Karakurian Chamber in his hands and stared down at the Inner Sanctum's stone door. He turned the cube over and over until he found the sixth full sail of the ship. He placed his thumb upon the sail, sliding it back until there was slight resistance and a faint click. The tall ship lifted, appeared to sail, and then vanished. A metallic trill sounded, and the skeletons on the next side began to dance. One by one, the old boneheads leaped and fell. The Karakurian Chamber shifted and flattened, the rough edges becoming smooth. Metal unraveled like thread and wound itself up tight. Round and round it went until a rod formed, and then the rest of the Shadow Key.

Rigby held the key aloft and shouted, daring the Sages to descend and tell him to be quiet. They did not show themselves, but something beneath the door stirred.

"Threaten me, will you?" Rigby grumbled. He shoved the Shadow Key into its matching hole and gave a violent turn. "I'll show you, Keaton, you and all the Dreamtreaders, I'll show you who really owns the Dream!"

He twisted the key once more, heard a thunderous boom from within, and felt a strange trembling wave beneath his feet.

But Rigby did not open the door. He stood upon it, keeping it down with his weight.

"Let us out!" came a raspy whisper.

"We yearn!" came another.

"Yes, yes, free us!"

"We must play."

"You will serve me?" Rigby asked.

"We are Scath. We serve no man," came the answer. "We are wild things!"

A chorus of laughter rasped underneath like a nest of rattlesnakes.

"I am the owner of the Shadow Key," Rigby declared. "You will do my bidding, or you can rot behind that door."

Some of the Scath cried out. "No, no!" one shouted.

"You bluff us!" another one said. "You want the Masters' Bindings!"

"Yes, I want them," Rigby admitted. "And I will have them. But you will not be free until you pledge to serve at my call."

"We did once, but you tricked us."

"Not this time!"

"We will not. We will not!"

"It is a hateful tease, releasing us for just one hour! Then you trap us again!"

"Not worth it. Not worth it."

"Is that what you think?" Rigby asked. "You underestimate me. Pity, for I have such big plans."

"Tell us, tell us!"

"He lies!"

"He is like Bezeal."

"I am *not* like that weasel," Rigby hissed. "Forget it, then." He bent down and twisted the key back to the left. Thunder sounded below. Thunder and weeping.

Rigby removed the Shadow Key and started to walk away.

"Wait, wait!"

"Come back, Walker!"

"We would hear your plan!"

Rigby hesitated until the Scath's screeching became a wailing storm. Finally, he returned the key to its place in the Sanctum door. "Now then," he said. He whispered into the keyhole and then gave the key a twist.

"We like it!"

"Yes, yes, ambitious and fun!"

"The teacher man is already there."

"Locked up tight!"

"We did as you asked. We can be trusted."

"I know you can," Rigby said. "But we need to have this understanding between us. I will set you free, but you must do as I ask and come when I call, no matter what."

"More than an hour."

"A day! A full day!"

"I will do better than that," Rigby said. "If you pledge to serve at my call, I will free you . . . forever."

All the rustling beneath the door ceased. It became eerily silent.

Finally, a tentative Scath voice said, "You are cruel, Walker."

"Twist our hopes."

"Be gone with you!"

Rigby rolled his eyes. "You underestimate me again. But I will prove it to you. I will set you free, and I will throw away this Shadow Key so that no one can ever lock you away again!"

"Dare we hope?"

"Risk it, yes, yes!"

"But we will be slaves."

"Not slaves," Rigby said. "Servants. There is a difference."

"We must do your bidding, come when you call?"

"But we remain free?"

"If you don't need us, can we do mischief?"

"Can we play?"

"If you will pledge me your service," Rigby said, "then you may do what you wish with your time until I call."

The shrieking rose to such a calamity that Rigby's ears rang.

"We will!"

"Serve the Walker!"

"He is Master now!"

"Free us, free us!"

"The Scath are yours to command!"

Rigby gave the key another quater turn. Then he took the corner of the door and threw it open.

A flood of shreds and shadows and peculiar shapes burst up from the gate. They streamed out and swarmed, screeching and chanting and spitting. And then, they were gone.

The Inner Sanctum yawned open for Rigby. He smiled and descended the stairs.

FOURTEEN

THE SHADOW KEY

"SOMETHING HAS CHANGED, ARCHER," MASTER GABRIEL said, pacing the room.

"I know. More breaches," Archer replied, seated on the edge of his bed. He flopped back and sighed. "Just as you suspected, Rigby's computer app is bogus. The breaches are all over Forms and Verse, and Bezeal's patching paste won't hold, not long enough—"

"Not just the breaches," the master Dreamtreader replied. "There's trouble in Garnet's Libraries, the Inner Sanctum."

"Not Bezeal again," Archer said. "Is it?"

"Most certainly Bezeal is involved. As much as it pains me to say, you are involved also, Archer."

"Me?" Archer plopped down on his bed. "I've been to Garnet, but I haven't messed around in the Libraries. I haven't set foot in the Inner Sanctum's vaults."

"No, but the Karakurian Chamber has," Master Gabriel replied.

Archer remembered the intricate silver puzzle box he'd liberated from the Lurker and delivered into Bezeal's hands. He dearly regretted making the deal with Bezeal, but now, it seemed, his error had been far worse than he'd ever imagined.

"But," the Master Dreamtreader went on, "I wear the weight of this mistake as much as you do. I should have seen it, should have realized."

"Seen what? Realized what?"

"The Karakurian Chamber was no mere curiosity for Bezeal, and no mere toy," he said. "It was a key."

"A key?" Archer squinted. "Sure didn't look like a key. It was kind of a mechanical box . . . all skeletons and ships and weird moving parts."

"The concealment was very detailed," Master Gabriel said. "I believe Bezeal designed the disguise to make certain no one would know that it was indeed a key. Understand, Archer, this wasn't just *any* key. This was the Shadow Key."

"The Shadow Key from the Creeds?" Archer blurted out. He sat bolt upright and tried in vain to rub the chills from his upper arms. "*The* Shadow Key? The one that opens the vaults of the Inner Sanctum and controls the Scath?"

"The very one," Master Gabriel replied. He reached into the fold of his cloak and retrieved a massive ring of dark metal upon which hung several keys. "These are the Masters' Keys, Archer. I am their caretaker now. But there was once . . . another . . . who guarded the Keys. In that charge, he failed. The Shadow Key was stolen, but for many ages, it was never used. Archer, this is a measure of time beyond your capacity to understand—so much time passed that the Masters, at my insistence, decided the Shadow Key had been lost."

"I read about it," Archer said. "It was kind of a good thing that it was lost, right? No longer a temptation for Dreamtreaders?"

"For a time, perhaps," Master Gabriel said. "But it would have been far better if the Masters had retrieved the Shadow Key long ago."

"I don't understand."

"We were wrong, Archer. The Shadow Key was never lost. It was merely hidden."

"Bezeal?" Archer said. "You mean Bezeal took the key and hid it?"

"The evidence points to that conclusion. Bezeal may have had help, but he is clearly behind it all."

"Wait," Archer said, sitting up straight. "But Bezeal acted like the Karakurian Chamber was something the Lurker had all along. Bezeal acted like it was something he couldn't get for himself. He used it to make deals with Duncan and Mesmeera . . . and with me."

"Yes," Master Gabriel replied, taking off his sunglasses. They vanished from his fingertips, and his eyes blazed. "Yes, Bezeal used it for that purpose . . . and he used our Dreamtreaders, including you, for his own purposes."

"But Bezeal's just a chump. He's a nuisance and a troublemaker, but he's no mastermind."

"Enough," Master Gabriel commanded. "I have warned you not to underestimate anyone, especially not Bezeal. You are right to recall that Bezeal duped all three Dreamtreaders last year. That required diabolical cunning."

"I won't ever forget that," Archer said. "But even then, Bezeal was just the Nightmare Lord's errand boy."

"Was he?" Master Gabriel asked. "Are you so certain it was not the other way around?"

If Archer's thoughts had been a speeding train, that train would have just run straight into a wall of cement. Archer squinted and said, "Bezeal, somehow controlling the Nightmare Lord? That makes no sense."

"Perhaps not," Master Gabriel said. "But we cannot afford to assume anything here, Archer. It is arrogance that prevents us from seeing through the mask of foolishness . . . to discover the devil behind."

Archer puzzled over that idea for several silent moments. "So,

Bezeal hid the Shadow Key in the Karakurian Chamber puzzle box. And . . . he gave it to the Lurker? Do you think the Lurker knew what it was? I mean, what it really was?"

"That is a very troubling possibility," Master Gabriel said. "It would not mark the first time that Bezeal and the Lurker seemed to be working together."

"But where is it now?" Archer asked. "Who has the Shadow Key? Bezeal?"

"The Shadow Key had been used, Archer," Master Gabriel said. "The Sages report that Bezeal and a great warrior entered the Libraries and produced the Karakurian Chamber to gain access to the vaults of the Inner Sanctum."

"Great warrior?" Archer echoed. "The Lurker?"

"It may well be," Master Gabriel said. "Though, I would expect the Sages to know him by name. Whoever it was, he and Bezeal first used the Shadow Key to release the Scath for a short time . . . for mischief. But now, the vault doors have been thrown open and left open. The Scath roam free."

"Why not just shut the door?" Archer asked. "You don't need a key to shut a door."

"Think of the door to the vaults as more of a binding rather than an exit. Once the key is turned, the Scath are bound to the one who turns the key, and they are free forever until the key bearer turns the key again, to lock them within."

"What will they do? The Scath, I mean."

"With endless freedom? Tragedies unnumbered." Master Gabriel nodded his head. His trench coat, secret agent garb, vanished. His Incandescent Armor flared to life. "They have forced our hand, Archer. The breaches are perilously close to a rift, and the Scath are abroad. We can no longer wait; we must have a third Dreamtreader immediately."

"Who?" Archer asked. "Will I have to do the awakening again?"

"I had hoped to wait," he said. "Time and maturity are almost certainly needed."

"Wait for whom?"

"Together, the three of you will have to handle two missions. The breaches must remain first and foremost. All is lost if a rift forms. Three Dreamtreaders can handle the breaches, but you will also have to find the Shadow Key. Get it back at all costs and shut the Inner Sanctum."

"Okay, already," Archer huffed. "I get it. But who will the next Dreamtreader be?"

"And, Archer, no matter what you find investigating the Libraries, you are not to touch the *Masters' Bindings*. Is that understood?"

"Of course, of course," Archer said. "Do you think I want to turn myself into some kind of monster?"

"I am relieved to hear you say that," Master Gabriel. "But making such a decision in your own room and standing in my presence is far different from what you might decide in the darkness . . . alone."

"You're stalling," Archer said. "Are you going to tell me about the third Dreamtreader or not?"

Master Gabriel sighed. With his sword swaying at his side, he strode to Archer's bedroom door, opened it wide, and said, "Go get your sister."

Northeast of Direton, just beyond sight of Shadowkeep, in the province of Warhaven, lay the ancient ruins known as Xander's Fortune. It was there, at the base of that dark mountain, in days long past, that a Dreamtreader began his infamous mining operation.

Rigby stood there now, looking over the fallen towers, shattered keeps, and scattered stone. Due to the battering of Intrusion waves over the ages, very little hint of structure remained. The stonework left was all but engulfed by soil, weeds, and tall grass. Anyone who wandered onto the site would be hard-pressed to imagine the gigantic masonry fortress that once stood there. But Rigby knew. He knew about it from the stories his Uncle Scoville told him as a little boy.

It all began when the dutiful Dreamtreader Xander Volkov found a white stone. He was on patrol in Warhaven when a glistening shape caught his eye. He'd thought at first that it was a new breach opening. But instead, it was a sparkling, pristine white hunk of stone. It was, Xander thought, unlike any stone of the Waking World. It was both hard and soft, heavy and light, rare and plentiful.

Xander called it *fulgenite*, meaning "lightning born," for he discovered that the stone drew strikes of lightning to it. And once struck, the stone became as light as cardboard and as pliable as clay. Warhaven was the only area of the Dream where the lightning stone could be found, but as Xander explored the region, he found its source. At the top of the nearby conical mountain, there was a crater filled with the brilliant white stone.

Rigby recalled that Xander was no fool. At least, not that kind of fool. He suspected at first that the mountain was indeed some sort of volcano. But after years of monitoring, research, and innumerable mining visits, Xander deemed it safe.

Xander built his fortress from fulgenite and even created a lightning stone stairway up the mountain. But one fateful night, while mining deep within the crater, Xander witnessed an amazing sight, one that took his Dreaming life.

A bolt of lightning struck the crater. This had happened frequently, given the attractive nature of the stone. This time, though, the strike seemed to activate a chain reaction within the stone. Lethal electricity discharged in a spiral until at last it drew down from the sky a brilliant bolt of lightning so massive that it kindled all the ful-genite to its molten state.

That vat within the mountain had stayed active and molten ever since. It was the perfect place to make things final.

Rigby alone climbed the lightning stone stairs. The light near the crater at the top was near blinding, but Rigby went straight to the edge. There was no heat, not like a fiery volcano in the waking world, but a sense of dread was there. The ferocity of the light blasting up from the raging cavity below created its own kind of terror. It was the terror of being unmade.

Rigby found himself wondering what Xander Volkov's final thoughts had been as the cataclysmic eruption of power took him apart, molecule by molecule. Rigby stood on the edge of the crater, awash in currents of power and virtually blind by the white light. He could almost imagine himself teetering, losing his balance, and fall-ing in. Falling and falling, maybe forever.

But no.

Rigby blinked for several moments. "What's wrong with me?" he asked aloud, his voice instantly swallowed up by the unrelenting roar of the cauldron below. He shuddered.

Something wasn't right. Rigby knew it. He felt it. He'd been changing, almost by the day, and it terrified him. It felt like ants were crawling all over his body, but just beneath the skin, itching but impossible to get at without doing more harm than good. And his thinking wasn't clear—an absolute rarity for him—and he'd been making mistakes. He'd seen this kind of thing happen before. It had happened to his Uncle Scovy right before his consciousness became trapped in the Dream.

"I won't let that happen to me!" Rigby shouted. From the deep pocket of his coat, Rigby withdrew the Karakurian Chamber, the Shadow Key. The *Masters' Bindings* had confirmed his theory. He would set his Uncle Scovy free, and he would keep himself from being imprisoned. There was a high price to pay, both to Bezeal and . . . to the world. But he must not fear the costs. He must not allow himself to turn away from his goals.

Rigby looked down into the furious molten fulgenite. This was a threshold, he thought, but he was an explorer . . . a discoverer. And, like Hernán Cortés destroying his ships so that his sailors would be forced to stay and conquer the new world, Rigby knew he needed to make certain there was no going back. He had to step past the point of no return. If it thwarted Archer Keaton in the process, so much the better.

"This is for you, Uncle Scovy!" he cried out, holding the Shadow Key high above his head. "And for me!"

Rigby reared back and heaved the Shadow Key with all of his might. He saw it just for a moment, shining white above the cauldron. Then an updraft of phenomenal power took the key from sight.

On the way down the lightning stone stairs, Rigby opened the mental connection that allowed him communication with the Scath. "Have you located the man?" he asked.

"Easily," came the first Scath reply.

"He is weak."

"He will not fight."

"Good," Rigby said. "I'm not surprised. You have your orders. Make it messy."

"Hehe. We like messy."

FIFTEEN

THE THIRD

"ARCHER, ARCHER!" KAYLIE CRIED OUT, SHUTTING THE door behind her. "I get to be a Dreamtreader! Just like you." She held up her fist for Archer to bump.

Archer bumped her but turned to Master Gabriel. "I knew she had the skills, but . . ."

"She more than has the skills, Archer," he said. "She is very powerful for one so young."

"Are you sure she can do this?" Archer asked. "She's only eight."

"Archer!" Kaylie objected. "I thought you wanted me to join you."

"I did," he said. "I mean, I do. But now that, well, now that it's happening, I dunno. I just don't want you getting hurt."

"Nor do I," Master Gabriel said. "That is why I must train Kaylie myself."

"Me and Gabe have been talking about it for weeks now," Kaylie said.

"Gabe?" Archer gulped.

Master Gabriel shrugged. "It comforts her," he said. "So I allow it."

"Wait." Archer turned back and forth between Gabriel and Kaylie. "What do you mean you've been talking for weeks?"

Kaylie stared at her feet.

"You didn't break into my new box? Did you?"

"Well, it wasn't especially difficult," Kaylie said. "I found your feather thing and threw it up in the air. Boom! Gabe showed up."

"The Summoning Feather?" Archer cried out. "Is nothing secret around here?"

"You shouldn't keep secrets, Archer," Kaylie said, hands on her hips. Her expression was so stern, so comically, childishly stern that Archer burst out in barks of laughter . . . and snorts.

Even Master Gabriel smirked. "We will begin your training tonight, Kaylie," he said.

"Sounds good, Gabe!"

Gabe. Archer shook his head.

Archer sat on a stone bench overlooking the waterfall near the little hamlet of Starcaster. *No wonder Mesmeera loved Verse District so much,* he thought, staring out over the cascading water sparkling with effervescent moonlight.

Archer waited for Nick Bushman to arrive. Their errands were urgent, but part of Archer wanted Nick to take a little longer. There was a saturating peace in this place. The dark water at the top of the falls seemed hardly to move at all, but after it crested the edge and poured over, it gained speed and energy. Halfway down, it flared alive with white fringes and spray. It crashed with a mighty but hypnotic voice in the stone-rimmed pool far below.

From there, the water became calm and dark once more, meandering a slow, curvy path through the midst of Starcaster. Small, irregularly shaped stone-and-mortar cottages sat amiably on either side of the water. Every chimney puffed lazy white smoke, and every window was lit with glad candlelight. It reminded Archer somehow of elderly friends gathered in a park to smoke their pipes and recount memories of full lives.

A screech overhead announced Nick's arrival. The long-maned valkaryx that the Australian called Rocky spiraled down and landed softly near the edge of the water not far from Archer's bench. His short-maned companion, Shocky, landed nearby.

Archer reluctantly left his bench. "How did it go?"

"Bonzer, mate," Nick replied. "I got the little breaches quick using a running whipstitch. My mum showed me that one. She was a surgeon in the Royal Australian Navy. But some of the bigguns were fair ripe with scurions. I had to sic the boys on them." Nick patted the pockets of his sleeveless canvas cargo vest. Boomerangs of several sizes filled each pocket.

"Nice," Archer said. "You sure you got them all?"

Nick rolled his eyes. "You know I didn't," he said. "I saw what you did there, mate. You took out most of the really outta-the-way breaches to make it easier for me. I saw it. That's why you gave me the Forms District in the first place. It's yours, right? You know it well enough to set up for me."

Archer tried not to laugh. He failed. "Guilty as charged," the Dreamtreader said.

"Look, Archer," Nick said. "You meant well. I'm new. But I'm not stupid or irresponsible. I've signed on. I'll pull my own weight. From here on, okay?" He held out a hand, and they shook.

Archer glanced up at Old Jack. "Done, with four hours to spare. That's good time."

"But we're not done, are we?"

"No, we're not," Archer said, climbing onto Shocky. "We're headed to the Libraries of Garnet."

"This is the coolest thing *ever!*" Kaylie exulted, riding the crimson vortex into the Dream for the very first time.

"It is quite random where the vortices drop you off," came Master Gabriel's voice in Kaylie's mind. "And so, you need to be prepared for anything."

"You mean, like flying turtles, talking radishes, or Porta-Potties that don't smell bad?"

After an awkward pause, Master Gabriel said, "I mean, like anything. Anything at all. The Dream is the ultimate untamed landscape."

Kaylie stretched out her arm so that she could touch the rapidly rotating Dream matter. "Ha!" she said, giggling. "It tickles." She leaned her head so that one of her pigtails got caught up in the vortex. "I love this."

"Now, remember what I showed you concerning the Intrusion waves."

"I remember, Gabe," Kaylie said. "Don't be such a worrywart."

"It is no simple matter, Kaylie," he argued. "The Intrusions waves are the resulting chaos of every dreaming person on earth's wildest dreams interacting with one another. If you don't dampen them immediately with your will, you won't be able to do anything."

"I get it," she said. "But it's no different than fluid dynamics, and the laws of motion and energy make waves easy to predict. I've used computer-generated art software to create and control my own worldsized oceans, so this should be a piece of cake."

"Hmph," Master Gabriel replied. "We'll see."

Grinning and laughing the entire way, Kaylie let the vortex take her on a winding descent until, at last, it dropped her off into the middle of absolute chaos. Translucent waves came crashing in from every direction. Eddies and rogue currents swirled this way and that. And a vicious undertow yanked at Kaylie's feet.

But the young Dreamtreader flexed just the smallest fraction of her will, and the tempestuous sea became as tame as water in a bathtub. "There," she said. "See? No problem."

Master Gabriel melted into existence beside her. "That . . . that was . . . well done," he said. "Don't let it go to your head."

Kaylie giggled and looked around. Without the untamed Intrusions, she saw that they were in the middle of a vast desert. Huge mounds of violet-colored sand and massive mountain-sized mauve dunes trailed off in all directions. Nearby stood a sparse forest of tall cacti, and each vertical arm wore a cowboy hat.

"I don't recall the hats," Master Gabriel said drolly. "Your doing?"

"Yup, yup," she said. "This feels like a western. You should be sheriff."

Before he could object, Kaylie used her will to clothe Master Gabriel in a tall cowboy hat, leather chaps, and a dark vest with a shiny gold sheriff's badge.

"I am not amused," he said. He blinked, and his Incandescent Armor returned. "Let's try to focus, please."

Kaylie blushed. "Sorry."

"Now, let's review the creeds," Master Gabriel announced. "I asked you to read the first three."

"I did twenty-one creeds. Is that okay?"

"You read twenty-one creeds?"

"No, I memorized them."

"Nonsense," Master Gabriel replied with bluster. "Creed four, verse nine."

"'We call this the Festival of Culling,'" she said, "'but it is hardly a holiday. This is an extremely perilous—'"

"Creed nine!" Master Gabriel blurted. "Verse eleven!"

"'Tread not heavily the moors of Archaia within Pattern. There the mist gathers, so beware.'"

Master Gabriel adjusted his sunglasses and said, "Uncanny." After a few moments, he said, "So I guess you know all about transportation options."

"Sure," she said. "Archer uses a surfboard, but I think he stole the idea from my brother Buster."

"Yes, well, that may be, and Nick Bushman uses a pair of creatures he's tamed here in the Dream. Have you given any thought to what you will use?"

"I want a dune buggy," she said.

"A dune buggy?" he repeated. "Is that some sort of flying insect?"

"No, silly!" Kaylie put her hands on her hips as if trying to be patient with a toddler. "It's a recreational vehicle with wide axles and huge tires that allow it to race across loose terrains such as gravel, soil, or sand. It'll be perfect for here."

"Very well," he said, shrugging. "Make one."

"What?"

"You had no trouble putting cowboy hats on the cacti . . . and on me. It shouldn't be hard to make a dune buggy."

Kaylie frowned and twirled a pigtail in her fingers for a few moments. Then she said, "You should put on your seat belt, Master Gabe."

"What?"

Suddenly, the master Dreamtreader found himself in some kind of iron cage. Kaylie was next to him, and they both wore bulbous, hard plastic helmets.

"Ready?" she asked, flexing her knee to give the dune buggy a little gas.

The resulting roar startled Master Gabriel. "Confound it, Kaylie! Ready your weapons. There is a dragon behind us!"

"There's no dragon," she said. "It's just the engine of my dune buggy. Here we go!" Kaylie stepped on the gas, and the vehicle lurched forward and raced up the nearest dune.

At the abrupt acceleration, Master Gabriel let out a sound. It was a sound that surprised Kaylie greatly. And once they'd come to a stop once more, Master Gabriel swore her to secrecy that she would never recount that event to anyone. Especially not to Archer.

Rigby threw open the gates of Number 6 Rue de la Morte, the Shadowkeep, and waltzed in as if he owned the place. He smiled at the irony. *I do own it,* he thought.

Sure, it had been built ages ago by the original Nightmare Lord, but he'd been evicted. It was Rigby's home now. Wearing his Victorian-era John Bull gentleman's top hat, a long black cape, and wielding a raven-headed walking cane, Rigby strode the shadow-strewn halls until he came to a double-wide stairway. Tapestries, darker than blood, hung from long arched windows far above. He raced up the stairs with eager anticipation.

"Tonight," he whispered, "tonight will be wondrous."

At the top of the stairwell, a large banquet hall lay quiet. The forty-foot table was set with plates, fine silver, goblets, and bowls, but the many chairs were empty. Rigby imagined a great feast there, with all of his friends and associates: the clink of glasses, the fireplace crackling, the thrum of conversation. *Epic parties*, he thought, leaving the table behind.

Rigby turned a swift corner, strode down the narrow passage that surrounded the throne room, and paused at the massive wooden door. It was ajar. Rigby frowned. He thought of himself as a man of extremes. When he left, the door was all the way open or all the way closed. Never, ever in between.

Someone else had been in the throne room . . . *his* throne room. And there was a possibility that whoever it was might still be in there. Rigby snapped his elbow. The walking cane became a black mace. He knew there was no easing open the door—it groaned like an old man on the stairs—and he wasn't about to slink into his own room, so he grabbed the brass handle and threw the door open wide.

Ready to bludgeon or flay the first person he saw, Rigby pounced into the room and yelled, "Who dares trespass here?"

He saw his throne from behind and a willowy thin, pale arm on the armrest. *His* armrest.

"Who are you?" Rigby demanded. "And give me one good reason why I shouldn't destroy you."

It'd better not be one of the confounded idiots from Dream Inc., he thought. They knew the boundaries. But as Rigby drew near, he felt cold creep into the pit of his stomach.

"Because I'm your partner," Kara said, and she leaned around the tall seat and winked.

This called for a change of tactics. This was different. Kara called for a certain kind of diplomacy. Rigby swallowed down a gallon of flaming bile and said, "Comfy?"

Kara beamed. "It is rather nice," she replied.

"Good. Now, get out of the chair," he said, cranking up the jokey tone while maintaining a base of iron beneath. He wanted her out of the chair, to know her place, but not to feel indignant.

"You aren't jealous, are you?" Kara asked. Her words lacked emotion but not thought. It felt like a doctor's questioning, trying to identify symptoms and be very diagnostic.

"Why would I be jealous of my partner?" Rigby asked, willing the mace back to its cane form. "You've just as much right to the throne as I do."

"That's sweet of you to say," Kara said, easing slowly from the chair. "But we both know you don't believe that." Kara strolled a semicircle around Rigby and lightly touched his shoulder. "Did you see the profit margins for last month?"

"Not yet. Good?" Rigby grinned, settling snugly onto the throne seat.

"As of November, Dream Inc. is the fastest startup company to reach a billion dollars in net profits," Kara revealed.

"Splendid, Kara," Rigby said. "Your marketing efforts have played a huge role in that success."

"If you're going to be this nice," she said, "maybe I'll sit the throne here more often."

"A billion dollars is a nice number," he said, sitting up in the massive seat, its color like midnight ice. "But really, I think it's just the first few drops of the storm to come."

"You think so?" she asked.

"I know so," he replied. "Dream Inc. is about to diversify."

"What do you mean?"

"I've been working with Research and Development on some new angles," he said. "We're stunting our growth by limiting Dream Inc. services to the rich and famous."

Kara stiffened. "But Archer said that bringing too many Lucid

Walkers in and out would destroy the Dream fabric. We can't do that."

"Archer said, Archer said," Rigby mocked. "When you went to Archer and asked him to teach you to Dreamtread, what did he tell you?"

Kara winced but kept her eyes riveted to Rigby's. "He told me I wasn't cut out for it."

"And do you agree with him?"

She blinked exactly once. "No. I've as much right to the Dream as he does."

"Exactly," Rigby replied. "You didn't put much stock in what Keaton said then, so don't treat him like some wise teacher now. If Keaton had his way, Dream Inc. would be shut down for good. Is that what you want?"

"Of course not," Kara replied. "But Archer's not stupid, and we don't yet know everything about the Dream and how it interacts with our world."

"Neither does Keaton," Rigby said. "And all he's got to learn from is some ancient book of creeds. We've got modern science on our side. The research is absolutely compelling and trustworthy. Besides, I'm not talking about letting the whole world go Lucid Walking."

Kara's eyebrows met temporarily over the bridge of her nose. "You aren't? I thought . . . you—"

"No, no," Rigby said. "While the data clearly shows that Keaton is overblowing the whole rift, 'collapse of the Dream' thing, I've no desire to share our secrets with the world. But what I would like to do is take advantage of other ways to assist the paying public with their dreams."

"Now, *that* sounds very interesting," Kara said. "I'd like to hear about it, but another time. My time's up. I need to head back."

Rigby stood and bowed. "Farewell, Queen Kara," he said.

She smiled and performed a curtsy. Then she was gone.

Rigby clenched his fist around the cane so tightly that it trembled. He waited a few carefully controlled breaths to make certain that Kara was gone, and then he exploded, "How dare she!" he muttered. "Bezeal was right all along. Kara cannot be trusted."

<hr />

"Y'know, mate, it would really help if I knew what we were looking for."

"Anything," Archer said, studying the engraved pattern that bordered the doorway of the Inner Sanctum's vault. The strange hinges on every slab of wood made it look more like a hundred doors than just the one. The stairs beneath fell away into an alluring darkness. "Anything and everything, really. We need to know who Bezeal's warrior friend is, why they let the Scath out, and why they left the door open."

"And Bezeal is who, again?" Nick asked.

"He's a shifty little merchant out of Kurdan. Hooded cloak, you can't ever see his face, but he has these little sparkly eyes."

"Sounds like a Jawa," Nick said.

"A what?"

"A Jawa," Nick repeated. "Don't tell me ye've never seen *Star Wars*."

"I'm not big on fantasy. Well, fake fantasy," Archer said. "Anyway, Bezeal is the one who showed up here with the Shadow Key, but he wasn't alone."

"I'm not sure I want to be a Dreamtreader anymore," Nick said.

Archer felt his heart suddenly quicken. "What? Why?"

"Well, you've not seen *Star Wars*," he said. "I don't think we can hang out."

"Very funny," Archer said. "C'mon, maybe we'll find a clue inside."

"We're going down there?" Nick asked.

"We have to," Archer said. "But listen, among the old books down there, are some ancient manuscripts called the *Masters' Bindings*. From what Master Gabriel says, they're extremely tempting to a Dreamtreader, but we need to keep away."

"If it's full of books down there," Nick said, "how will we know which ones to avoid?"

"The *Masters' Bindings* are seven thick volumes," Archer said. "And they are welded into iron cases. It should be fairly obvious."

"If you say so, mate," Nick replied. "Just to be safe, I think I'll keep my hands in my pockets."

The stairs led straight down, and the darkness gave way at first to amber light and then to something closer to red. Archer's first thought when he could see the interior of the vault was that it reminded him a little of Rigby's basement. There was a long hallway punctuated by doorways. Each doorway led into a chamber filled wall to wall, floor to ceiling with books. Each room also had a desk with a small lamp and a sturdy chair.

Archer led Nick in and out of the rooms until they came to the end of the hall, where a broad room with a very low ceiling opened. This room was different. Pillars of stone, some floor to ceiling and others more like platforms, studded the chamber. There were also massive war chests, huge sunken-pirate-chest things stuffed with all manner of weaponry: swords, axes, staffs, spears, mauls, and maces.

"Looks like an armory," Nick said. "Fairly odd, don't you think?"

"Very odd," Archer replied, scanning the chamber. Other than the overstuffed chests, everything in the vault seemed in order. The bookshelves all appeared full. There was no sign of Bezeal or anything left behind. Then Archer saw something very irregular. He shook his head. "I don't know what this means," he said. "Look."

He pointed to the central pillar. It was the only pillar in the vault that didn't have at least one bookcase built on top of it. The central pillar had hunks and scraps of metal, the remnants of seven iron cases. And they were empty.

Nick said, "I think I can guess what we're seein' here. The temptation got the better a' someone, and he stole the *Masters' Bindings*."

Rigby climbed to the tallest tower of Shadow Keep, the bell tower, and reached for the rope that hung from the high belfry. "Too bad you couldn't be here for this, Kara," he said. "You're missing out on all the fun."

With both hands, he gave a mighty pull. Instantaneously the hammer struck the bell, sending the first low toll to roll across the Dream. Again, he pulled the rope. And again. A total of six tolls, he rang.

"Come, hounds," Rigby said. "Come and meet your new master."

SIXTEEN

TAKEN

ARCHER FELT SOMETHING WAS VERY WRONG EVEN BEFORE he touched the well, his anchor, and departed the Dream. He awoke in his bed to find Kaylie with an iron grip on his arm, shaking him and crying hysterically.

"Archer!" she howled. "Wake up, now! Oh, please, wake up!"

"I'm awake!" he yelled, jouncing upright in his bed. "Kaylie, what's going on? I thought you had Dreamtreader training with Master Gabriel."

"I did!" she cried, her face three shades redder than it should have been. "But when I got back from the Dream . . ."

"What?"

"Dad is gone!"

That was all Archer could get from Kaylie for some time. She continued to sob and wail. Archer hugged her and shushed her and picked up Patches every time she dropped the stuffed scarecrow.

When she calmed down a little at last, Archer asked, "What do you mean Dad's gone?"

"Somebody took him!"

"Aww, Kaylie," he said, "don't get so worked up. I'm sure Dad just went up to the Quik-Mart."

"His car's still here," she said. "And I've been waiting an hour."

Archer didn't want to set Kaylie off by voicing his thoughts, but he stood up and led her by the hand. He went to the places in the house where his father might likely be found. He wasn't in the basement on the computer. Archer even cracked open the basement work-side door and called in. There was no answer. He wasn't in his chair in the den. He wasn't on the screened-in porch, where he went to smoke cigarettes.

But there on the porch, Archer stopped. There was a travel mug sitting on the table next to his father's chair. It was three quarters of the way full of coffee, but it had gone cold. The nearby ashtray held remnants of dozens of cigarettes past, but there was one cigarette resting in the corner of the ashtray. It was burned to ash down to the filter.

"See, Archer?" Kaylie said. "He was here. He was here."

"But where would he go?"

But Archer thought of the answer before Kaylie replied.

"The well."

It was close to sunup, but not close enough to have much natural light. Archer fetched a large flashlight from underneath the kitchen sink and went back to the porch. Kaylie snuggled her blanket and Patches close and followed Archer through the porch to the outside door. As soon as the door shut behind them, Archer turned on the flashlight.

Kaylie inhaled, making a shrill gasping sound. The little glass table was on its side and shattered. All the deck furniture had been tossed around as if a hurricane had hit. *Not likely in December*, Archer thought, and he found himself remembering Amy's phone call about the missing teacher. "There was sign of a struggle," he whispered.

Archer was torn now. He didn't know whether to send Kaylie in the house or take her with him. Neither way seemed safe or responsible. He decided she would come. Archer shone the light on the deck stairs that led down into the backyard. They were still snow covered, but there were man-sized footprints in the snow. And there were dozens of other smaller prints, prints he'd seen once before but hadn't understood.

Archer searched the ground with the flashlight, scanning the beam across the snow and through the clouds of his own breath. The cold didn't phase him, but he could feel Kaylie shivering next to him. He took her hand and said, "Come on."

The two of them followed the strange pattern of footprints, large and many small, through the yard, and down the hill. The trail led right up to the well. Archer felt the bottom drop out from his stomach. He had to look over the edge. He had to look down into the well. But he had a dreadful certainty about what he would find.

Kaylie started weeping again. "Did Dad go . . . did he go down there?"

"I don't know," he said. "I'm going to look."

"I wanna see, too."

"No," he said, holding her back gently. "No, you let me look first. I mean it, Kaylie. Wait here."

Through her sniffles and flooded eyes, she nodded.

Archer passed through the phantom vapors of his own frozen breath and approached the well. He swallowed, said a prayer, and then looked over the edge of the well. He trained the flashlight down into the well's depths . . . and then gasped.

"You say you were asleep when it happened?" the uniformed police officer asked.

"We all were," Archer said, rubbing his temples. "Kaylie was the first to wake up."

"And Kaylie is . . ."

"My sister," he said. Archer pointed to the long couch in the living room, where Kaylie and Buster sat mutely sipping hot cocoa. "Kaylie woke me up. We woke up my brother, Buster, last. Officer, we've already told you all this. Isn't there something—"

"Tell me more about the well," he said, still scribbling on his notepad. "You said you suspected he went to the well. Why would you suspect that?"

Archer sighed. "The well was special to my mom. She died eight years ago. Dad often went to the well to think, you know, for quiet time."

"Even on a snowy night?"

"I don't know," Archer said. "It was just a hunch."

"And you said you went out there looking for your father?"

"That's right," Archer answered tightly.

"And you looked into the well?"

"Right," Archer said. "He wasn't there."

"Tell me why you looked into the well again," the officer said. "Did your father enter the well often?"

"No, of course not," Archer said.

"Then why look into the well? Wouldn't it be dangerous for your father?"

"It could be dangerous," Archer said.

"Was your father mentally stable?"

"What do you mean by that?" Archer exclaimed.

"Just routine questions, young man." The officer scribbled a few lines on his notepad. "And what did you find when you looked in the well?"

"Ice," Archer said. "The water in the bottom of the well was all ice."

"And that's unusual?"

"I've never seen it turn to ice," he said. "Even when the temperature outside is below zero, seems like the water in there is somehow insulated."

"But now it's ice?"

"I already told—"

"Archer!" Amy shouted from the front door. She ran for Archer. Her mother, wrapped in a thick fur coat, elbowed past the police officer to follow her in.

"I am so sorry, Archer!" Amy said, hugging him. "So sorry."

"This is terrible," Amy's mother said. "Do the police have any leads?"

"And who are you exactly?" the police officer asked.

"My name is Cassandra Pitsitakas," she said, anger simmering on each syllable. "As in Commissioner Pitsitakas. That's my father, you understand. Now, are you finished with Archer and his siblings?"

"I'm sorry, ma'am," the officer said. "Yes, yes, we're finished . . . for now. But . . ."

"But what?"

"We haven't been able to reach any next of kin," the officer explained. "And . . . uh . . . our forensics unit will be all over this house. The kids can't stay here."

"Of course they can't," Cassandra said. "The very notion! They will come home with me until our fine police force here brings their father back home safe and sound. We have plenty of room. Will that be all right with you, Archer?"

He looked at Amy, who nodded emphatically. "That's very kind of you, Mrs. Pitsitakas. Just until my father's back home."

"Of course, dear," she said.

"I need to run up to my room to get a few things."

"Get whatever you need, Archer," she said. "I expect your brother and sister might need a few things also."

She strode over to Kaylie and Buster. "No long faces," she told them. "Pouting and worry never fixed anything. In our house, hope springs eternal."

When the alarm went off the next morning, Archer awoke in a strange room. It took him a few heart-pounding moments to remember. It was the guest room at Amy's house. *I am a guest in their house because my father has been taken.* The rage boiled up within him like a geyser, but Archer tamped it down a few notches. He needed to think. To plan.

Archer had ruled out coincidence. It couldn't be. For his father to go missing just a few days after Archer had confronted Rigby? No, there had to be a connection. One way or the other, Archer would find out what exactly Rigby had done. And Archer would get his father back.

He flicked the alarm to radio mode and listened to the news. The new snow and cold temperatures hadn't been enough to get the day off from school, so that complicated Archer's initial plan. He would have to go to plan B. Archer shook his head and got dressed.

An hour later, Archer got off the bus and headed into school. He knew Amy was trailing him at a distance, hoping to make sure he didn't do anything stupid. Her mother had tried to convince Archer not to go in at all. He'd just suffered a family tragedy. He'd had very little sleep. He was upset.

All true, Archer thought. *Also true that I'm about to do something stupid.* Archer didn't go to his locker. He passed his homeroom by and kept walking. It was near time for the warning bell to ring. *That's my life*, Archer thought. *Controlled by bells.*

He glanced back over his shoulder and, as he'd hoped, Amy was caught in the crowds scurrying to get to homeroom on time. Archer wasn't scurrying; he was plowing. He hadn't been looking. He rammed straight into Brett Kiefer, the starting middle linebacker for the Dresden High varsity football team.

"Watch it, Smurf!" Brett bellowed, flexing shoulders that bulged even covered by a thick letterman jacket. "What's your prob—"

Archer wasn't sure what happened. Immediately after smacking into Brett, Archer felt a tingling sensation. In his hands, on his shoulders, down his arms, even across his face . . . especially around his eyes—it was like tiny crawling streaks of lightning. And the image of a wolf became crystal clear in his mind. Archer clenched his fists, heard his own knuckles crackle, and glared at Brett.

"Whoa," Brett muttered, backing away. "Nah, man, it's cool. It's all good. My fault."

Archer blundered on. He had to get to Rigby before the late bell rang. Archer turned down the band hallway. Rigby usually held court next to the trophy showcase there until the bell.

The hallway was jammed, but even so, students seemed to be giving Archer plenty of room to walk. *I could get used to this*, he thought.

Then Archer saw him. Wasn't hard. After all, Rigby was one of the tallest kids in the school. Archer blinked. Was he wearing . . . a top hat?

He was. Like the Planters Peanut guy, or maybe more like the

Mad Hatter from the Batman comics . . . Rigby was wearing an honest-to-goodness top hat. Archer couldn't believe it. School had rules against wearing hats indoors, and Rigby Thames wears a top hat. *The nerve of this guy*, Archer thought as he pressed forward.

Rigby was surrounded by a dozen of his closest suck-ups. Kara was there too. There was no way to do this without making a scene. Probably no way to do this without getting suspended. Archer didn't care.

Just before he invaded their circle, Archer felt a brief pang of reluctance. It was like a breath of wind through his mind, something telling him not to do what he was about to do. But other images were there too: Kaylie weeping hysterically, the mute distance in Buster's eyes, the burned-out cigarette in his father's ashtray, and the footprints toward the well.

Archer burst through the circle of teenagers and rammed his fists into Rigby's jacket, lifting the larger boy up from the ground and slamming him against the trophy showcase. Someone screamed.

"What did you do?" Archer demanded, spitting the words. "What did you do, Rigby?"

"Put . . . me . . . down, Keaton," Rigby hissed. "Don't make me humiliate you in front of your peers."

Shocked by his own strength, Archer pressed in on Rigby. "I know you did it," he said. "It had to be you."

"I . . . ow! Archer, I'm warning you," Rigby said, lifting a fist full of threat.

"You want to sit with the trophies?" Archer warned. "All I want is my father back. What'd you do with him, huh? What'd you do?"

"Keaton, have you lost your mind?" Rigby bellowed. He twisted free of Archer's grasp and shoved him back. "Never touch me again."

"What did you do with my father?"

"Look, Keaton," Rigby said, "I don't know what you're talking about."

A chant of "Fight, fight, fight!" rose up in the hallway. A deep voice somewhere nearby shouted, "Break it up!"

"You're not fooling me, Rigby, not this time," Archer said. "My father went missing last night, and I know you have something to do with it."

"Terribly sorry to hear of your dad," Rigby said. "But get some rest, Keaton. You look ill. I 'ad nothing to do with it."

"I said *break it up!*"

A chill like icy rain spilled down Archer's back. Archer grabbed Rigby by his jacket lapels and slammed him into the trophy case again. He had to stand on his toes, but he put his face right in Rigby's face and said, "It was you. You took the Shadow Key. You let the Scath out. You reckless—"

A strong hand took Archer's shoulder and pulled him away from Rigby. "Break it up, break it up!" Mr. Bohrs commanded. The assistant principal stood between Archer and Rigby, holding his hands out like a traffic cop. "Back off, Keaton."

"Mr. Bohrs," Rigby said, "I wasn't doing anything, and Keaton here comes pushing me around. Is this how things go here?"

"Save it, Thames," Mr. Bohrs growled. "Seems to me you've been suspended for fighting once before too."

"He's telling the truth, Mr. Bohrs," Kara said, appearing by the assistant principal's shoulder. "Archer just shoved in here and attacked Rigby."

Archer shot a red-eyed glare at her. "No one asked you, Kara!" he growled.

"Enough of that, Keaton," Mr. Bohrs said. "C'mon. We have a little trip to take."

He led Archer to the main office. Archer waited in the administrative conference room for close to an hour. Mrs. Mears, the principal, entered the room, closed the door, and sat down across the table from Archer.

"I've been in touch with the Washington County Police Department," she said. "They told me . . . well, they told me about your father. I'm sorry, Archer. This has to be very tough on you. I want you to know that we—the school—won't hold this altercation with Mr. Thames against you. You're under a lot of strain here. But maybe you need to take some time off. Maybe talk to someone." She nodded to the conference window, and Mrs. Anders, the school counselor, came in.

"Hello, Archer," she said, and she handed him a business card. "This is the contact info for a very highly recommended teen therapist. She's especially good with . . . well, with helping us with difficult times . . . or loss."

"We've also been in touch with Mrs. Pitsitakas," the principal said. "She's on her way here to pick you up."

Through it all, Archer said nothing.

"It's been a long day," Mrs. Pitsitakas said. "Buster's already asleep. You should sleep too."

Archer stretched and yawned. "I'm worn-out," he said. "C'mon, Kaylie, we need to hit the hay."

"Kaylie, you can stay in my room tonight," Amy said.

"I can?" Kaylie asked, blinking.

"Sure, I'll show you."

The three headed up the long staircase. "Amy, your house is

huge," Archer said, gazing at the vast room below and the long hall full of doorways above. There was a grand piano in one corner of the living room; long couches divided the space into a kind of L-shape. Glass tables bordered with gold inlay rested in front of and between the couches, and a dazzling chandelier hung down from the ceiling. "Just huge."

"Cut the small talk," Amy said. "C'mere." Once they were all up the stairs and around the corner, she said, "I know what you're up to. You're gonna do that Dreamtreading thing, yep."

"Shhh!" Archer warned.

Kaylie looked thunderstruck. "She knows?"

"I might know," Amy said coyly. She winked at Archer.

"She knows a little," he whispered. "But don't worry. Amy's cool."

"I know she's cool," Kaylie said. "But I didn't know she knew."

"So, I'm right, then?" Amy said. "You're going Dreamtreading tonight?"

"Yes," Archer said. "But first we need to talk to our superior, Master Gabriel."

"Ooh, he sounds cool," Amy said. "Like a Jedi or a ninja or something. Can I meet him?"

"Uhm, I don't think so," Archer said. "Not tonight anyway. He doesn't like surprises. But listen, Amy. I'm worried."

"Of course you're worried. Your father—"

"It's more than that," he said. "First, it was Mr. Gamber, then my dad. You told me you thought you saw shadow people in your room."

"Freaked me out," Amy said. "I screamed for my mom, but they were gone. I'm not even sure I really saw them."

"I think you did, Amy," he said. "I think something really bad is happening. Rigby Thames did something, and things from the Dream are intruding in our world. I want you to be careful, Amy.

Sleep with a light on."

"Will light protect me from the shadow people?" Amy asked.

"Honestly," Archer said, "I don't know. All I know is that light drives out darkness. But be careful."

"I will, Archer," she said. "I will turn my bedroom into the Kingdom of Bright Light."

DREAMTREADER'S CREED, CONCEPTUS 8

Meddle not with the Masters, Dreamtreader, for they have many errands. Each to their own territory, their own tasks. They will assist you in your business, but the Masters are not themselves the shepherds of that realm. You, Dreamtreader, must manage your own duties. You must abide by the Creeds. You must vanquish the evil that dwells in nightmares.

But . . .

Should the Nightmare Lord's master ever make himself known to you, do not dare to fight alone. Not even if all three Dreamtreaders join forces, do you attempt this task. He is a greater foe than your modest abilities will abide. It is then that a Master should be called. It is his task to face the dark one.

SEVENTEEN

FIRST PRIORITY

"WHAT IS THIS PLACE?" MASTER GABRIEL ASKED. "AND why have you summoned me here?"

"This is Amy Pitsitakas' home," Archer said. "We're . . . staying with her family for a while."

Immediately, Kaylie broke into tears, dashed forward, and hugged the master Dreamtreader.

"Uh, hmph, hmm," Master Gabriel said, clearing his throat. "Kaylie, what's gotten into you?"

She didn't answer but sobbed all the more.

"Archer?" Master Gabriel said, his armor flaring white. "What's wrong?"

"My father," he said. "Someone took my father away."

Master Gabriel sighed as if weary, but his eyes still kindled a defiant flame. "Storm and madness!" he grumbled. "This is Scath doing."

"And I think I know who has the Shadow Key," Archer said. "I think I know who let them out."

"Your Lucid Walker friend?"

"Rigby Thames," Archer said. "But he's no friend. I confronted him about the breaches that his Lucid Walker business was causing. I warned him to shut it all down. I think he let the Scath out to spite me, to target me and hurt me."

"That may well be true, Archer," Master Gabriel said, "but if you'll accept my counsel, I would advise you to see a bigger picture."

"What do you mean?"

Master Gabriel knelt and drew Kaylie away. "Do not fear, child," he said. "Fear is an invitation to darkness."

"But my daddy," she said, her voice a bare whimper.

"Listen to me, Kaylie," Gabriel said. "I will do everything in my power to bring your father back to safety. Do you understand?"

"Uh . . . uh-huh," she whispered, nodding.

"What did you mean by 'bigger picture'?" Archer asked once more.

Master Gabriel patted Kaylie lightly on the head, rose to his full height, and said, "Rigby may indeed bear you a great deal of ill will, enough to attack people you love, but for someone to risk letting the Scath out for good? That speaks to a larger plan. A fouler plan. I believe this Rigby fellow desires to become ruler of the Dream."

"Like the Nightmare Lord?" Archer asked.

"Yes, but worse. At least the old Nightmare Lord knew better than to release the Scath. They are unpredictable and treacherous. No, Rigby is power hungry and power mad. He wants to rule the Dream, even if it means destroying the Waking World in the process."

"So we stop him," Archer said.

"We must," Master Gabriel replied. "If you're right, and Rigby has the Shadow Key, you must get it back and lock up the vaults of the Inner Sanctum."

"Where do we begin?" Archer asked. Kaylie tugged on his shirt.

"I suggest you divide and conquer," Master Gabriel said. "There are three of you now."

Again, Kaylie tugged on Archer's shirt. "Wait," he whispered. "Where should we look?"

"Shadowkeep, for one," Master Gabriel said. "Bezeal, of course. And maybe seek out Lady Kasia as well. If there's a rumor about, she'll know it. If time permits, you might try to intercept Rigby at the Libraries of Garnet."

"Okay, I understand," Archer said. "We'll go tonight. But you'll have to get Nick on board."

"I will see to it," Master Gabriel replied. "The three of you will meet at the Cold Plateau, in the center of your territories. Make your plans, seal off the new breaches, and find that key."

Archer said, "Got it."

"Archer!" Kaylie cried out. "What do you mean? We can't go looking for some stupid key. We have to find Daddy."

"The Shadow Key might be the reason Dad was taken, Kaylie," Archer said, keeping his tone gentle. "We get it back, we might get him back too."

She scrunched her nose. "But we don't know that," she said. "All we know is that Daddy's gone and the creepy things took him. We gotta go into the Dream and find him."

"I understand how you feel, Kaylie," Master Gabriel said. "But you must understand you are a Dreamtreader now. Your duty is to preserve and protect the Dream and the Waking World. You must be strong and carry out your duty."

"But Daddy might need us, Archer," she said plaintively.

"I know, Kaylie, I know. But getting the Shadow Key back is the way to help him now."

The moment he was certain Kaylie was safely tucked in with Amy, Archer locked the guest room door and tossed the white Summoning Feather into the air once more.

In a furious sparkle, Master Gabriel appeared. "Honestly, Archer, what is it now? I have other errands, you know."

"I'm sorry," he said. "But I'm worried."

"I know, Archer. Your father—"

"I'm worried about Kaylie."

"Explain."

"Are you sure she's ready for this?" Archer asked. "I mean, I know you trained her a few times. But I had months before I went active duty."

"We do not have the luxury of time," Master Gabriel said. "She is already better at Dreamweaving breaches than you are."

"I'm not worried about breaches," he said. "But Rigby, the Lurker, the Scath . . . and any other beastie the Dream has to offer. I mean, I was thinking of having Kaylie watch over the Libraries in Garnet, but suppose Rigby does show up? What if he tries to hurt her or take her captive?"

"In that case, I pity Rigby," Master Gabriel said without a hint of a smile. "Do you have any idea the kind of mental power Kaylie wields? If Rigby does challenge her, I just hope she doesn't kill him."

Rigby picked at the vast tray in the studio's green room, glanced at the television, and went to switch it off.

"Wait," Kara said. "I want to see that." She rushed to the TV and turned up the volume.

The handsome gray-haired anchor was saying, "The second abduction in recent weeks, sparking a statewide manhunt. If you have seen or have any information about Phillip Gamber or Brian Keaton, both of Gatlinburg, please call . . ."

"First, Mr. Gamber from Gatlinburg Elementary," Kara said. "And now, Archer's father. I can't believe it."

"Why?" Rigby said. "It's a rough world. Bad things happen."

Kara eyed him coolly. "You didn't have anything to do with that, did you?"

"Oh, please, Kara," he said. "Don't tell me you're buying into anything Keaton said today. He's delusional."

"You forget, I've known Archer a long time. I've never seen him that angry. It's not like him at all to barge in and throw you up against a trophy case. He was furious with you."

"He didn't throw me up against the trophy case."

"You didn't answer my question, Rigby," she said, her voice dropping an octave. "Did you have anything to do with Archer's father?"

Rigby shrugged. "It's all about leverage."

"I didn't sign up for kidnapping, Rigby."

"You signed up to rule the Dream," he warned. "This is what it costs."

"They're ready for you, Mr. Thames, Ms. Windchil."

Rigby switched off the television. "Come, partner," he said. "We have a world to win."

⚷

"What took you so long, Archer?" Kaylie asked.

"Yeah, mate," Nick said. "It's freezing here!"

"Well, it is called the Cold Plateau," Archer said. He turned a brief circle with his arms outstretched. They stood upon a relatively flat, snow-covered elevation high above the Forms District. "You could have just willed a big bonfire."

"Oh," Nick said. "Color me gobsmacked. I keep forgetting."

"We went to bed at the same time, Archer," Kaylie said, peeking out from the hooded parka she wore. "You usually fall asleep pretty quick."

"I was planning," he said.

"Right then," Nick said. "So, what's the plan?"

"We all anchor here," Archer said. "We head out, shut all the breaches in our own districts as fast as we can. Then Nick, you go to Bavanda. Talk to their leader, Lady Kasia. See if she knows anything about the Shadow Key, but be wary. She's a little touchy."

"What does that mean?" Nick asked.

"You'll see," he said. "Just don't let her charm you or feed you anything black."

"Gort, right," Nick said.

"I'm going to check out Shadowkeep first, and then I'll look for Bezeal. Kaylie, I want you to go to the Libraries of Garnet. Keep a watch for Rigby or Bezeal. If either of them shows up, you need to let us know."

"How will I do that?" she asked.

"My secret weapon," Archer said. "Razz!"

There came a crackling double puff of purple smoke, and then Razz hovered there in front of Archer. "Hiya, boss!" she said.

"Awwwww!" Kaylie clapped. "It's a flying squirrel!"

"I'm not an *it*," Razz said, turning her back to Kaylie. "I am a *she*, as my outfit plainly shows."

"Cute!" Kaylie said. She leaped up, grabbed Razz out of the air, and snuggled her up to her cheek.

"Hey!" Razz cried out. "Hey, leggo! How undignified!"

"Razz," Archer said. "You go with Kaylie tonight."

Razz squirmed out of Kaylie's grasp, swooped up in the air, and hovered in front of Archer's nose. "Really?" she said. "Really, boss? She thinks I'm a stuffed animal."

Archer grabbed Razz out of the air so fast that her acorn beret whirled. "Listen to me, Razz. You go with Kaylie. And don't you dare bail on her."

"I wouldn't dream of it," she said indignantly.

"Right," Archer said. "You stay with her, answer her questions, and if there's a threat, any threat at all, you come get me. You understand?" He opened his hand and let her out.

"I understand, Archer," Razz said. "I won't let you down."

"Good, Razz," he said. "Thank you." He turned and looked from Kaylie to Nick and back. "We meet back here before the Stroke of Reckoning. You two entered the Dream first, so you'll need to get back before I do. Leave some kind of sign to let me know you got here and got out safely."

"Bonzer plan, mate," Nick said. "So, I'll anchor down here, then?"

"Right," Archer said, loosing the rendering mallet and an anchoring stake from his back-hanger sheath. "We all do." He slammed the mallet down onto the anchor's striking plate and the shaft pierced the snow and ice. Instantly, Archer's wishing well appeared. He turned to watch the others.

Kaylie gave her anchor stake a few heavy smacks with the mallet, and Patches, her favorite stuffed doll, appeared. Only this version of Patches was much bigger than a teddy bear.

More like a grizzly, Archer thought. And he thought he knew why his sister had made this gigantic version of Patches the Scarecrow to be her anchor. He might have let his imagination wander back to the previous year's climactic battle with the Nightmare Lord, but he wanted to see what Nick's anchor would be.

Nick wandered a few yards away and slammed his anchor stake into the ice with one strike of the mallet. Rising from the snow, came a sprawling tree with a mix of dark green and dark red foliage. Small berries or seeds hung from the ends of the branches.

"Tell me about your anchor, Nick," Archer said. "If it's not too personal."

"No worries, Archer," he said. "This here is the crab apple tree my little brother Oliver and I used to climb at our granny's house back when we were little."

"That . . . is cool," Archer said.

"Makes me want to climb it right now," Kaylie said.

"Maybe later, kiddo," Nick said. "We've got work to do."

"Everyone clear on your mission?" Archer asked.

"Absolutely," Nick said. He whistled for his valkaryx. Instantly, the sound of large wings flapping came out of the gray gloom overhead.

"Kaylie, you feel okay about everything?"

She blinked at him, her eyes big blue marbles, all too ready to be washed again with tears. "I'm . . . I'm good." Her sky-blue dune buggy with huge knobby tires appeared around her. She cranked the engine and roared off.

Archer watched her go. It already felt like a mistake.

"This is compelling stuff," Ned Aimsley, TekTime Network anchor, said, leaning forward. "So what you're saying is that you can essentially give everyone in the world good dreams."

"That's right, Ned," Rigby said, glancing at Kara and then

grinning for the cameras. "Ms. Windchil and I have built upon my Uncle Scoville's research and have isolated the source of nightmares. We've created a proprietary herbal formula that will absolutely rid a person of bad dreams."

Ned raised an eyebrow and said, "For a price."

"These herbs are rare," Kara said, "and very expensive. There's a purification process necessary, as well, and that's costly."

"But we plan to keep the price point low," Rigby said, "especially for subscription services."

"We want everyone to be able to afford Sweet Dreams," Kara said, flashing teeth.

"That name should be trademarked," Ned said, laughing.

"It already is," Rigby said.

"When will your herbal supplement appear in stores?" Ned asked.

"It won't," Rigby said. "It'll ship directly from our warehouse. You can order online wherever you are, and we guarantee you'll have it in your hands and be nightmare-free in less than a week."

"There you have it, folks," Ned said, picking up the black-and-silver bottle from the table. "Sweet Dreams are waiting for you, just a phone call away."

EIGHTEEN

SEARCH AND RESCUE

BY THE TIME THE VALKARYX NAMED ROCKY DROPPED
Nick Bushman just outside the trellised city of Bavanda, he was feeling quite good about his efforts. "Heaps of breaches mended, and
not even winded," he muttered to himself. "Now, to find this Lady
Kasia."

Nick whistled, and Rocky took to the air. Then Nick jogged the
winding path to the gated town. From the outside, the place looked
like a rain forest interspersed with cottages, towers, and winding
stairs. "Stone-cold gorgeous," he whispered as he drew near.

"Hail, traveler!" an armed guard called out from a large stone
gatehouse.

"What weapons do you intend to carry into the green city of
Bavanda?" a second guard asked.

"G'day," Nick said, not certain if a bow was proper, but bowing
anyway. "These?" He pointed at his vest.

"The L-shaped things, yeah," the guard replied. "I've not seen
their like."

"These are boomerangs," Nick said, loosening a pair, one in each hand. "Watch." With a low-to-high fling, he launched the two boomerangs.

The guards gasped as the boomerangs rotated and soared through the air. Then they startled and stepped fearfully backward. One even expelled a decidedly unmanly scream: the boomerangs had become great and fierce eagles.

The winged predators swooped down low, just above the guards—eliciting two more very unmanly screams—before transforming back to wooden boomerangs and landing in Nick's waiting palms.

"Verily!" cried one of the guards. "You are the new Dreamtreader we've heard about!"

"Sir Nick, is it?" the other guard asked.

"No, mate, it's just Nick," he said. "But yeah, I'm one of the two new Dreamtreaders. How'd you know?"

"Well, truly your impressive display of power for one," the guard explained. "But also, we heard of your doings by word of mouth. Bavanda is kind of a center of information, if you take my meaning."

"I do indeed," Nick said. "And information is why I have come. I need to meet the Lady Kasia."

"Oh, she'll be happy to meet with you," said one of the guards with a snicker.

"Hehe, yeah," the other guard said. "Welcome to the city, Dreamtreader. You'll find the Lady Kasia in the domed garden, taking tea, I should think."

Wondering about the guards' mischievous giggles, Nick entered the city and made for the massive domed garden near the center.

Kaylie sat in a camouflaged stand within a thick tree canopy less than a hundred yards away from Garnet's Library. She had an excellent view of the surreal building in a tree. Not that there was much to see. Dream citizens went in and out all afternoon, forcing Kaylie to stare through the will-summoned telescope to search their faces for Rigby or Bezeal. Some climbed up the library's trunk, but most hitched rides with strange batlike creatures Kaylie had never seen before.

"This is a waste of time," she muttered, glancing away from the telescope to check Old Jack. "My dad's trail is getting cold."

"What do you mean?" Razz asked as she gnawed an orb of acorn meat. "Why is the trail cold? Is it snowing where you live?"

"No, well . . . yes, it is actually, but that's not what I meant." Kaylie thought a moment. "It's a figure of speech," she told Razz. "It just means the longer we wait, the harder it will be to find my father."

"Oh," Razz said, crunching the last of the acorn.

"Could you take another loop?" Kaylie asked. "We can't afford to let Rigby or Bezeal sneak in some hidden entrance."

"On it, boss!" Razz said, leaping into the air. "Back in twenty minutes!" With hardly a sound, the flying squirrel vanished through the leaves and branches.

Kaylie sighed and went back to her lonely duty at the telescope. A few moments went by, and she found herself zooming in on a strange couple standing just down the hill from the library tree. They were dressed in shadowy gray and didn't seem to be in any hurry to enter the library. Kaylie hadn't seen them arrive. When the larger crowd thinned out, these two were just kind of there. The expression on their dark faces looked so serious, and they were deeply engaged in conversation.

A voice came to Kaylie: "Will never guess, will she?"

She couldn't tell if it was just in her mind or something audible.

"No, no, never guess," a second voice answered. "Master is too clever for her."

Kaylie blinked and pressed her face tighter to the telescope eyepiece. It couldn't be. She was too far away. But the words she heard perfectly matched the lip movements of the two strangers in gray.

"Shame shame," said the first voice. "She won't find him in time."

"I wonder if there will be anything left of him."

They both laughed, a sound like a pair of rattlesnakes.

"Who are you talking about?" Kaylie whispered.

Both figures in gray turned immediately and seemed to stare directly into the telescope. "Your father!" they hissed, just as they vanished.

Kaylie heard rustling in the limbs below her stand. A shadow passed by her window. A second and third time. Something scratched outside her stand's wooden walls.

Kaylie readied her will. All went quiet.

"You were listening after all," came a whispery voice behind her.

"Thought we might as well come visit," said a second voice.

Kaylie squeaked, spun, and saw the wispy shapes. They were like human shadows but somehow with volume, and little knobby segments like joints wherever there was a bend in a limb. Worse still, their eyes gleamed pale fire.

"Any last words?" Kaylie asked, suddenly wielding a will-summoned flamethrower. She gave the trigger a feathery pull, and it burped a brief fiery plume.

"Silly fleshling," one of the shadow men said. "Fire harms us not!"

"This isn't just for fire," Kaylie said. She didn't even glance down. The flamethrower morphed into a wide-bladed exhaust fan. "I don't like you. Good-bye." And she switched on the fan.

A hurricane-force gust blasted from the fan blades. The shadow beings filled with wind like gray sails until they could no longer keep their footing. A harsh gust launched them against the wall, flattening like melted gum. All the while they shrieked and hissed and screeched.

"Foolish . . . fuh-fuh-fuh-fleshling!"

"Never tell you . . . where to find him, *eeeee!*"

"Who?" Kaylie demanded, cranking up the fan to an even higher level. "Tell me now!"

"Yes, yes!"

"We tell you!"

Kaylie shut off the fan. The two shadow men peeled off the wall, slithered to the floor, and began to wriggle around, inflating at last to their original form.

"You play rough, little one," one shadow being said.

"Who are you calling little?" Kaylie asked. She furrowed her brow and raised the fan gun threateningly.

"No, no!"

"Okay, now listen, Scath," Kaylie said. "You are Scath, aren't you?"

Both shadow beings nodded.

"Fine," Kaylie said. "I want to know who took my father away and where he is now."

The Scath leered at Kaylie and muttered, "The Lurker."

"Took him or has him now?"

"Both, *ssss*, both!"

"Thank you, Scath," Kaylie said. "See, we can play nice." She made the fan gun vanish and strode toward the Scath. "If you two are lying to me, I'll dream up something that'll trap you forever. And my traps won't have keys to let you out."

The Scath tripped all over themselves trying to get out through the stand's window. When they were gone, Kaylie left a note for Razz and descended from the tree. She called up her dune buggy and revved the engine while she scanned her Dream realm map. Then she stepped on the gas pedal and raced west toward Archaia.

⚷

Archer had fully expected to find Rigby or Kara or both of them at Number 6 Rue de la Morte. The entire fortress had been re-furnished . . . and recently, but there was no one around. In Kurdan's marketplace, however, Archer found his quarry selling piles of useless junk in the center of the marketplace.

Bezeal finished with his last customer and scraped the thin gold coins—eighteen gossamers, all told—off the greasy table and into the satchel at his side. When he turned around, he found Archer tow-ering over him.

"Dreamtreader tall, how come you to my stall? Can I . . . help you at all?" Bezeal's eyes shrank to the tiniest pinpricks of light.

Archer had been mentally rehearsing how he would approach Bezeal. The little hooded merchant was very clever and deceitful. If Master Gabriel was correct—and he almost always was—no intel-ligent person would underestimate Bezeal. Archer knew it would tax his mental will fiercely, but he was beyond caring. He would endure no trickery, no foolishness from Bezeal. Not this time.

Archer grabbed a fistful of Bezeal's hooded cloak just below his neck and flung the merchant one-handed into a high-security bank vault. The vault hadn't been there a second before, but Archer's will made it happen just in time for Bezeal to crash into it.

Archer raced inside the vault just as the multilayered titanium steel door slammed shut. He used his will to spin the inner tumblers, and the lock clicked tight. There was total darkness except for Bezeal's tiny eyes and the angry red smoldering in Archer's hands.

"What is this foolish thing you do?" Bezeal squeaked. "We're trapped just us two. Release me now; I'm warning you."

"You lying, scheming scab!" Archer yelled, fire flaring in his fists. "You tricked me into getting the Karakurian Chamber. You knew all along it was the stolen Shadow Key, and you used me to get it."

Bezeal's eyes grew, and a tiny white glimmer of his smile appeared. "Of course I knew it was the key. It was right where I wanted it to be. But I needed you to give it back to me."

"You used me," Archer repeated. "Come to think of it, you used Duncan and Mesmeera too. Because of you, they're dead."

Bezeal's laugh startled Archer. It was a crackling sound, low, and full of malevolent glee. "As I recall, it was you who killed poor Duncan and Mesmeera."

Bezeal's sudden lack of rhyme unnerved Archer. He took an involuntary step backward but then grew angrier for his own cowardice. "You listen to me, runt," Archer growled. "I want the Shadow Key back, and I want it now."

Archer felt a pulse in his will, a throbbing kind of strength, aching to be exercised. He decided to make a statement. He turned his palms down toward the floor and set loose streams of flame that hit the floor and slithered across to widen at Bezeal's feet.

As Archer stepped toward Bezeal, the flame rose a little higher until at last it encircled the merchant and rose up to form a cage of flame.

Bezeal's voice was shrill and fearful. "Do not burn your faith— your faithful servant. I have not the key, no matter how much you chant. The key to give you, I—I can't."

"I'm through playing around, Bezeal," Archer said. "Give me the Shadow Key."

With a sound like a scream, all the fire blew out. The vault plunged into total darkness.

"Ah, the sweet smell . . . of arrogance," came a voice Archer didn't recognize. "You have no idea what real fire is."

Flaming red eyes appeared and widened, growing to become windows of blood and fire. Archer could not help his reaction to this sudden terror before him. It was a physical thing, the sudden impulse to flee, a frantic instinct to escape.

Archer's will took apart the bank vault, wall by wall, sending them flying out into the Dream. Archer ran. He didn't look back. He ran until he had the presence of mind to summon his surfboard and find an Intrusion wave.

Then he took all the speed the wave could offer and fled. The towns and regions and minutes passed by, and Archer arrived first at the rendezvous point on Cold Plateau. He was early by an hour, and there was no sign of Kaylie or Nick.

Archer rubbed his arms, but truly the temperature from the icy environment wasn't nearly as troubling as the chill from his confrontation with Bezeal. He couldn't shake that no matter what he tried.

⚷

"How do you like your tea?" Lady Kasia asked, her lips still hovering above her own cup.

"Bonzer, love," Nick replied. "Best tea I've had in years."

"Did you just call me . . . love?" she asked, putting down her teacup with a clink. Her table was covered with a pristine white cloth and fully set with fine porcelain. They sat at the table for tea surrounded by lush trees and hibiscus shrubs with blooms the size of dinner plates. It was a lovely place for a conversation, but Nick couldn't help feeling out of place for some reason. Lady Kasia drew out a long fan, spread it with a flourish, and began to cool herself. "We've only just met."

Nick felt the blush bloom in his cheeks. Now, at last, he understood Archer's warning. "No disrespect meant," he said. "Just a friendly term, you understand."

"Friendly?" Lady Kasia repeated, frowning as if the word tasted sour. "So, tell me, Dreamtreader Nick, what is the occasion for this *friendly* visit?"

Nick put down his teacup. "The Dream is in danger," Nick said.

"The Shadow Key?" Lady Kasia said with a flutter of eyelashes.

Nick struggled to keep his jaw from dropping. "Dooley! You know about the Shadow Key?"

"Of course," she replied. "I am the eyes and ears of the Forms District, you understand. There are very few goings on that I don't know about."

"Was it Bezeal?" Nick asked.

"Bezeal alone?" she asked. "Oh, I don't see how. I have it on good account that there were others involved."

"Who?"

"Well, now," she said. "You certainly seem eager."

"Of course I'm eager," he said. "Someone cast open the vaults of the Inner Sanctum and let the Scath loose. Until we get that key back, the Dream fabric will decay at a fair rapid rate."

Lady Kasia stood, whirled so that her vivid red dress brushed the low ferns and purple flowers. She flounced back to her chair, leaned over the table, and propped her chin upon her fists. "I'll tell you what," she said coyly. "I wouldn't be a bit surprised to discover that the Lurker's been a part of this from the beginning."

"The Lurker?" Nick replied. "The wacky hermit out in Archaia?"

"The very same," she said. "Of course, I might know a few more teensy, weensy details."

"Tell me."

"I might," Lady Kasia said. "But you have to do a little something for me first."

Kaylie was brilliant. She could calculate pi to a million digits in her head. She could hack into just about any computer or security system. And she could memorize books whole. But there was one thing she was terrible at: reading maps. And the map of the Dream was rough at best. The place kept changing. Sure, it was always roughly triangular and always divided into three districts, but some of the landmarks moved a little. And a little was enough to get Kaylie discombobulated.

The newest Dreamtreader had to stop her dune buggy to ask directions three times, but in the end, she found the Lurker's home in Archaia. Everyone she spoke to about her destination warned her to avoid the Lurker at all costs. Kaylie thanked them, but moved on anyway. She didn't fear the Lurker like the other citizens of the Dream did. She knew who he was.

Kaylie marched up the incline, a kind of foothill on the Archaian moors, in the midst of craggy rocks and slowly churning mist. A very wide arched doorway had been built into the top of the incline just below the rooty overhang.

Kaylie knocked on the door.

She heard the thunder of her knock echo behind the door, but there came no answer in return. She knocked a second time and a third, but still there was no reply.

She tried the door and found it unlocked. It was heavy, but nothing her will-enhanced strength couldn't handle. This was a door that had struck terror in the hearts of Dream citizens for ages past. It was a door that turned away seasoned warriors. But, in spite of all that, in spite of the warnings, eight-year-old Kaylie Keaton entered the Lurker's lair.

Waiting impatiently for his Dreamtreading partners to show up, Archer paced the plateau. If possible, it had gotten colder up there, and an odd bluish-tinted snow had begun to fall. The flakes were much larger and longer than those of the waking world. They looked like feathers, as if someone far above had been ripping pillows open a thousand at a time.

How long has it been? Archer wondered, glancing up at Old Jack. Too long. He'd worn a path in the snow, almost a perfect figure eight in and around Nick's crab apple tree and Kaylie's big Patches doll. All three anchors were flecked with fresh snow and looked somehow lonely. No, more like old and abandoned.

Archer stopped pacing. A shadow approached from the eastern side of the plateau. It was a dark bulky figure, obscured by the snow but advancing rapidly.

"Whoever you are," Archer called out into the swirling wind and snow, "I am a Dreamtreader, and this is our protected territory. Who are you, and what is your business here?"

The dark figure continued undeterred, a sooty specter in the white landscape. There was something magnified about this being, as if, beneath the heavy hood and cloak, a great power resided. Archer clenched his fists at his sides like a gunslinger and readied his will. "Last warning!" he called out, deepening his voice for effect. "Announce yourself and your purpose, or face the wrath of a Dream-treader!"

The hooded and heavily dressed stranger stopped a dozen yards from Archer and said, "G'day, mate!"

"Nick?" Archer said, sighing deeply. "Is that you under all that fluff?"

"Hey, fool me once," Nick said, "shame on you. Fool me twice, shame on me. I hate the cold."

"You had me a little worried, walking up here all cloaked like that. I could have thrown a school bus at you."

"Yeah, sorry about that," Nick said, dropping his hood and winking. "But, ah . . . since we're on the subject: 'Face the wrath of a Dreamtreader'? A little dramatic, don't you think?"

"Maybe," Archer said. "A little. Okay, yeah, it was way over the top. Still, you're all bulky in that outfit. You must have fifty pounds of weather gear on."

"Like I said, I hate the cold."

"I bet it wasn't cold around Lady Kasia," Archer said.

"No indeed," Nick said. "A might too friendly."

"Did she have any information?"

"Yeah, heaps. She told me the Lurker is working with Bezeal, that he has some connection to the Shadow Key. Might be we need to pay the Lurker a visit."

"I agree," Archer said. "That it?"

"Well . . ." Nick hesitated. "I think she knows more, but she wouldn't tell me unless . . ."

Archer raised an eyebrow. "Unless what?"

Nick mumbled something.

"What?" Archer asked. "I didn't quite catch that."

Nick sighed. "Unless I accept her proposal for marriage."

Archer blinked. "That . . . well, that would be kind of an issue, huh?"

"Ya think?" Nick shook his head.

"Well?" Archer asked, shifting back and forth on his feet.

"Well, what?"

"Did you—"

"No, I did not agree to marry her! Think I'm mad? Dooley, that woman is three kinds of creepy."

Archer stifled a laugh. "Yeah, you meet all kinds here in the Dream."

"Never met her kind," Nick said. "Hope I never do again. How'd you do?"

"Shadowkeep was deserted," Archer said.

"What about Bezeal . . . did ya find him?"

It was Archer's turn to hesitate. "Yeah, I found him," he said. "I—I didn't get much from him. But he told me that he doesn't have the key."

"You believe him?"

"This time?" Archer said. "I think I might. I think he wanted me to know that someone else has the Shadow Key. I think he's taunting me, daring me to find out."

"Who is it, then?"

"The Lurker, maybe," Archer said. "Or it could be one of the Lucid Walkers."

"Who?"

"Trespassers in the Dream," Archer explained. "Through research and sleep science, they've found a physiological technique to enter the Dream."

"That explains a lot," Nick said. "I've seen others here. Long before you woke me up. At first it was just one or two, doing things that other Dream citizens couldn't do. But, I dunno. Over the last year maybe, I've seen a lot more of them."

"That's because of Rigby Thames, Kara Windchil, and their company, Dream Inc." Archer gave Nick the short version of Rigby's recent endeavors. He didn't spare any details or feelings.

"Get out!" Nick said. "So that's why the Dream's been full of a buncha ankle biters. That's why there are heaps of new breaches all the time. You think this Rigby fellow has the Shadow Key, then? Think it's all his doing?"

"I confronted him," Archer said. "Back in the Waking World. He hates me—that's for certain. But would he be so reckless as to let the Scath out? Honestly, I don't know."

Nick nodded. "No one said this would be easy."

"You're dead on right there," Archer said, thinking of Bezeal. "In fact, we were warned that things may be even harder than we can imagine. The Creeds tell us that."

"Guess I haven't read that far," Nick muttered.

Archer nodded, but he was lost in thought, weighing how much, if anything, he should tell Nick about Bezeal's ominous transformation in the dark. The red eyes lingered . . . it was almost like he could see them, luminous like bloody lights in the falling snow.

"Archer?" Nick queried.

"What?"

"You there? Seemed like you blinked out on me."

"Sorry," Archer said. "A lot on my mind."

Nick glanced over Archer's shoulder and nodded. "Kaylie should be back soon, shouldn't she?"

Archer turned and looked up to Old Jack. "She should have come by now, but we'll wait."

"I've only got about an hour," Nick said. "That's by Dreamtreader law, right?"

"Law number three in the Creeds," Archer replied. "I've got about twenty minutes more than you, so I'll stick around." *C'mon, Kaylie,* he thought. *Where are you?*

Kaylie knew her time was running out, but the Lurker's stronghold still had tunnels, passages, and doors she'd not yet searched. She felt certain her father was there somewhere, if she could just find the right door.

She finished exploring a vast vaulted chamber filled with old storage chests and peculiar furniture, and moved on to a kind of cell block that seemed promising. There were eighteen barred alcoves, all locked . . . and all empty. Kaylie began to despair.

I don't have enough time, she thought. *Daddy, I need to find you, but I can't wait much longer.*

She began to move recklessly, ricocheting from chamber to chamber until, in a shadowy corridor, she plowed into a freestanding coat of armor. It tipped over and crashed, making a horrendous ruckus. Kaylie half expected her father to come running around the corner to yell at her.

She wished he would, but no one came. She hurriedly picked up the pieces of armor and tried to reassemble them on the frame, but failed miserably. That was when she noticed the door.

It had been hidden behind the coat of armor, a narrow door nearly the same color as the stone of the corridor. She tried the handle. It opened.

It was pitch dark, so Kaylie willed an oil lantern and carried it down the steps. Down and down the stairs she went, into the dank chill of the underground. Near the bottom of the steps, the lantern revealed a series of huge vats. They reminded Kaylie of the huge wooden pens at the European amusement park where the staff would dance around, crushing grapes for wine. If the smell of this subterranean chamber were any indication, however, the Lurker hadn't been mashing grapes.

Kaylie set foot on the chamber floor and turned up the wick on the lantern to get a little more light. It showed a cavernous room full of all manner of surreal twisting and turning pipes and pipettes, tall cylinders, networks of flasks, and barrel-sized beakers, each filled to varying degrees with putrid colored liquids.

It's like a giant's chemistry set, she thought, wandering between the great vats. There didn't seem to be any prison cells or anything that would obviously hold captives, but Kaylie continued on.

She found one of the vats had a movable ladder hanging from its high lip. When she climbed to the top, she held out the lantern to see inside. From the stairs, the vats had seemed empty. And this one mostly was. Mostly.

Adjusting the height of the flame, she saw that there were a few lumps or globs of something at the bottom of the vat. She leaned forward even more. She recognized the shapes. They were bulbous, long, eellike creatures, each with several circular sets of leech teeth. Scurions. Now that she could see better, they were unmistakable. But these were larger than most of the scurions she'd encountered while sewing up breaches. They were the most unpleasant part of that nightly chore.

Gross-o-rama, she thought. These were even nastier than . . . than—

A realization. Kaylie's brilliant mind had been spinning the variables until the correct conclusion arrived. "Someone's been breeding scurions," she whispered. Quickly, she clambered down the ladder. Her foot hit the floor, and she froze.

Squee-eeak!

Kaylie spun around and shone the lantern. She thought she'd heard something . . . a chirp or a wooden creak, maybe. The light showed nothing.

She rounded the vat and found a large pipe secured at its base. It ran from the vat to some kind of junction at the wall. Other pipes from other vats met there as well. Kaylie investigated. The pipes were metal, and each had numerous hatches and pressure wheels. Kaylie followed one to the wall, opened up its hatch, and held the lantern up.

There were more dead scurions in the pipe. She lowered the lantern into the pipe and looked down its length as far as the light would cast. More scurions—a trail of the dead, but going where?

Kaylie gasped. Like one of her encryption apps unraveling chains of computer code, her mind spun. The last element fell into place. She stood up sharply and closed the hatch.

"No wonder we can't keep the Dream stable," Kaylie whispered. "The Lurker's been breeding scurions to rip open breaches below the surface. Breaches we would never fix because we'd never see them."

The raspy voice came from the huge shadow at the top of the stairs. "I really wish you hadn't seen that."

"You need to get back," Archer said. "I've got a little more time. I can wait."

"Look, mate," Nick said, "I wouldn't worry. Kaylie's newer at this than I am, right? And she's so young. She probably just lost track of time."

202

"That's what scares me," Archer said. "She could be in trouble somewhere out in the Dream."

"Or, maybe she went back to the Waking World before either of us got here. Young people don't always think before they do."

Archer had to smile at that. "Yes, we do a lot of that kind of thing."

"See, that's probably it, mate," Nick said. "Old Jack still says I've got a little bit of time, ten minutes. If Kaylie is still out here, that's all she's got as well. You should go back to your home and see. If she's there, all's well. If not, at least you have a little time to come back and hunt for her."

Archer nodded. "That makes sense," he said.

"Right, then. I'm off," Nick said. "Good luck, mate." With that, Nick leaped up, grabbed the lowest branch of his crab apple tree, and vanished.

Archer took a hesitant step toward his anchor. "Razz!" he called out. "Razzelestia Moonsonnet, get over here!"

She didn't answer. She didn't appear. While not unheard of, it was still odd for Razz not to answer for so long a period of time. *If I could talk to Razz,* he thought, *and just know that Kaylie went back early, then I'd be fine.*

Archer shook his head and reached for his anchor.

NINETEEN

HOURGLASS SANDS

WHEN ARCHER AWOKE, HE WAS IN A STRANGE ROOM. The curtains had a floral pattern. They weren't his. The closet was in the wrong place. There were two lamps, not one. The dim light from the hallway had a burnished brown cast, not the bright yellow of his home. Something was very wrong.

Archer sat up and rolled out of bed. The disorientation lingered. He went to the bedroom door, saw the length of the hall, the numerous rooms, the crown molding, intricate light fixtures—details of luxury—and then it dawned on him: *I'm at Amy's house. Why do I keep getting confused like this?*

Kaylie.

His consciousness rolled in like a tidal wave. He had to make sure Kaylie had come back. He charged down the hall to Amy's room and froze. Her door was shut. What was he going to do? Barge into a young woman's room in the middle of the night? That would be awkward at best, but if Amy's mom got wind of it? Archer didn't want to think of that.

But Kaylie was in there. He had to get to her. "Duh," he muttered to himself. He knocked three times on the door. They were sharp knocks, enough to wake most sleepers.

After a few seconds, "Mom?" came Amy's sleepy voice.

"No, it's Archer. Sorry to wake you, Amy, but it's important. Can you check on Kaylie?"

"What?" Amy asked, cracking the door and looking out. "What are you talking about? She's right there on the bed. She's fine."

"Wake her up," Archer said. "Please. I don't have time to explain. Please just wake her up."

Amy let the door drift open a little more. She wore a long flannel nightgown. "Okay," she said.

Archer watched her waddle back to the bed. He heard her call to Kaylie, saw her give Kaylie a little shake, and then a more solid push. Archer heard Amy's voice rise, calling again for Kaylie to wake. Archer watched in horror as Kaylie's form remained as still and silent as stone.

"Archer!" Amy cried out. "Kaylie won't wake up!"

Coma.

Archer had heard the word before. Once, his mother had an adverse reaction to a cancer treatment. She'd slipped into a coma for a few long days. It was a terrifying thing. But somehow, seeing Kaylie like this was worse. Far worse.

The trauma doctors and pediatric surgeons could find no reason for the coma, no other symptoms. The coma just was. But Archer knew why. He hunched over in the waiting room, buried his head in his hands, and the tears drained out.

He absently felt Amy's hand patting his back and Mrs. Pitsitakas's steadier hand on his shoulder.

"No, no, no," he muttered. This couldn't be happening. Kaylie was trapped in the Dream. She'd stayed beyond her Hour of Reckoning, and now, like Rigby's Uncle Scoville, she was reduced to a comatose prisoner.

"I tried, Kaylie," Archer whispered, holding her small hand through the hospital bed rail. "I tried . . . but I just couldn't fall asleep. I couldn't come look for you. I'm sorry . . . so sorry."

The tears on his cheek dried, almost as if they'd flash-boiled into vapors. Archer's breath quickened. He let go of Kaylie's hand and felt the heat of rage surging up within. He reached into his coat pocket and withdrew the summoning feather. He tossed it in the air and watched absently as a bluish glow slowly bordered the hospital room door.

Then Master Gabriel materialized.

"I'm going to kill him!" Archer hissed.

"Calm yourself, Dreamtreader!" Master Gabriel thundered often like this, and when he thundered, his Incandescent Armor flashed like lightning. "Rigby may not be to blame here."

"But it's Kaylie!" Archer railed, his voice high and desperate. "She's just eight. Eight! Look at her!"

Master Gabriel moved to her bedside. Archer watched his mentor's face carefully, saw him swallow deeply, saw his eyebrows loosen, and the slight tremble in his lower lip. But, in a blink, the Master Dreamtreader's expression turned stony once more.

"My sister," Archer whispered. "My kid sister, and now she's trapped in the Dream, forever."

"Not forever, Archer," Master Gabriel replied quietly.

"Oh, great. So she's trapped until her physical body dies! That's no comfort. Rigby's got to pay."

"There is a broad and treacherous difference between justice and revenge, Archer. Do not tread in that gulf."

Archer paced the guest room. "But Kaylie? She's just a little girl."

"Archer, know this," Gabriel said. "She had only trained for a short while, but she isn't just some little girl. She is a full-fledged Dreamtreader and one of the most powerful in a dozen generations."

"It didn't keep her from missing the Stroke of Reckoning," Archer said somberly.

"No," Master Gabriel said, "you are right. That she did miss the bell toll is not in doubt, but who caused her to miss it very much is. You will need to Dreamtread again tonight. You will need to search."

"Wait, I can't go back," Archer said, the pitch of his voice growing brittle and frantic. "I've been two nights already. The Nine Laws—I can't go. No, no, that was the night before last. I'm confused. It's getting so hard . . . I can't keep all this straight."

"Yes, you can," Master Gabriel said, his voice full of steel. "You can keep this straight. You must."

"But with my regular duties? The Dream nearing a rift? Patch up the breaches, find the Shadow Key, find Kaylie—how can I do all that?"

"You will have Nick to help you," Master Gabriel said.

"He's good," Archer said. "I'm just not sure if the two of us together can handle this."

"You are Dreamtreaders, Archer. You and Nick are gifted beyond reckoning and skilled. And now, unfortunately, there is no one more motivated than you."

"I'm not sure what I'll do," Archer said. "I mean, if I find whoever's responsible, this anger inside . . . I'm worried I'll do something I'll be sorry for after."

"We do not know yet who is responsible," Master Gabriel countered. "But when we do, we will pursue justice."

"What kind of justice?"

"Archer Percival Keaton, you leave that to me." The Incandescent Armor flared suddenly. There was a sharp crack of thunder, and Master Gabriel was gone.

Archer sat down across from Buster at the Pitsitakas' kitchen table. Buster didn't seem to notice. He didn't flinch. He had a thousand-mile stare. Archer wanted to join him, to disconnect from it all. How nice it would be to just go on vacation mentally and leave it all behind. But while Archer knew it was natural to feel that way, he also knew it would be intensely selfish for him to take that way out. People were counting on him. Starting with the person in front of him.

"It won't always feel like this," Archer said quietly.

Buster said nothing. His gaze was still far away.

"What I mean is, right now, it hurts. It hurts bad, and it feels like it's never going to get better. It seems like nothing will ever feel good again."

Buster blinked. His eyes changed. He wasn't making eye contact, but he was there, in the moment.

"I feel it too, Buster," Archer went on. "Tragedy is hunting our family at every turn. First Mom dies of cancer. Then Dad kind of breaks down. You get a concussion. Dad disappears. Kaylie goes into a coma. It's too much. We're just kids. We shouldn't have to deal with this kind of stuff. Sometimes, I just want to shout at the sky, 'Enough!'"

Archer's outburst startled Buster, and the two made eye contact at last. Archer could see it in his eyes. Buster was right there with him now. "Thing is, Buster," he said, "shouting at the sky doesn't make sense. It's not God's fault all this has happened. There's evil in this world, and evil's gonna do what it always does. The question is, will the people God's put here—the ones who know what's right and have the strength to do something about it—will we climb out of our pits and fight?"

Buster's expression didn't change. His eyes remained riveted to his brother's eyes. And Archer saw Buster's hand slowly close into a fist.

"We need to fight it," Archer went on. "And we're going to. But it's going to take some faith. You gotta believe it's not always going to feel this bad; it's not always going to be this bad. Better times and better days are coming. You gotta trust that God put us here and let us endure all this for a reason. Do you hear me, bro? Do you?"

Buster nodded slowly. A tear rolled down his cheek. "I hear you," he whispered.

"Good," Archer said. "That's strength, Buster. Remember that. Faith equals power. And I'm going to need you to be strong. I'm going to need your help. See, I think I know who took Dad. I think I know how to help Dad and Kaylie."

Buster's eyes grew huge. "Dude, you need to tell the cops," he said.

"It's not something the police can help with, Buster," Archer said. "I can't explain it all right now, but I'm going to find them, Buster. I'm going to get Dad and Kaylie back . . . somehow. And while I'm fighting that fight, I need you to pray. Pray like you're trying to beat down the gates of heaven with your fists. Tell God everything you feel and everything we need to beat down the evil that's come after our family."

"Bro," Buster said, his voice gaining strength. "You mean, I can fight this . . . by praying?"

Archer nodded. "You probably don't remember, but Mom always prayed for us at bedtime. She thought I was sleeping, but I heard her. She always asked God to make us tender warriors, to have caring hearts but the ferocity to protect the weak and fight for what's right."

"Mom . . . prayed that . . . for us?"

Archer nodded.

Buster blinked back tears and said, "That's righteous."

"Yes, it is," Archer said. He turned. Out of the corner of his eye, he saw Amy pass by the kitchen on the way to the den. "I'll be back in a minute, Buster. Maybe we'll have something to eat. Okay?"

"Yeah, 'kay," Buster said. "I got you."

Archer couldn't help but be encouraged by his brother. He gave him a very brotherly fist bump and headed for the den.

He found Amy sitting on the hearth by a guttering fire in the fireplace.

"I didn't want to interrupt you," she said. "It looked serious, yep."

"It was, but I wanted to talk to you, Amy."

"About Kaylie?"

"Yes. Is there anything you remember, Amy?" Archer asked. "Anything at all? You were with Kaylie when she fell asleep. Did she say anything?"

"Before she went to sleep?" Amy clarified. "No, she didn't say anything. But . . . she woke me up once. She was talking in her sleep. I didn't understand much of what she said. She sounded angry, like she was threatening someone. Then she was quiet for a long time. But just as I was drifting off to sleep, I think I heard Kaylie say something about the library. But the rest was kind of mumbled. She kept saying 'Scat' or 'scratch' or something. Does that mean anything to you?"

Archer got chills. "Yes, it does," he said. "I know where to start looking."

WAYNE THOMAS BATSON

Archer surfed down the gray stair. The Sages of Garnet's Library were not happy about it. Not even the least little bit. They hissed and shushed Archer relentlessly. He ignored that and raced down the corkscrew, using his short surfboard to navigate the hairpin turns. The ruckus was horrendous, a staccato *Smack! Smack! Smack!* as the back end of the surfboard hit every other step.

Their normal warnings ignored, the Sages went to their plan B: shrieking at Archer from all directions, shriveled hands opening and closing like claws. Archer couldn't ignore that. He ducked and swerved as best he could, avoiding injury until one of the Sages hit him from behind.

Like many experiences in the Dream, the attack was surreal. Archer saw the Sage fly just overhead seconds before he felt the delayed pain of its strike. It was that fast. Archer winced and spun around to face his attacker.

Of all the Sages Archer had seen, this was the most demented-looking apparition: gray and black shreds of what once had been a hooded cloak, nasty pale skin, sunken eyes, and a ghastly, "next time I'll eat you" grin.

Archer felt cool air from the rip in the back of his leather duster. The pain hit as if someone had fired up three identical blowtorches and run them across his left shoulder blade. Archer yelled out to no avail.

The Sage seemed to think that was hysterically funny. Archer heard the thing's maniacal laughter as it wheeled around and prepared for another pass at Archer.

Still wincing from the slow-healing wound, Archer kept one eye on the Sage and one on the gray stair. He wasn't close to the bottom yet. Halfway, if that. The Sage was inbound with a vengeance, still laughing and accelerating to hit Archer on his next turn.

The Dreamtreader was more prepared this time. He will-summoned a Louisville Slugger, slammed on the surfboard's air brakes, and broke the bat on the Sage's mottled skull. The ghostly creature careened down the stairs in front of Archer, shrieking and spitting as it went.

Archer gave his surfboard a shove and raced down the stairs after it. He turned the corner and was shocked to find the Sage on its feet, poised to attack. And now, the creature had an enormous scythe.

Okay, Archer thought, *so how'd the Sage get a big old grim reaper weapon?*

Archer wasn't about to stop and ask. In fact, he'd just about had enough of this Sage and all his buddies. They were wasting Archer's time. And Archer was in no mood to be delayed.

The scythe swishing wildly in front of it, the Sage leaped into the air and rushed Archer like a sudden storm. The Dreamtreader called up his will, adding an extra measure to make sure his actions were final, and a bank of laser-guided sidewinder missiles appeared at his elbow. Archer fired once, twice, and a third time, using his will-summoned laser to direct the missiles at the incoming Sage.

The first explosion burst directly in front of the Sage. The blast sent the scythe flipping from its hands and froze the enraged creature in midair. The second and third sidewinders never had a chance to reach their mark. With a shriek, the Sage whipped out of the hall as fast as it could, the two missiles chasing after it. Two distant explosions rocked dust into the air.

Archer turned in a slow circle, and the missile launcher turned with him. The other Sages, closing on Archer like a noose, seemed to skid in the air. They halted immediately and retreated, soaring to the vaulted heights of the Sanctum.

Archer had no more trouble from the Sages on that visit. He arrived at the bottom of the gray stair in peace. After passing through the strange curtain, he found himself bathed in suffocating shadows. But some sixty yards ahead, a conical beacon of light shown down from above, illuminating the Inner Sanctum, the vault door thrown open and its dark entrance gaping.

Archer approached cautiously. When he and Nick came to the Inner Sanctum before, they hadn't seen a single Scath. But maybe Kaylie had come down here. Maybe she'd had a very different experience. For all Archer knew, the whole horde of Scath might be in the vault waiting for him, and he didn't want to be caught off guard. "Kaylie!" he whispered urgently. "Kaylie, are you here?"

"No, she is not," came a voice from the opening in the floor.

Archer froze. He heard footsteps climbing the Inner Sanctum stairs. A black top hat appeared, seated snugly on a tangle of drift-wood-brown hair, then long, knifing sideburns, arched brows, eyes like brown embers, and a slanted smile that somehow communicated both vast intelligence and vast arrogance. Feature by feature, Rigby Thames rose up from the steps.

Archer summoned his flaming sword, and blue fire whooshed up the length of its blade.

"Now, is that any way to treat a friend?" Rigby asked.

"Where is she, Rigby?" Archer demanded. "What have you done with Kaylie?"

"And just what do you fancy you'll do with that sword?" Rigby asked. "You can't kill me."

"I don't know about that," Archer said. "You and your dream company have done such damage to the Dream fabric, things aren't as certain as they used to be."

"Hogwash!"

"No, I've seen things happening. I missed my Stroke of Reckoning by a few seconds, but nothing happened to me."

"So? We all stretch things a bit. I know I have."

"That's just it, Rigby," Archer said. "You don't stretch laws. You know science. It doesn't work that way. The Rift is near. The fabric is fraying. There's a frozen electricity climbing up from the horizon. Even the creatures here are creating now."

Rigby teetered on the top step. "What do you mean, Keaton?"

"You haven't seen it?" Archer barked out a laugh. "The creatures in the Dream are creating just like us. They're becoming lucid."

"You're a fool, Keaton," Rigby said. "These creatures, they're figments of people's sleeping imaginations. They do what they do, but they cannot create from nothing."

"Believe what you want," Archer said. "But I've seen enough lately to wonder if my sword might do more damage than you think. And I'm willing to test my hypothesis."

"Sure, test your hypothesis," Rigby said. "And if it works for you, you'll never get Kaylie back."

The flame on Archer's sword spluttered and went out. "There's . . . there's no way to get her back," he said. "She's trapped now, right? She's trapped forever."

"Trapped like my Uncle Scovy?" Rigby said, making his voice a feigned whimper. "Oh, no, whatever will you do? Poor little Kaylie."

Archer felt the blood rush to his face. His sword blazed with new azure fire. "Don't push me," he growled. "Tell me what you know. Tell me everything."

Rigby laughed. Tiny red fingerlings of lightning coursed down his forearms and hands. Similar spider veins of red appeared momentarily around his eyes.

Archer rocked on his heels. "What was—"

"If I were to tell you everything I know," Rigby said, "we'd be here for a hundred years. But I will tell you this: Uncle Scovy and your sweet Kaylie are not trapped forever. They can return."

"How?"

"It's quite simple, really," Rigby said. "Amazing what you'll learn from one of these." Rigby held up a book.

"Is that . . ."

"One of the Masters' Bindings?" Rigby finished and grinned. "Why yes, yes, it is."

"You're the fool, Rigby," Archer said warily. "Those books aren't made for us, not even for Dreamtreaders. They'll change you . . . turn you into something . . . something monstrous."

"Is that what your Masters told you?" he asked. "Not surprising. The truth is, Keaton, reading these books *will* change you. They *will* turn you into *something* . . . they'll turn you into a Master."

Archer stepped toward Rigby and said, "If that's what you think, you're crazier than I ever imagined."

"*Crazy* is such an unenlightened term," Rigby said. I guess you prefer to stay unenlightened, then? A shame for Kaylie."

"Stop!" Archer commanded. "Don't use my sister as a bargaining chip. Say what you want to say or don't. I am a Dreamtreader. I already know all I need to know about the Dream."

"Really?" Rigby asked. He doffed his top hat, rolled it down his arm to his hand, and then back up to land perfectly on his head. "Well, depart then. But before you go, know that there is only one way Kaylie will ever consciously return to the Waking World."

"What is it?" Archer said. "Spit it out."

"All you have to do," Rigby said, "is stop weaving up the breaches."

Archer squinted. "But that would cause a—"

"A Rift," Rigby said, "precisely. If we induce a Rift, the Dream fabric and the Waking World will become enmeshed. Uncle Scovy and Kaylie will be free to move between. You see, Keaton, this is what I've been after all along. And now, it seems we have similar motivations."

"I'm a Dreamtreader," Archer said. "I won't let a Rift happen."

"Even at the loss of your sister?"

Archer could barely force out the words. They caught in his throat and tasted acidic on his tongue. "I love Kaylie, but . . . even . . . even for her, I cannot."

"You can't have it both ways," Rigby said. "Either you let a Rift form and have your sister back, or you honor your so-called Creeds and leave your sister to rot. What a struggle it is for you. I marvel at that. Fortunately, I have made the hard choice all the more easy for you. I've destroyed the Shadow Key. I tossed it into the raging furnace of Xander's Fortune. You'll never close the Inner Sanctum, and the Scath will shred the Dream fabric. You'll have Kaylie back before you know it."

DREAMTREADER'S CREED, CONCEPTUS 9

T he Dream is a vast triangle of territory, divided into three
districts: Forms, Pattern, and Verse.

You will find that each of the three districts is in constant
motion, prone to great changes and mysteries. But you shall
also find features that endure for so long that generations of
Dreamtreaders will find them ages after you are gone.

Forms, the most vigorous District, is the largest span of the
three. The markets of Kardan have always been and will always
be. Direton is always dangerous, and Number 6 Rue de la Morte
seems to weather even the worst of storms.

Pattern is the most static of the three. Change comes there
little. Only the experienced Dreamtreader should dare to shepherd
this place, for there are ancient things there: ancient and danger—
ous. Tread not lightly the moors of Archaia within Pattern. There
the mist gathers, so beware.

Verse is the most beautiful of the three, vast and changing,
stunning to behold and often deadly. It is said that in view only,

that Verse is what leaves the Waking Mind craving the Ethereal Realm, and perhaps that is so. If true, then Verse is also the Waking Mind's thorn, reminding the dreamer with painful clarity that he is yet far from the Ethereal.

TWENTY

DEMANDS

"YOU LUNATIC!" ARCHER CRIED OUT. FLAMING SWORD held high, he leaped at Rigby, plummeting like an azure fire comet.

KERRANG!

Archer's sword met Rigby's raven cane, now crackling with spiders of red lightning. "I can play this game as well as any Dreamtreader," Rigby said, the sarcasm especially thick and dripping on the title.

Momentarily stunned, Archer fell backward, but he recovered, turning the fall into a somersault. He lunged forward with a thrust. Rigby parried, leaping sideways and swiping his cane high to low. Archer whirled and struck low, but again, Rigby's weapon met his.

Archer rolled backward and came back to his feet. He yelled in anger. "You'd sell out your entire world? For what? Money? Fame? What, Rigby?"

"What's wrong with love?" Rigby asked.

Archer's mouth closed with a snap.

"You have no idea how important Uncle Scovy is to me," Rigby said. "He was the first one to believe in me, to see my genius for what it was. He was a father to me, a mentor. All his hard work, all his research, he didn't deserve to be locked up, trapped forever. No one does. Certainly not a little girl like Kaylie."

Rigby's daggers of conviction struck home. Archer knew what it was like to lose a parent. When his mother withered away from cancer, it had torn out a piece of his heart. Now, his father was gone, taken away in the middle of the night. And Kaylie. Doomed to spend the rest of her life in the Waking World, hooked up to a battery of machines. It wasn't fair.

No, Archer thought, *it's not fair*. He hovered on the edge of explosion. "You did it, Rigby!" he screamed. "All of it. You released the Scath, you commanded them to take my father, and you trapped Kaylie!"

"I can't take credit for everything," Rigby said with a twirl of his cane.

"I want them all back," Archer said. "Give them back to me, Rigby!"

"I already have," Rigby said, his eyes flaring red. "When the world's merge, it'll all be better."

Archer gritted his teeth. He wanted to believe that. But he shook his head. "No," he said, "even if we save the ones we love, we can't just let the world burn."

"That's the trouble with you Dreamtreaders," he said. "You always assume you know how things should be. You'd really let little Kaylie rot, would you? That's so cruel, even for you, Keaton."

"It's not like that," Archer shot back. "I love Kaylie, I—"

"Apparently, not enough to save her."

"How can you justify one life while throwing away thousands, maybe millions of others?"

"And how can you possibly believe that? How do you know the two worlds weren't meant to become one?"

"They don't become one!" Archer shouted, exasperated. "They

destroy each other! Do you have any idea what will happen? People won't know dream from reality. People will die by the millions. There'll be chaos—"

"Freedom, you mean," Rigby said. "Who's to say, Keaton? I mean really, who's to say mankind wasn't meant to live, free to dream?"

"Dreamtreaders say so," Archer said, but his words lacked conviction. "Dreamtreaders are the caretakers of it all. We didn't make the rules. We just follow them."

"Follow them blindly," Rigby muttered.

"I'm not the blind one here!" Archer shot back. "You call it freedom, but how can you not see that some freedoms can be abused? Some choices should never be made!"

"So says the Dreamtreader," Rigby grunted, holding his raven cane and studying the weapon. "Easy to say such things when you have the power. But not anymore, not just you. There's really only one question left to answer. Do you know it?"

"Rigby, you've got this all wrong," Archer said. "It's not about keeping the power or putting anyone down. This is about safety. It's—"

"I'll take that as a no," Rigby said, tilting his cane. "I'll tell you, anyway. The only pressing question is: what color should the flame on my cane be? I was thinking green." Immediately, green fire leaped up Rigby's blade. "Hmmm. Not sure that's the right color for a villain. I am the villain, aren't I, Keaton?"

"Of course, you're the villain," Archer growled, calling up buckets of his will. "You don't care who gets hurt, who dies, as long as you get your way."

"Perhaps, purple," Rigby muttered as if Archer weren't even in the room. The green flame winked out, replaced a second later by raging purple fire. "I could just as easily call you the villain; you know that, Keaton? It's all about creeds and rules with you. No room for love.

No room for freedom. That sounds like a villain to me." He paused, considering his fiery weapon. "Hmmm, no. Why fight it? I think I like being the villain. And . . . I know it's cliché, but . . . let's go with red!"

Again, the crimson electrical charges flickered on the cane, but with a roar, red fire engulfed Rigby's weapon as he vaulted up to the height of the arched chamber and dropped toward Archer. The red and blue flame met and met again, causing a strange swirl of color to flash around the two combatants. They moved back and forth across the chamber floor, ducking and dodging, leaping the doorway to the Sanctum's vault and careening around the room.

After an exhausting exchange of strikes and counters, Archer found himself panting and frustrated. Forty feet away, Rigby crouched.

"This is rather pointless," Rigby said. "Don't you think?"

"You've got to be stopped," Archer muttered.

Rigby stood up. When he tossed his raven cane into the air, it vanished in a streak of red flame. "See, now, that's what I'm trying to explain, Keaton. I cannot be stopped. What's done is done. The Scath are free and working for me, the Shadow Key is destroyed, Dream Inc. thrives, and the breaches are multiplying far beyond your ability to weave them up." Rigby shook his head. "You don't even know the half of it. A Rift is inevitable, Keaton. Get over it."

"I'm a Dreamtreader," Archer said. "I can't get over it."

"Yeah, well, that may be," Rigby said. "But don't you think it's time you put your family first? I mean, just this once? Where's your father? Where's Kaylie? And poor Buster back at home . . . all alone."

The sound that burst from Archer's lungs was primal and ferocious and, in some distant part of his consciousness, he was frightened to hear that sound and to know that it came from himself. Terror and rage propelled Archer forward. He crossed the forty yards in a blink, raised his sword . . . and crashed hard into a real brick wall.

Archer crumbled to the ground. He was already healing from the collision when Rigby made the brick wall vanish. "See there, Keaton," he said. "It does you no good. You summon a sword; I summon my cane. You charge; I make a wall. You create a tank to blast through the wall, I'll make a bomber to blow up your tank. Back and forth we'll go until one of us finally—finally—gets too tired to fight. And by the look of things, that's going to be you, Keaton. In the end, your family suffers. All these rules you follow, all these codes, and what really matters . . . your family, the people who love you . . . will suffer. You can't win."

"I beg to differ, ya bloomin' ankle biter."

The boomerang hit the back of Rigby's head and sent him sprawling gracelessly, face-first, to the floor.

"Seems you've underestimated the Dreamtreaders, mate," Nick Bushman said, striding out of the shadows. "We don't work alone."

Rigby lifted his head from the stone and shook away the cobwebs. He rolled over onto his back just in time to see a swarm of boomerangs streaking his way from all angles. Rigby called up a metallic dome and used it as a shield. The boomerangs clanged and clattered off, but the moment Rigby lifted his shell, a single boomerang took him in the jaw.

"I've got heaps of them," Nick said. "Now, be good, and tell Archer here what he wants to know, or I'll be forced to let the boys get busy again."

Rigby wiped a trickle of blood from his chin and sneered. He made the shield shell vanish and clambered back to his feet. "You're new at this, aren't you?" Rigby asked. "A bit of beginner's luck, that's all."

Archer leaped to his feet and came at Rigby. The Lucid Walker raised his hands only to find himself handcuffed with heavy, dark metal manacles.

"You don't have beginner's luck, Keaton" Rigby said, smiling. "Whatever kind you had has run out."

A strange rope appeared, dangling down from somewhere unseen far overhead. Even with his cuffed wrists, Rigby reached above his head and gave the rope a sharp pull.

A distant bell tolled. Once. Twice. All the way to six.

Howls. Howls echoed across the landscape.

"Hounds!" Archer exclaimed.

"Sounds like heaps of 'em," Nick said. "Not far away."

"Call them off, Rigby—!" But the words died on Archer's lips. The handcuffs Archer had summoned lay empty on the floor.

Rigby was gone.

TWENTY-ONE

POWERS

"I'm TELLING YOU, WE HAVE TO FIND HER!" RIGBY YELLED, pacing the throne room of Number 6 Rue de la Morte. "This can't wait."

"Isn't it enough that she's trapped here?" Kara asked. She stood in front of a body-length mirror on the far side of the chamber.

"You have no idea the kind of power she wields," Rigby said. "She could tip the balance back the other way."

Kara crossed her arms and frowned at her own reflection. "She's just a little kid, Rigby."

"A once-in-a-lifetime brilliant little kid," Rigby growled. He sank low into the dark chair.

"Twice," Kara said. "You mean twice-in-a-lifetime, right? Your uncle is that smart."

"Right, fine. Yes, twice."

"But what's the urgency?" Kara asked, spinning on her heel. "She's here in the Dream. She's contained."

"Are you even listening?" Rigby asked, spluttering mad. "She

225

is not contained. In fact, being stuck in the Dream amplifies her power here."

Kara abruptly went still. "You haven't mentioned that before. How . . . could being stuck here amplify her abilities?"

"Again, like my uncle." Rigby pounded his fist on the armrest. "He didn't earn the Lurker nickname for nothing. Since being trapped here, he's become savagely powerful."

"But why?"

"Brain physiology," Rigby replied. "When the brain no longer needs to function in the Waking World, it devotes more of its resources to the subconscious. New neural pathways open up. You become beastly strong."

"And Kaylie was already strong," Kara thought out loud.

"You see what I mean, then," Rigby said. "Now . . . I've led Keaton and his Aussie pal to believe I have her, but if they find her first, it could ruin everything."

"What will you do?" Kara asked.

"What?"

"If you find Kaylie," Kara said, "what will you do with her?"

"I don't know," Rigby said. "I'm not even certain the two of us together could hold her here."

The throne room fell into dreadful silence. Rigby leaned forward in the black seat and became very still. Kara waited for him to say more, but he sat, motionless as a cemetery. His eyes even had that faraway look like the blank-eyed statues, the monuments to the dead.

It was Kara's turn to pace. She paced until she heard her bell toll nine, and a flash of red light near the throne took her attention. "What was that?" she asked.

Rigby didn't answer right away. He was staring at his own right hand. Tiny spidery pulses of crimson electricity jittered along his forearm, his wrist, and even to his fingertips.

"Rigby?"

He blinked and looked up. "I'm sorry," he said. "What?"

"What was that?" Kara asked. "I've never seen you do that before."

"Nothing," he said. "Just a little trick I learned from the Masters' Bindings."

Kara crossed her arms again. "I don't like it," she said.

"Well, I'm sorry," Rigby said. "Sorry that it troubles you. I can control it mostly, but . . . sometimes, when I'm deep in thought, it just happens."

"What were you thinking about just now?" Kara probed. "You seemed out there . . . like, just gone."

"I was thinking there might be another way to neutralize Kaylie."

Kara squinted. "What do you mean?"

Rigby gave a dismissive wave of his hand. "Something outside of the Dream might actually be better."

"I don't think—"

"I hope I'm not interrupting something. But Number 6 has no doorbell for me to ring. And it shouldn't wait . . . this news I bring."

In the dark archway, two glistening star-point eyes appeared.

"What's he doing here?" Kara asked.

Rigby shrugged. It was not an expected visit. *I hope he hasn't come to collect,* he thought. *I'm not ready for that yet.* "What is it, then?" Rigby demanded. "What's this news?"

"The tidings I bear are sure to be a thrill," Bezeal said, shuffling into the throne room. His eyes were brighter than usual and somehow eager. "It just couldn't wait for parchment, pen, and quill. For Kaylie, the enemy, lies in the sure grip of Scoville."

"What?" Rigby exclaimed. "Are you certain?"

The merchant's Cheshire Cat grin appeared. He nodded.

"Well," Rigby said, clapping his hands. "Problem solved. Now, there's nothing Keaton can do. I hold all the cards."

Kara walked slowly back to the mirror. She saw the glint in her own eye as she thought, *All the cards . . . except one.*

Archer steered his longboard toward a less violent Intrusion wave, one headed east, to get a better look at the Forms District. He called up his will to engage Visis Nocturne. The breaches were raging. He shut off the will-draining vision and gazed out to the horizon. The ice-fire was spreading upward. It reminded Archer of the front windshield of the family car a few years back. A tiny rock had flown up from the road and nicked the glass. For weeks, all that showed from the rock was that tiny little nick. But then, over time, the crack blossomed into meandering streaks until the windshield was so shot through with cracks that it needed to be replaced.

"This is too much," Archer muttered, kick-turning onto another Intrusion wave. "It's like no matter what we do, the Rift is going to happen anyway." The wave was just forming, but Archer had seen its type before. The Dream matter behind it was surging in from several directions, feeding a more or less innocent-looking wave, but it would rise up, and soon.

Archer felt the sudden altitude forming beneath his board. It was curling now, and he took every bit of its height and speed, using it to propel himself forward as fast as he could go.

"Archer!"

The voice was so urgent, so sudden, that Archer lost his balance. The board got away from him, and he went headfirst into the

Intrusion. The violence of the turbulent Dream wave threw Archer end over end, bouncing him roughly from image to image. Snippets of dreams, hundreds and hundreds of dreams, came raging to Archer's thoughts, drowning his rational thought in a chaotic mishmash of other people's subconscious.

Archer found himself tumbling down a long hallway in a colonial country home. Tall windows rose up on either side. Suddenly, at the end of the hall, a young girl appeared, screaming. Her screams echoed into something visible—a bouncing spiderlike thing with hollow red eyes. Thorny limbs took Archer by the shoulders and yanked him into a room where dozens of people were seated.

They were all dressed in black, and no one so much as turned to look at Archer. They all stared straight ahead. There was something there on a kind of stage or platform or . . .

The spider thing heaved Archer forward and flew past the people in their seats, racing forward toward an open casket.

"No!" Archer cried out, but it was no use. His trajectory was fixed, blasting toward the coffin. He fell into it, and all went black . . . until, at last, he broke the surface of the Intrusion surf.

It used a ton of mental will for Archer to pull himself up out of the muck and into the air, but he managed, clawing above the swelling Intrusions long enough to summon his surfboard.

"Snot rockets!" he muttered, resting safely on his board once more. He'd been riding Intrusion waves for a long time, but rarely had he wiped out like that.

His thoughts raced. *Who called me?*

"I did."

Archer was a little more ready this time. He didn't lose control. And this time, he recognized the voice. "Where have you been?" he asked. "I could have used your help, like, a hundred times."

"It is of no consequence where I have been," the Windmaiden replied. "Listen to me: there is a new Nightmare Lord."

"Rigby," Archer muttered. "Tell me something I don't know."

"He must be stopped, and soon," she said. "Everything depends on it."

"How?" Archer asked. "So many things have gone wrong that I don't even know where to start."

"Start with the Scath."

"That's a dead end," Archer replied. "Rigby's destroyed the Shadow Key."

"No!" the Windmaiden exclaimed. "He tried, but it still exists. I have seen it, down deep in the heart of Xander's Fortune. It is beyond my reach, lying on a ledge in the midst of electrical chaos."

"You can't get to it," Archer said. "But you think I could?"

"Perhaps," she said. "But I was thinking of someone more powerful . . ."

TWENTY-TWO

MASTER AND STUDENT

"SO NICE OF YOU DROP BY," THE LURKER SAID, SIPPING from a massive gray goblet. "It's a shame you won't be more agreeable. Throwing water balloons full of liquid explosives is no way to make friends."

In the corner of the chamber, a cramped dining hall filled with rigid chairs and an octagonal table, was a luminous cube . . . with Kaylie inside. "Rrrr, I don't want to be your friend!" she growled.

"Pity," the Lurker replied. He scratched at the wiry white hair that clumped in, around, and behind his ear. "I have'na got a clue as to why you'd be so obtuse."

"You have me trapped in this . . . this." Kaylie stretched her arms as wide as her elastic prison would let her. It surged with pulses of electrical color wherever she touched it. It was some kind of stretchy cube but made of something that pulsed with its own energy. "I don't even know what to call this thing, but I hate it."

"I hate it too," the Lurker said, eyes bulging. He smacked his lips and traded his goblet for a massive brownie. He nibbled at its corner and asked, "But what can I do? You went down in my subbasements;

you saw things. I can't set you free from my little *oubliette*—oh, sorry, that's French for a secure little prison—"

"I *know* what an oubliette is!"

"That's right," he said. "You would . . . being the precocious little Dreamtreader that you are. But, as I was saying, I don't think I can see a way t'set you free from the oubliette . . . unless . . ."

"Unless what?"

"That's the trouble with the youth of today," he said, taking a bigger bite of his brownie. He was a large man, broad of shoulder but strangely proportioned, even awkward. His jaws didn't seem to meet quite right, but he still managed to carve a hunk from the brownie. He chewed quietly for several seconds and then said, "Always in such a hurry. Fast food. Fast love. Fast living. You need t'learn t'savor life like I do."

Kaylie crossed her arms. "What did you mean? You might set me free, if what?"

"I don't want t'talk terms right now," he said. "I prefer t'have a civil meal first. Won't you put aside your haste for just a moment? Share a bite with me first, and then maybe we can make some sort of arrangement."

"Oooh," Kaylie grumbled, kicking at the wall of her oubliette. It glowed in the spot she'd struck but didn't flex more than an inch. "What good would any kind of arrangement do anyway? Everything's all messed up already. I missed my Stroke of Reckoning. I'm trapped here."

"Like me," the Lurker said. "Trapped away from home and family. You must be so very sad."

Kaylie screamed and lashed out with her will, throwing massive whirling bolts of destruction at the translucent membrane that contained her. But it didn't budge. Her willed energy dissipated in harmless puffs of smoke.

"You won't git out of the oubliette that way," he said calmly. He put down his brownie and leaned forward. His wispy white hair flowed around his head and face as if underwater and his eyes blazed. "You aren't the only genius in the room, you understand."

"It . . ." Kaylie growled, continuing to push and punch and stretch the oubliette. "It feels like being trapped in bubble gum."

The Lurker laughed quietly. "Bubble gum. That's cute. Far more complex than that, though. I've been here long enough to study the Dream fabric. Did you know it has mathematical properties? It does, of course. And, as you've demonstrated yourself, the Dream fabric is quite malleable. I've recently learned to create the Dream fabric equivalent to a Penrose triangle. Use your mind. Play with the oubliette all you want; you'll find it has no end. An infinite loop, and I am the only genius in the room smart enough to get you out."

Kaylie's face flushed angry red. She trembled furiously a moment. The tears came, fresh and hot, rolling down her cheeks and between her fingers, even dripping from her chin.

"Awww, this is too much for you," the Lurker said. "I know. I know. It really is, but don't worry. We can fix things."

"How?" she sobbed.

"First, dine with me," he said, sliding the platter of brownies toward Kaylie's side of the table.

She eyed the brownies hungrily. They were so dark and rich looking, almost totally black. "How can I . . . if I'm stuck in here?"

The Lurker grinned, yellowed teeth appearing for a moment. He nodded, and a small divot appeared on the surface of the oubliette. It enlarged, becoming an orange-sized hole in Kaylie's enclosure.

"I can reach through?" she asked, her hand hovering at the opening.

He nodded.

Kaylie took a brownie and eyed it suspiciously, as if, at any moment, the Lurker might make it disappear.

"No tricks," the Lurker said. "It's all yours."

Kaylie took a massive bite of the brownie and chewed thoughtfully while the Lurker looked on. He watched her swallow and said, "There now. I think we can be friends."

Kaylie nodded and took another bite. "Delicious," she said, though her words sounded like echoes from far away.

"We won't be needing the oubliette any longer," the Lurker said, gesturing his left hand in a circular motion. Kaylie's enclosure became awash with brighter colors, but threads began to pull away . . . spiraling round and round until the oubliette was threadbare and then . . . gone.

"You . . . you're letting me go?" Kaylie asked.

"Now that we've broken bread together, I see no reason to hold you back." He gestured at the platter of brownies. "Gort brownies are my favorite."

"I like them very much," Kaylie said. "Thank you."

"Oh, you're welcome," the Lurker said. "Of course, now you'll do whatever I ask, won't you, Kaylie?"

"Yes," she said. "I will serve only you."

"Good," the Lurker said. "First, forget what you saw in my subbasement. And then I need your help with something."

"What?"

"My nephew, I'm afraid, has made a very foolish mistake. I need you to fix it."

When Archer awoke, he locked the Pitsitakas' guest room door and went straight to his suitcase. He removed the summoning feather and tossed it into the air.

Master Gabriel appeared in a flash. No unusual clothing. No Incandescent Armor. Just a plain brown robe.

"I've never seen you wear that before," Archer mumbled.

"No . . . I rarely need it. It is a Restoration Robe. I wear it when I am very weary. Now, what have you to report? What of the Shadow Key?"

"Rigby told me he threw it into the volcano in Xander's Fortune."

"It should have been named Xander's Folly," Master Gabriel said, his shoulders slumping. "That turbulent, volcanic mount. If Rigby threw the Shadow Key into the pit, it's gone. We will have to find some other way to neutralize the Scath."

"The key didn't burn up," Archer said. "It landed on a ledge just above the destructive . . . lava or whatever it is."

"Who told you of this? Bezeal? I suspect he would like nothing more than to have the remaining two Dreamtreaders clambering the precarious edges of Xander's Fortune."

"The Windmaiden."

"Her." Master Gabriel stiffened and paced the room. His robe made warbling *shoosh* sounds with each step. "The woman's voice you've heard but seldomly?"

"Yes," Archer replied. "She's helped me before, saved my skin more than once."

"But . . . you have never met her? Never seen her?"

Archer shook his head. "No . . . I haven't. But she's never steered me wrong before."

Master Gabriel pulled at the fringes of his beard. "What interest does she have in the Shadow Key?"

"She doesn't want the Scath loose either. She doesn't want the Dream fabric to fail."

"She seems to have extraordinary power," Master Gabriel said. "Why doesn't she simply retrieve the key herself?"

"She told me her power isn't enough for that. She said the forces inside Xander's Fortune would unmake her."

"She's likely right," Master Gabriel said. "It would unmake you, also. Tell me, Archer, have you seen anything else like Xander's Fortune in the three districts of the Dream?"

"No."

"Do you know what that mountain is?"

"I know the stories about the lightning stone . . . the stairway, but no, I guess I don't really know what it is."

"The later creeds speak of it, but, even so, it is complex." Master Gabriel wandered around the guest room, then paused and gestured to an oil painting of the seashore. "What do you see here?"

"The beach."

"Yes, yes, the ocean and the sand. It is beautiful, part of creation. But you realize that, over time, the wind and the rain are eroding that beach, eating away at it."

"Erosion, right," Archer said. "Last year this weird line of storms called a *derecho* came blasting through. It tore up the Ocean City shore so badly they needed to dredge up more sand."

"Quite right," Master Gabriel replied. "The worse the storms, over time, the worse the damage. The Dream has a similar phenomenon. Every time breaches form and the Dream fabric frays, there are by-products—matter from the Waking World leaks in while Dream matter leaks out. That matter is corrupted."

"Okay, that makes sense. What does it have to do with Xander's Fortune?"

"The storms in the Dream—the massive, never-ending tempests that cause the crimson vortices you ride into the Dream—those storms act as a kind of living filter. They collect any stray matter that leaked in from the Waking World, what we call Temporal matter, and funnel it up into the heart of the storm."

"The lightning," Archer said. "Oh, oh, I get it. The Temporal matter causes the lightning that set off the chain reaction in Xander's Fortune."

"Not quite," Master Gabriel corrected. "The Temporal matter doesn't cause the lightning. It is the lightning. That's how dangerous it is. And that cauldron is stewing with a thousand centuries of that power."

Archer warded off a wave of shivers. "But if the Shadow Key is there, don't we have to try? The Windmaiden said that someone with enough power could possibly—"

"Possibly get you killed," Master Gabriel said. "Or worse. Hear me on this, Archer. Neither you nor Nick have the kind of power to attempt Xander's Fortune."

Archer crossed his arms and stared at the bedroom window and the darkness beyond.

"I have seen that look before, Archer," Master Gabriel said.

Archer shook his head, tentatively at first, but then with more and more conviction. "No," he said, "I won't go to Xander's Fortune. I confess I am tempted, but I trust your wisdom."

Master Gabriel eyed the young Dreamtreader shrewdly. "I feel as though you have something else in mind."

"Well, actually I was thinking that *you* could get the Shadow Key."

Master Gabriel stepped backward, bumping the desk and rattling the lamp. "I told you before, Archer," he said, "I cannot intervene in this way."

"I remember what you said," Archer replied. "But I thought, well . . . I thought since you are the keeper of the Master's Keys now that maybe you could go get the one key that's missing. No one has power like you have."

The master Dreamtreader sighed but didn't seem angry. But the wrinkles and creases on his careworn face seemed to deepen. "Archer, I would help . . . if I could," he said. "But even if my duties permitted me, I could not do this thing."

"Why?"

"If a Master draws near to that place, the presence of his power would cause Xander's Fortune to erupt. It would be as if a Rift formed, and there would be chaos. I would never get to the Shadow Key."

Archer shook his head. "So, we just leave the key there?"

Master Gabriel stared at the floor. Archer had never seen him look so worn down. "There is one who might attempt it," he whispered.

"Kaylie?"

Master Gabriel looked up, eyes dreadfully wide. "You know?"

Archer nodded. "The Windmaiden suggested Kaylie might be able to do it. Could she?"

"Have you found her, Archer?" Master Gabriel asked. "Do you know who caused Kaylie to miss her Stroke of Reckoning?"

"It's Rigby's fault," Archer said, anger simmering on each syllable. "I think he has her locked up somewhere. And Rigby's gotten stronger, some kind of red electricity stuff."

"He's been reading the *Masters' Bindings*," Master Gabriel said. "Poor fool. He doesn't understand the power he's playing with. And Kaylie? Oh, I am so very sorry, Archer." When he spoke, his other-worldly glow seemed to dim. "I should never have pushed her so hard. She just wasn't ready."

Stunned, Archer took a tentative step closer. "Last year, after what happened to Duncan and Mesmeera, you told me something about tragedies. You said, 'Poor choices aside, there is a very real enemy who lives to cause nightmares. He is the root.'"

Gabriel seemed to inflate a little, seemed to glow a little brighter. "But, Archer, that enemy is not to blame. He is no more."

"There's a new Nightmare Lord, remember?" Archer said. "Maybe not as full-fledged and ancient as the original, but Rigby Thames is making up for it with pure hate. It's his fault the Inner Sanctum's vault is stuck open. It's his fault the breaches are multiplying. His fault that people I care about are being taken, and his fault that Kaylie missed her deadline. His, not yours."

Master Gabriel put a hand on Archer's shoulder. "Thank you, Archer," he said. The room became brighter once more as the master Dreamtreader's Incandescent Armor appeared in place of the plain robe. "You give mercy when you could spite. And your hard-won wisdom will not abandon you."

Archer smiled, but it was forced, and it occurred to him quickly that it was the same sort of smile his father had barely managed all these years after the death of his wife. "What do we do now?" Archer asked.

"We do not despair," Gabriel said, "for that is a tool of nightmare. We are Dreamtreaders, and we deal in hope. Your kindness provides me some relief from stifling guilt. At the very least, I can return the favor by reminding you of our hope and our purpose."

"Our purpose?" Archer echoed. "You mean, what the Creeds say?"

Gabriel nodded. "Archer, listen to me. There's a very real danger that a Dreamtreader will dutifully do his—or her—job night after night, and do it well and yet lose sight of why."

"I haven't lost track of why, Master Gabriel. I was born with this ability, the ability to do things in dreams, things that help people. That's why I do it."

"That is part of it, Archer," Master Gabriel said. "But you do not Dreamtread simply because you can. There are many around the world who can or could, but many are unwilling to answer the call. Make no mistake, Archer; you have been called to this journey to fulfill the Creeds and turn aside darkness so that mankind may have hope and truth. There is a third realm, you know."

"The Ethereal," Archer whispered.

Master Gabriel's increased glow lit up the room. "Yes, yes, the Ethereal. It waits for mankind as a gift from the Maker of All Dreams, but mankind will not receive it without hope or without truth."

Archer flexed his neck and shoulders, feeling strangely empowered. "I guess I never thought about it that way before."

"Well, start thinking about it that way," Master Gabriel bristled. "Your world is adrift, losing its anchors one at a time over the years. But you, Archer Percival Keaton, are kind of a shepherd of the subconscious realm. You must fight to preserve hope and truth."

"How?" Archer asked. "Everything's gone wrong."

"Not everything," Master Gabriel said. "Not yet. Things can get worse. They may get a lot worse, but that just means we fight harder. Archer, this is your charge: you and Nick will need to manage the breaches, and by 'manage,' I mean patch, paste, quick-stitch—any means to slow their progress. We cannot do business as usual now. Manage the breaches, but leave yourselves time for other tasks. You must find your family, especially Kaylie. I am not certain why, but Kaylie is the key to much of this. If you're right about Rigby, he certainly seemed to think Kaylie was worth his attention."

"I will find her," Archer whispered. "I will."

"That's the spirit," Master Gabriel said. "You must go back to the Dream tonight,"

"I can't," Archer said. "The Laws Nine. It'll have to be tomorrow."

"So be it," Master Gabriel said. "But perhaps, it will be better this way. There's something I want you to do before you Dreamtread again."

"What?"

"It remains to be seen what you will think of it. But I think it will be good for you."

"I'll go right now," Archer said. "Before sun-up."

"I think that is for the best," he said. "You need to go back to your home."

"Home?" Archer glanced at the guest room window. "But the police—"

"Have completed their investigation and come away empty. But there is something there that only you can discover."

"How . . . how do you know all this?"

"Archer, I am not unaware of things that go on in the Temporal." Master Gabriel smiled mischievously. "Go home, Archer. And go to the basement. You'll know it when you find it."

TWENTY-THREE

THE PRICE

"Is someone there?" the man called out to the darkness. There'd been a sound, a creaking of the gate, but not even a glint of light. There were slow footsteps, as if very cautious. Then came a low, mournful voice, not intelligible yet, merely muttering sadly.

"Do not taunt me again!" the man called out. He jerked against his chains and growled. "I won't be threatened, you hear me? You can't scare me. I'm an elementary school teacher."

"What happened? Am I dead?" came a weak voice from the darkness. There was shuffling movement.

"Wait right there!" the man commanded. "Don't come any closer!"

"It's so dark," the other voice said. "Am I dead?"

"What?" the chained man replied. "You aren't one of them, are you?"

"One of who?"

"No, you aren't," the chained man said. "And you aren't dead. You're just imprisoned . . . like me."

"I was on my screened-in porch," the new arrival said. "These things—shadows with eyes—they swarmed me. They threw me

242

down . . . threw me down my well. But the well's in the backyard. How did I get here?"

"I was at my computer working on lesson plans," the chained man said. "The same creatures came right out of my monitor. It's what I get for splurging on the thirty-four-inch screen."

"Wait, your voice sounds familiar. Mr. Gamber?"

"You know me?" the teacher replied. "Who are you?"

"Brian, Brian Keaton. You taught my kids: Archer, Buster, and Kaylie, for a little while."

"Keaton!" The chains jangled. "Yeah, yeah, I remember you. Great kids. Kaylie—wow, talk about smart."

"I wish I could see your face," Mr. Keaton said. "I don't mind night so much, but this is different."

"It's a kind of separation, isn't it?" Mr. Gamber said. "By design, no doubt."

"Mr. Gamber?" Mr. Keaton asked. "Can you tell me where we are?"

"It's Phillip," he said, holding out his hand. "Oh, oh, right. You can't see my hand to shake it."

By feel, their hands met. "Is this real, Phillip? I mean, it can't be, can it?"

"I wish it weren't," he said. "But I was wide awake when those things came." He laughed, a sad, sickly sort of sound. "At least, I think I was awake."

"How can we know?"

"Well, what did you experience when they took you?"

"It felt like being buried in a thousand spiders," Mr. Keaton said, a jitter in his voice. "I heard their voices. I felt the cold air outside. No, I've never had a dream that real before."

"Nor have I," Mr. Gamber said. "I don't understand what this is, why it happened, where we are, or what we've done wrong."

Mr. Keaton felt around until he found the wall. He slid down and took a seat next to the teacher. "I have a theory," he said. "But you'll probably laugh."

"I've had a few of those since I've been here," Mr. Gamber said. "Lay it on me."

"Well, I was born in the South, in a good Christian family, and I guess I always believed, y'know? But when . . . when my wife died of cancer, I said some pretty horrible things to God. Those things . . . those shadows with eyes . . . well, I'm wondering if maybe that's God's way of telling me something."

There was no reply.

"Phillip? I guess I was hoping you'd laugh at me." Mr. Keaton waited and still no reply. Then he heard a very long sigh, a dreadfully dry sound full of regret and no small amount of frustration.

"I didn't laugh," he said. "Because it's not funny. God's not like that, Brian. No, definitely not. Whatever those things were, they are not Godsent."

"That's a little encouraging, I guess."

"Yeah, and we can't dwell on the why stuff, you know?" Mr. Gamber said. "We've got to think of a way out of here. You aren't chained?"

"No."

"Well, that's something," Mr. Gamber said. "You any good with your hands?"

"Actually, yeah," he said. "I am."

"Archer."

Archer froze. He had barely left his room when the whisper came out of the dark hallway behind him. He took one more step.

"Archer, where are you going?" Amy whispered from her room's doorway. "It's four o'clock in the morning!"

"Would you believe that I'm going to the bathroom?" Archer asked, already sure of her answer.

"When people go to the bathroom in the middle of the night, they don't tiptoe like they're trying not to get caught." She stepped out of her room and crossed her arms. "Now, what are you up to?"

"I might ask you the same," Archer said. "Look at you. You're wearing jeans and a sweatshirt. Going somewhere?"

"Wherever you are," Amy said. "Yep."

"You aren't going to let me say no on this, are you?"

"Nope," she said, falling in behind him. "Now, where to? I want to leave a note for Mom."

Archer spun on his heel. "A note?" he said. "Are you crazy?"

"Not here," she whispered, giving him a little push down the hall. Together, they sneaked down the spiral staircase, past the sprawling living room, and into the kitchen, where a small light gave a fluorescent glow.

"Okay," she said, "we can talk here, but not too loud."

"Right," he said. "You want to leave a note for your mom, but you're worried that she'll hear us sneaking out."

"It's not like that," Amy said, slowly opening a drawer. She removed a piece of stationery and a pen and went to work on the note. "Look, Archer, I don't know how you do things with your folks, but, after my dad left us, my mom and I vowed we would never break each other's trust. If I go somewhere, I leave a note or a text or something. You're the crazy one if you think I'm going to run off at night and not let my mom know, with all these kidnappings or whatever they are. No way. Now, where are we going? Are we going to bust into Rigby's place and steal his secret dream whatcha-ma-jigger?"

"Uh, no," Archer replied, rolling his eyes. "We're going to my house."

"Your house?" Amy stopped writing and blinked at him through her owlish spectacles. "Why?"

"I'm not exactly sure," he said. "Master Gabriel told me I need to look around for something?"

"He, the chief Dreamtreader?"

"You know about him?"

"Kaylie told me." She shrugged. "Hey, we're girls. We share."

"Great," Archer replied, wondering what else Kaylie had told Amy. "Anyway, yeah, that's him. He didn't tell me what to look for but said I'd know it when I see it."

"That's mysterious," she said. "Yep."

⚷

The Lurker had given Kaylie very clear directions to Xander's Fortune. She flew most of the way across Forms, barely getting tired, so great was her mental strength. But northeast of Direton, she figured she'd better conserve as much energy as possible for the dangers ahead. She gave Number 6 Rue de la Morte a wide berth, sprinting along the tree line of Drimmrwood and darting from thicket to thicket, keeping low and out of sight.

"So Rigby let the Scath out," she muttered as she leaped down a hillside and raced toward the ruins ahead. "And he wanted them to stay out too, if he tried to throw the key into a volcano. Too bad he messed up." She leaped from stone to stone, passing through Xander's stronghold without leaving so much as a footprint, until a fuzzy blur passed so close to her face that she blinked.

Her next step was less than accurate. She slid off a corner of stone and tumbled into a thicket of brambles. She will-summoned a pair of electrified machetes, hacked her way out, and crouched, ready to fight.

"I've finally found you!" came a squeaky voice from behind.

A pair of tiny feet lighted for a moment on the top of Kaylie's head, leaped away, and then there was Razz, hovering just a few feet in front of her.

Kaylie sighed and willed away her machetes. "You're lucky I didn't cut off one of your tails," she said.

"They grow back," Razz replied offhandedly. "But where have you been? You left me at the library in Garnet, and I had to fight a couple of Scath. I followed your scent all over Verse and into Archaia in the Pattern District. What were you doing there? You weren't messing around with the Lurker, were you?"

"I can't stand here and talk," Kaylie said. "I'm on a mission."

"A mission?" Razz squeaked. "We were already on a mission, remember?"

"I'm sorry," Kaylie said. "I'm not on that mission anymore."

"What?" Razz blurted. "You're a Dreamtreader!"

Kaylie shouldered past Razz. "You'd best get back to Archer," she said.

"Without you?" Razz asked. "No way! Why do you think I've been looking for you for so long? Archer sent me to keep you safe, and I lost you. If I go back to Archer without you, he'll kill me!"

"I'm not the Kaylie you once knew," she said. "But I'd like you to take a message to Archer. He deserves that at least."

Razz shot toward Kaylie's face and put a little paw on her forehead. "Are you sick?" Razz asked. "You're talking nonsense."

"Please tell Archer I'm sorry I failed. Tell him I ate some gort."

Razz gasped. "No!"

"It was in a brownie, and I ate it. Tell Archer I said that, please, Razz."

"Who gave you the gort?" Razz squeaked.

"The Lurker," Kaylie said. "He tricked me. I serve him now, and I am on an errand for him. Tell Archer."

"No, Kaylie," Razz said, sniffling. "No, no, no . . . you can't serve him."

"I cannot do anything but serve him," Kaylie replied, looking toward the mountain and the lightning-streaked sky behind it. "Now go, Razz."

"I won't leave you."

"You have to," Kaylie said. "I don't want to hurt you, but I can use my will. If you won't take my message to Archer, I can put you in a little box so you'll keep out of my way."

"You wouldn't!" Razz said indignantly. She crossed her arms. "Hmph! Well, I guess you're going to have to do it, then, because I'm not leaving you."

"Suit yourself," Kaylie said. She reached into her rich imagination and called a glowing cube that was just Razz's size. It shimmered and pulsed, and then suddenly, a gap in one side opened. It darted toward Razz and scooped her up.

"Big deal!" Razz said, her head appearing briefly on one side of the box. "I'll just go *POOF*!"

"No, you won't," Kaylie said. "The Lurker has taught me some things."

Razz nodded, winked, and blinked. She snapped her fingers and bounced up and down, but she was not able to *POOF*.

"I'm sorry, Razz," Kaylie said again. "But this is good-bye. And don't worry; this box thing won't last forever. When I'm sure you can't mess with my plans, I'll release you."

"No, wait!" Razz cried. "Wait!"

With a wave of her hand, Kaylie sent the mini-oubliette soaring across the terrain until she was certain it was out of range of the lightning that struck almost constantly in Xander's Fortune.

Then Kaylie looked up at the mountain. "Time to get back to work," she said, leaping across a small fence of white stone. As she hit the upslope, she noticed the two wisps of white mist that had been following her ever since she left Archaia. The Lurker's wraithlings, but they weren't keeping up anymore. In fact, they seemed to be turning back.

It's about time, Kaylie thought, and she raced toward Xander's Fortune, where she hoped to find the Shadow Key.

Archer and Amy ducked under the yellow police tape that surrounded the Keaton's home.

"What if the police come back?" Amy asked. She followed close behind Archer as they disappeared into the shadows of the carport.

"They won't," he said. "I guess they've found all the clues they're going to find here. Besides, what are they going to do? Arrest me for breaking into my own house? We're not even breaking in, really." Archer clambered up onto a two-seater bench, reached into the birdhouse, and took out the spare key. "See?" he said.

Even though it was his own home, Archer still felt a little sneaky as he turned the key in the lock. The two of them slipped inside as fast as they could.

"What do you think Master Gabriel wants you to find?" Amy asked.

"I really don't know," Archer said. "It's been driving me crazy. I can't imagine what we could find that the police missed. And . . . I can't imagine anything that'll help."

"Help with what?"

"Bringing Kaylie back," Archer said. "My dad too . . . and Mr. Gamber. So many things have gone wrong."

"I know," Amy said. "I'm sorry."

"Not your fault," Archer said, closing the door behind them. They passed through a narrow laundry room, and from there, to a wide den. Archer had been in there in the dark before, many times, but it seemed strange and somehow threatening now. The couches, chairs, end tables, cabinets—all had a blue-gray tint from the predawn twilight ghosting coming in through the picture windows from outside. Nothing moved. It was absolutely silent, the kind of silence that lets you know that no one else is in the house.

Amy's hand on his shoulder made Archer jump.

"Sorry!" she whispered. "Jumpy much?"

Archer exhaled in a puff and shook his head. "C'mon," he said as he led her past his father's favorite chair and out of the den. He paused at the stairs going up to the bedrooms. A wave of nostalgia slammed into him. He was little again, waiting at the bottom of the steps with Buster and watching his father and mother coming down those steps. His mom carried baby Kaylie and was as relaxed as could be. But, as usual around the baby, Dad was moving his hands and arms every which way, just in case.

Then it was gone, the warmth of remembering replaced with an empty cold. Archer shivered. It was more than emotion. It really was cold.

"The temperature in here just dropped," Amy whispered.

"Did you leave the side door open?" he asked.

"No way," she said.

"I don't think we should stay here too much longer," he said. "Let's get to it."

The door to the basement stairs was just around the corner. Archer reached for the knob and then jerked his hand away: it was freezing. His hand throbbed, especially where the strange red scar had formed.

"What's wrong?" Amy asked.

"Cold," he said. "So cold it burns." He turned toward Amy. "It's like—" He felt his voice catch in the back of his throat. "Amy . . . Amy don't move."

"Not funny, Archer!" she hissed. "You're scaring me."

Archer stared over Amy's shoulder. "Don't move."

A shadow form was nosing around in the kitchen. Its red eyes glimmered as it half walked, half slithered, half shambled closer.

"There really is something there?" Amy squeaked.

Archer dove, sprawling hard on the kitchen floor. The Scath slipped through his fingers and darted away. Away toward Amy.

"No, you don't!" Archer growled, rolling onto his back and throwing his arm forward. There was a faint crackling sound. Archer's hand tingled and an honest-to-goodness bullwhip appeared in his hand. In that single motion, it was suddenly there, and he snapped it, wrapping the leather cord around the Scath's neck. Archer yanked back on the whip and jerked the snared Scath with it.

"Not fair!" the Scath hissed. "You can't do that here, Dream-treader! Scath rule here." The shadow form's eyes glowed vicious red. The creature reared its head back and clamped its jaws down on the whip. It struggled with the leather, bit through it, and wriggled free.

Archer, still stunned from the whip's appearance, hesitated, allowing the Scath to make another play for Amy. "No!" Archer cried out, but he wasn't fast enough.

The Scath coiled around Amy's right leg. Instantly, another Scath appeared from the hallway and slithered around her midsection. A third came out of the ceiling and went for Amy's neck and began to pull.

Archer scrabbled to his feet in time to watch as a rippling bog of ashen, black, and gray mud pooled in the air behind Amy. It was a constantly moving, writhing blog, spreading and growing as if it might swallow Amy and the Scath.

In that moment, something came over Archer. It had the shrill electricity of fear, coursing across his shoulders, down his back, and in his limbs. It wasn't terror. It was rage.

This—what was happening right before his eyes—was so utterly wrong that something seemed to snap in Archer. All of it, the troubles of his family: his mother dying of cancer, Buster's concussion, his father being taken, Kaylie trapped . . .

Troubles in the Dream: the multiplying breaches, Bezeal's treachery, the Scath . . .

And troubles in the Waking World: Rigby, Kara, Dream Inc.'s army of Lucid Walkers . . .

It was all undeniably, impossibly, wretchedly *wrong*. And Archer was going to put a stop to it . . . right . . . now.

The Dreamtreader took a deep breath, felt his will surging like never before, and—in one mighty effort—stomped his foot down to the ground as he shouted, "*No!*" A thunderclap sounded in the word and shook the house.

The Scath not only lost their hold on Amy but were blown back into the whirling sludge portal. Archer reached out with his hand spread wide and then made a sudden fist.

The portal collapsed and vanished, the Scath with it.

Eyes wide with fright, lips moving soundlessly, Amy looked like a fish out of water. She managed a little communication at last. "What . . . what, how? How did you do that?"

Archer figured he looked pretty much like a fish himself. He said, "I don't know."

Amy fell toward Archer and embraced him. "They were trying to take me, weren't they?" she asked. "Like Mr. Gamber . . . like your dad."

"Those were Scath," Archer said. "Rigby set them free in the Dream. And . . . yeah, I think they were trying to take you."

"Those were the shadow things I saw that night," she said, "the night Mr. Gamber was taken."

Archer nodded.

"Why?" Amy asked, stepping back. "Why me? What have I done?"

"Not you," Archer said. "Me. Rigby has tapped into some new kind of power in the Dream. It's a long story, but he's found a way to control the Scath. If they hurt you, they hurt me."

Amy blushed. She'd never had a friend put it so plainly before. She mattered to Archer. It was time to change the subject. "But what about Mr. Gamber?" she asked. "Why take him?"

"He was my teacher in elementary school," Archer muttered, thinking aloud. "Buster and Kaylie's too. He even tutored Kaylie for a little while, until she outgrew him, at least."

Amy squinted and nudged her glasses to rest higher on the bridge of her nose. "But . . . if Rigby was trying to hurt you, I don't see . . ."

"You said you saw the Scath that night," Archer suggested. "I think they came for you, but you scared them off."

"Hey!" she muttered. "My bedhead's not that bad."

"Maybe it was your night breath," Archer said.

Amy gave him a playful slap on the shoulder. But then everything about her demeanor softened. "Thank you," she said. "Thank you for what you did. You were very brave."

Archer looked away, looked at his hand, looked at his feet—anything to avoid the vulnerable, melting-ice look in Amy's eyes.

"That was Dreamtreader stuff, huh?" she asked. "The whip . . . the shockwave and thunder?"

Archer was slow to nod. "I've never done that before."

"Huh? I thought you did that kind of stuff all the time. Isn't that what Dreamtreaders do?"

"In the Dream," he said. "We're in the Waking World. I've never done anything like that here before."

"Well, you knocked the snot out of those Scath critters."

"Yeah," he said absently, his mind reeling. *Decay.* That was the word. The fabric of the Dream was degrading, unraveling. That had to be it. The details seemed to fall perfectly into place.

The first sign of the Dream fabric weakening had been more than a year ago when Archer brought back the Tokens of Doom, the first physical objects he'd ever carried back. Then Rigby had supernaturally disarmed Guzzy Gorvalec, the school bully, turning his knife into a bouquet of daisies.

Now, as the fabric frayed even more, the creatures in the Dream showed will, showed the ability to create. The Scath were able to manifest in the Waking World and physically drag people into the Dream. And lastly, Archer's sudden outburst of Dreamtreader power—outside of the Dream—taken together, it could only mean one thing: a Rift was near.

"We should leave, right?" Amy asked, breaking Archer's trance. "We need to go . . . before they come back."

Archer craned his neck to see the windows on the east side of his home. There was a pink glow in the woods outside. "I think we're okay for now," he said. "The sun will be up soon, and I don't feel that weird cold."

"No," she said. "You're right. It feels . . . normal."

"I still want to see what's in the basement," Archer said. "Especially now."

"What do you mean?"

"The Scath tried to take you," he said. "But they were already here. They put their ice touch on the basement door, and they attacked as soon as I touched the knob."

"So?"

"So, whatever's in the basement, I don't think they want me to find it."

Dreamtreader's Creed, Conceptus 10

Dreamtreader, you must always know upon what you stand. Yours is not a casual employment, not a trade, not an occupation. Dreamtreading is a high calling and a vital one.

The Waking World must dream or it will languish in despair that there is nothing more, wilting until there is little left but a dead husk. But the Waking World must not be mistaken for Dream, for that kind of vision without conscience, without wisdom, would be chaos.

Should you and your Dreamtreader brethren fail, doom will come to both Dream and Walking realms. People will sleep with no dreams and rise with no waking. It will be as carnal and miserable as a nest of eaglets left to starve. They will turn and consume each other. Some will fly too soon and die in the effort. Others, too late, and they will wither.

Do not let it be so on your watch, Dreamtreader. Not on your watch. For the shattered glass might be glued back together, but it can never be unbroken.

TWENTY-FOUR

THE DEEPEST WELLS

U couldn't wait until morning? KARA TEXTED, GLARING AT her glowing smartphone.

No, came Rigby's reply. *As u know, many things can happen at night.*

What's so urgent?

We need to plan a dinner.

What? R U KIDDING?

No.

Kara knew Rigby's odd sense of humor, but texting at five a.m. about a dinner? That was bizarre, even for him.

A special dinner, Rigby texted. *In the Dream.*

I don't get it.

We need to lay things out for Keaton and his DT friend. They need to see we've got this.

Why rub it in? Kara asked. *Why play with fire?*

There was a long pause before Rigby texted back, *You don't think this is wise?*

It was Kara's turn to pause. She had to tread carefully here.

Whatever U want, Rigby, she texted. *What's the plan?*

After a diabolically long wait, Rigby's text came. It was so long that her phone broke the message into six segments.

A creeping chill trickled down Kara's back after she read it. And, not for the first time, Kara wondered if Rigby truly was insane.

The lightning was relentless.

Kaylie stood on the edge and stared down into the inferno of that tempest in the midst of Xander's Fortune. "I'd rather find a needle in a haystack any day," Kaylie muttered, thinking that, at least haystacks didn't usually take you apart cell by cell until you were nothing.

Between the caustic electrical discharges, the rising vapors, and the blinding light, Kaylie couldn't see. She willed up a set of headgear she'd read about in one of Archer's steampunk adventure novels. It fit less than snugly over her head, so she tucked her pigtails up and under. Several sets of geared lenses clicked and clacked into place. She worked at the dials and levers until she got the shade and magnification she wanted. And then she leaped over the edge.

With Amy on his heels, Archer eased down the stairs. His basement was rectangular, with one L-shaped half being finished, furnished, and comfortable. The other half? Not so much.

Archer turned on a pair of lamps and took a look around. "Yup," he said with a sigh. "It's my basement."

"Nothing different?"

"Not that I can tell," he said. "I was just down here less than a week ago. It looks the same to me."

Amy frowned. "Think about it," she said. "Your leader, Master Gabriel, did he give you any hint at all?"

"'You'll know it when you find it,' was all he said." Archer shook his head slowly. The Scath attack and the sudden use of power in the Waking World had caused a surge of adrenaline, but it was wearing off. The realities fell back into place like dark curtains. Rigby, Kara, Dream Inc., his father, Kaylie . . .

"Some kind of message, maybe?" Amy asked, tapping the space bar on the computer. It didn't wake. "Think detail. What about these paintings? They look kind of strange."

"We've always had those," Archer said, looking at the oriental prints. "My dad got them from my granddad, who was in the Korean War. They are kind of weird."

"Should we open stuff? Drawers? The little fridge behind the counter?"

"I feel like it should be something more obvious, but I'm not seeing it."

"What about in there?" Amy asked, pointing to the paneled door on the other side of the desk.

"Nah," Archer said. "It's just my dad's shop. He hasn't used it in years, not since Mom . . ."

"Right." Amy put her hands on her hips. "Still, it is part of the basement. We should at least look."

Archer shrugged. That single bad memory of the basement work side came knocking, but he wasn't about to give that mental airtime now. He knew Amy was right. At least they had to check, a brief look around. *Whatever*, Archer thought. *This night's been more trouble than it was worth.*

Reluctantly, he opened the work-side door. "C'mon," he said. "Let's get this over with—"

Archer smelled it before he saw it. It was pitch dark on the work side, but the scent was unmistakable: fresh cedar wood. That rich, earthy smell filled Archer with more joy than a thousand trophies because he hadn't smelled it—not in the basement—in a long, long time.

Archer flipped the light switch and might have gasped but couldn't catch enough breath to do so. He hadn't been in the work side of the basement for a while, maybe more than a month. But the last time he'd been in there, the room was just as it had been for many years: abandoned, piles of mismatched pieces of scrap wood, work tables built from sawhorses or old kitchen counters, tools everywhere—the few still hanging up were so shrouded in cobwebs it'd been near impossible to identify which tool was which. It was a junk room, a place for discards and forgotten things. It had become a graveyard for hope.

But now, the wonderful scent of cedar filled the air once more. The scrap wood had been organized, the tools too, a few new ones shining up their ranks.

"Oh!" Amy said, gasping loud enough for the both of them. "Oh . . . my . . . word, Archer! Who did this?"

He didn't bother swiping the tear on his cheek. "I . . . I think my dad did."

Archer and Amy stepped lightly, silently, as if the room were too sacred now to disturb. On every work bench and table, crafted with intricate detail, mostly from cedar but a little balsa and fir also, rested an assortment of wooden wishing wells.

"I . . . I can't believe it," Archer said. "Dad is woodworking again. He hasn't touched this stuff since Mom died."

"Oh," Amy said. "You mean that night . . ."

Archer nodded and looked away. "You know how much my mom loved our well in the backyard? Well, when Mom first got sick, Dad started making these little wooden wells. He made them for her, just to cheer her up because she couldn't walk to see it anymore. They were so good that she made him sell a few, but he still made more. It was something he could do to make Mom smile.

"But, when she died, Dad came down here and flew into a rage. He wrecked the room and destroyed every last wishing well. I never saw him set foot in the work side after."

"He's making the wishing wells again," Amy said. "That's gotta be a good thing, yep?"

"It's miraculous is what it is, Amy. It means there's a spark of real life still left in him. Now I know why Master Gabriel wanted me to come back here. He wanted me to see . . . wanted me to know."

"Know what?"

Archer leaned over one of the wishing wells and inhaled deeply. "That broken things—even people—can be rebuilt."

Flying was tricky for most Dreamtreaders, and exhausting too. But Kaylie had more mental energy to spend than most and managed to fly like a hawk on her first try.

Even still, flying back and forth across the guts of an active volcanic crater was no small feat. Kaylie rode thermals, lifts of warm air, whenever she could see them first, but others buffeted her unexpectedly, slamming her against the stone innards of the crater or throwing her dangerously off course.

Worse yet, the crater vomited up energy discharges, randomly and without warning. Kaylie's quick thinking saved her more than once, calling up shield after shield of plated steel to bear the brunt of the violent discharges.

She leaped from ledge to ledge, careening across the violent gulf dozens of times but still coming up empty. "Where are you, stupid key?" she growled. While not perilously low, her will was weakening. The flight, the dodging, the conjuring—it all took its toll.

Kaylie sought a moment's respite on a thin jagged ledge that curled about fifteen feet on the interior. She landed, pressed her back flat against the stone, and panted. Suddenly, the right lens on Kaylie's headgear system fell into place. It was a magnetic filter of some kind, allowing Kaylie's eyepiece to pierce the vapor for just a moment. It was long enough to see the most foreign thing: a black object on a very low ledge. It wasn't really a ledge, though, but rather, a small crop of stone, and it wasn't nearly far enough from the violent miasma below. Kaylie had the will. She could get to it, but that didn't mean she wouldn't be annihilated by a discharge on the way.

"I need that key," she growled, taking flight once more. She dove, let herself plummet twenty feet, and then swooped up to take a more gradual descending route to the key.

Several things happened at once. Kaylie saw through her lenses that a great bubble of electrical energy had risen below her and was growing rapidly. She called up a shield, but didn't have a chance against the bolt of lightning that spidered down into the crater. It struck the metal, with the shock of impact blowing Kaylie off course.

She crashed into the ledge and started to fall. She scrabbled for a handhold, knocked stones and dust free, and then struck something else. The Shadow Key spun on the stone and teetered at the edge.

Kaylie held on for dear life and almost got herself all the way onto the ledge, when the electrical bubble below . . . burst.

Archer and Amy's eventful early morning became even more eventful when school beckoned. The two of them raced around the Pitsitakas' home, grabbing up books, lunch money, backpacks, and an assortment of key disk hard drives.

Mrs. Pitsitakas entered into the morning chaos and said, "Amy, I got your note."

Archer froze, and that was a little awkward because his arm was shoved into his backpack up to his shoulder.

"I trust whatever you were doing at Archer's house was good, right, and noble?" Mrs. Pitsitakas asked gently.

"It was, Mom," Amy said, pecking a quick kiss on her mother's cheek. She zipped and slung her backpack. Archer finally moved and did the same.

"All the same," Mrs. Pitsitakas said, "your decision made for a short night of sleep. Are you sure going to school today is wise?"

Archer had the distinct impression that he and Amy were being measured somehow. Mrs. Pitsitakas' eyes hovered lightly on him and then Amy, slowly meandering back and forth between them. Archer was dead tired, and here Mrs. Pitsitakas was giving them a perfect out from school. But again, there seemed a kind of measurement involved. It was as if he were standing on the Great Scale of Justice. His decision now would change the balance one way or the other.

"I think we should go," Archer said quietly. "The extra rest would be nice, but we made the choice to sacrifice sleep. We've got to live up to the other side of that choice."

Mrs. Pitsitakas' smile was so subtle that Archer barely caught it. Just a tiny impish upturn in one corner of her mouth—that was it. But it was enough. Archer felt certain he'd given the correct response.

"I have returned," Kaylie said. At a table deep within the Lurker's study, she found her master feasting on a platter of succulent morsels, strange steaming shapes—some recognizable, some not. Kaylie felt her stomach roil. "I almost didn't make it, Lord Lurker, but here I am."

He glanced down at her and sucked the last bit of meat and sinew from a large bone that looked like some small creature's rib cage. Then he said, "Darling Kaylie, you don't have to call me Lord or any such thing. And certainly not Lurker. I despise that name. I know! Why don't you call me Uncle Scovy?"

"Very well," she said. "Uncle Scovy, I have brought you a gift."

The Lurker let the chicken bone fall from his fingers and snatched up a cloth to wipe his hands. "Oh, I hoped you would!" he said, spinning in his chair. "When my wraithlings returned and reported your doings, I had such confidence that you'd succeed. Oh, oh, oh . . . is this what I think it is?"

Kaylie nodded and smiled. She held out a very large, dark key. "It's exactly what you think it is."

In spite of the rightness of his decision, Archer was weary and fighting off sleep all through the morning. Doing a lab in Biology helped a little. He was up and around and had the ever-cheery Amy to keep him awake. But later, in Literature and Composition, Archer was struggling. It wasn't the teacher: Mrs. Mangum had a way of making most lessons fun. It wasn't the assignment: unlike most of the tenth graders in the advanced class, Archer actually liked writing essays. For him, it was just practice learning to think and communicate, to argue more effectively.

But the book? *The Prince and the Pauper* by Mark Twain? That was another matter. The Tudor-era English was tough to translate when he was fully focused and awake. "Thou speakest well; thou hast an easy grace in it. Art learned?" Twain's tale was brilliant and accurate in the telling, but not very easy on the sleepy mind.

Archer found himself nodding. Time passed, and the class moved from activity to activity with Archer scarcely noticing. Until Mrs. Mangum called his name.

"Archer Keaton," she said. "What . . . are you doing? Are you falling asleep in my class?"

Archer sat bolt upright and blinked. "I'm sorry, Mrs. Mangum," he said. "I didn't get much sleep last night. I—"

"Of course you didn't, you absurd loser."

Archer blinked. Mrs. Mangum was glaring at him. Her lips were moving, but in a kind of dreamy slow motion, and her voice was no longer her own. It was Rigby Thames.

"That's right, Keaton," Rigby spoke through the teacher's lips, "I'm talking to you. Have I got your attention?"

Archer's head turned as if on a swivel. No one else in the class had changed expression. They gave no sign of anything unusual happening. *Unbelievable,* Archer thought. Watching and hearing this wonderful woman, his favorite English teacher, speak with a teenage boy's deep voice was just . . . creepy.

"Don't worry, Keaton," Rigby said. "Only you can hear me. We're gaining some pretty incredible abilities in the Waking World. Have you noticed?"

Archer nodded. He was half-tempted to will up an Atomic Foot Stomp and see how Rigby liked it. "What do you want, Rigby?" he asked instead.

"It's not so much what I want," he said. "A rational mind looks beyond emotions and petty lusts. I've been thinking that we're going about this all wrong. I've made it too personal. And we've got to fix things. You should have your family back. I want you to have your family back. We need to talk."

Archer squinted and looked again at the other students.

"No, not here," Rigby said, the look on Mrs. Mangum's face completely different from *his* words. "And not just us."

"What do you mean?"

"This needs to be decision by committee," the Rigby-voiced Mrs. Mangum said. "Kara, my Uncle Scovy, Bezeal, you, and Nick Bushwhacker, or whatever his name is. Bring your Master Gabriel, if you want, not that I'd expect him to come. Seems like the Masters don't like to get their hands dirty these days."

"Why should I trust you?" Archer asked.

"Really? That's all you've got in this dramatic moment? 'Why should I trust you'? I'd 'ave expected something less clichéd. Point is, you can't trust me, but you don't 'ave a lot of choice in this. Therefore, Keaton, you are hereby cordially invited to a grand dinner. Sleep at eleven, the party's one hour past, at Number 6 Rue de la Morte. RSVP now or someone might just suffer."

Archer didn't hesitate. "We'll be there."

"Good," Rigby said, and the voice changed back to Mrs. Mangum's voice in mid-syllable. "Mr. Keaton, please read the passage now."

"I'm sorry," Archer said, noting that half the class was staring at him like he was wearing a flowerpot on his head. "Uh . . . uh, what was the passage . . . again?"

Mrs. Mangum sighed. "We're talking about Twain's tendency to use irony and metaphor together. Page seventy-seven, Miles Hendon's speech at the top."

Naturally, Archer was on the wrong page. He madly flipped through the book until he came to the right spot. He scanned the words at the top of the page, not really registering what they meant. "Okay," Archer said, "I've got it." He began to read from Twain's tale: "'After a little, he went on, 'And so I am become a Knight of the Kingdom of Dreams and Shadows! A most odd and strange position, truly, for one so matter-of-fact as I. I will not laugh . . .'"

Archer read the rest of the page on autopilot, his mind reeling from what he'd just seen.

"That was well-read, Archer," Mrs. Mangum said. "You might have a future in acting."

The class murmured a laugh, but Archer didn't pay attention. He spun in his chair and grabbed Amy's book.

"Hey!" she whispered. "What's up with that?"

"Just a sec." He hurriedly flipped to page seventy-seven in Amy's book. He had to see, had to know if it was in her book too or just his. But there it was again, Twain's original words: "And so I am become a knight of the Kingdom of Dreams and Shadows!"

Archer's heart swelled with hope and passion. He felt the reservoir of his will flooding with power.

"Archer," Amy said, her eyes big green worlds. "What is it? You look . . . different."

"I am different," he said. "Better. I know what I'm going to do."

Mrs. Mangum's abrupt redirection cut that conversation short before it could really begin. But that was okay with Archer. He had plans to make.

TWENTY-FIVE

ENSLAVED

THE CRIMSON VORTEX THAT DELIVERED ARCHER INTO the Dream was more violent than he'd ever experienced. For one bone-rattling moment, the wind current shifted and, like a strong riptide, the wind yanked Archer outside of the funnel. He flailed a thousand feet above the Dream landscape until the vortex gobbled him back up.

When he finally reached the ground, Archer was so dizzy that he walked around like someone just off of a Tilt-A-Whirl. It was a point of personal pride that he had never—not a single time—thrown up in the Dream. As nauseous as he felt, he fought through it.

Archer summoned his surfboard and took off on a speedy wave toward the moors of Archaia. The Dream felt strangely quiet. Pattern District could be a most violent place, but not today. Today, the calm was welcome, and probably deceiving. Looking sideways, Archer scanned for breaches. There were many, but they would have to wait. Visis Nocturne off, he looked toward the horizon . . . and felt a dire chill form across his shoulders. There, climbing into the sky almost as high as Old Jack, was the ice-fire.

If something doesn't change . . . Archer wouldn't complete the thought. He carved between two waves and bunny-hopped onto a third. He reflected on his meeting with Master Gabriel right after school. Master Gabriel had taken some persuading, but in the end, decided that Archer's plan might actually be the only way to turn back the destruction of the Dream, in a world-altering Rift.

The other reason for their after-school rendezvous was this: Archer wanted Master Gabriel to attend the "special" dinner that Rigby had planned. But Rigby had been right: no amount of Archer's pleading could persuade the Master Dreamtreader to attend.

Gabriel's final words on the matter echoed in Archer's mind: "Just as you have a District to shepherd in the Dream, I have certain responsibilities, Archer. I can provide you the same assistance and support that I always have. Nothing more. This is the word of my Superior, and His plans always work out best."

Archer didn't understand it. Master Gabriel clearly had otherworldly power. He wore armor and a sword most of the time, but he was apparently fighting other battles.

Archer surfed in peace and quiet until the border of Archaia. The Intrusion waves stopped at the border of that fell land as if hitting a wall. He took to sprinting across the ragged, craggy landscape and came to the copse of trees overlooking the Lurker's valley, the meeting place he'd selected.

Archer ducked under some low-hanging limbs and darted into the tiny clearing. But Nick wasn't there. Or so it seemed.

"G'day, mate!" Nick said cheerfully.

When Archer turned around, he saw nothing but a gangly tree. But as if made of wax, Nick's face melted into the bark of the upper trunk.

"That's pretty good camouflage," Archer said.

The rest of Nick's body materialized. "Thanks, Archer. I figured we might need to keep a low profile."

"Right about that," Archer said. "Master Gabriel fill you in on the plan?"

Nick nodded and said, "You're a bonnie loon is what you are. Do you know how many dominoes have to fall just right for this to work?"

"Yeah, I know it's crazy."

"It'll be a real ripsnorter," Nick said. "I'm in. All the way, Archer. Count on me." The Aussie put his hand on Archer's shoulder.

"Thank you, Nick," he said. "You ready?"

"Aye," he said. "Let's give it a burl."

Archer and Nick broke into the Lurker's ridge stronghold by coming in from the north . . . and opening the broad, dark iron door.

"Well, color me gobsmacked," Nick said. "Why wouldn't it be locked?"

Archer shrugged. "I don't know, but really, what good is a lock against Dreamtreaders?"

"Good point."

The two snaked inside and followed the path Archer remembered to the Lurker's laboratory. Like a pair of spider-men, they scaled the walls and found a place to wait upon a ledge.

"He'll have Kaylie in some kind of cell," Archer said. "It'll have to be something special because Kaylie can think her way out of anything."

"Quite the little genius hacker, is she?"

"You have no idea," Archer said. "Brilliant. Stunningly brilliant."

"I mean no disrespect, but how do ya suppose the Lurker caught her?"

"I wish I knew," he said. "We'll ask her. Let's go."

The two Dreamtreaders came out of hiding and fled the lab. They navigated a half-dozen passages but found only empty cells. They found several experimentation chambers, each with what looked like an operating table surrounded by fearsome implements and tools. Archer swallowed and thought about his little sister. It was a thought he couldn't bear. He only knew that the Lurker would pay if he caused Kaylie any kind of pain.

So distracted with that line of thought, Archer almost blundered right into the Lurker's study. Nick held out his arm and physically blocked Archer. "Voices inside," Nick whispered.

Archer scanned inside the door. The study was a vast library built right into the black rock of the landscape. Bookshelves reached up three stories to a border of natural stone.

The voices were close by, likely just inside and around the corner. "C'mon," Archer whispered, and the two quickly swept down an adjacent passage. Archer searched the left-hand side until he found it: a staircase.

The thing looked like it had been hewn from wood that had been born old. It creaked and squeaked with every step, so Archer and Nick used a bit of will to lighten their steps. Up above they found a kind of attic that spanned the perimeter above the study. Like most attics, it was dusty and full of boxes.

Archer and Nick dropped to the ground and crawled as close to the edge as they dared. Peering out from behind a crate, Archer saw that it was indeed the Lurker, but he wasn't alone.

Kaylie! The Lurker and Archer's sister sat at the end of a short rectangular table, piled half with books and half with platters of food.

Archer's mind spun. *Why is she just sitting there? Why doesn't he have her locked up? Why doesn't she do something?*

"I have to hand it to you, my dear," the Lurker said, plopping what looked like an olive into his mouth. "Few have dared to attempt Xander's Fortune and lived to tell about it."

Archer's eyes widened.

"The mountain's dynamics are similar to a volcano," Kaylie said, wiping her lips daintily with a napkin, "but I didn't have too much trouble."

"Remarkable," the Lurker said. "I am fortunate to have such a capable ally."

Ally? Archer couldn't comprehend what he was hearing.

"I'm grateful," Kaylie said. "And thank you again for this meal."

"We will share many meals together, you and I," the Lurker said. "I have missed intelligent company."

Nick slithered up beside Archer. "This doesn't look good, mate," he whispered. "You want to explain what's going on here?"

"I wish I could," Archer said. "It doesn't make sense. I don't know why she's—wait. No, no, no." Archer looked at the platters of food, all manner of dishes, but some contained specks of black.

"What?" Nick asked.

"He's enslaved her," Archer said miserably. "The Lurker's enslaved my little sister with gort."

"Oh, mate," Nick said. "That's bad. Is there anything we can do?"

The Lurker's voice silenced the Dreamtreaders. "Well, my dear, you are free to amuse yourself for a few hours. I won't need anything until this evening."

Kaylie got up from her seat and dutifully pushed in her chair. She hesitated a moment. "I have a question," she said, "if I may?"

"Of course, Kaylie. What is it?"

"I guess I'm trying to understand something."

"And what is that?"

"Well, Rigby's your nephew, and he threw the Shadow Key into Xander's Fortune to destroy it. So why would you have me retrieve it?"

Archer felt his blood run cold. *No, Kaylie,* he thought. *No, please, no.*

"Rigby made a mistake," the Lurker said. He removed a long metallic object from his jacket pocket. "Oh, sure, it's all well and good to let the Scath loose for a little mischief now and then. They have their uses, but you would never want them to stay loose. They are . . . well, like a chemical fire: too hard to control."

The Lurker held up the Shadow Key and whirled it in his fingers like a rock drummer with a drumstick. "Yes," he said, "there are times when we elders have to clean up the mistakes of our beloved youth. No matter how well-intentioned, an error still is an error."

"And what will you do with the key now?" Kaylie asked.

The Lurker stopped the whirling motion and put the Shadow Key back into his jacket. "I'll let Rigby find out for himself just how volatile the Scath can be," he said. "And then, I'll give Rigby the key back . . . along with a lusty 'I told you so.'"

Kaylie laughed as she left the chamber. Somehow to Archer, that laugh sounded both joyful and sinister.

Nick turned to Archer. "This changes things, doesn't it?"

Archer motioned for Nick to come away from the overhang, and they retreated a few feet back into the attic area. "This changes everything," Archer said.

"All right," Nick said, "let's break this down, then. We've got no shot at getting the Shadow Key from Xander's Fortune . . . because Kaylie already got it. And she gave it to the Lurker, so that means we've got to get it from him."

"And he's intending to give it to Rigby," Archer said. "We can't let that happen."

"And Kaylie's under the Lurker's power by some hypnotic chemical stuff, right? But how far under is she? Will she recognize you? Would she listen to you?"

Archer frowned. "She would recognize me," he said, clenching his fists. "But she wouldn't listen to me. She wouldn't be able to defy the Lurker's commands."

"Okay," Nick said, "so that's a bigger problem. What if we're taking on the Lurker, and Kaylie comes into the fray on his side? What then?"

"Then we get our collective butt kicked," Archer said. "I won't fight my sister, and even if I did, she and the Lurker are two of the most powerful minds ever to enter the Dream. We're pretty good Dreamtreaders, but the two of them together? They'd vaporize us."

"Okay, so definitely not good," Nick said.

Archer sighed again. "This just doesn't make any sense," he said. "Kaylie's way too smart to eat anything with gort in it. She already knows the creeds better than I do."

"The Lurker's a tricky bitzer, right?" Nick asked. "Maybe he fooled yer sister. Or maybe he scared her into eating it. I dunno."

"I can't believe it," Archer muttered.

"Isn't there something we can do for Kaylie? Isn't there any way at all to get her out of the Lurker's control?"

Archer started to shake his head, but then he remembered something. The knowledge crystallized, but it led to a conclusion too horrible for Archer to even consider.

"What?" Nick asked. "What is it, mate?"

Archer exhaled slowly. "Last year, we discovered that the Lurker had been gort-enslaved by the Nightmare Lord himself. It was crazy. It made the Lurker betray his own nephew. But when we put an end to the Nightmare Lord, it freed the Lurker."

"So to free Kaylie," Nick said, "we need to take out the Lurker? Well, that's not such a bad thing, is it? We were planning to anyway, right? Him and Rigby and Kara and Bez—"

"I don't mean just beat him, as in making him surrender or putting him in some kind of prison. To set Kaylie free, we'd have to kill the Lurker."

Nick was thoughtful a few minutes. "Well, I'd say he has it coming. How can a human being ever enslave another? I've never understood that."

"I . . . I don't know if I could do that," Archer said.

"Of course ya can," Nick said. "You wiped out the Nightmare Lord. Why? He was threatening the two worlds you're sworn to protect. So is the Lurker. There's no difference, except for maybe the fact that he's made a slave of Kaylie, bitzer that he is."

Archer understood Nick's point of view. He was right, in a way, but that still didn't sway Archer concerning the prospect of killing again. Twin visions of fire and agony lit his imagination. Duncan and Mesmeera, hidden in the tree trunks.

Archer shook his head.

"Look," Nick said. "You've got doubts. Fine. I don't. If it comes to it, I'll take out the Lurker myself. But I think we have to act fast."

Archer nodded at that, and the Dreamtreaders ventured back to the edge to make sure the Lurker was still there, at his table in the study three stories below.

"Look at him," Nick whispered. "He looks like he's in a food coma. He's dozing. We've got him."

Archer whispered, "Okay, but let's go in quick and try to knock his feet out from under him. We want to get the Shadow Key before the Lurker even knows what hit him."

Archer and Nick inched closer to the edge. It would be a sudden, silent drop. *Maybe Nick is right*, Archer thought. *With Kaylie out of the chamber, this might be their best chance to deal with the Lurker.*

Archer held up three fingers. Then two. Then . . .

Someone tapped on Archer's shoulder. He and Nick spun around, but something clamped down over their lips to silence them. Archer's eyes widened in recognition.

TWENTY-SIX

DINNER IS SERVED

RIGBY LOOKED OUT THROUGH THE CHAMBER WINDOW AT Old Jack. "Uncle Scovy is running rather late," he said.

"I'm sure he'll be along soon," Kara said, gazing at the long bare dining table. "Madmen aren't especially well-known for their punctuality."

"Bezeal made it on time," Rigby countered.

The merchant's beady eyes narrowed. "If that was your humor," he said, "it was dreadfully bad. Not such a surprise from someone so sad. For I am neither man, nor mad."

Kara chuckled, but Rigby's ensuing glare silenced her.

A bell chimed in the distance, but it was not Old Jack. "Ah," said Rigby, "here he is at last."

In a minute, the hulking figure of the Lurker strode into the chamber. "What?" he said. "No food? I was told there would be quite a feast."

"Look again," Rigby said. He gestured toward the table. It blurred, colors and odd shapes melding into the smeared sight. When it was clear once more, the table sat laden with enough food and drink for a score of gluttonous kings. Roast turkey, beef, rack of lamb, dozens of steaming split lobster tails with pools of warm butter at the ready; herb-rubbed potatoes, pots of rice and gravy, piles of fresh vegetables, salads, and fruit jostled for space among a myriad of cakes, pies, and pastries.

"Impressive," the Lurker said. "You willed it up all at once."

"He can do the rabbit in the hat trick too," Kara quipped. "Show him, Rigby. Take off your top hat."

"You're full of laughs tonight," Rigby said, giving her a tip of the hat. He turned back to his uncle. "Where is Kaylie?" Rigby asked. "We need her here."

"Oh, she's here. Come along, Kaylie. No need to be shy. These are friends."

Kaylie emerged from the dark doorway. Eyes large and blinking, she hurried and stood at the Lurker's side. "So this is Number 6 Rue de la Morte?" she asked.

"Yes, yes," the Lurker replied. "The one and only home of the Nightmare Lord. Or used to be."

"You were a little late, Uncle," Rigby said. "Any trouble along the way?"

"Nothing I couldn't handle," the Lurker replied. "Shall we?" He held a chair out for Kaylie, and once she sat down, he took the next chair.

"We need music," Kara said. She glanced into the far corner of the chamber, where large crimson tapestries with gold-laced fringes hung. "I much prefer rock, but tonight feels a little more old school to me. How about a quartet?"

Four simple wooden chairs appeared first. Two men and two women in concert attire blinked into existence. They sat down in their respective chairs and, in a flash, each held an instrument: two

violins, a viola, and a cello. A moment more, after each had a stand
with sheet music, and musicians began to play a lively sonata.

"Well done, Kara," Rigby said. "It does somehow fit the mood."

The gatehouse bell rang out once again.

"The time has come for which we have strived," Bezeal said, taking his seat near the head of the table. "For us, victory will be no
longer deprived. It seems our guests have arrived."

Rigby took his seat with Bezeal at his right hand, Kara at his left.
The Lurker and Kaylie sat on Bezeal's side. Rigby folded his hands,
but then he frowned. "Wait," he muttered, and the music stopped.
"I almost forgot." He flipped his left hand toward the dormant fireplace, and a merry, crackling blaze sprang up.

"Now, we're ready," Rigby said. "Carry on."

The string quartet struck up the sonata with whimsical abandon,
playing with rousing fervor as two figures entered the chamber.

"Keaton!" Rigby announced, making a show of rising from his
seat to rush over to his guests. "Right on time." He shook Archer's
hand and turned to Nick. "And you must be the infamous Nick
Bushlander."

"It's Bushman, mate," Nick said.

"Right, sure," Rigby said. "Well, there we are. All here. Welcome
to the feast of the future. Please come and take a seat."

But as soon as Rigby stepped aside, Archer cried out, "Kaylie!"
He ran to her.

"Uh, I wouldn't," Rigby cautioned.

But Archer paid no mind to the warning. He ran to Kaylie's chair
and embraced her. "Kaylie, I'm sorry. I'm so sorry I wasn't there for
you before the Stroke of Reckoning. Are you all right? They haven't
hurt you?"

Kaylie did not return the embrace. Her head turned slowly. Her expression might have been curiosity, but nothing more. "I am no longer my own," she said quietly. "I belong to Uncle Scovy."

"What?" Archer said, releasing her and backpedaling as if he'd been stung. "No! Kaylie, it's me, your brother, Archer."

"I know who you are, Archer," Kaylie said, her voice empty of emotion. "I am a gort-slave now. I will do what Uncle wants . . . and nothing else."

Archer flashed to Rigby and shoved him. "You did this!" he yelled. "It wasn't enough to have her miss her Stroke of Reckoning? You had to enslave her? What kind of—"

"Please," Rigby said, his voice, in contrast to Archer's outburst, a strangely unnerving kind of quiet.

"Please, Archer," Kara said, "Take a seat."

"C'mon, mate," Nick said, pulling Archer back. "Let's hear 'im out."

"That's good, Bushman," Rigby said. "We need a calm mind. Haste and fear have been the source of all kinds of grave mistakes . . . for all of us."

Archer allowed himself to be led to a chair. He and Nick sat across from the Lurker . . . and Kaylie.

"I know you may not feel like it," Rigby said, "but please, eat. It helps to take the edge off."

"Yeah, sure. Poison us all with gort?" Nick asked. "We're not bloomin' shark biscuits at this, y'know?"

"Colorful expression," Rigby said. "Be assured, there is no gort here. Not now. You can pick at everything. Tear it to shreds with your fork and knife. You won't find a speck of gort. Or, if you like, fill a plate, and then give it to me. I'll eat every morsel."

Archer stared at Rigby and said, "I'm not hungry."

"Fine," Rigby said. He strode back to his chair. "Then let's get to the point, shall we? The Rift that Dreamtreaders are sworn to stop is inevitable."

"The Rift we *will* stop," Archer said flatly.

"No," Rigby replied, "you won't. Even if I wanted to, I couldn't stop it now. We've gone past the point of no return. And I want to be the first to admit I didn't see this all the way through before I started. My app substantially underrepresented the extent our Dream fabric has frayed."

Archer shook his head. "You think?"

"Your frustration is more than justified here, Keaton," Rigby said. "But hear me out. We've both erred, we Lucid Walkers and you Dreamtreaders too. You denied the inevitable out of fear when, in reality, the Dream and the Waking World were always meant to be together. And we, well . . . we pushed it to happen too quickly. Now, the new world is on the horizon, and we're not ready."

Archer turned to Nick and said, "He's stark-raving mad."

"Maybe," Nick replied. "Or maybe he needs us."

"I do," Rigby said. "I absolutely do. Things are about to change, and it's going to be dangerous for a lot of people who just won't understand what's happening. It won't be safe—or profitable—for us to be fighting each other in the midst of all that's about to happen. The world will need us, Keaton, all of us. Without a team of experienced Walkers like us, the world doesn't stand a chance. With all due respect to your history, three Dreamtreaders just isn't enough."

"What do you want, Rigby?" Archer countered. "Just say it."

Rigby took off his top hat and placed it upside down on the table. "I want a partnership. Dream Inc. and Dreamtreaders, working together, not to keep people from really living in their dreams, but rather, to help them do so safely. I want you to stop fighting the

Rift and start planning with us, putting our minds together so that we can teach the masses what to do and how to do it without killing themselves or others."

"Even better, Archer," Kara said, "if you're with us, like before, you get your father back . . . and Kaylie."

"But the gort," Archer whispered.

"There are ways around the gort," the Lurker said. "Kaylie is bound to my will, but if I wish her to be free—to be utterly back to normal—then she must obey."

"And once the Rift occurs," Rigby said, "she won't be trapped any longer."

"We'll be free again," the Lurker added.

"What about Mr. Gamber?" Archer asked.

"What, the teacher?" Rigby laughed. "He was . . . an accident, a bit of Scath mischief."

"You wanted Amy first, didn't you?"

"Guilty as charged," Rigby said. "I just wanted to distract you. But listen to me, Keaton. The teacher will be free too. We all will be free."

The room grew silent except for the crackling fire. Archer stared at Kaylie. She stared back but with no expression. Archer bowed his head.

"Look, Keaton, I know this isn't easy," Rigby said. "I never meant it to work out the way it did. Truth is, I just didn't know. But now, this is the responsible thing to do. The world will need us. All of us."

Archer lifted his head, but his shoulders were still hunched forward, his hands in his lap. When he spoke, his voice was barely audible. "What do I have to do?"

Rigby smiled and put his hand lightly on top of Kara's hand.

"I told you he'd come around," Kara said.

Beneath that dark hood, Bezeal's Cheshire Cat smile spread, broad and luminous.

"Let me make some room," Rigby said. With a quick wave of his hand, the meat, the veggies, the desserts—the whole spread—vanished.

"But I wanted the chocolate," Bezeal muttered, the lack of rhyme communicating his displeasure.

"I've drawn up a contract," Rigby said. "It is binding to us all." He snapped his fingers, and a parchment scroll appeared in his fist. He slid it down the table to Archer and Nick. A quill pen and a bottle of ink appeared next to the scroll.

"Read it, Keaton," Rigby said. "And then, sign it. You too, Bushman."

Archer untied the lace around the parchment and spread the scroll out so that he and Nick could read it. Archer traced his finger down the page, line by line. He looked up suddenly. "It says here that if you violate any part of the contract, Dream Inc. becomes my property, or the property of whomever I designate as heir. Why would you do that?"

"I know my own tendencies, don't I?" Rigby said. "If I didn't put that in there, I might get tempted on a few points. Of course, you have your own checks and balances. Read on."

Archer did, but Nick had read ahead. He pointed to a line in the second paragraph. "No bloomin' way."

Archer read it. "Gort?" he exclaimed. "You want us to take gort from you?"

"It's the only way," Rigby said. "Surely, you see that. I've got to be able to trust you. There are a lot of lives on the line. We have to make this work."

"By making Dreamtreaders into your slaves?"

"You've got it all wrong, Keaton. Just read on a bit."

Archer gritted his teeth and read on. Then he nodded. "You pledge not to abuse your control," Archer muttered. "Why am I not encouraged?"

The Lurker pounded his fist on the table. "Enough of the snide," he exclaimed. "We'll never work together if he keeps this up."

"You'll have everyone back, Keaton," Rigby said. "Think about it. Your father, Kaylie—even the teacher—you'll be free to live your lives the way you wish. It's all there in the contract. So long as you assist Dream Inc. in training people to know how to live, in preparing educational materials, and marketing, your life will be your own."

"So the gort is just to make sure that Dreamtreaders don't interfere with . . ."

"With company business," Rigby said. "That's exactly right. If you like, think of it as more of a treaty than a contract. That's what it is."

Archer picked up the quill pen and plunged it down into the ink bottle.

TWENTY-SEVEN

JUST DESSERTS

"WAIT." ARCHER'S HAND FROZE IN THE AIR, THE TIP OF the quill pen, wet with ink, just inches above the contract. "I'm not sure I can sign this yet."

Rigby spluttered, "Why . . . not?"

"See, I'm a Dreamtreader," Archer said. "But I'm kind of like a captain or a field commander, not a general. I don't really have the authority to make a decision like this."

The Lurker shifted uncomfortably in his seat. He glanced at Kaylie, who remained expressionless, her eyes riveted to something distant.

"Well then, Keaton," Rigby grunted, "who has such authority?"

White light flooded the chamber. "I do." His voice was thunder, and his blazing Incandescent Armor was lightning.

Bezeal hissed, rose from his seat, and backed toward the roaring fireplace.

Master Gabriel barely fit through the arched doorway, ducking his snowy head at the last moment. He towered over the gathering, standing with one hand on his hip, the other on the hilt of his great sword. "I have the authority over the Dreamtreader Division, and I absolutely reject your ridiculous contract."

Rigby bounced out of his chair. Crimson electricity danced on his fingertips and in his eyes. "Keaton, you backstabbing, conniving—"

"Hey," Archer said, "you're the one who told me to invite him."

"Now, you listen to me," Master Gabriel boomed. "Your so-called treaty is a manifesto of madness, a greed-infested, godless blasphemy!"

"Blasphemy?" Rigby spat. "That's always the cry of the oppressor. Always so certain of your righteousness while pushing down the common man."

Master Gabriel's armor flared. "We protect not just the common man but every man!" he bristled. "We pour ourselves out for the good of all. While you—*you*—speak of license and freedom as if they are one and the same. You sing of oppression to line your pockets and warm your hands over the world burning."

Rigby's eyes bulged. "You indescribably pompous . . . fool! I'll show you burning. My contract was your last chance. I will burn the Dreamtreaders to ashes! There will be—"

"Be silent, fool!" Master Gabriel thundered. "Your endless talk has made you mad. Listen, for once. You have spent your advantage. All is undone. Archer, make his situation clear."

"Dr. Scoville," Archer said, "I know what you've been doing. I know all about your secret deep tunnels, the scurions eating breaches unseen beneath the ground."

Rigby's mouth dropped open. Kara glared at him. The Lurker appeared ready to leap over the table. "How could you . . . how could you possibly know about . . . about that?"

Archer tensed before he said, "Kaylie, I think it's time."

"I'm sorry, Uncle Scovy," she said. "I told Archer about your tunnels."

"But—you couldn't. I control—"

"I never ate the gort," Kaylie said. "Every morsel of gort I put into my mouth went right into a capsule I willed up, one I could tuck into my cheek and spit out later. No harm done. Gort, really? How stupid did you think I was?"

Rigby turned to the Lurker. "Uncle?"

"I . . . I watched her eat the gort," Scoville said. "She obeyed my every command."

"I acted," Kaylie said. "I like to act."

"Now, we've a fair dinkum bit of work ahead," Nick said, "but we're going to close up all the breaches, starting with the under-ground."

"I'm stuck here," Kaylie said. "I can work on breaches all day and all night. No clock for me to worry about anymore."

"We're going to stop the Rift, Rigby," Archer said. "It's over."

Rigby's rage simmered, but he mastered it and took a more relaxed posture. "Have you forgotten?" he asked. "We are past the point of no return. A Rift is inevitable now. I have thrown open the Inner Sanctum. The Scath, even now, are punching so many holes in the Dream fabric, you'll never fix it in time."

"Except that they're not," Archer said. "Not anymore. See, I have the Shadow Key."

Bezeal hissed again. "You said you destroyed it!"

"I did destroy it!" Rigby yelled. "I threw it into Xander's Fortune!"

The Lurker reached into his jacket pocket. "Actually, nephew," he said, "the key never made it to the bottom. It landed on a ledge." He held the Shadow Key aloft. "See, I have it here."

Rigby exhaled. "Ha, Archer!" he crowed. "You are sorely mistaken."

"Uh, Uncle Scovy," Kaylie said. "That key's kind of a fake. Sorry." As she said the words, the key began to decay until it was nothing but ashes falling from the Lurker's hand.

"What is this?" he growled. "Where is the real Shadow Key?"

"I gave it to my brother," Kaylie said, her pigtails bouncing.

"And I gave it to the Windmaiden," Archer said. "Right about now, I imagine she's locking up the Scath for good."

"No!" Rigby rasped. "This can't be."

"It is, trespasser," Archer said.

"You've stepped in it this time," Nick chided. "Master Gabriel, Kaylie, Archer, and I? We're more than enough to take you down for good."

"Now, do you want to end this peacefully?" Archer asked. "Or do you really need to learn the hard way. Please, please say the hard way."

Kara stood and edged toward Rigby. The Lurker did the same. But Bezeal pulled at Rigby's elbow until he bent low enough to listen. The merchant whispered in his ear.

"There won't be any more deals, Bezeal," Archer said. "Save your breath."

"Archer, look out!" Kaylie cried out.

Kara had will-formed a great spear and, in the blink of an eye, had hurled it. It sped through the room. Kaylie's conjured shield protected Archer, but the spear sped past him and buried itself deep in Master Gabriel's chest.

"Nice try, Archer," Kara said. "You almost had me fooled."

Archer's shoulders fell. Master Gabriel began to dissolve. Like a sand sculpture in the wind, the figure of the master of all Dreamtreaders vanished, and the spear clattered to the floor.

"Now!" Rigby yelled. The torchlights and the fire flickered and went out.

A bell sounded, ringing out six mournful tolls.

"Kaylie, Nick, form up on me!" Archer called out. "We fight together!"

"Light!" Nick yelled. "We need blasted light."

White fireballs like shooting stars launched up from the chamber and lodged at intervals in the arched ceiling, bathing the chamber in silvery light. "That work?" Kaylie asked.

"Much better," Nick replied.

"Where are they?" Archer yelled. He leaped over the dining table and searched the far wall, but Rigby, Kara, the Lurker, and Bezeal—they were gone. And then, came the howls. First just a lone cry, then an answer. In moments, the night was drowned out by hundreds of feverish howls. The hounds were coming.

"That's a lot of doggies," Kaylie said.

"These are not doggies," Archer said. "Nightmare Hounds. Huge, ferocious things."

"Good luck getting in here, ya bitzers!" Nick shouted, looking at the fortress around him. "These walls are—"

The eastern wall of the chamber began to tremble. It bulged and then collapsed in a pile of rubble and smoke. Huge red eyes waited on the other side.

An immense black hound stepped over the debris. It had a mane like a lion's, only black, and it flared out upon its massive shoulders as the creature broke into a rippling snarl. It lunged for Kaylie. Archer dove to her aid but found himself knocked out of the air and sprawling against the north wall of the chamber. He healed up his bruises even as he stood, wondering, *What in the world hit me?*

"Bad dog!" Kaylie shouted. There was a yelp, and Archer saw Kaylie wielding a rolled-up newspaper that had to be at least three feet wide and ten feet long.

"Bad dog, heel!" Kaylie shouted, whopping the hound on the snout repeatedly.

"Kaylie," Archer called out. "You're going to need something stronger than that!"

"I dunno," she said. "It's the way Dad did it with Bingo."

"Bingo was a poodle!" Archer yelled. "These are Nightmare Hounds!"

Fierce growls announced the leaping attack of too many hounds to count. Archer found himself tumbling among snapping jaws and claw swipes. All the while, he heard Nick shouting, "Take that, ya flea-bitten bitzer! And that, yeah! Hooroooo!"

Archer bounced snout to snout before falling to the ground and being battered by the mess of paws and legs. "Too much chaos!" he yelled, and he drew up his will and thunder-stomped the ground.

The shockwave took the nearest hounds. They cartwheeled backward and crashed to the floor ten yards away. They yipped and whined as they righted themselves but then slunk away limping. But others came behind them. Dozens of other hounds. And there was something else. A grating sound like stone.

Archer looked up and caught a glimpse of starlit sky through a crack in the high ceiling. "Dreamtreaders!" Archer called with will-infused volume. "Watch your head! The roof's caving in!"

Archer saw the crack widen. A car-sized panel of fused stone tumbled loose and fell. It crash-landed a few feet away from Nick. The Aussie Dreamtreader gaped wide-eyed and exclaimed, "Whew! That was close."

As the stones began to fall, the hounds' fury increased. They pounced. One knocked Archer to the ground, and Nick leaped onto its back. He slung out massive chains, wrapped them around the beast's neck, and yanked backward.

Archer called up his flaming blue sword and drove it into the creature's rib cage. He and Nick heaved the thing to the side just as a swift wind whistled up. It howled louder than the hounds. Dust and debris all but blinded Archer and Nick.

A huge section of the chamber's roof tore free, but it didn't fall. It was sucked into the sky. The added light gave Archer a window to see. Kaylie, still wielding her giant rolled-up newspaper, was fighting off a pair of hounds. But she didn't see the other two approaching from behind.

"I'm on it!" Nick yelled. "I'll show those bitzers!"

Archer launched forward to help, but an invisible barrier struck him down. "Archer, no!" a female voice yelled in his mind. "Leave her. She and Nick can handle things here!"

"What? You?" Archer called aloud. "Your windstorm?"

"Yes," the Windmaiden replied. "Listen, you have to go now!"

"What? Where?"

"Rigby has gone back. He's gone back to the Waking World. He means to kill Kaylie."

"But Kaylie's here—" Archer's mouth snapped shut as he realized. "No, he can't be."

"Rigby sees Kaylie as his greatest threat," the Windmaiden said. "He's going to the hospital. He'll destroy the machines that keep her alive!"

"Can you zap me there?" Archer asked desperately. "Please!"

"I cannot," she said. "But I can return you to your anchor."

Archer watched as Nick called up an electrified fence behind Kaylie. The two hounds rammed into it, yelped, and streaked away.

Archer leaped over a pile of rubble and landed between Nick and Kaylie. "I have to leave," he said.

"What?" Nick yelped. "No, we work together, right?"

"I'm sorry," Archer said. "There's something I've got to do."

"What is it, Archer?" Kaylie asked. "We'll come with you. We can help."

"No!" Archer barked, much louder than he meant to. "I'm sorry, but you need to secure Number 6. Find Dad and Mr. Gamber. They'll be in the dungeons below, I think. But I can't wait."

"Why, Archer?" Kaylie asked. "Why would you leave us now?"

How many times will I let you down? The thought just about crushed Archer's heart. He could barely speak. "Please understand," he said. "I'm trying to help."

"Archer," Kaylie said, "you're scaring me!"

Archer stepped backward and cried out to the Windmaiden, "Now! Do it!"

Storm winds swept Archer up, encircled him, and he was gone in a cloud of dark turbulence. He opened his eyes, saw his mother's favorite well, and lunged for it.

TWENTY-EIGHT

A DARK IMPASSE

A TOUCH OF STONE. THEN COLD, AND ARCHER WAS BACK.
He leaped from the bed and screamed for Mrs. Pitsitakas. But there
was no answer. He burst through her bedroom door and found the
bed made . . . and the room empty. Archer turned and raced back
down the hall. "Amy! Buster! Anyone here? Anyone home?"

There was no answer. "Snot rockets! Where is everyone?" He
thumped down the stairs, half sliding down the last three. There was
no sign in the den or living room. No one in the sitting room or the
kitchen—a note. There was a note stuck with a magnet on the hood
above the stove.

"Archer, went to a midnight movie. Sorry, you were asleep and
Amy said it was important not to wake you. We'll bring you back
something. Mrs. P."

The last time Archer felt this helpless was when he stood outside
his mother's door, listening to his father weeping. There had been
nothing to do then. And it felt as if there was nothing to do now. He
had no ride to the hospital, and it was fifteen miles away. If Rigby
was already there . . .

Stop. Stop. Can't think like that. But there's no time. There's no time to wait for a ride. There's no time to get there. No time to do anything.

Anchors. Remember your anchors, Archer. Master Gabriel's words rolled in. *You must fight to preserve hope and truth.*

He paced the kitchen and spoke his thoughts aloud, "How can I fight when I'm too far away?"

Things can get worse. They may get a lot worse, but that just means we fight harder.

Fight harder, he thought. *How?* The split second the idea arrived, Archer was off like a shot. He thundered up the stairs, dove onto the guest room bed, and snatched up his cell phone.

He used an app to find the hospital's telephone number and dialed. The hospital's automated line picked up and asked him which department he wanted. Cardiology? Pediatrics? Archer hammered the "0" on his keypad and prayed for an operator.

"Gatlinburg General Hospital. To whom may I direct your call?"

"Get me hospital security!"

"Hold please."

"Hospital security," a tired male voice answered.

"I need you to listen. My sister is in Room 17 on the pediatric wing. Kaylie Keaton is her name. She's in a coma. She . . . she was injured by this guy . . . a neighborhood bully, his name is Rigby Thames."

"Okay, I see her name in our registry. What's the problem?"

"Thing is, Rigby said he's coming up to the hospital now to finish her off."

"He said that?"

"Yeah, he said it. Rigby's dangerous. Please, you have to get up to my sister's room. Rigby's tall. He doesn't look like a teenager. Brown hair, long sideburns, English accent. Please just go. I think he's already there!"

Archer hung up. He sat on the edge of his bed, waiting. Waiting while Kaylie's life hung in the balance.

"No," he said aloud. "I'm not just going to wait." He shoved his phone in his jeans pocket and ran back downstairs and out into the front yard. It was a long shot, but he had to try. The Dream fabric had been weakening, day after day. Archer had developed some Dreamtreading powers in the Waking World. Why not this one?

Archer ran across the front porch, calling up all the will he could muster to fly. There was some lift but not nearly enough. He didn't fall full speed, but he did fall, coming down on top of Mrs. Pitsitakas' bushes. He huffed, cracking through the brittle winter branches and losing his footing in the snow. But he didn't stop. He tried flight again. And a third time, but the best he could get was about ten feet of hover time. He wasn't getting anywhere close to fifteen miles anytime soon.

"Rigby!" Archer's scream echoed down the quiet suburban street. Archer kicked the snow once, twice, a third time. It wasn't any good. At that very moment, Rigby could be pulling the plug.

Archer froze. The last bit of his breath snaked out of the corner of his mouth. The idea that presented itself turned Archer's stomach, but he found himself absently checking to make sure his cell phone was still in his pocket.

The idea went against everything he believed in, everything he stood for, but he found himself sprinting down the street toward his neighborhood.

If Master Gabriel got wind of this idea, Archer knew he'd have no way to justify his actions. The idea itself was shameful, but Archer found himself turning the corner and using his will-enhanced speed to charge the last four blocks to Rigby's house.

Archer balled his fist and banged hard on the front door. No answer. He heard the animals barking, chirping, cawing, yelping, and carrying on . . . as they always did when someone was at the door. Archer banged again. No one came. Rigby's parents were always overseas. But the house wasn't empty. Rigby's Uncle Scoville was there. He was always there.

Archer summoned up his will, but instead of thunder-stomping the ground, he snapped his foot forward and kicked in the door.

Rigby had immobilized the hospital security guards easily enough. One got an open-hand strike to the throat. The other had drawn his gun. Rigby had turned the weapon into a snake. When the guard looked down at the thing wriggling between his fingers, Rigby knocked him unconscious with a will-conjured bat.

All that ruckus had gotten Rigby far too much attention. He used a variety of will-created barriers and a few illusions to get to the pediatric wing. From there, it was a matter of following the room signs.

At last, there it was: Room 17. He turned into the doorway and ran straight into a doctor. He grabbed the startled physician by the lab coat lapels and threw him bodily across the foyer into the nurses' station. Then, his will surging, he called up a solid wall of granite to block the only way into the hospital room. "Now, Miss Kaylie," Rigby said. "No one will disturb us."

Archer strode quickly down the stairs to the basement. At the base of the stairs, on the left, stood the new security door Rigby had installed. "I'm not as smart as Kaylie," he whispered. "So I'm just going to use a key."

He summoned up a sledgehammer, pulled from his will to aid the strike, and struck the door on the side where the internal hinge mechanism was hidden.

Archer took a quick step backward. "What was that?" he asked aloud, his breathing swift, heart pounding. When Archer connected with the door, something had gone wrong with his vision. The door seemed to flex and bend. In fact, Archer's entire field of vision had warped momentarily.

The animals in Rigby's basement zoo went berserk. The noise was deafening. Archer turned back to the door and took another swing. This one hit so hard that Archer's ears rang, and he saw a slightly larger shadow between the door and the jamb. Again and again and again he swung the sledge. There was a visible gap. The hinge was stressed near to breaking. It was no match for a thunder-kick.

The security door fell inward, crashing into a cabinet frame. It set off a buzzing, howling alarm, but Archer yanked out the wires. He turned, and there as still as death, lay Dr. Scoville. Archer stared at the body of the man he had known in the Dream as the Lurker. It had been his research that led to all of it: the Lucid Walkers, Dream Inc., Rigby's obsessions—Dr. Scoville had begun it all.

But did he deserve to die?

Archer looked at the trail of wires leading from the machines. He followed their trail back to a central power junction. There was no plug to pull, but there was a circuit breaker. If he opened that little metal door and pulled the switch inside down, Dr. Scoville's life support machines would stop running. The man would die.

I'm no judge, Archer thought. *How can I be executioner?*

Archer pulled out his cell phone, double-checked that the video chat was active, and made the fateful call. While it rang, Archer prayed Rigby wouldn't answer. If he didn't, Archer would have no leverage. There'd be no reason to—

At the fourth ring, Rigby's face appeared on the tiny screen.

"Keaton?" Rigby's voice sounded odd. Thin. Strained. His face looked odd. Sickly. "Keaton, is that you?"

"Don't do it, Rigby!" Archer demanded to the little face on his phone screen. "Don't hurt her. She's just a little girl!"

"Who told you—never mind. Archer, I—I have to."

"No, you don't. You can just walk out of that hospital. I promise, we'll leave you alone. You can have your Rift, and we'll leave you alone."

"I wish I could believe you, Keaton," Rigby said. "I really do. But you've got your code. And you really can't help yourself, can you? I'm sorry, Keaton, but Kaylie's just too powerful. I can't allow—"

"No! No, don't! Rigby!"

"Relax, Keaton, I haven't done anything yet. Look here; see for yourself."

"Please," Archer said quietly. "Let me see her." He glanced back at Dr. Scoville. Rigby hadn't noticed yet, hadn't seen where Archer was. He ran his hand through his hair. "Rigby?"

Kaylie appeared on the tiny screen. She was there, tucked into the hospital bed. Her chest rose and fell because the machine breathed for her. She looked so small, so fragile. "Please, Rigby, for the love of God . . ."

"Really, Keaton?" Rigby's face returned to the screen. "As if I've ever known real love . . . or God."

"You said you did."

"What?"

"You told me that's why you needed the Rift to happen," Archer said. "For your uncle. You said he was like a father to you. You said you were motivated by love."

Rigby glanced away from the screen. "I . . . I am, I guess." Rigby covered his face with his free hand. "Ah, no, how did I get here? How did it all get like this?"

"You can change direction, Rigby," Archer said. "You can turn. You don't have to do this."

Through tears, Rigby faced his phone's camera again. "But . . . I . . . do. Can't you see, Keaton? It's the only way."

"You act like it's some kind of fate, like an equation that has to have a certain answer. There are other answers."

"I don't think so," Rigby said, and Archer could tell he was turning toward the hospital bed again. "I'm sorry for all of this, but I 'ave to see it through."

"Don't you touch those machines, Rigby!" Archer yelled. "Don't touch them or I'll—"

"You'll what?" Rigby asked. "Kill me? Do you 'ave any idea how powerful all this will make me. I'll—"

"I'm here with your Uncle Scoville, Rigby."

Fear washed smug from Rigby's face. "You-you're what?"

"I'm in your basement, at your house. I'm a foot away from the circuit breaker that would end your uncle's life."

"You're bluffing."

Archer turned the camera of his smart phone. "See?"

"You . . . you can't, Keaton," Rigby said. "You're a Dreamtreader. You can't."

"This is where you've—" Archer blinked. The room seemed to bend inward again. It warped and then sprang back. Archer shook his head. "This is where you've pushed me, Rigby."

"No, no. Keaton, you don't understand," Rigby said. "You can't blame me. This is on you. You don't want to do that. You're not a murderer."

"It's simple," Archer said, trying to sound convincing. "You get away from my sister, right now. Or I'll shut down your uncle's life support."

"You're not that type, Keaton," Rigby said. "You never were, but I am." The call disconnected. Rigby's face, the little corners of the hospital room, the last glimpse of Kaylie . . . all were gone.

"Rigby!" Archer screamed. In a blinding rage, Archer spun toward the circuit breaker. He snapped open the small metal door and put his finger on the breaker switch. His fingers felt heavy.

But his heart felt heavier.

There's my big boy, Archer's mom said from memory. *Perfect timing, too, because I'm so thirsty. Can I feel that bucket? Oh my goodness, that's so heavy! How did you bring it all the way up the hill from the well? You're strong for your age, son. I bet you'll do great things one day.*

Tears came, hot and messy, streaming down from Archer's eyes and blurring his vision. But his fingers did not move.

"Kaylie, I'm sorry," he whispered. But his fingers did not move.

No. It was a single brief thought, a single word. But it was potent. Archer exhaled deeply and pulled his hand away from the circuit breaker.

"It's really quite simple, my boy," came a gritty voice from behind. "Just a little flick of the fingers, really. Like . . . so." An arm moved in a blur. Just a flick of the wrist, and the circuit breaker clicked off. The life support machines died.

Dr. Scoville did not.

TWENTY-NINE

STONE COLD

ARCHER ALMOST LOST IT. HIS HEART BEAT SO FAST HE could scarcely breathe enough to keep up. "Dr. . . . . Scoville?"

"I'd say at your service," he replied with a slight bow. "But I'm really not."

"How?"

"Don't you know?" He scratched at the wildly waving gray hair above his ears. "I thought you Dreamtreaders were smart."

"The Rift?"

"It's happening, Keaton boy," Dr. Scoville said. "The Dream fabric has failed at last."

The warping in my vision, Archer thought. *That was the Dream's last gasp.* "Now, what?" he asked.

"Now what?" Dr. Scoville echoed. "Now, you get out of here. I owe you one for not killing me when you could. Indeed, I owe you *exactly* one." A mischievous glint came to his eye, just as a wickedly sharp dagger appeared in his right hand.

Archer took a step backward.

"That's right," Dr. Scoville said, his bloodshot eyes bulging, "the one I owe you is right here. It's me not killing you. Door's that way. Get lost."

Archer raced up the stairs. With each step, his experience of reality flickered. Left foot: a cave laboratory. Right foot: Rigby's house. The stairway railing warped and bent. It was there, and then it wasn't. Archer fell and slid back down a few stairs.

"You can do better than that, Keaton boy!" came a maniacal voice from below. The animals barked and screeched and howled.

Archer staggered to his feet and threw himself up the stairs with will-energized strength. He charged around the doorjamb, flashed through the kitchen and hallway, and out through the wrecked door.

There, on Rigby's snowy front porch, Archer stopped. The door was not the only thing wrecked.

A second moon lit the neighborhood, and the sky itself seemed to be tearing. The ice-fire burned through the dark starlit canopy in streaks like the mauling of some great beast. Archer's entire field of vision filled with warping images: clouds bending as if they had corners, houses expanding and shrinking as if they were breathing, and the roads rippling as if preparing to slither away.

Sirens cried out from ten directions at once, and a car skidded around the corner into Rigby's court. It swerved violently and then drove right through the front picture window of Rigby's nearest neighbor.

Chaos.

The Rift.

How many will die? Archer shook away the thought. Kaylie needed him. Needed him now . . . if it wasn't too late.

He felt his will practically bursting from his veins, and then he leaped into the air and soared above the trees.

He'd been to Gatlinburg General Hospital many, many times, but most of those had been when his mom was sick, eight years ago. He knew the general route but had to descend to street level to watch for blue signs with the big white *H*.

Not far now, Archer thought, breathing heavily. The Rift had happened, he knew. He could feel the increase in his mental energy, his will. He could fly . . . in the Waking World. *Or whatever it's called now.*

Archer flew over trembling suburban neighborhoods, warping strip malls, schools, and office buildings, and over a lake that seemed to be burning. Thankfully, at this time of night, he knew most people were settling down for bed or already asleep. They might not discover the massive changes until the morning. But when they did . . .

Archer shook his head and soared toward the hospital. The Rift and all its consequences would have to wait. He had to go to Kaylie. He had to find out.

The building stood at the elbow of a boomerang-shaped road. An ambulance with flashers pulled into the emergency entrance, even as Archer landed in the parking lot. There were a lot of people there, running around in terrified circles. Some stopped to attend to the ambulance. Others ran away from it, screaming.

Archer sprinted inside, passing scrub-clad doctors and nurses. He rounded the corner and found a directory. The pediatric department was on the third floor. Archer glanced at the elevator. "No," he muttered. "Stairs will be faster." He plowed through the door and literally flew up the stairs.

He found the floor frantic with activity and raced ahead, weaving between medical personnel and security. He counted rooms as he went, all on the left side. Odd numbers.

Room 9, Room 11, Room 13, Room 15.

Archer didn't need to search anymore. A massive slab of granite, otherworldly and out of place in the sterile hospital hallway, stood as an impenetrable guard in front of Kaylie's room.

A shadow came rushing toward Archer, tackled him, and slammed him against the wall. "Archer, son! Oh, God, thank you!"

"Dad?" Archer whispered. "Dad, you . . . you're here."

"Something changed, didn't it, son?" Mr. Keaton said, pulling back. "I was in the dark forever, but there was this Australian guy . . . and Kaylie was there, but everything went nuts. The sky split open, and suddenly I was back here. I thought . . . well, it doesn't matter what I thought. Son, son, I'm so glad to see you. But something's wrong. The doctors told me Kaylie was still in her hospital room. It doesn't make sense. I just saw her. But . . . nothing makes sense. And there's this!" He pointed at the wall. "We can't get inside Kaylie's room."

Mr. Keaton dragged Archer toward the granite. "They've got a crew coming," Mr. Keaton said, his voice getting frantic and breathy. "But her signals . . . they've all gone flatline."

"Stand back, Dad!" Archer yelled.

His father blinked at him, not comprehending.

"Stand back, please, Dad. I'll get us in."

"How can . . ."

Archer put his hand up to the granite wall. It was solid, horribly so. Maybe a thunder-stomp or thunder-kick would get through, but then Archer might send shards of granite into the room.

Archer ducked into the room next door to Kaylie's and found it blessedly empty. He went to the adjoining wall and used his will to harden his hand. Then he thrust his hand through the drywall and began tearing at the studs. Soon he had enough torn away to see. Rigby stood at the side of the bed, but his back was turned, and Archer couldn't see anything beyond.

"Rigby!" Archer called. "Tell me you didn't do it! Tell me . . . you didn't do it!"

There was no reply, and Archer wasn't waiting. He tore chunks at a time and flung them away. The hole grew wider. Archer saw the edge of Kaylie's bed. "Kaylie!" he yelled. "Kaylie!"

Finally, enough of the wall gave that Archer could push himself through. He stepped into the room behind Rigby, but Rigby didn't turn around. Archer heard a strange sound . . . a wheezing or choking.

Archer grabbed Rigby and tried to spin him around, but it was like he was caught in a vise grip.

"Hello, Archer," came a female voice, but it wasn't Kaylie. "You know, for the record, Rigby did pull the plug. It just wasn't Kaylie in the bed."

Rigby seemed to hover to the side. There, with a gloved hand around Rigby's throat . . . was Kara Windchil. "You aren't the only one who can play the disguise game, Archer," she said. "It was your brilliant ploy with the fake Master Gabriel that gave me the idea."

Archer's mouth barely worked. He mouthed, "Kaylie?"

"She's safe," Kara said. "In another room down the hall. Probably wide awake right now and wanting ice cream. Of course, she could just will up the biggest ice cream sundae in the world . . . if she wanted. She is very strong."

"Let . . . let—ugh—me—go!" Rigby struggled, but it was obviously no good. Kara walked him over to the hospital room window. Holding Rigby up with one arm, she didn't look like she was even breaking a sweat. Archer had always thought Rigby the more powerful of the two.

"What . . . what are you going to do?" Archer asked.

Urgent voices came from behind Archer. "Archer! What are you doing?"

"Oh, we can't really have visitors right now," Kara said. "It's after hours." She waved her free hand. There was a violent rush of wind, and the wall bricked itself up.

Archer blinked. "That was a pretty neat trick," he mumbled.

"No trick," she said. "That was real. That's what 'real' is now. I gotta hand it to you, Archer. You have helped me so much all along. I mean from the very beginning. Getting all jealous of Rigby? That gave me such an in. He was so eager to share his uncle's Lucid Dreaming secrets with me."

Archer felt a rapid chill forming on his neck.

"Of course, I'd already been Lucid Dreaming for years," Kara went on. Rigby hissed and spat and continued to struggle.

Archer raised a hand and took a tentative step toward Rigby.

"Oh, don't tell me you're worried about Rigby," Kara said, smiling sadly. "I'm not going to kill him. I'm not as cold-blooded as he is. No, I'm going to let the Scath have him. They were so angry at him for not keeping his promise of freedom . . . when I locked them up. I figure, I'll just lock Rigby in the Inner Sanctum with the Scath . . . and see what shakes loose."

"You—you locked up the Scath?"

"C'mon, Archer," she said. "Connect the dots. Maybe this will help." Kara reached into the long pocket of her jacket and pulled out a dark piece of metal: the Shadow Key. "Like I said, you have helped me so much, you and Kaylie. Without the two of you, I'd have never gotten this. The Rift would have happened, and I would have lost control of . . . well, everything. But you put the Shadow Key right in my hand and basically delivered Rigby to me on a platter." She laughed.

"I gave the Shadow Key to the Windmaiden," Archer muttered. "You . . . you're the Windmaiden?"

"Poor Archer," she said. "You never had a clue, did you? Not even from my last name? Really? No? Well, now you know. It has been a good ride, Archer. A brilliant game of chess. But this is checkmate. Good-bye, Archer Keaton."

Kara thrust her free hand forward. The window and the wall bowed outward and appeared to melt into a hollow. Archer ducked as the wind picked up. Furniture from the hospital room flew through the opening and vanished.

Kara slung Rigby toward the pulsing portal, but hesitated and said, "There will never be another Nightmare Lord, Archer, be sure of that. No king will sit on that throne. But there will be a queen."

She started to turn, but Archer lifted his foot and slammed it to the hospital room floor. The shockwave battered Kara, and she nearly dropped her captive.

"This isn't checkmate!" Archer shouted, will-infused thunder-clapping with each pause in his words. "You won't be a queen. You'll only be a nightmare. And I know just what to do with nightmares!"

Kara sneered. Her eyes widened, and Archer saw the same spidery red lightning dancing there that he'd seen in Rigby's gaze. Archer knew then that Kara had been reading the *Masters' Bindings*. She was changing. But into what?

Archer gathered all of his will, but before he could strike, Kara stepped into the portal and drew Rigby in with her.

Eerie, warbling wind moaned and shrieked as they vanished. Just before the portal closed completely, Archer could have sworn that he saw Bezeal's star-point eyes and Cheshire Cat grin.

But Archer didn't have time to dwell on what he'd just seen.

"Archer!"

There came a crackling, and bits of granite fell away, until a full door appeared in the barrier Rigby had created. Archer's father stood there . . . and Kaylie. They raced forward. Archer lost himself in their embrace.

Sirens howled outside, sounding eerily like hounds. People were screaming in the hospital. Archer's father said, "Everything's gone crazy."

But Archer just held his family tighter. Things were broken, but he knew they could be repaired.

ACKNOWLEDGMENTS

I, WAYNE THOMAS BATSON, DO HEREBY ACKNOWLEDGE that the following remarkable people invested great love, energy, sacrifice, and kindnesses in ways that I will never be able to repay. *Search for the Shadow Key*, like all my novels, couldn't have happened without your support and presence in my life. To you, I offer these simple thanks:

Mary Lu Batson: gorgeous wife, best friend, co-dreamer, and life-mate—to you I offer the greatest human thanks. You committed your life to me, a rare thing these days, and extraordinarily precious to me. Navigating life with four teenagers, teaching, and trying to be a writer would be absolutely impossible without your fantastic support.

Daughter Kayla: Your passion and initiative, dreams and drive to help others are nothing short of inspiring. Love you, K-doodle!

Son Tommy: You are a tender warrior, my son. I love the joy you find in God's creation, everything from noticing the gold light before dusk or the smell of wood smoke on a chill evening. You are a constant reminder to me that God's richest blessings are never ending.

Son Bryce: You are the quiet strength, my son. I love the way you become a student of what inspires you, learning every facet and detail, and then *explode* into action. You are committed to excellence. May God use you to do great things.

Daughter Rachel: Upon you, God has also placed His creative touch. You are a teacher and a storyteller, a singer and a songwriter. I am thankful for the bubbly life you inject into every day. You have a heart full of love to give, and I'm grateful to shepherd you . . . for a little while.

Mom & Dad Batson: I don't know how else to thank you. You gave up forty-five-plus years of your life to directly or indirectly help me be a better son, friend, man, employee, writer, and husband. Thank you!

Mom & Dad Dovel: You gave me your daughter and much love besides. Thank you!

Leslie, Jeff, Brian, Edward, Andy, Diana, your spouses, significant others, families, and friends—thank you for creating a landscape of adventure. It is no small thing to be able to raise a sword with such as you.

Doug & Chris, Dave & Heather, Chris H. & Dawn, Dan & Tracey, Warren & Marilyn, Todd W., Alex & Noelle, Alaina & Greg, and all friends past and present: I can't thank you enough for the camaraderie and adventures. May there be many, many more.

Folly Quarter Dreamers: Erin, Kirsten, Julie, Regina, Barb, Sherrie, Dreia, Lindsay, Susan—you are one amazing group of teachers! Verily, to you I cry out in a loud voice: Deer!

Students present and past: You have no idea what precious blessings you are to me and the world. Pip-pip, cheerio!

Sir Gregg of Wooding: Agent and friend. Thanks for being among the first to believe in my stories. It is an honor to know you, my friend.

Steele Filipek: Well met, sirrah! Seriously, you are an amazing editor. Thanks for chipping away the chaff so this series could emerge.

Thomas Nelson / HarperCollins: You opened the door for me back in 2004. Thank you for the long and incredible ride.

Christopher Hopper: The disciples told Jesus, "We have left all to follow you. What shall we have?" The Lord replied, "Truly I tell you, no one who has left home or wife or brothers or sisters or parents or children for the sake of the kingdom of God will fail to receive many times as much in this age, and in the age to come eternal life." God is true to His word. He linked us in friendship, and I'm grateful. How many zero-dark-thirty writing sessions have we shared? How many laughs? Thanks for your friendship, bro. Through airships, flatulent barrister gnomes, spiders, and much more—it has been an honor to ride together. Right.

The fantastic staffs of G. L. Shacks, Glory Days, O'Llordan's, Ramshead Tavern, and other haunts for putting up with me writing there at all times of day . . . or night. Special thanks to Oscar's in Eldersburg for being the authentic "Cheers" for me and my family. Ralph, you are Da Man!

My Army of Faithful Online
Reader Friends

Laura Mary Firemel · Aaron Russell · Ryan Paige Howard · Andrew Bergk · JT Wilt · Gracie Wilt · Tom Wilt · Kaysie Wilt · Mimi Lincicome Wilt · Cameron Strauss and family · Elizabeth Liberty Lewis · Kaleb Kramer · Ethan Park · Nikita Maves · LoriAnn Weldon · Kathleen Fleeger Edwards · Noah Cutting · Josh Vallance · Kaye Whitney · Addy Buxton · Brian McBride · Rachel O'Malley Brown · Brent Bourgoin ·

Chris Deanne · Rachel Herriman · Ashton Poole · Lindsay Renea · Brent Ammann · Morgan Babbage · Elizabeth Hornberger · Jadi Verdin · Jay Goebel · Declan Ross (You know who you are!)

THE "I BEAT THE AUTHOR"
SCROLL OF HONOR

During the crafting of this novel, the following writer/warriors did engage me in battle and exceed my efforts and production. Their friendly competition didst verily inspire mine own writing in countless ways. They are to be commended and showered with gifts and affection.

Petra Hurley • Josiah Boss • Imogen Elvis • Sarah Spradlin

First and last: I offer thanks to you, Lord Jesus. You ransomed me; you lifted my chin; you gave me a mission and the means to complete that mission. In short, you made my dreams come true. Let the words of this story ring the bells of Glory for you throughout the heavens and the earth.

About the Author

Wayne Thomas Batson is the author of several bestselling novels, including The Door Within trilogy, The Isle series, and The Berinfell series. A middle school reading teacher in Maryland for 22 years, Wayne tailors his stories to meet the needs of the young people he cares so deeply about. Wayne writes meaningful adventures set in imaginative locales because he believes that on a deep level, we all dream of doing something that matters and that we all long for another world.

SAVING THE WORLD
ONE DREAM AT A TIME

Fourteen-year-old Archer Keaton is a dreamtreader, one of three people in the entire world destined to defeat evil forces in the Dream World by using the power of imagination. The dreamtreaders are working to stop the Nightmare Lord, who terrorizes the dreams of innocent people all over the world. But as Archer's adventures in the Dream World become more threatening, so too does his waking life.

As Archer faces two foes in two worlds, will he be able to quell the nightmares haunting his dreams and reality?

THOMAS NELSON
Since 1798

AVAILABLE IN PRINT AND E-BOOK

There is an unseen world of good and evil where
nightmares are fought and hope is reborn.

Enter The Door Within.

Aidan's life is completely uprooted when his parents
move the family across the country to care for his ailing
grandfather. But when he begins having nightmares and
eerie events occur around his neighborhood, Aidan finds
himself drawn to his grandfather's basement—where he
discovers three ancient scrolls and a mysterious invitation
to another world.

By Wayne Thomas Batson

www.tommynelson.com

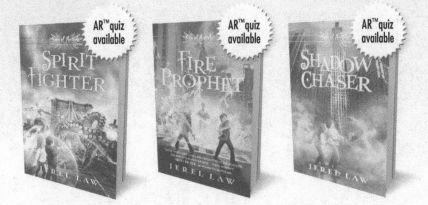
9781400321995-A

9781400318452-C